WILDLIFE
OF THE
LOW COUNTRY

JOANNE YOUNG

Disclaimer from the Author

Please know that I did my absolute best in identifying the enclosed wildlife by their proper name. Whereas we know they do not wear name tags and several of the species have a strong resemblance to each other. Also noting that all markings are not always visible in the positioning of the photograph. If I happen to misname anyone, my deepest apologies to them and to you.

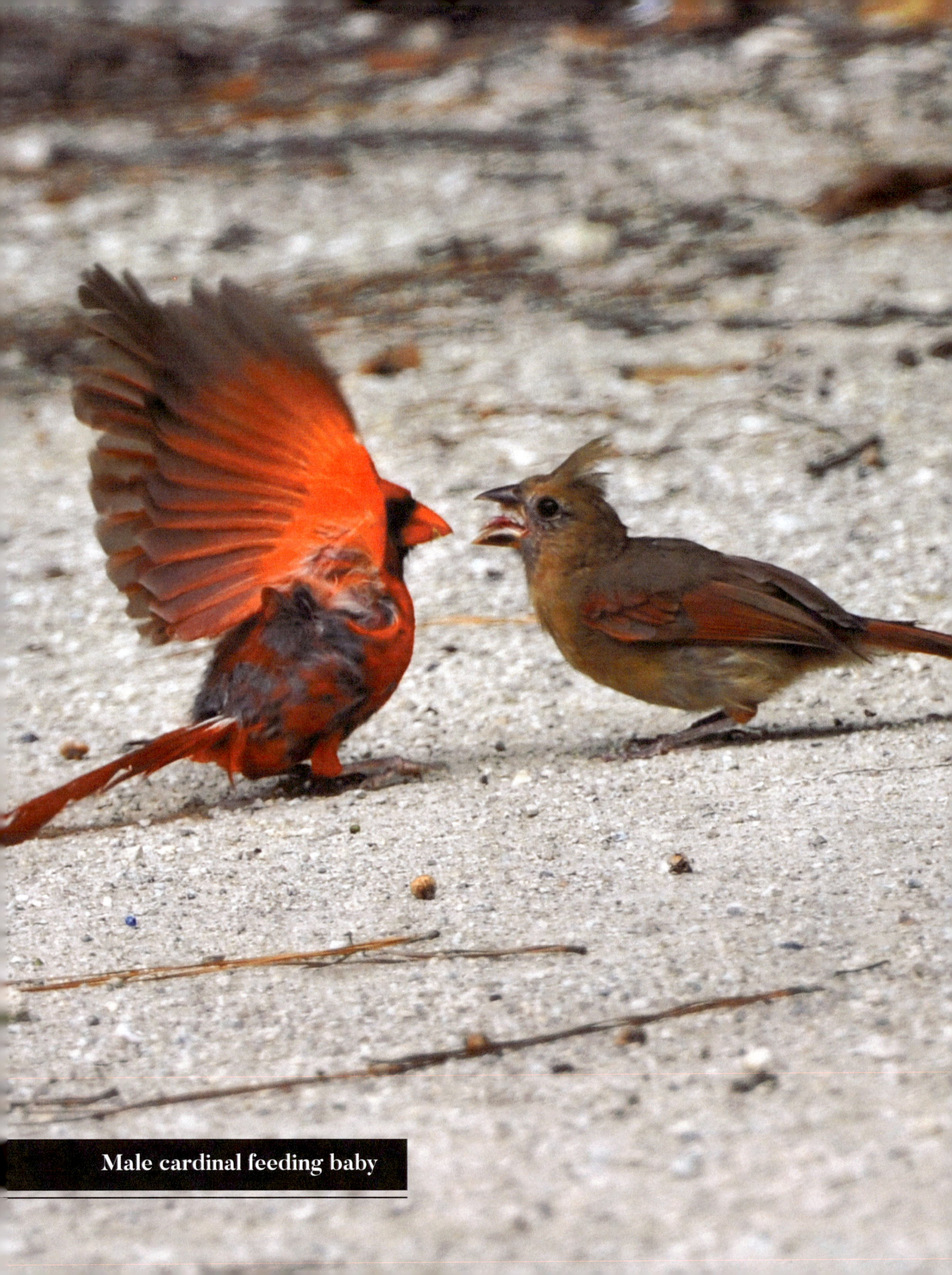

Male cardinal feeding baby

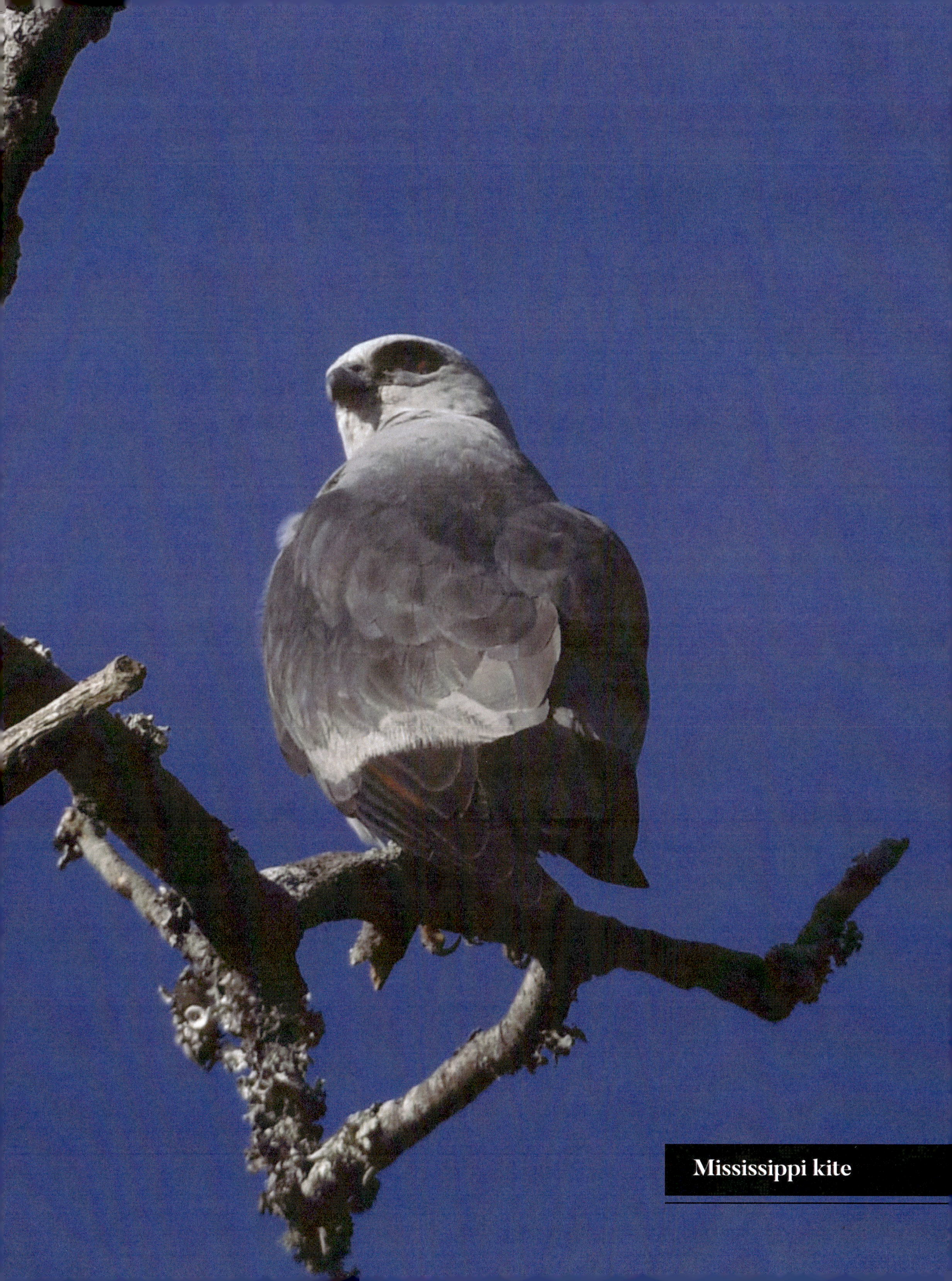

Mississippi kite

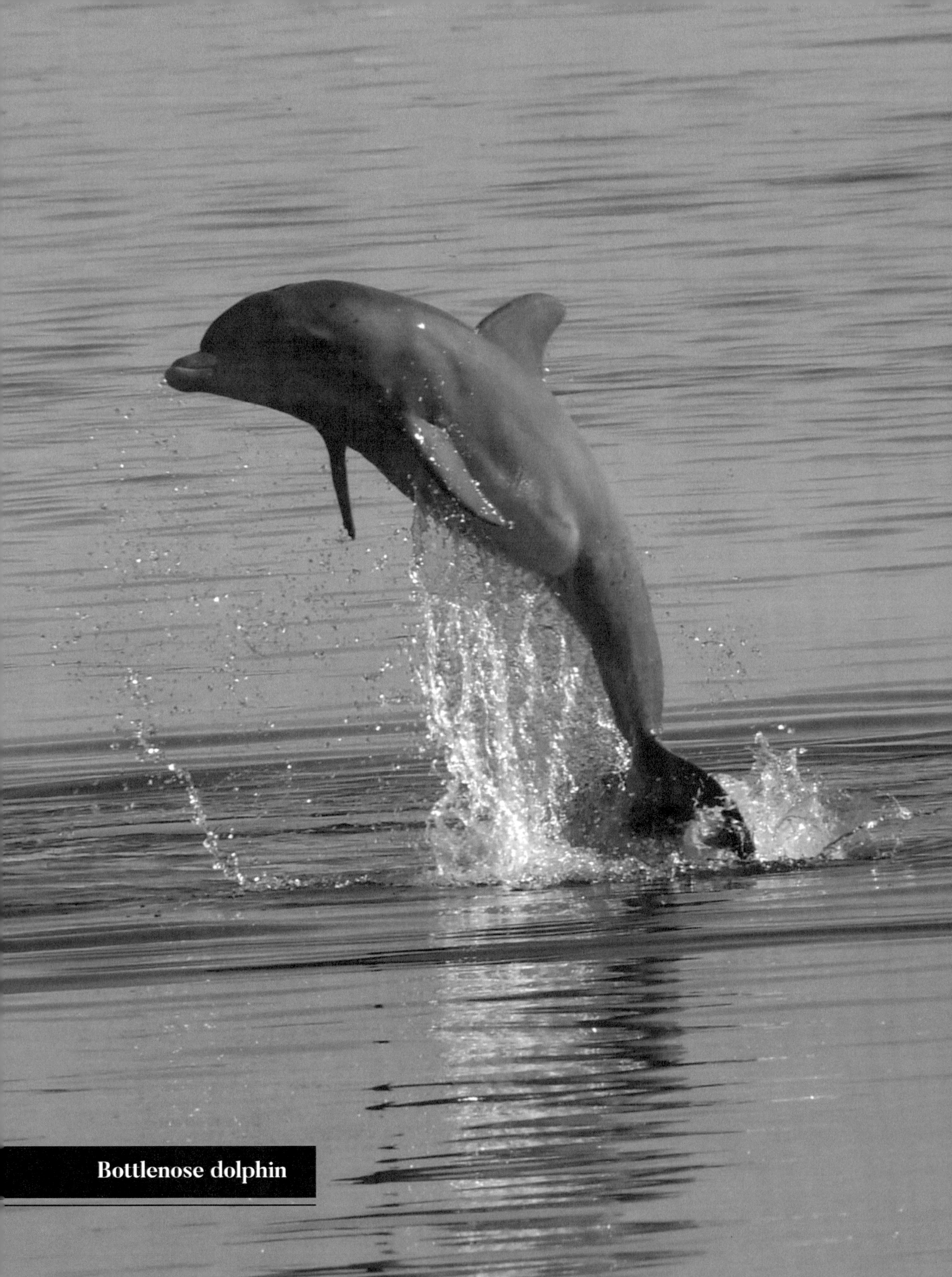
Bottlenose dolphin

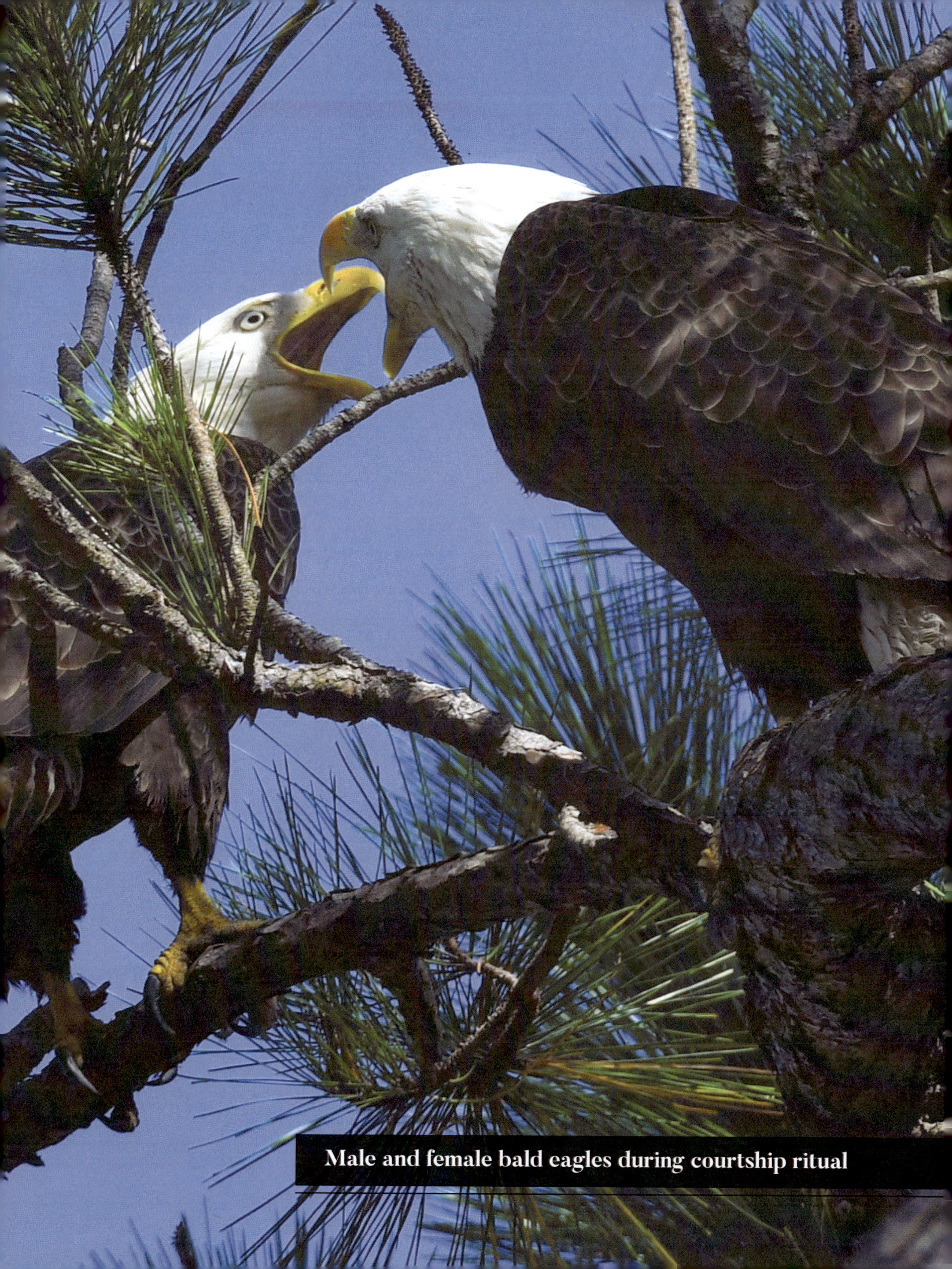

Male and female bald eagles during courtship ritual

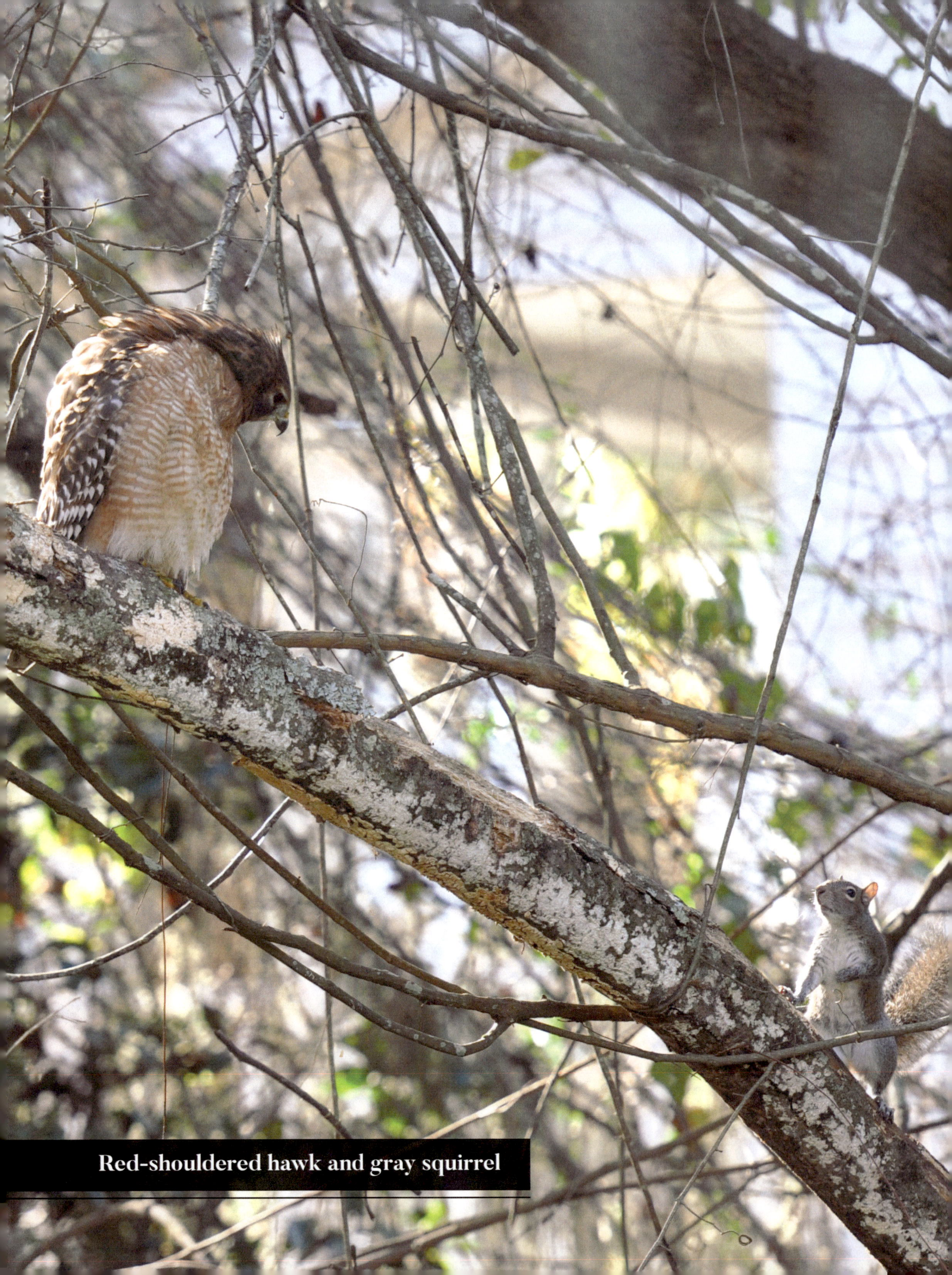

Red-shouldered hawk and gray squirrel

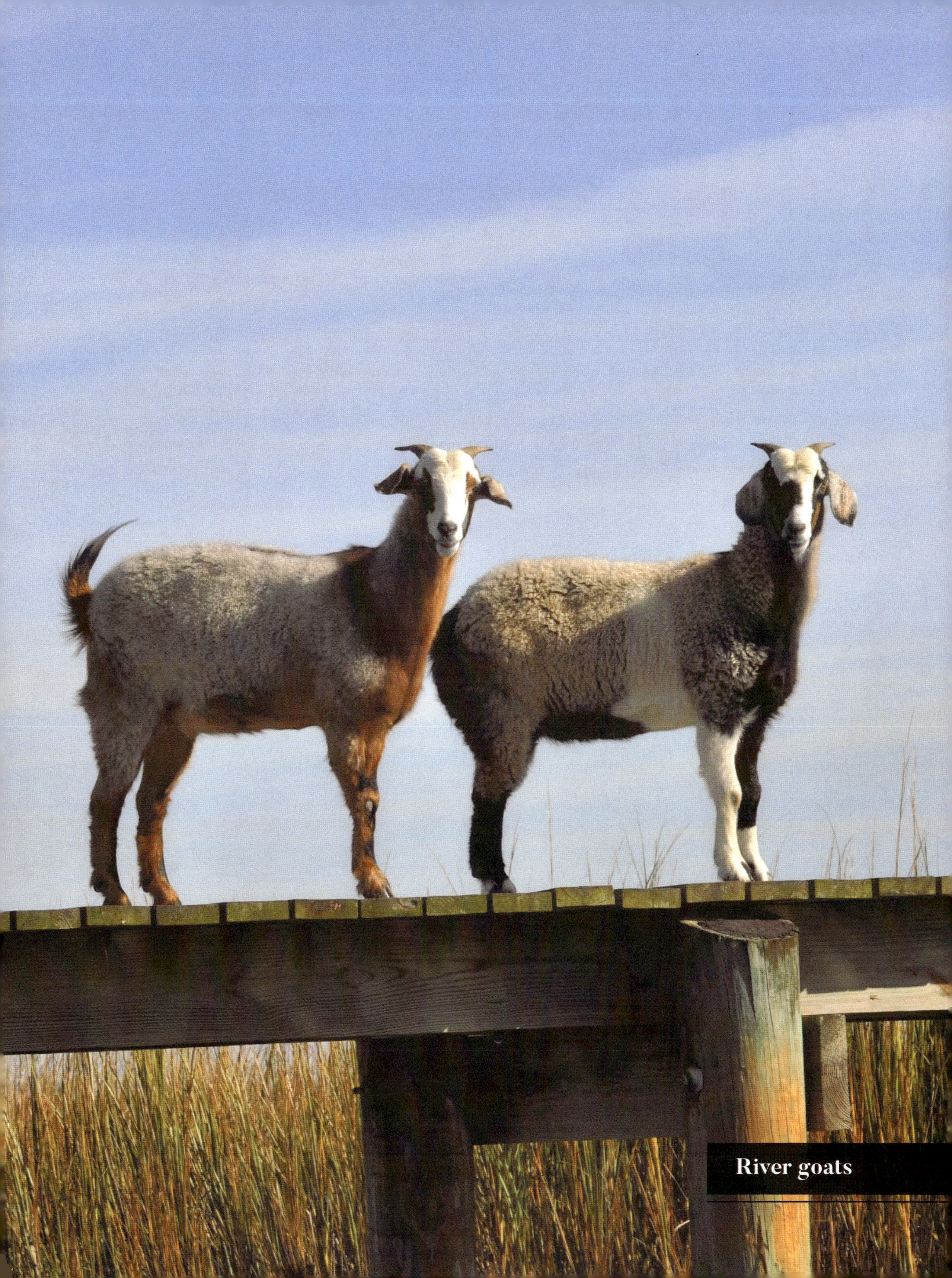
River goats

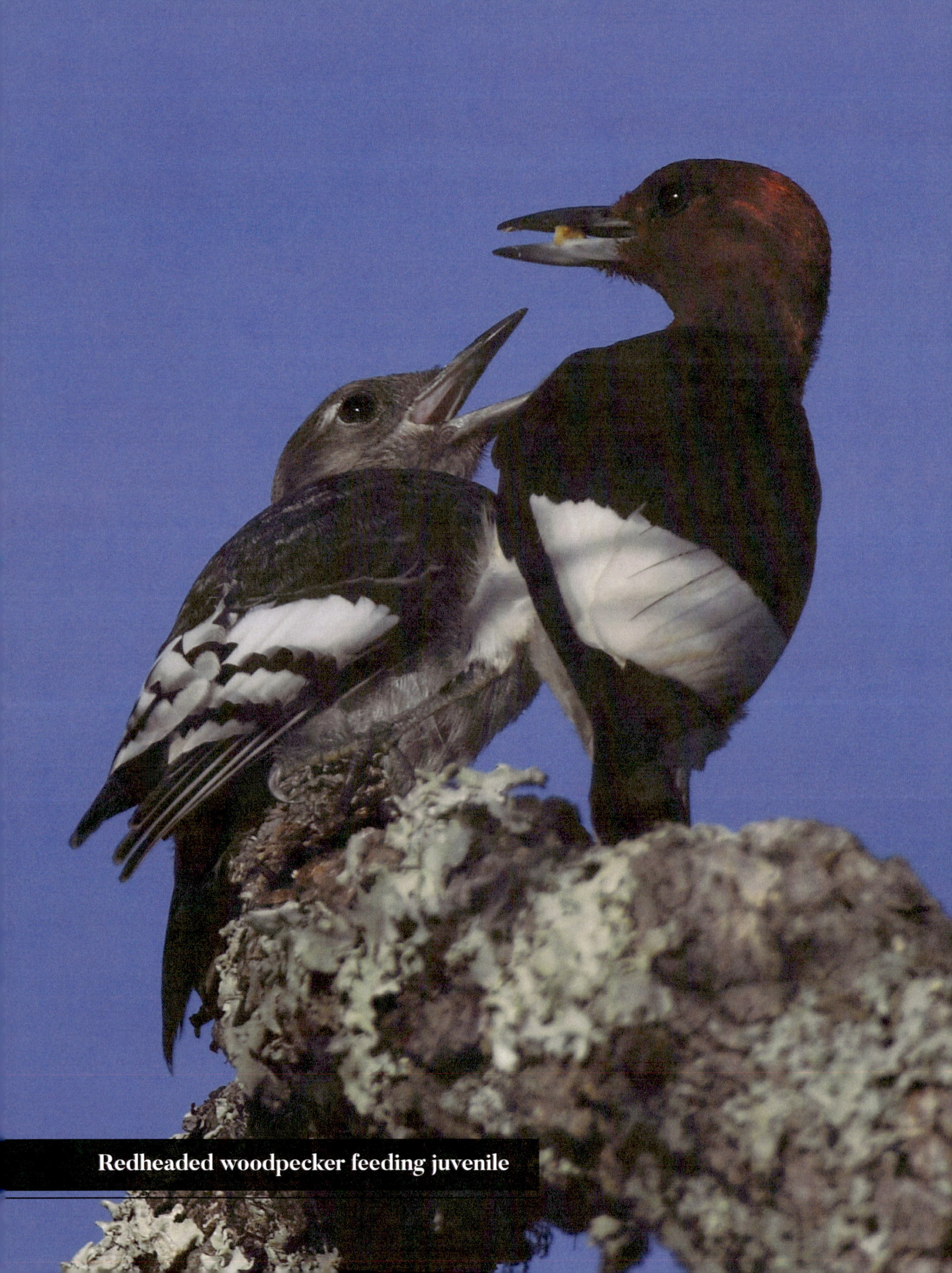

Redheaded woodpecker feeding juvenile

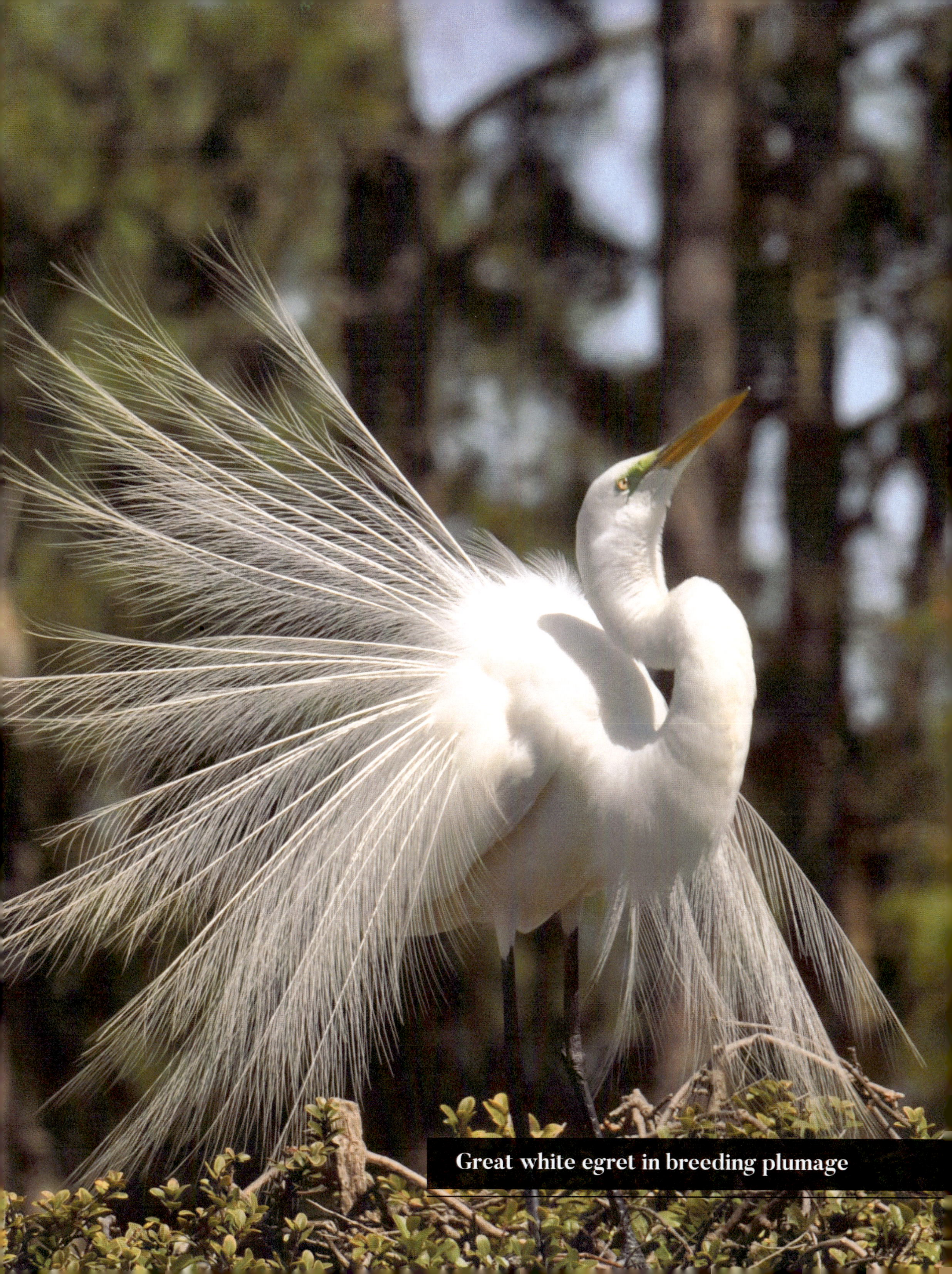

Great white egret in breeding plumage

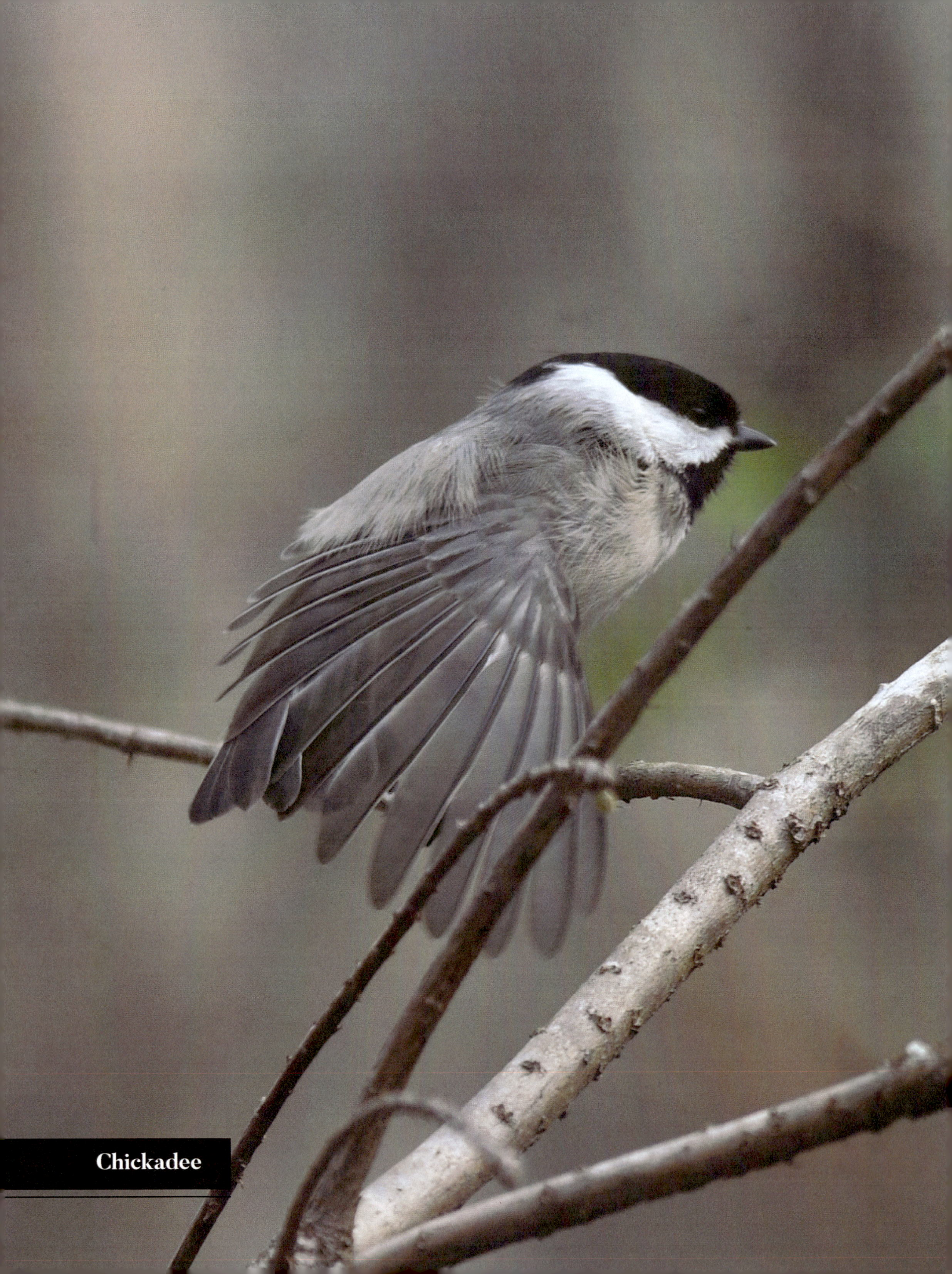

Chickadee

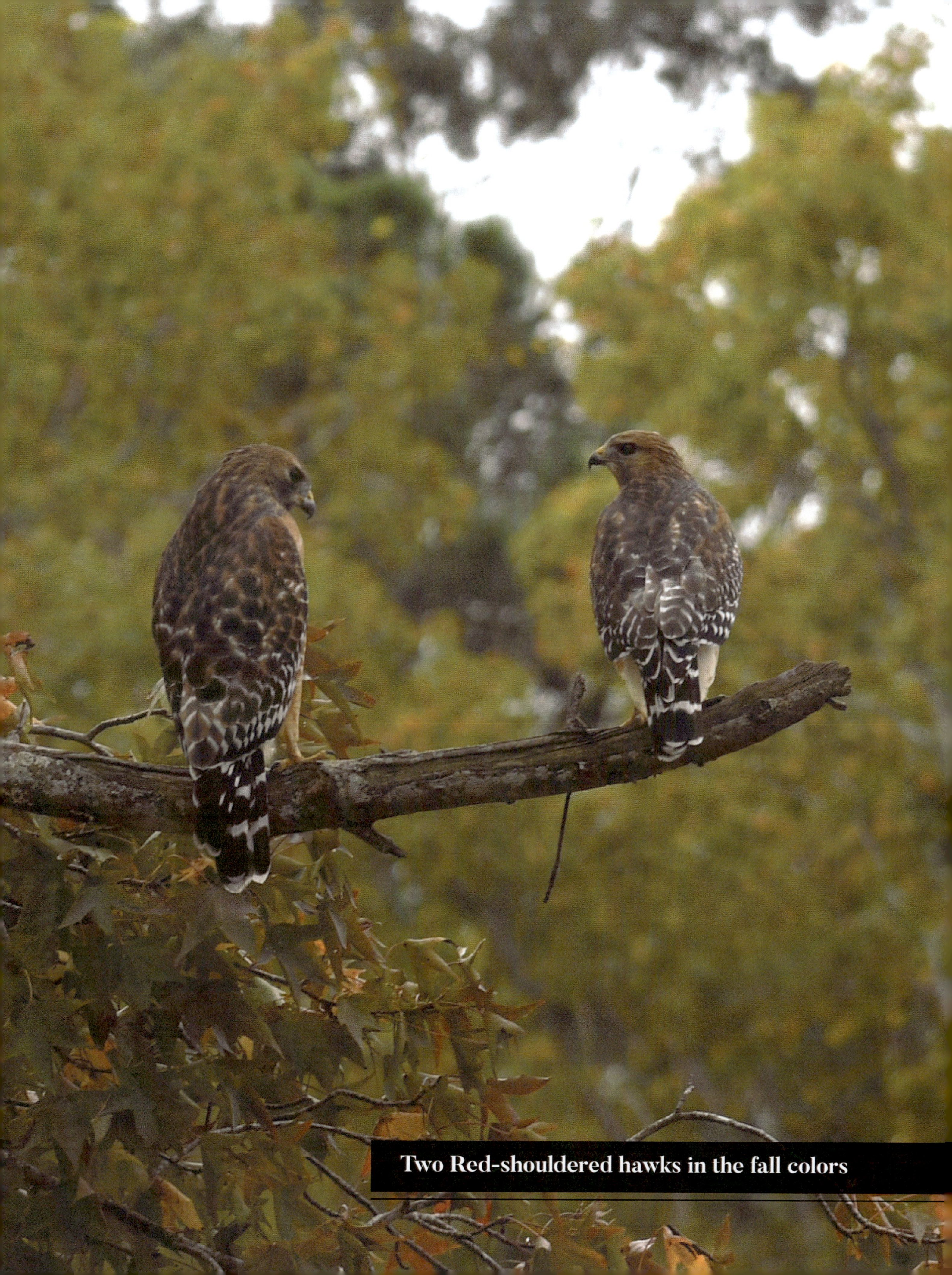

Two Red-shouldered hawks in the fall colors

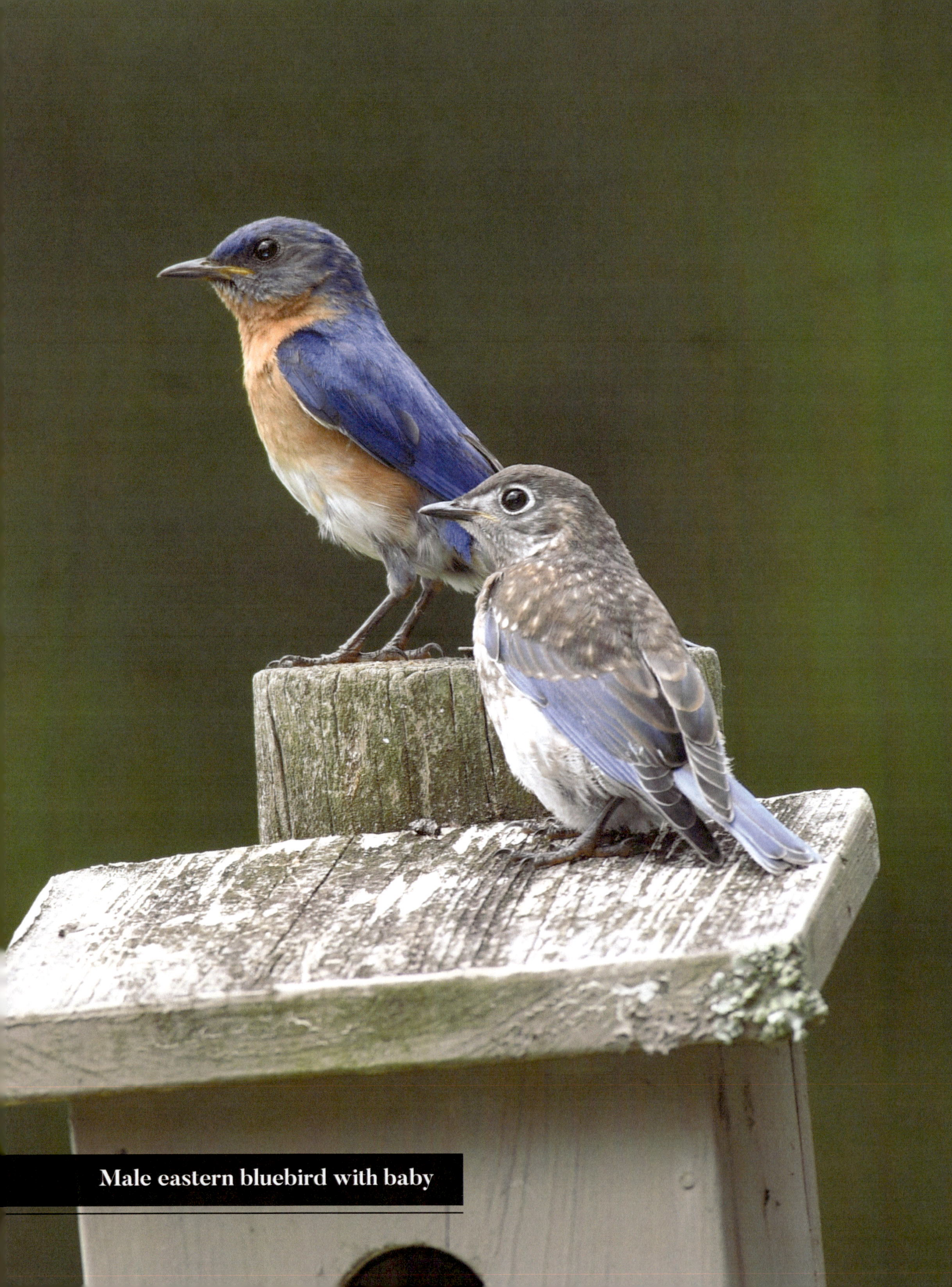

Male eastern bluebird with baby

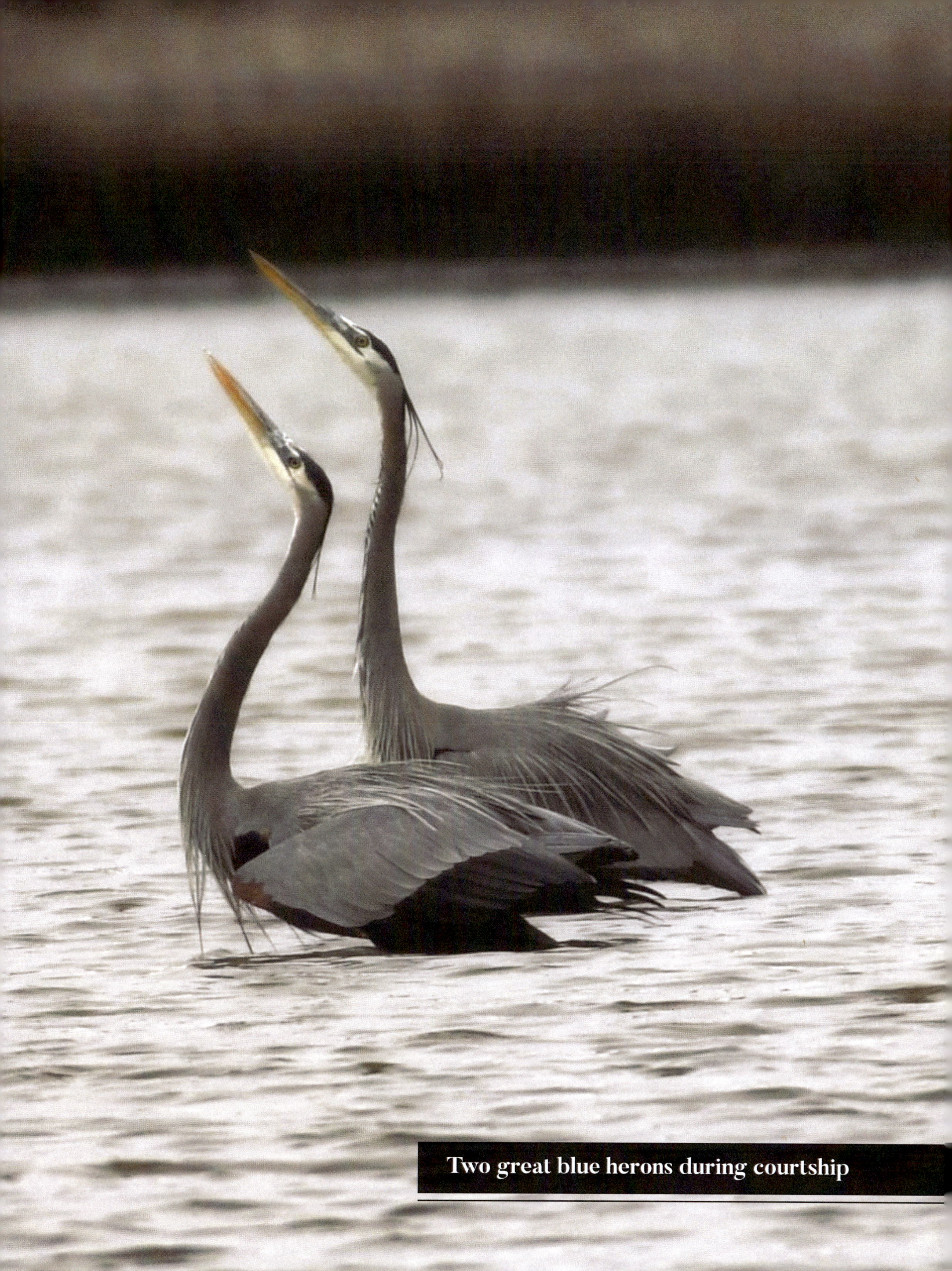

Two great blue herons during courtship

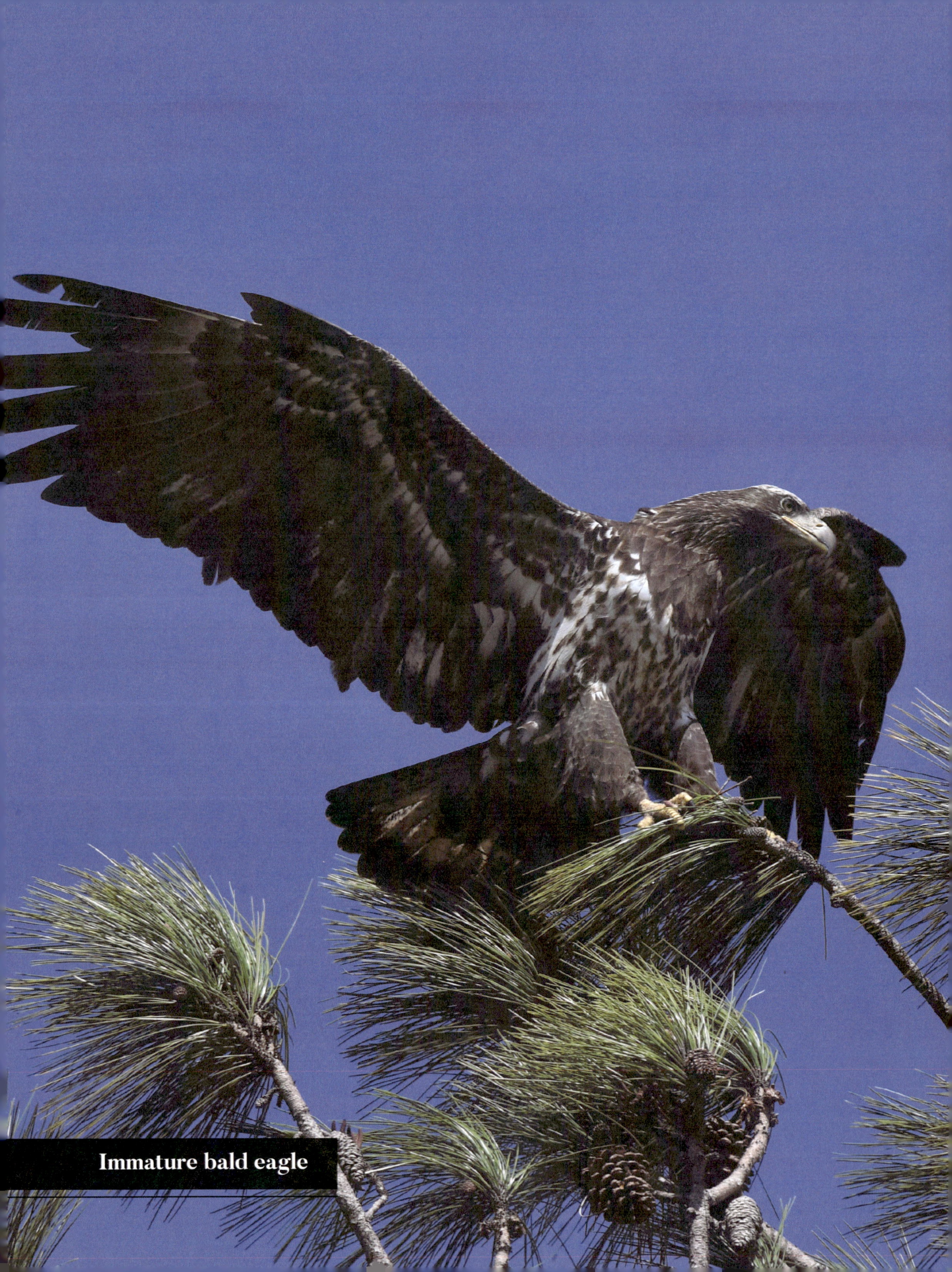

Immature bald eagle

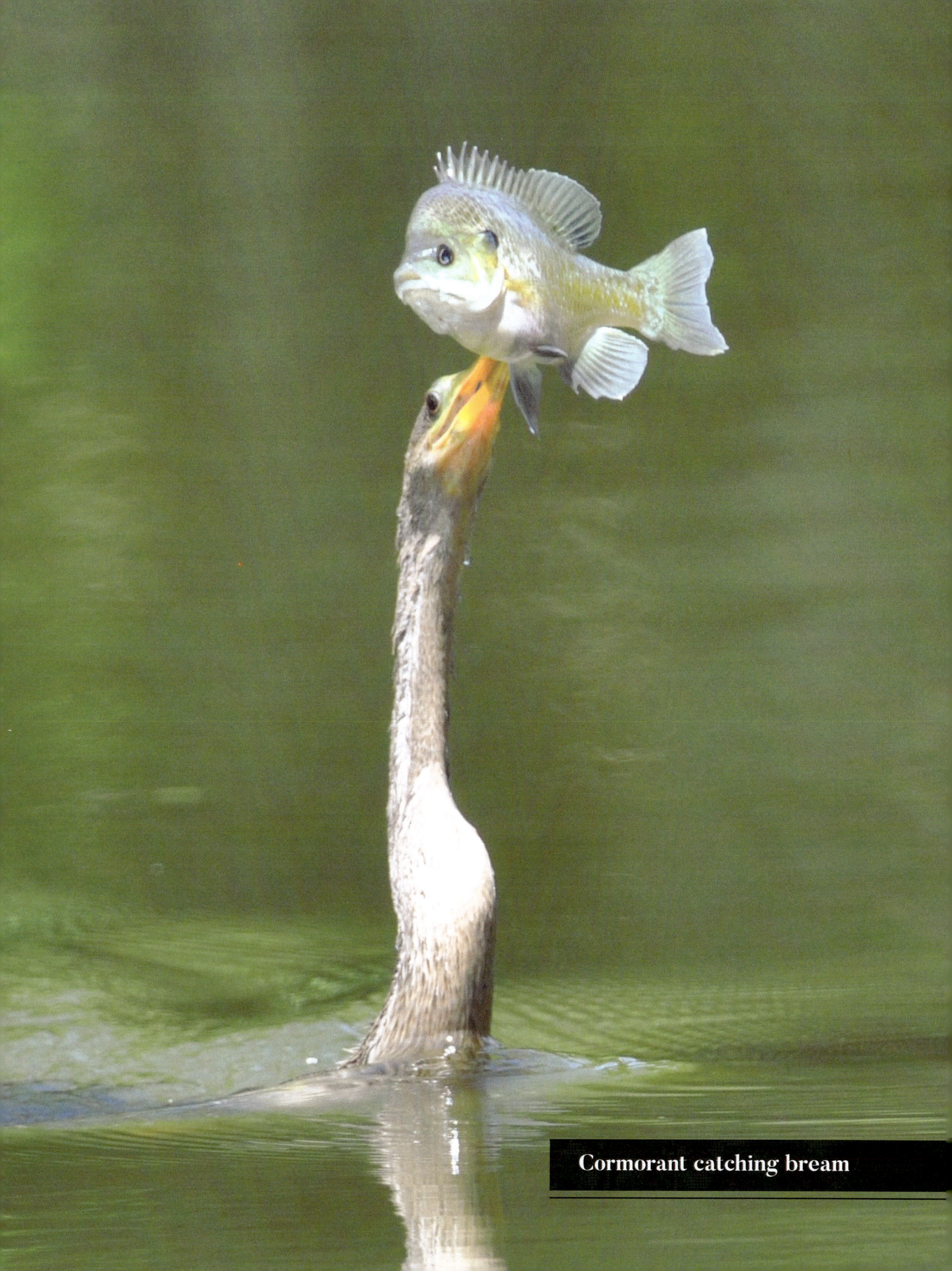

Cormorant catching bream

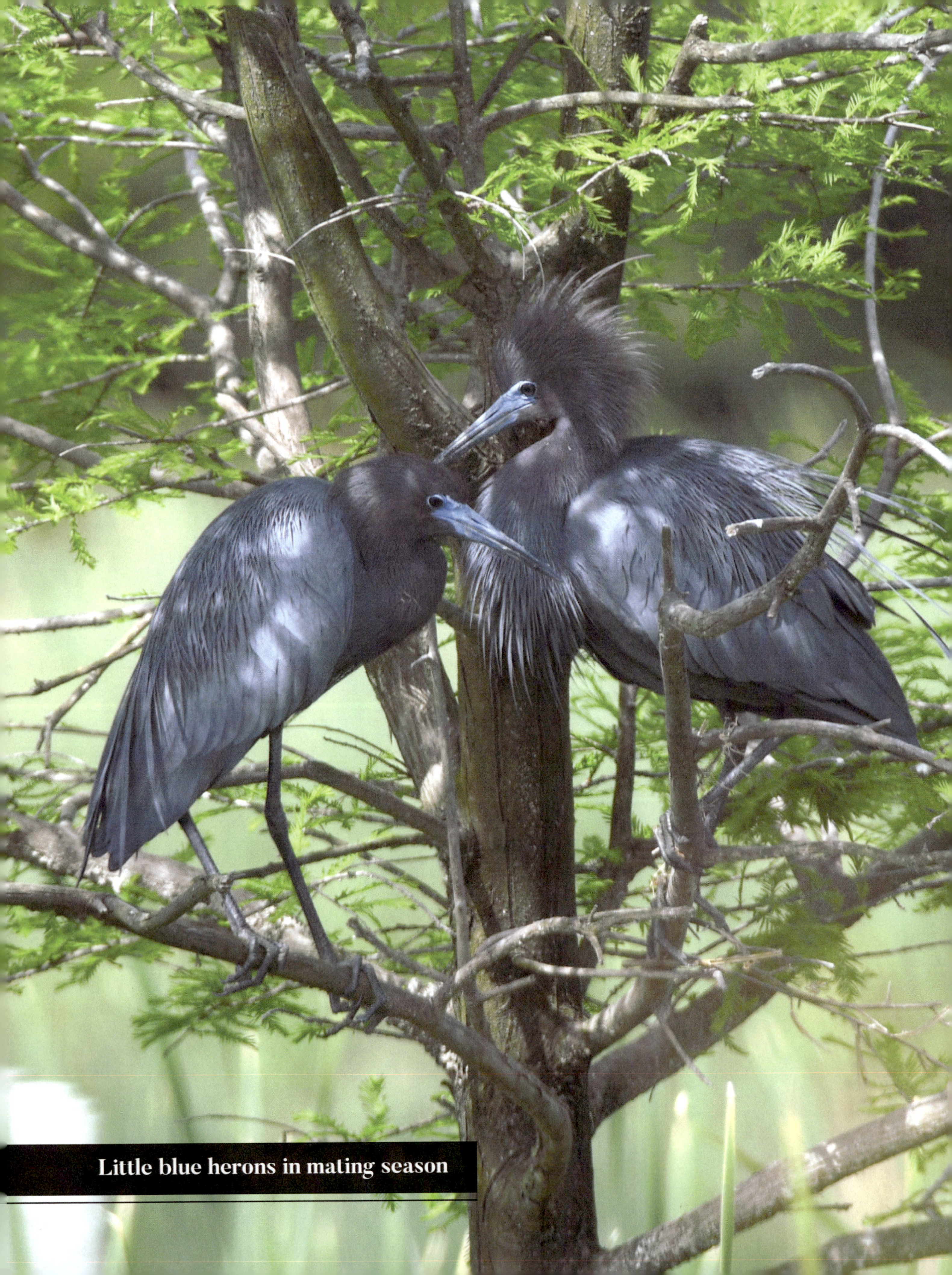

Little blue herons in mating season

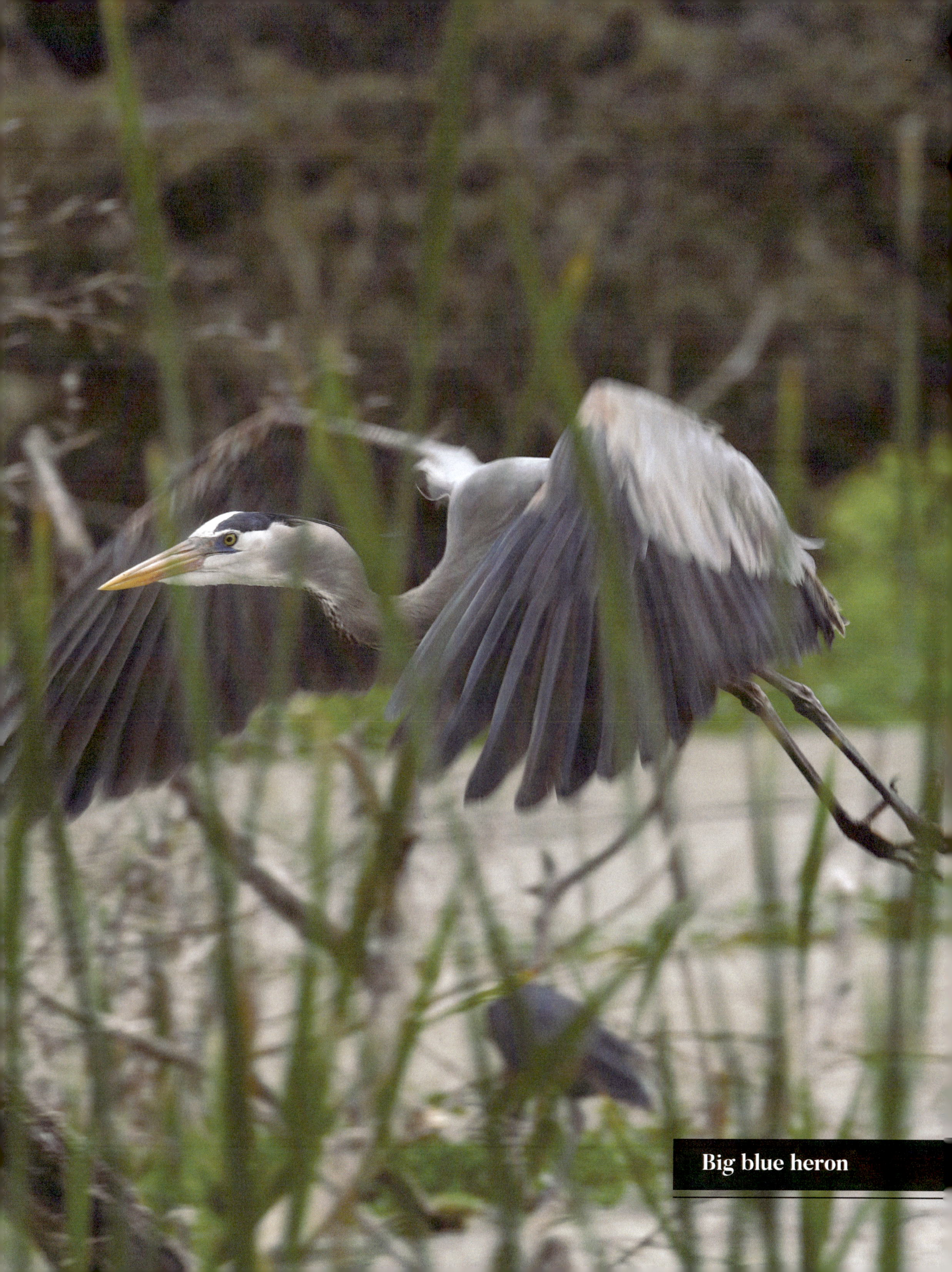
Big blue heron

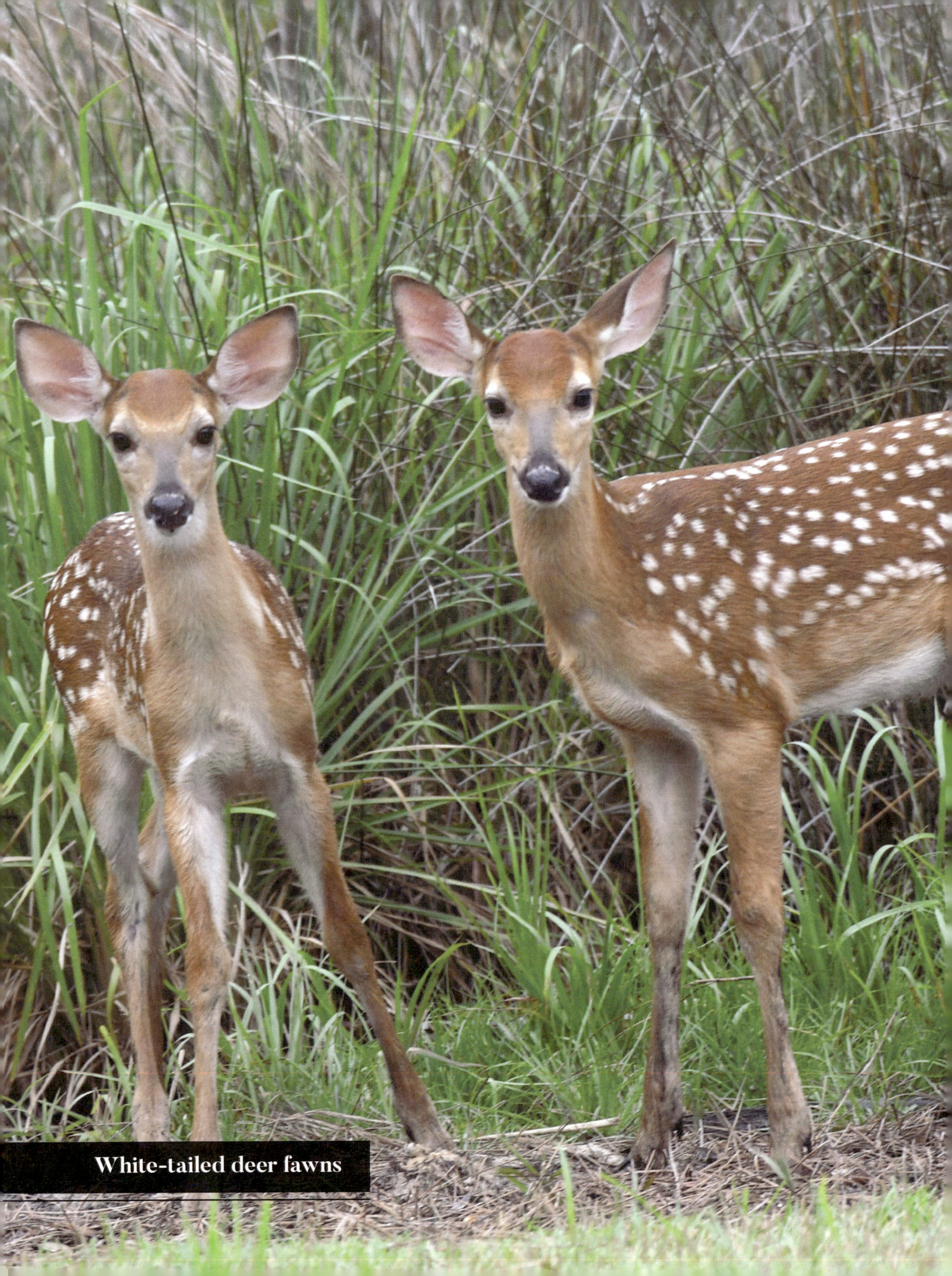

White-tailed deer fawns

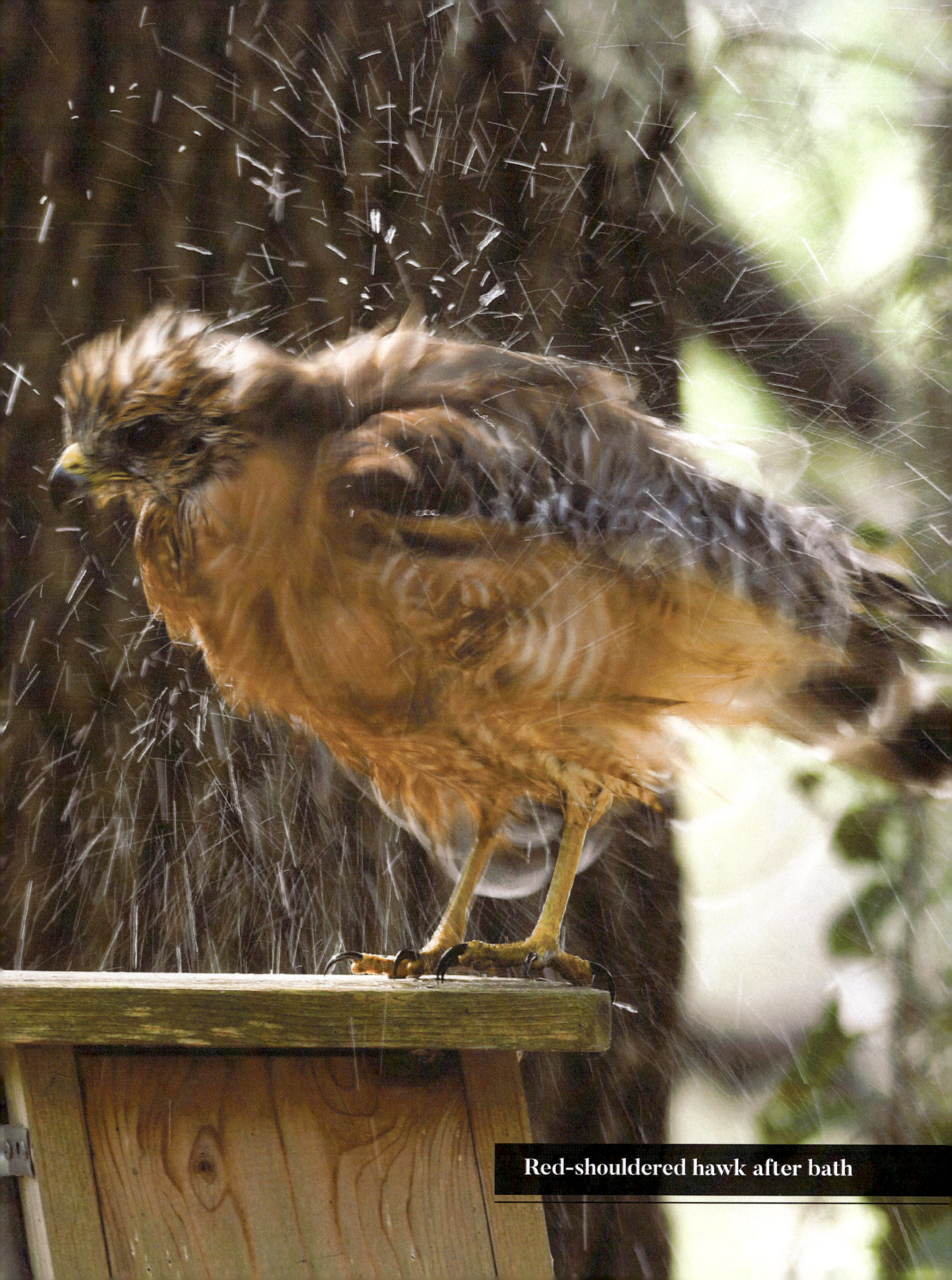

Red-shouldered hawk after bath

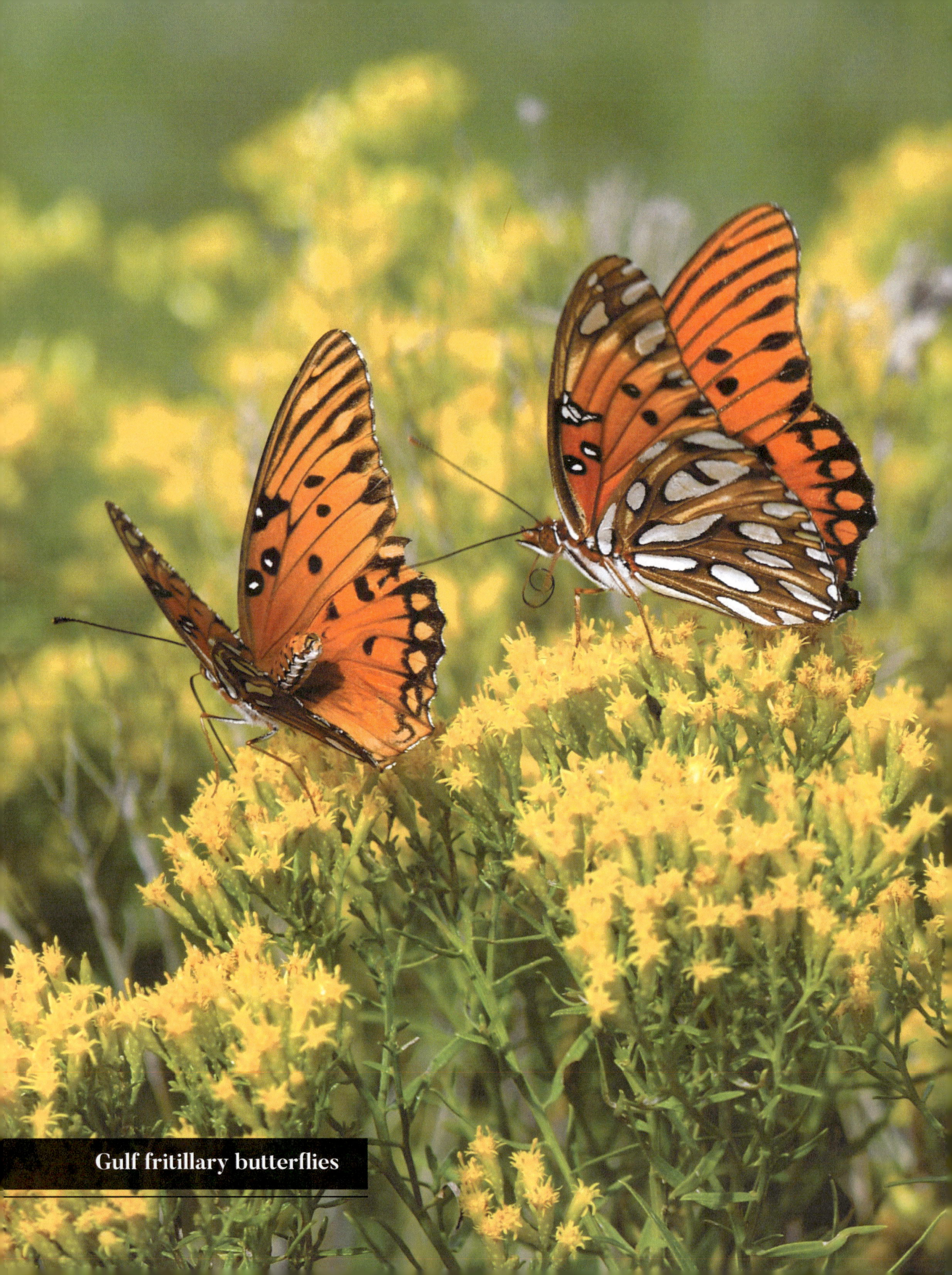

Gulf fritillary butterflies

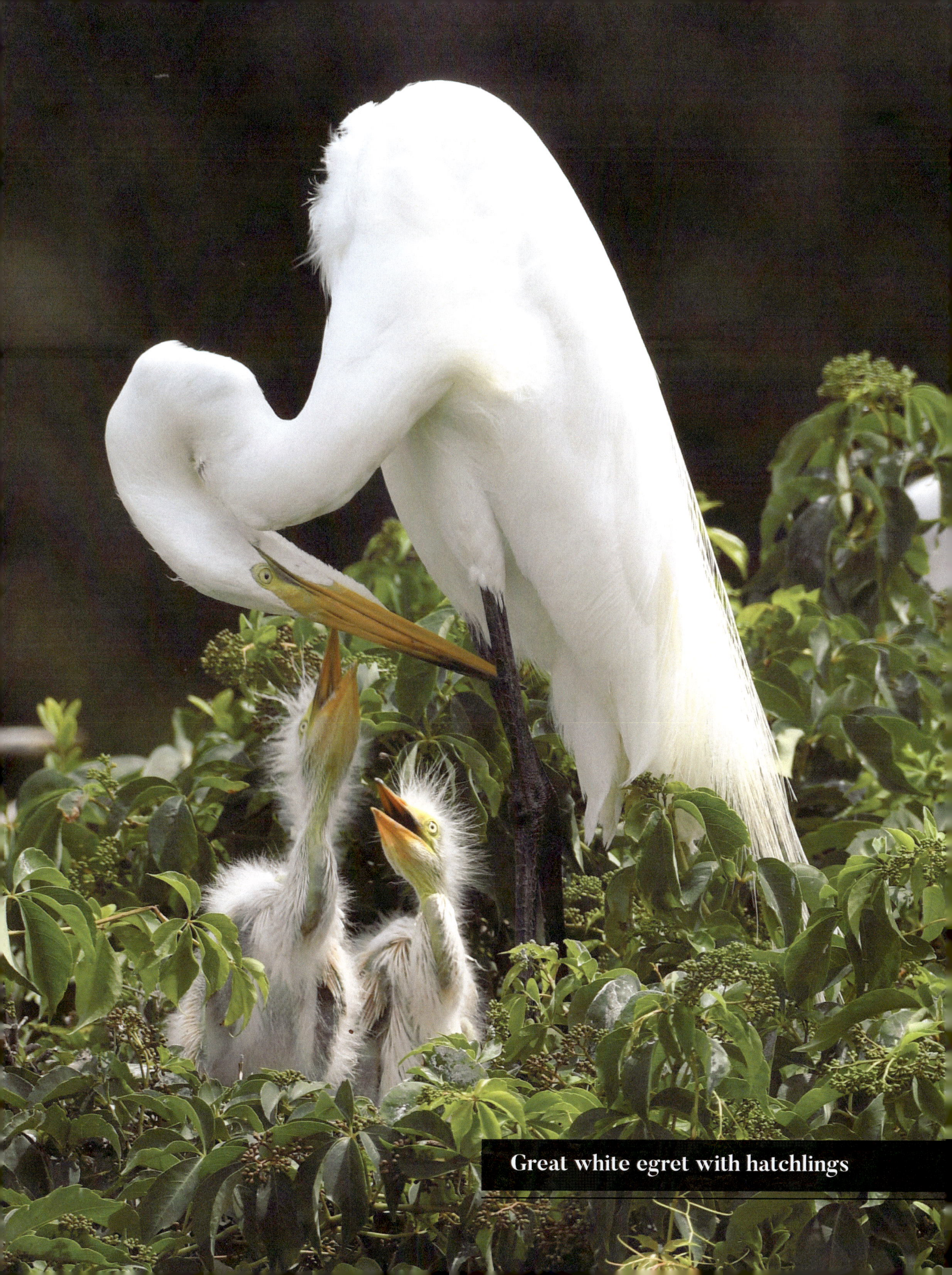

Great white egret with hatchlings

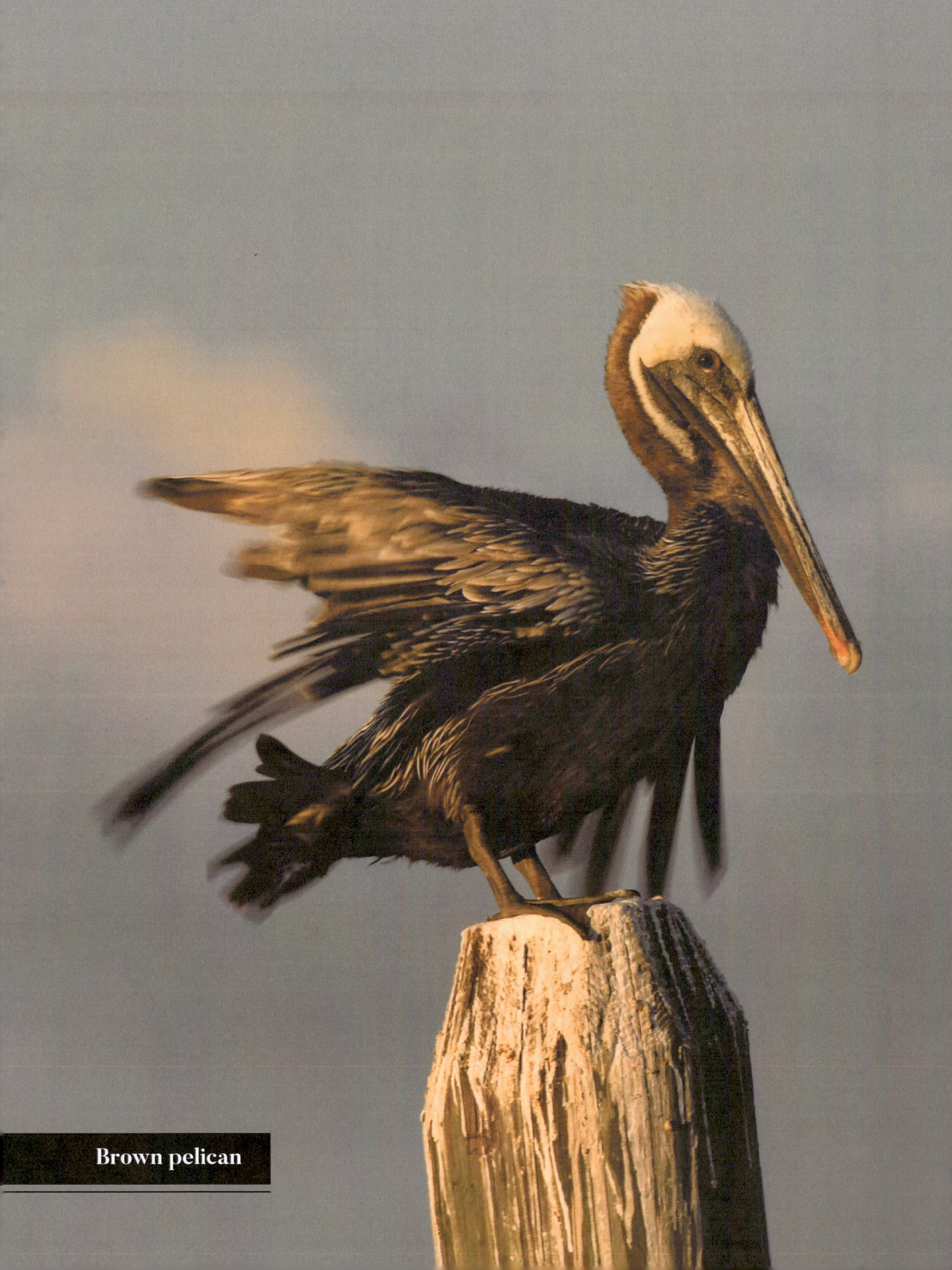

Brown pelican

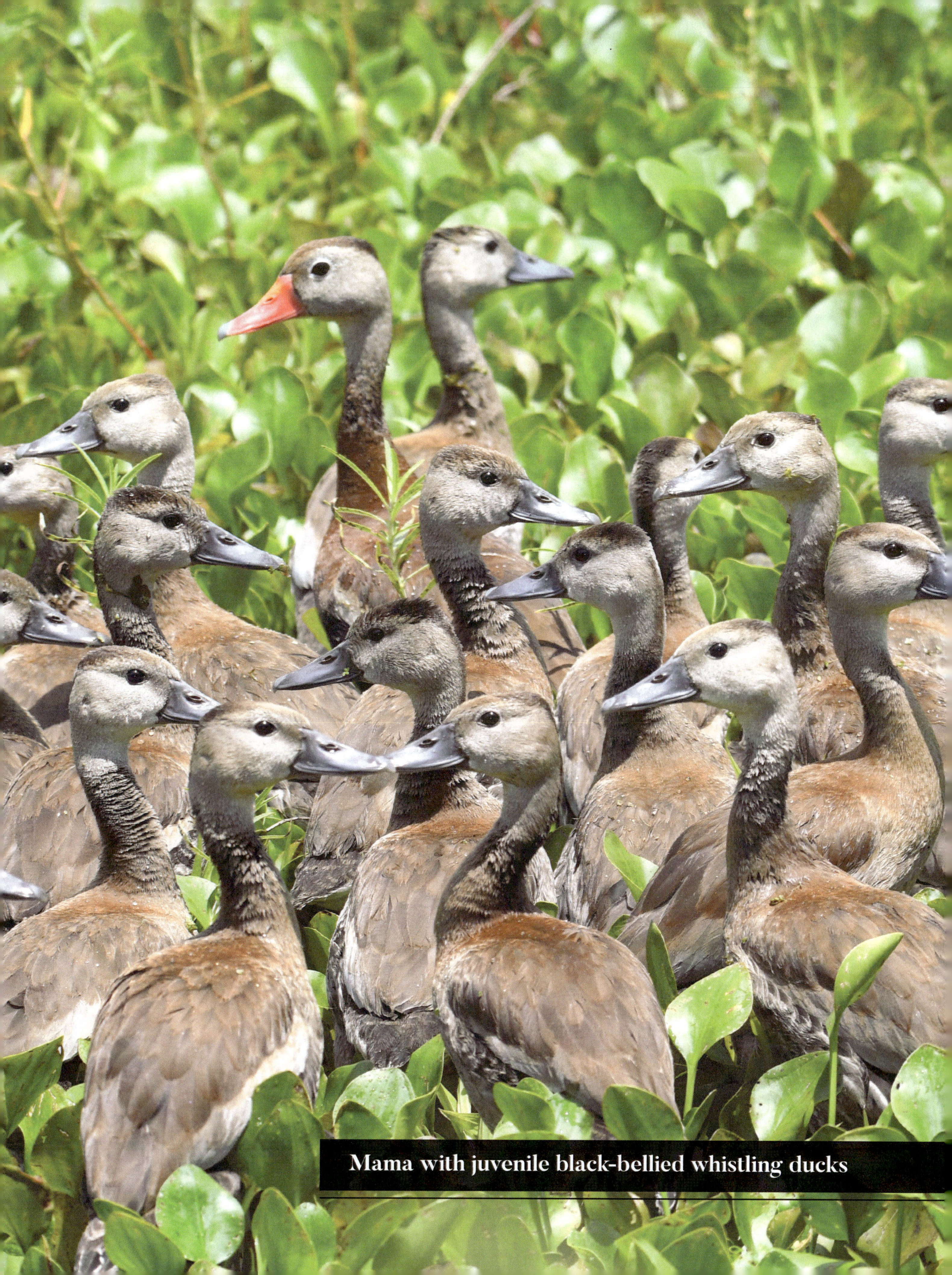

Mama with juvenile black-bellied whistling ducks

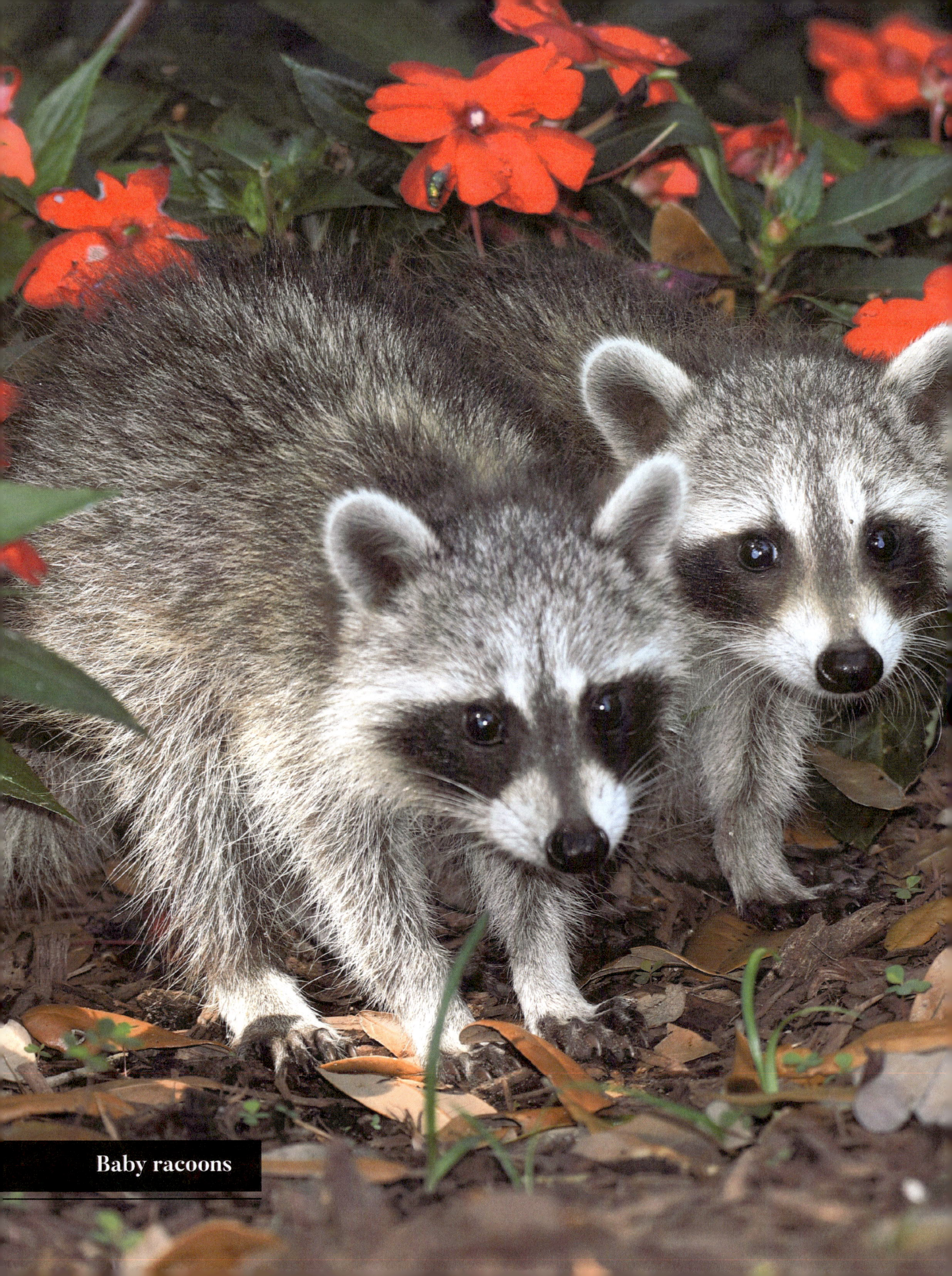

Baby racoons

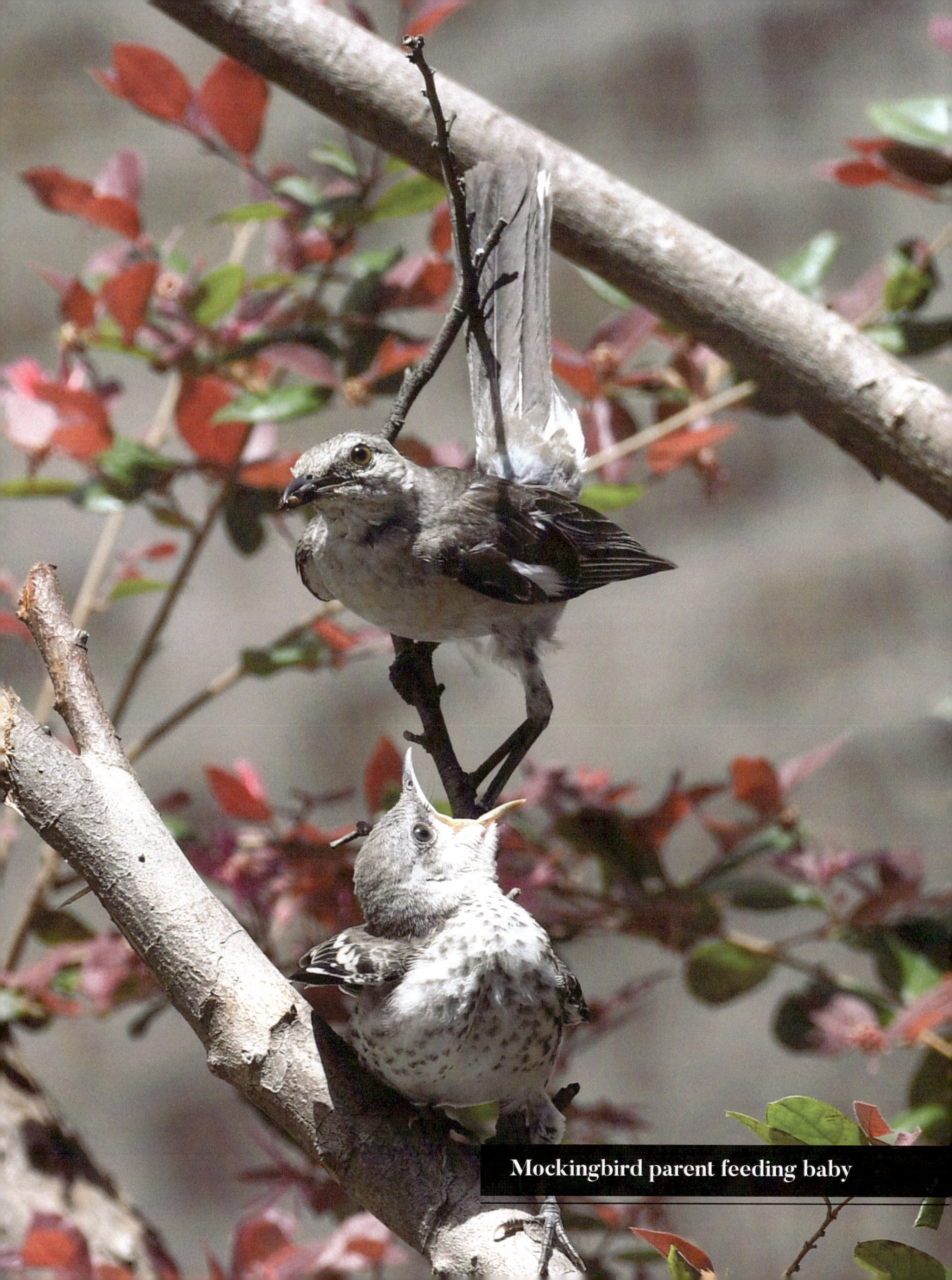

Mockingbird parent feeding baby

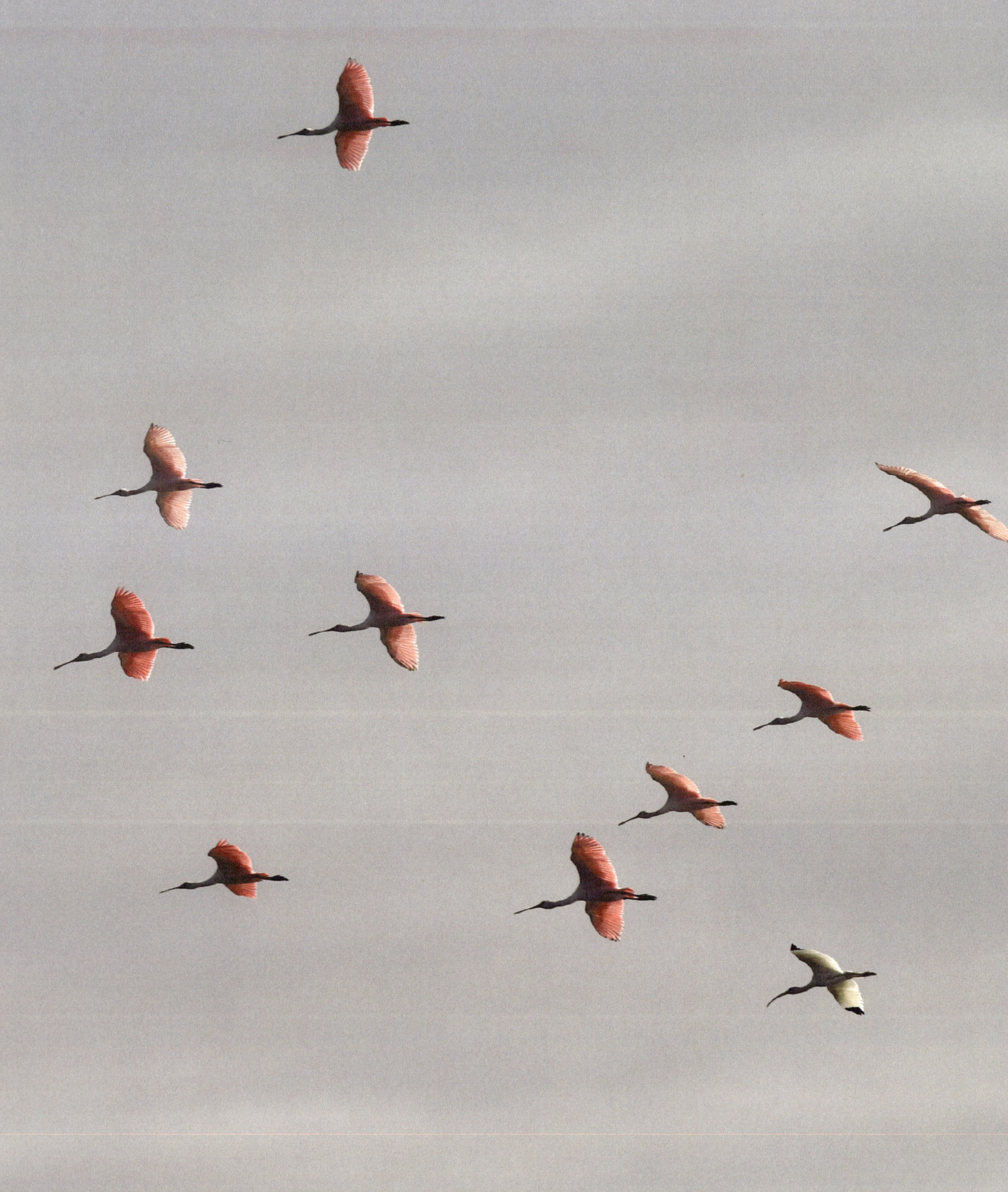

Flock of roseate spoonbills and wood storks

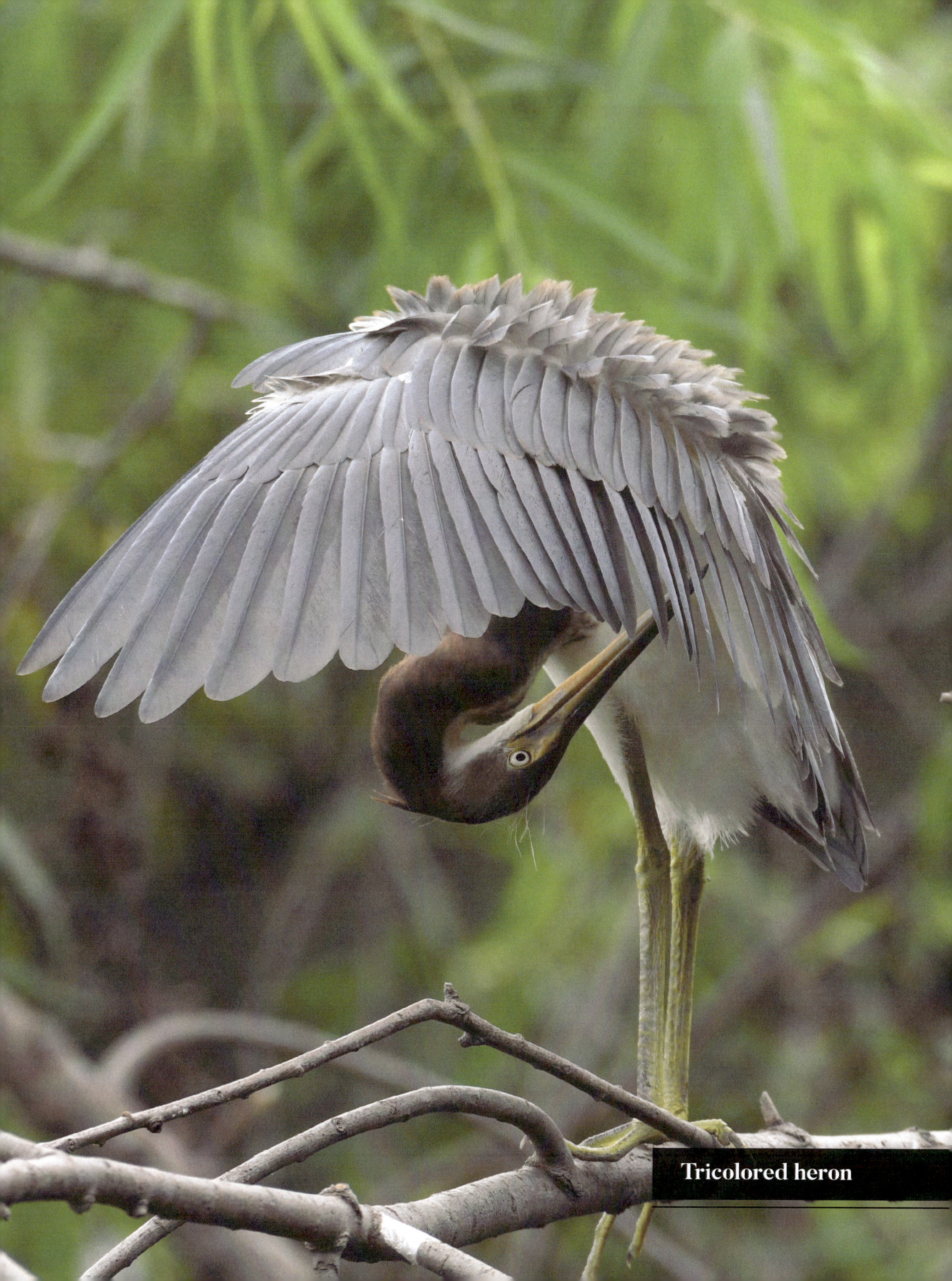

Tricolored heron

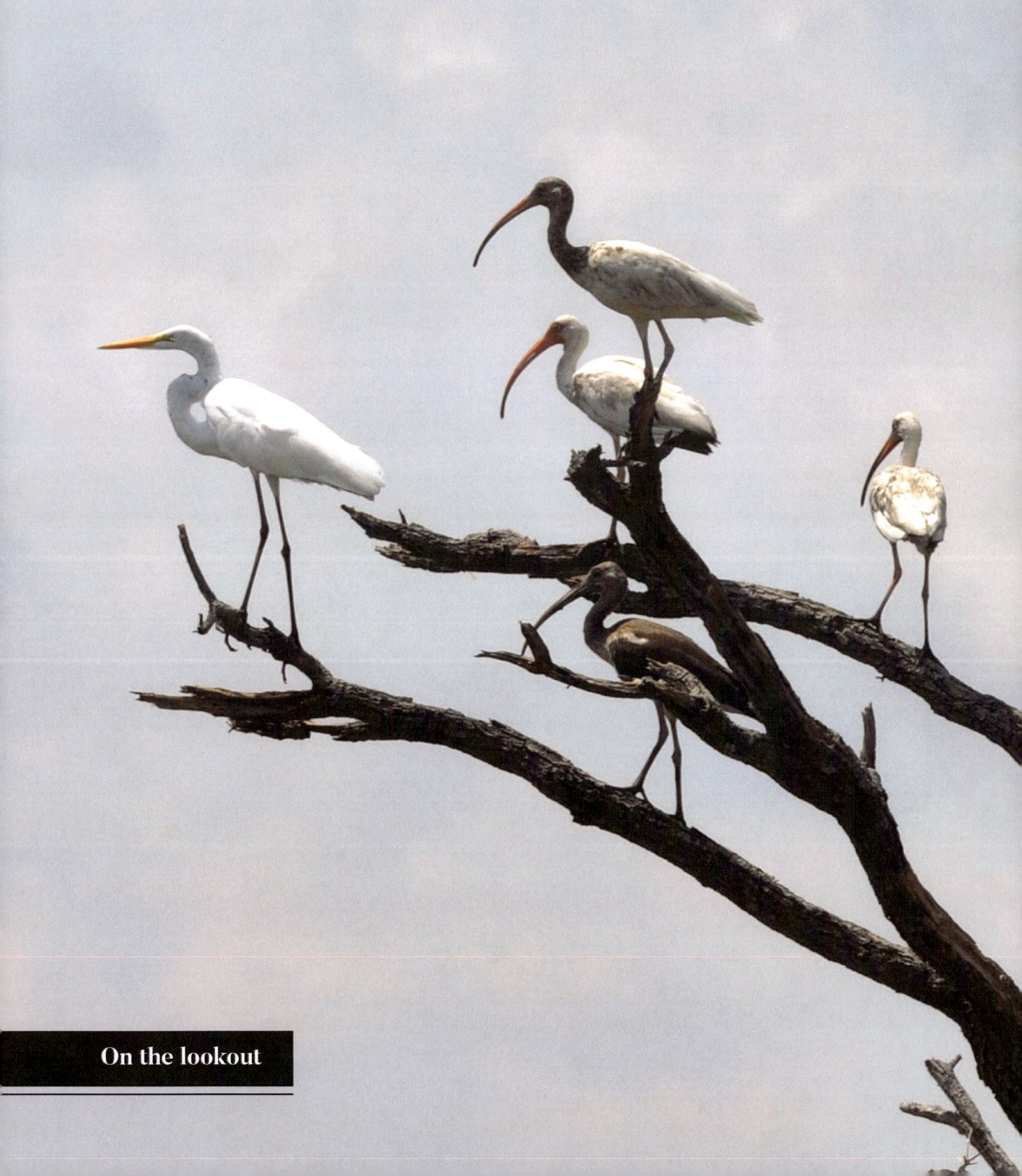
On the lookout

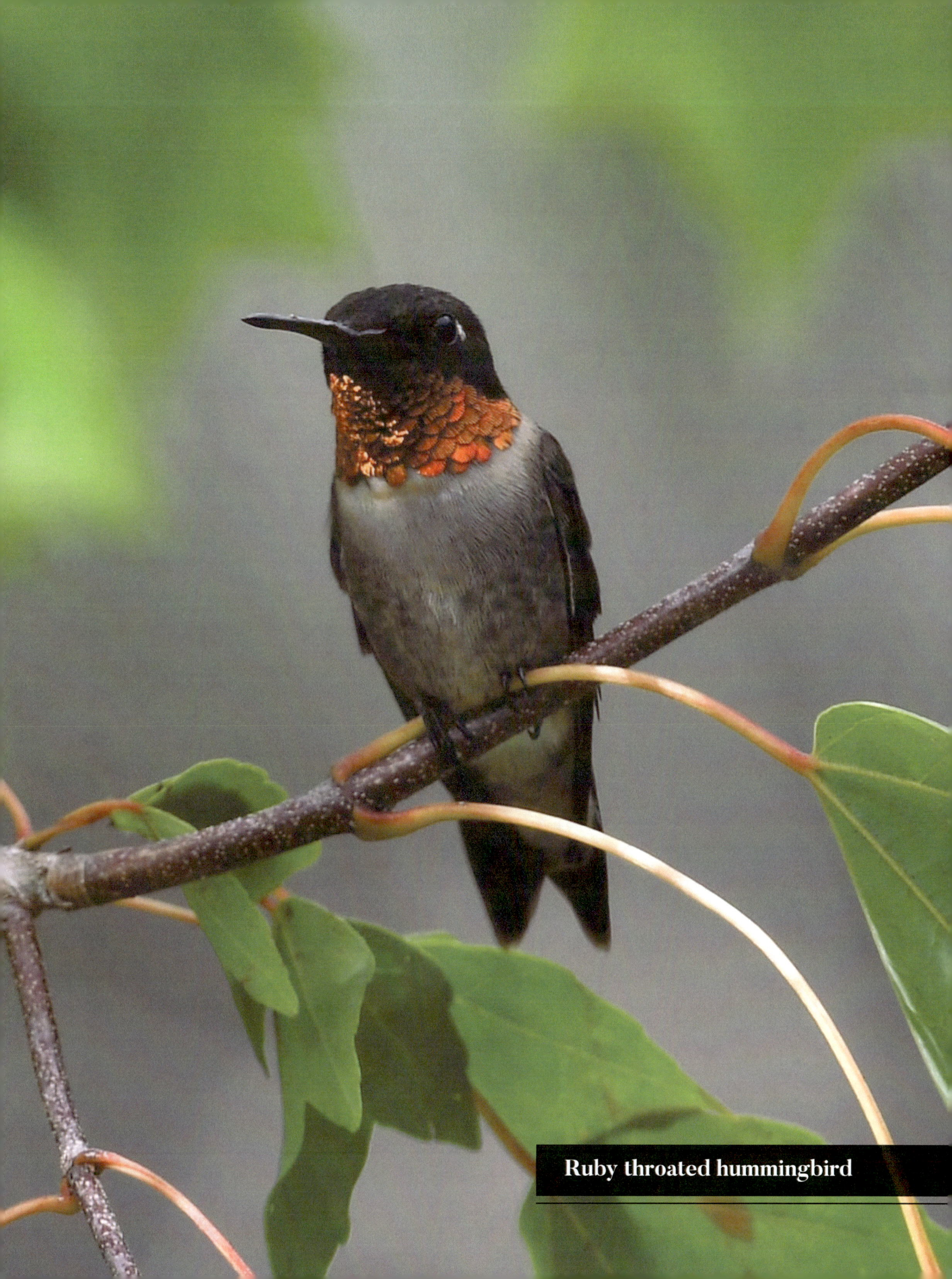
Ruby throated hummingbird

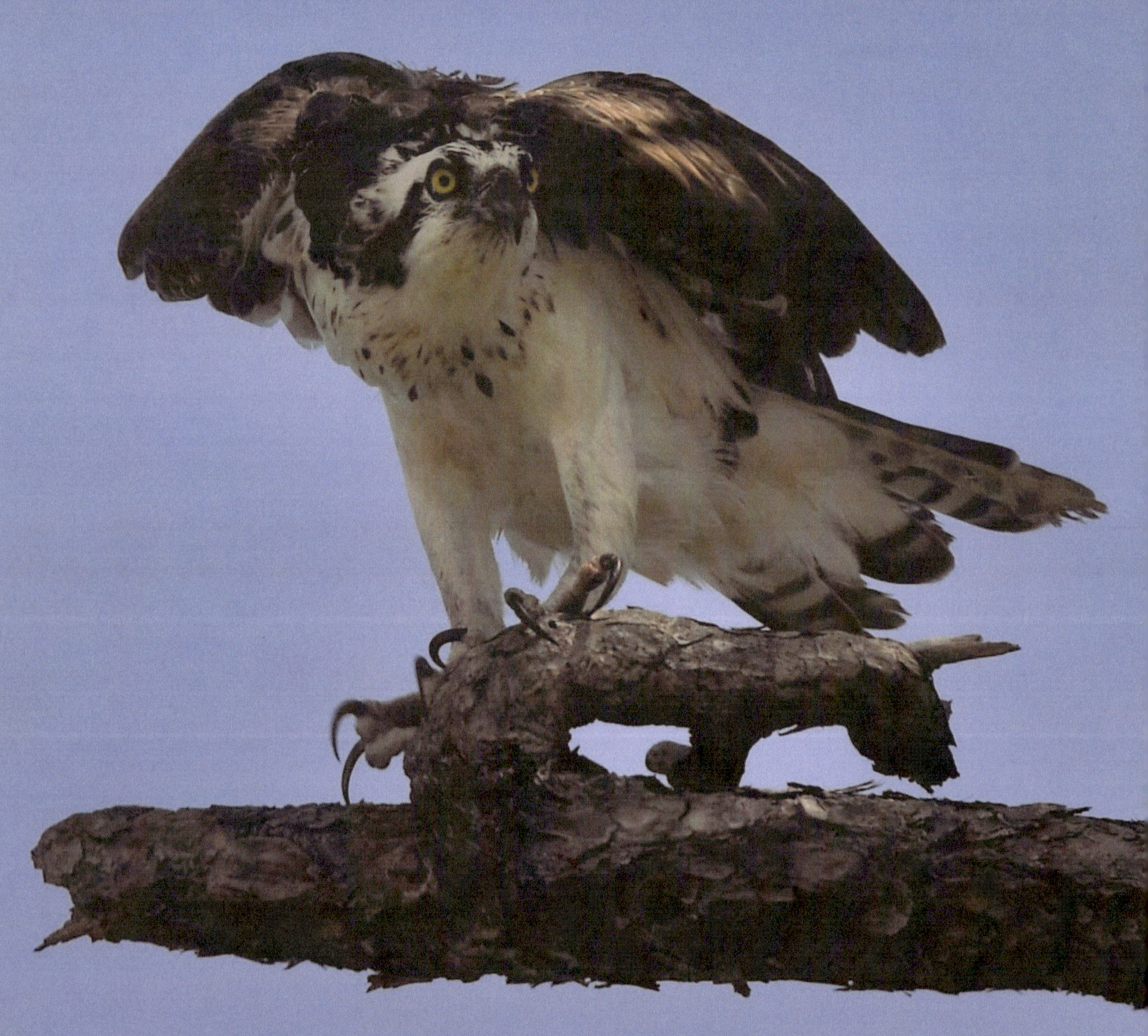

Osprey

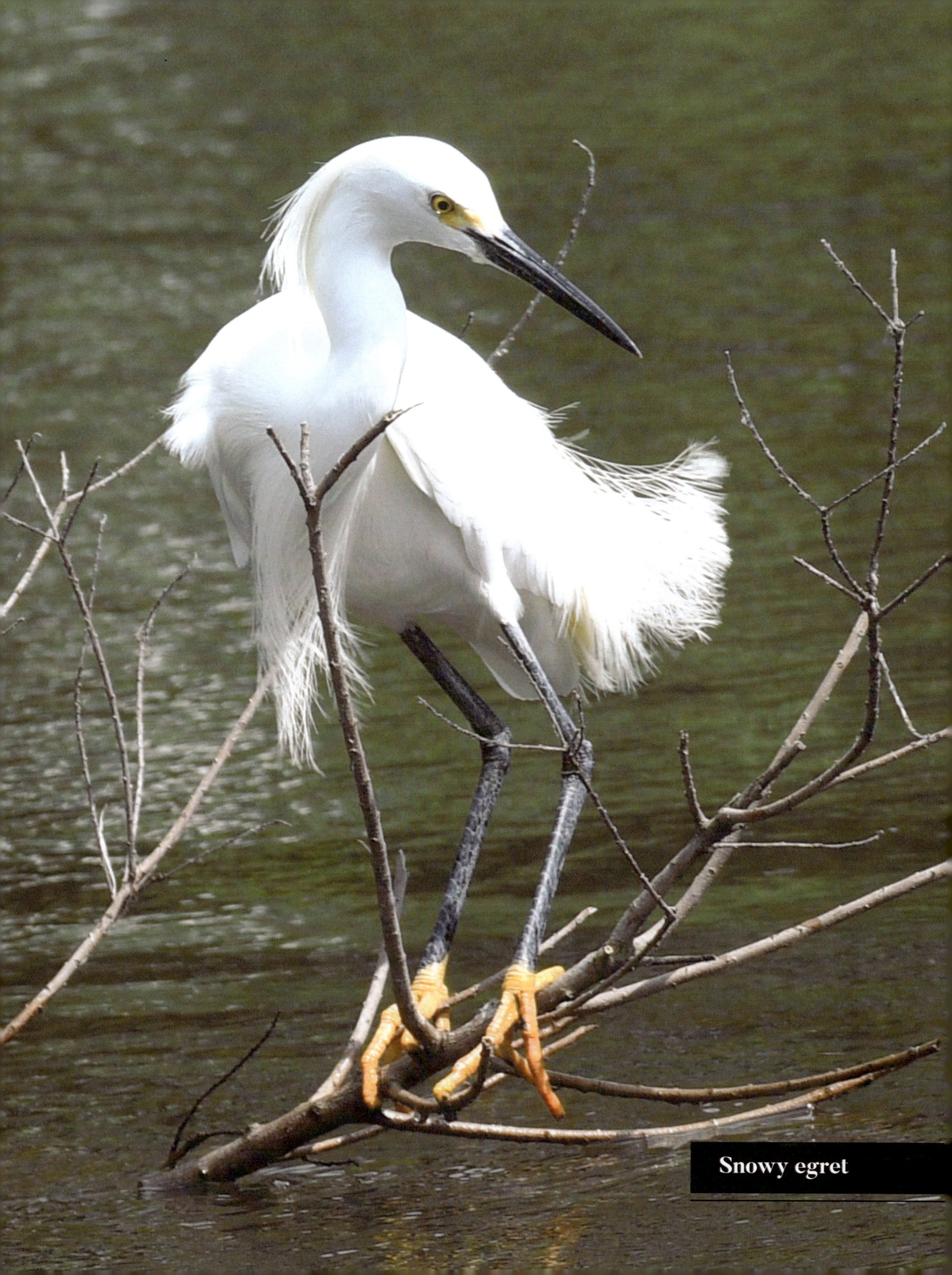

Snowy egret

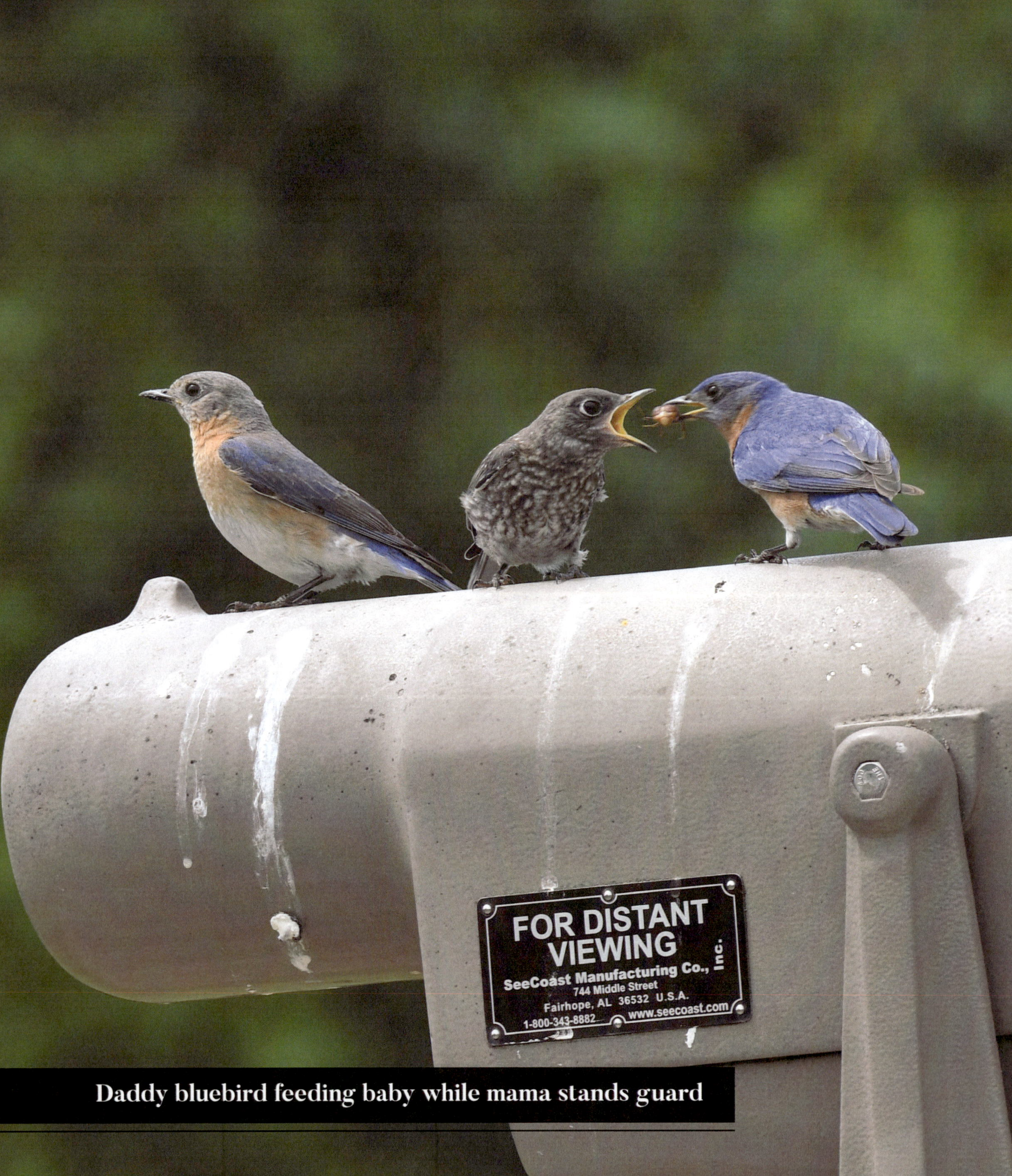

Daddy bluebird feeding baby while mama stands guard

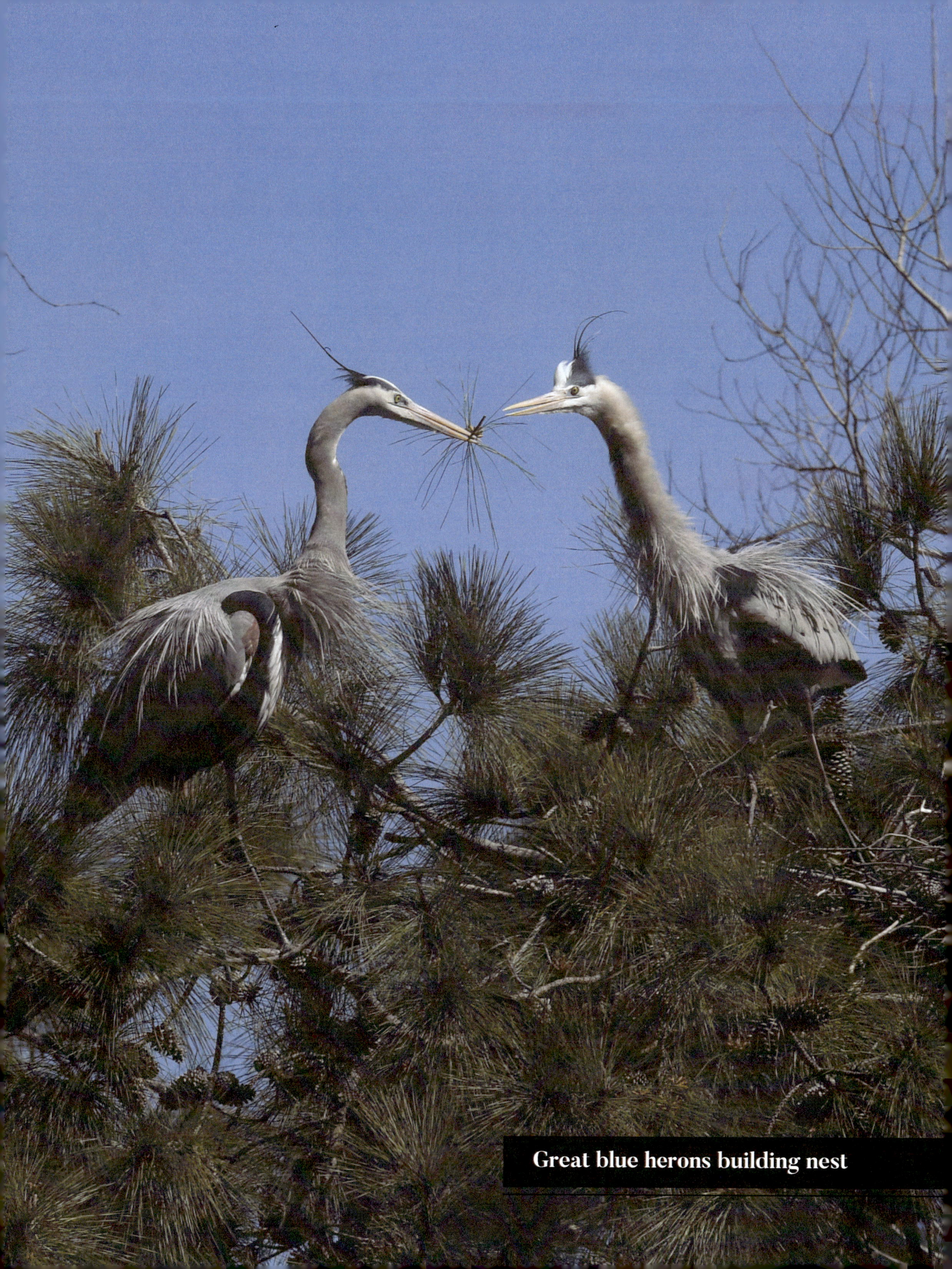

Great blue herons building nest

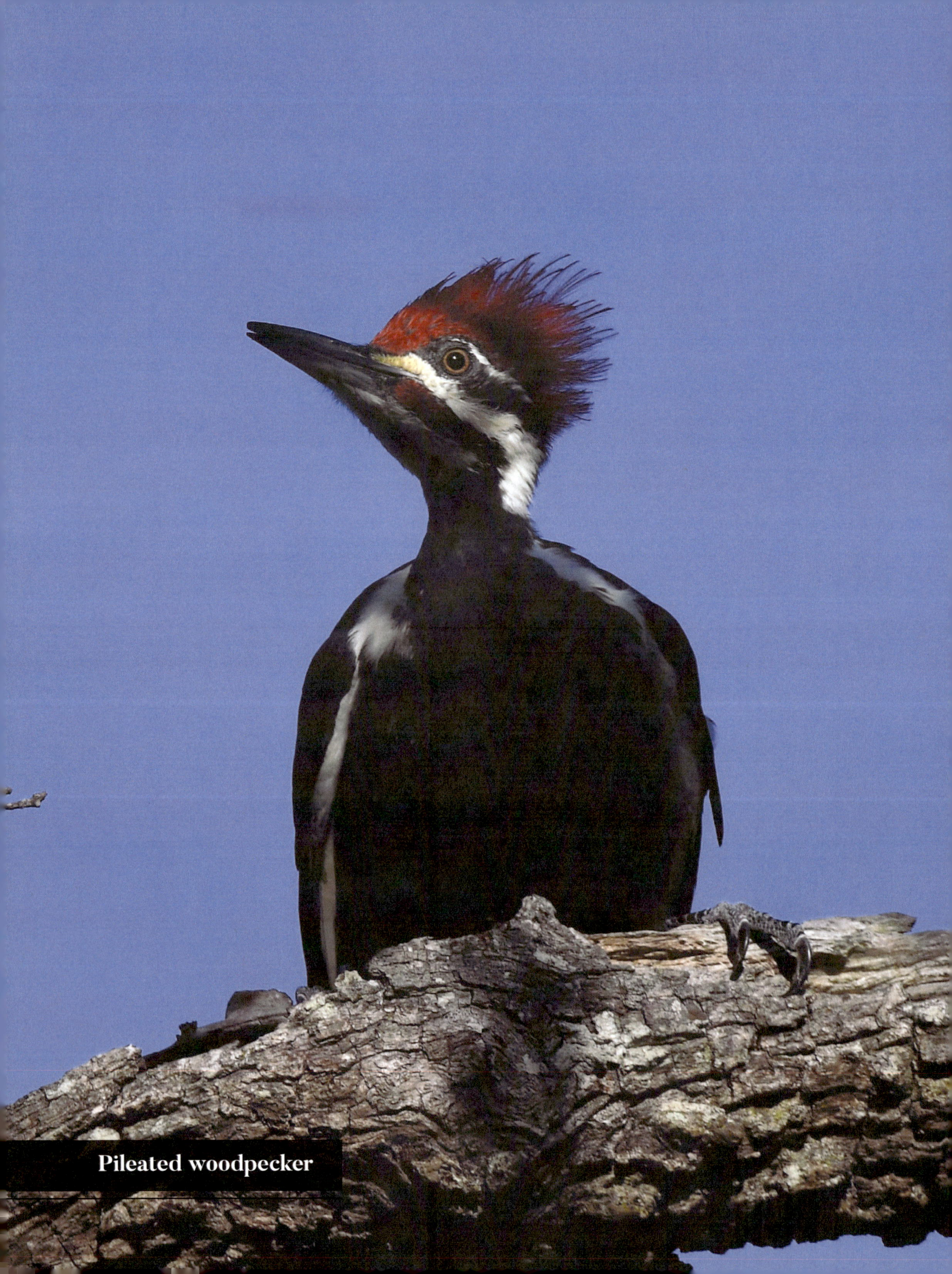

Pileated woodpecker

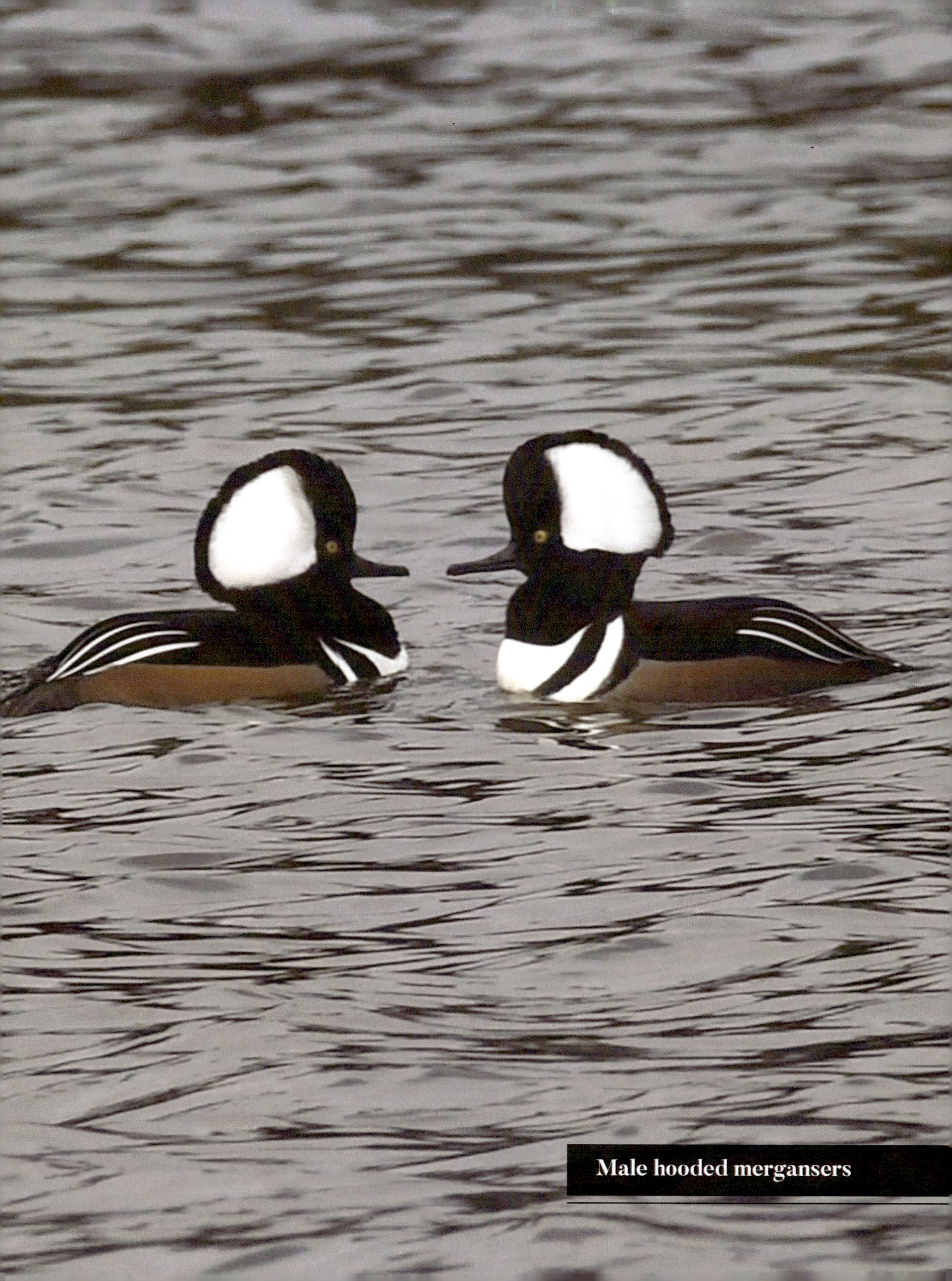

Male hooded mergansers

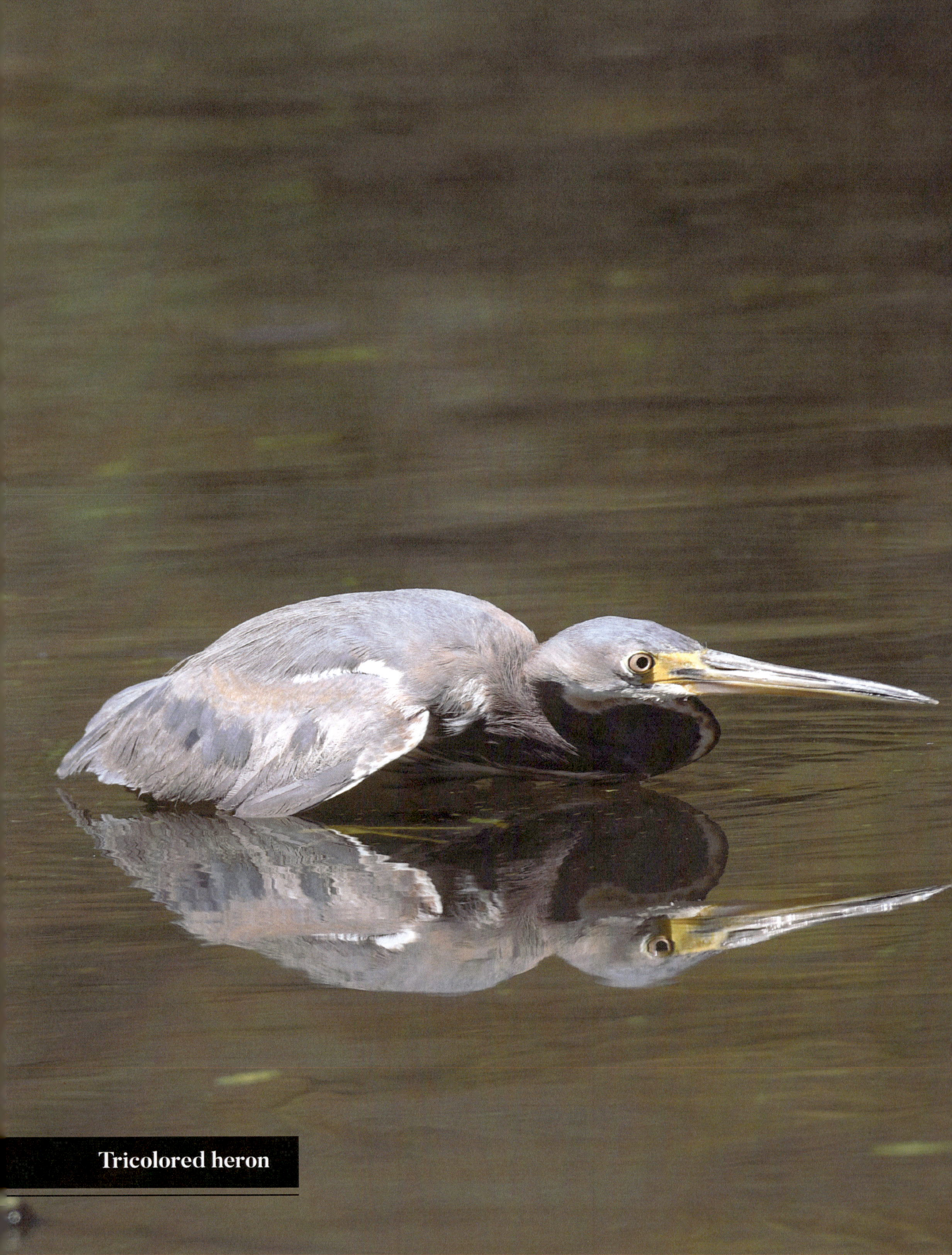

Tricolored heron

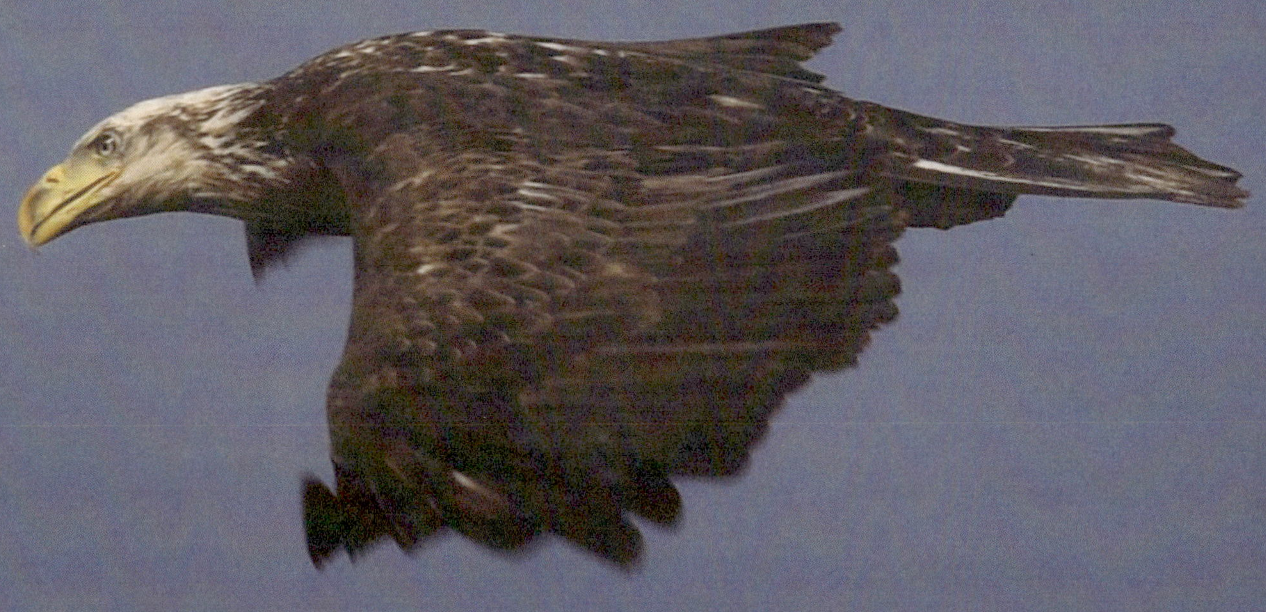

Immature bald eagle

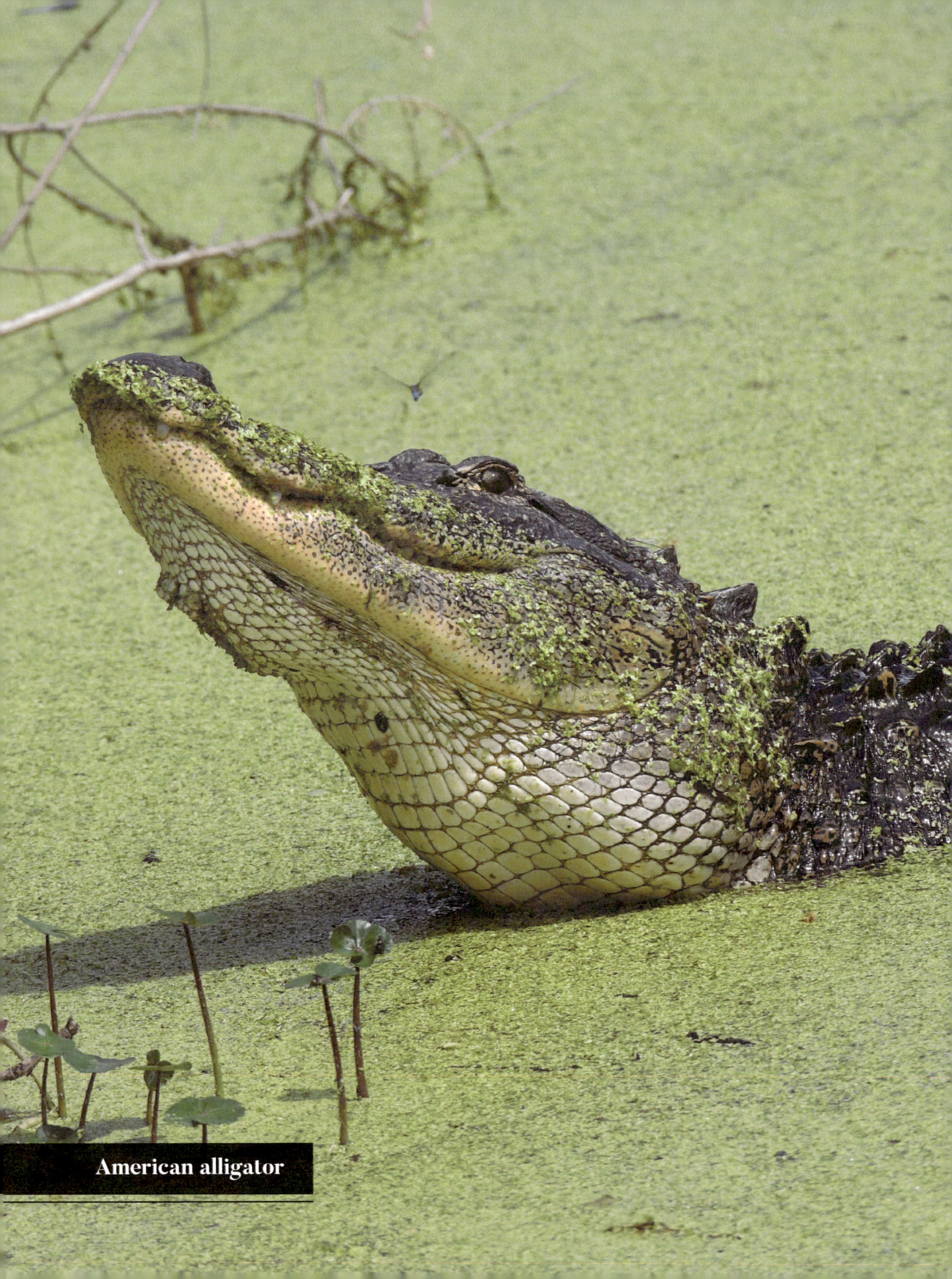

American alligator

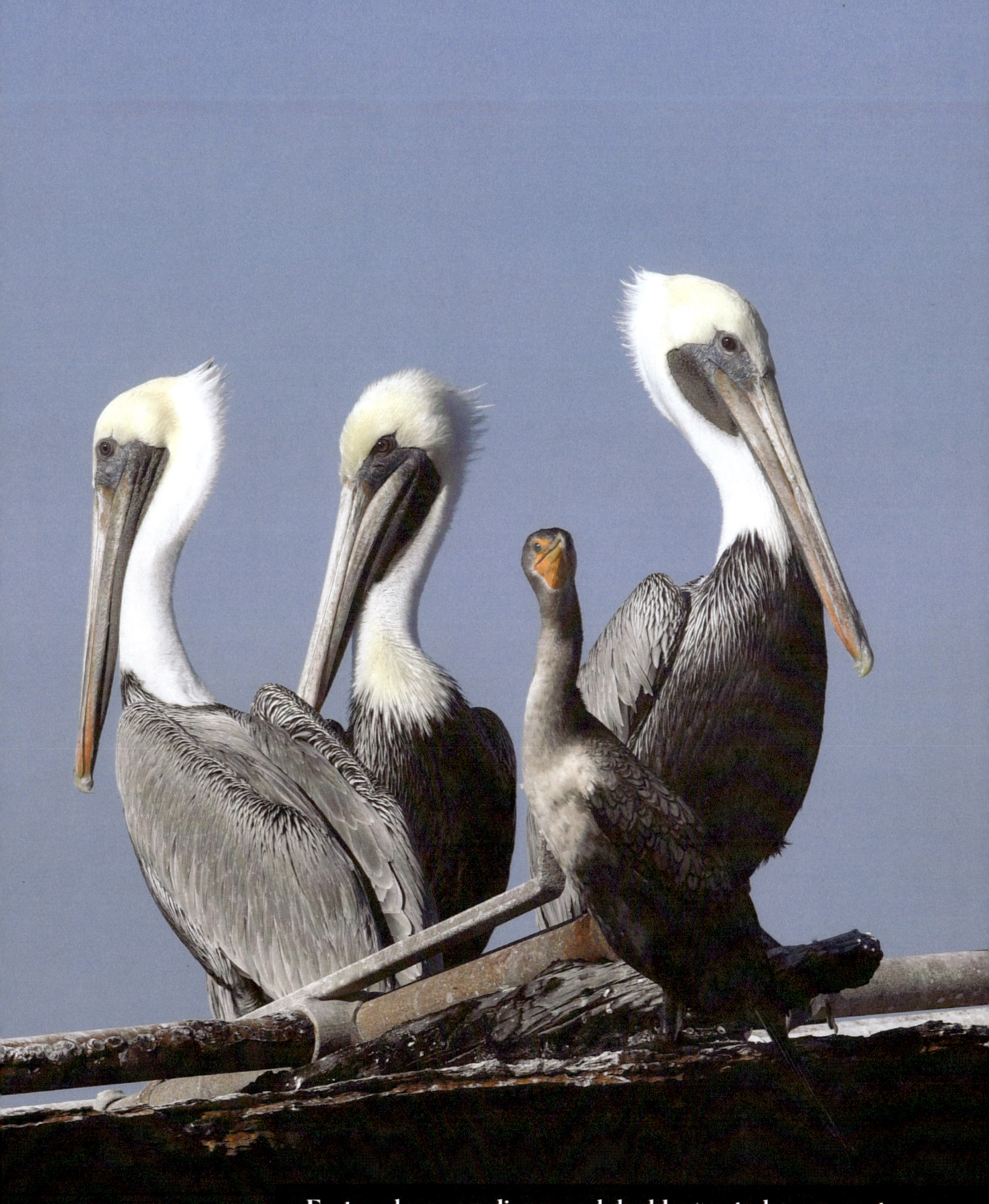

Eastern brown pelicans and double-crested cormorant

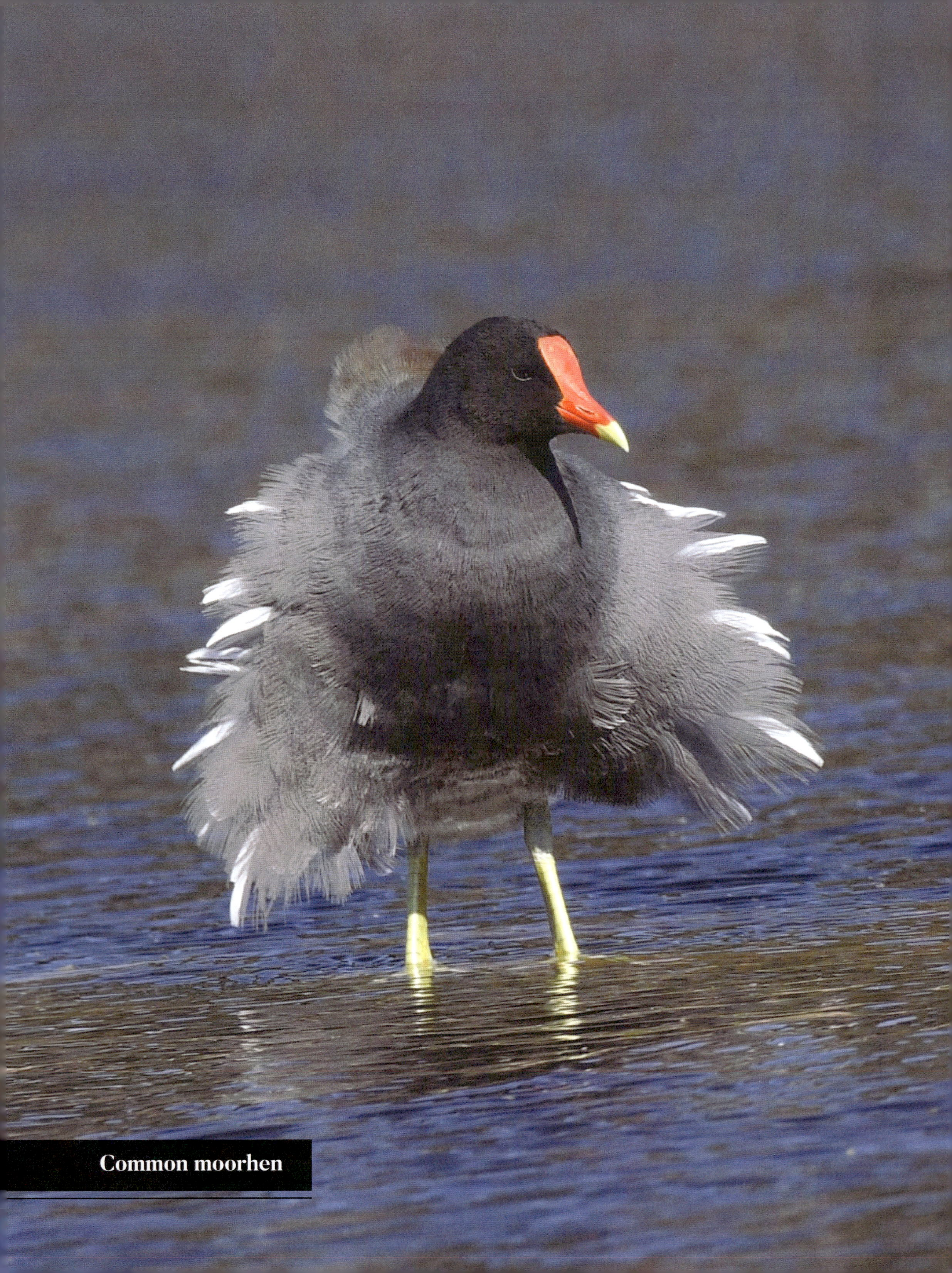

Common moorhen

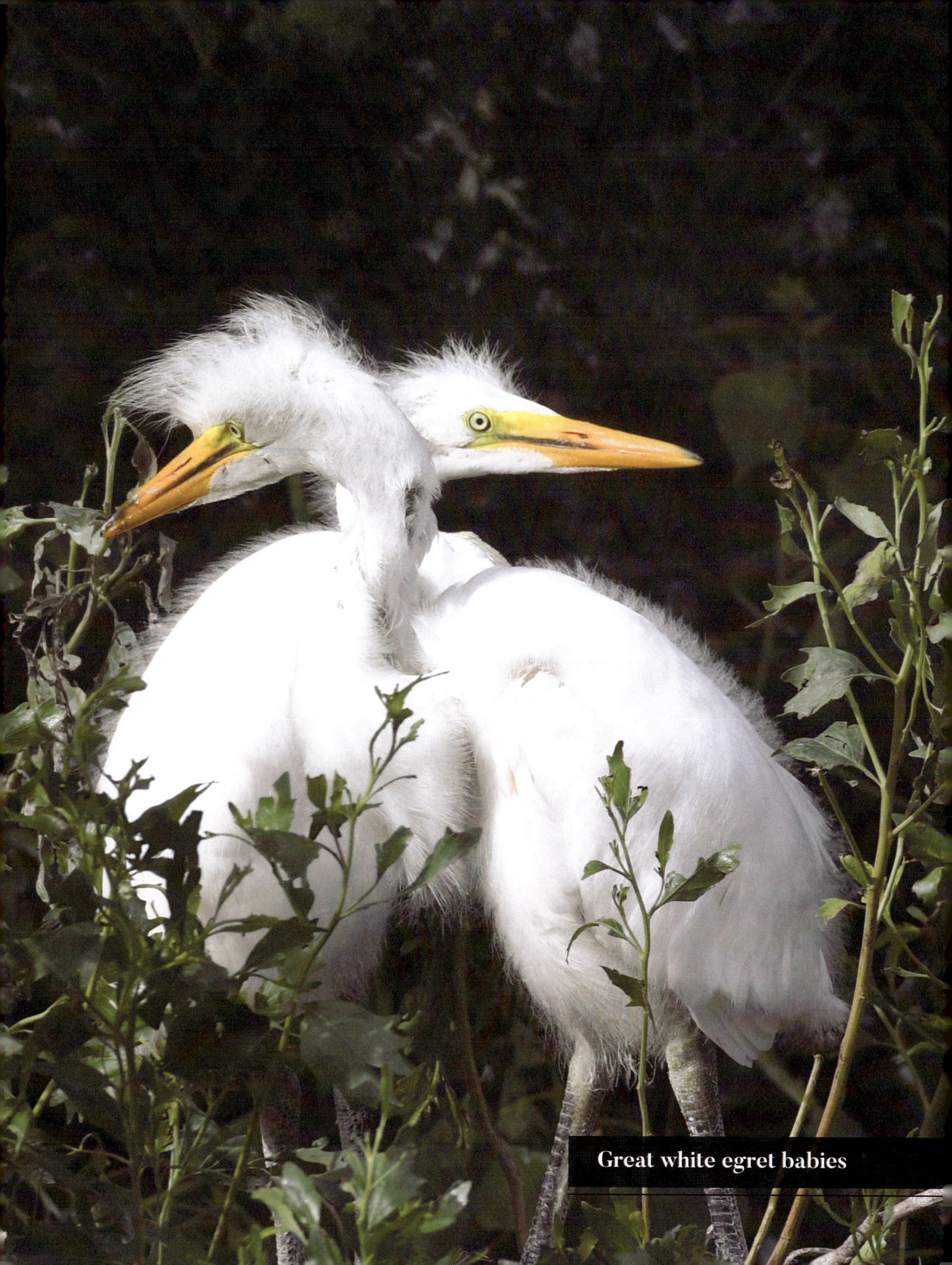

Great white egret babies

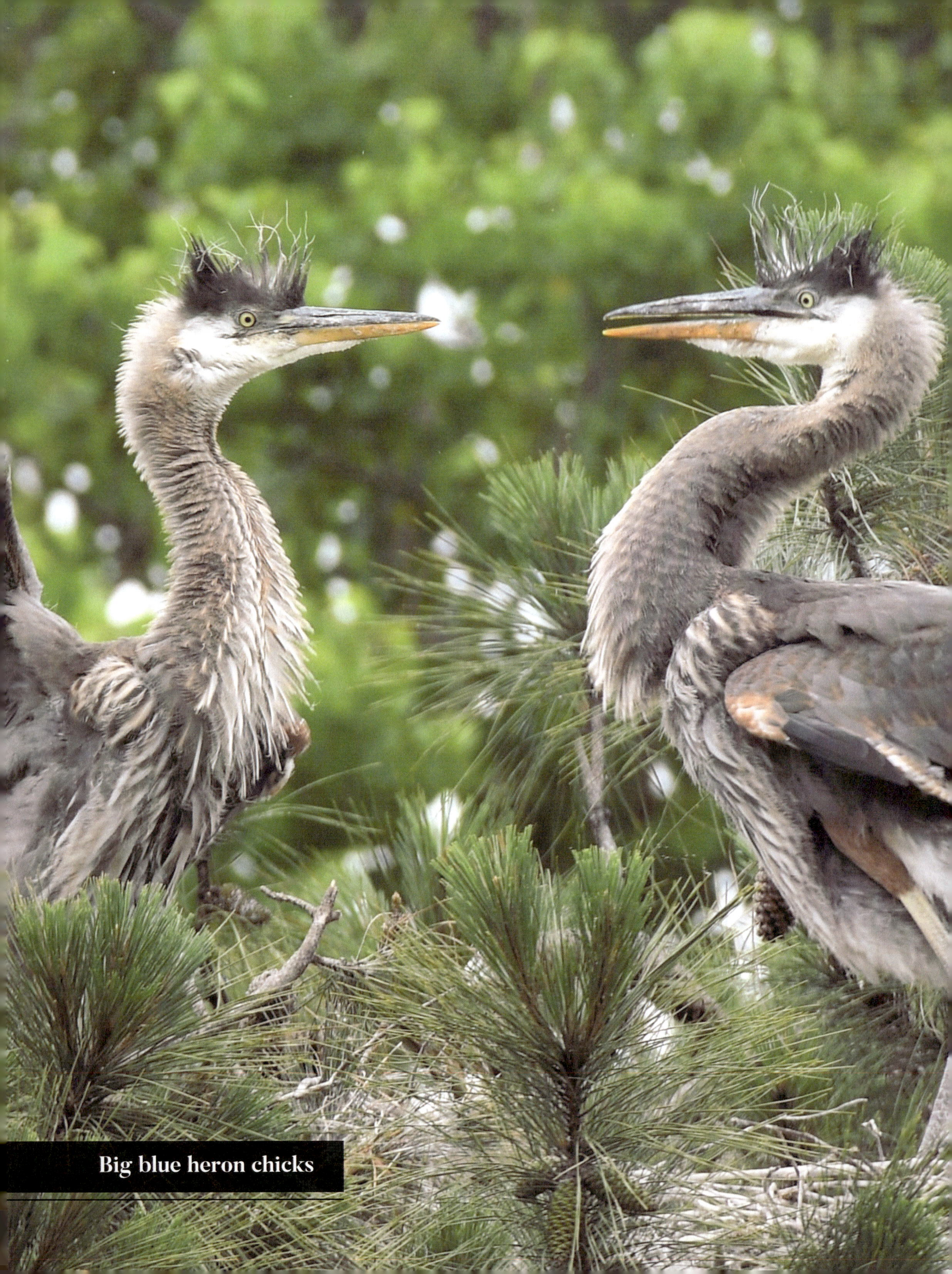

Big blue heron chicks

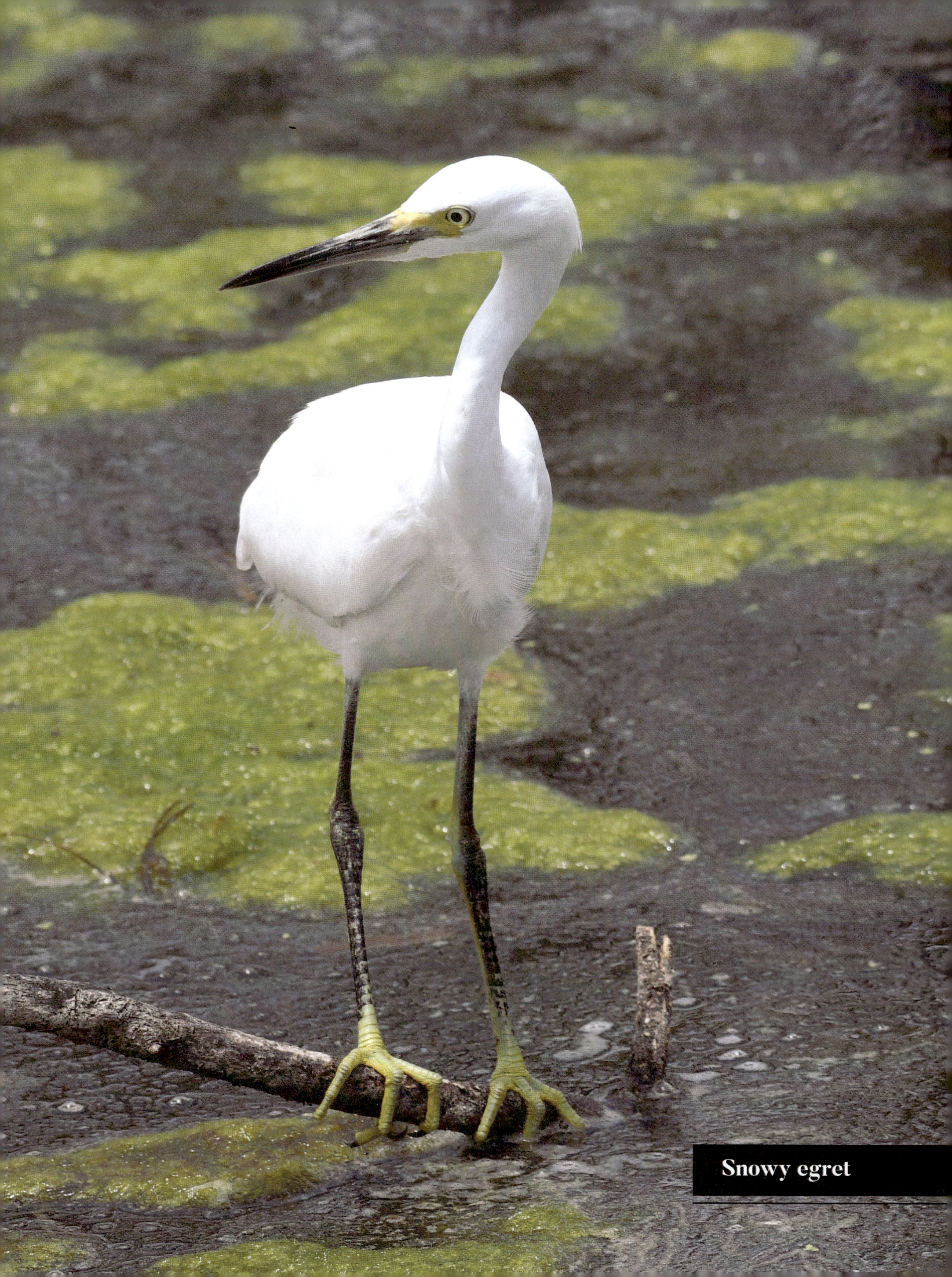

Snowy egret

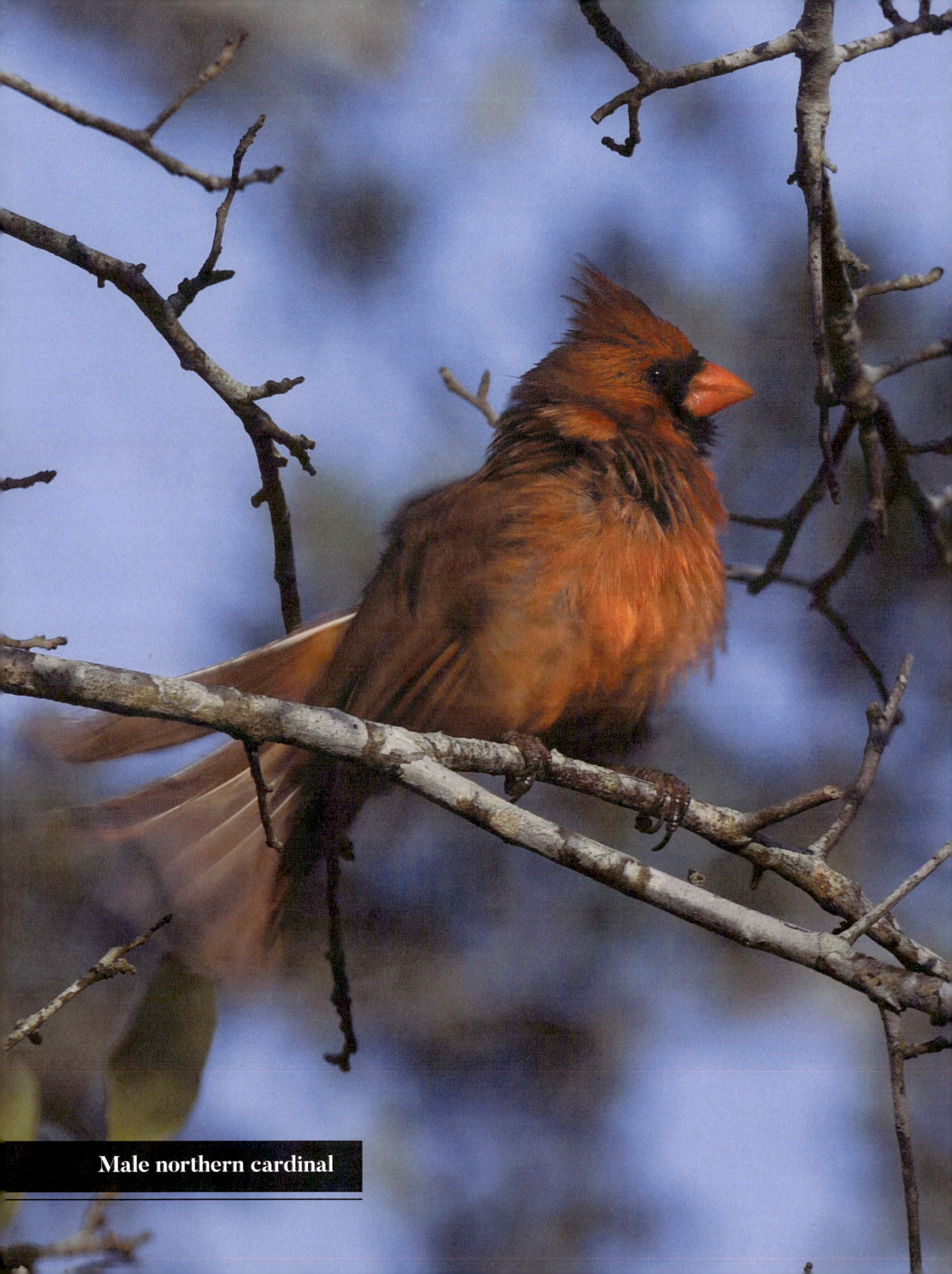

Male northern cardinal

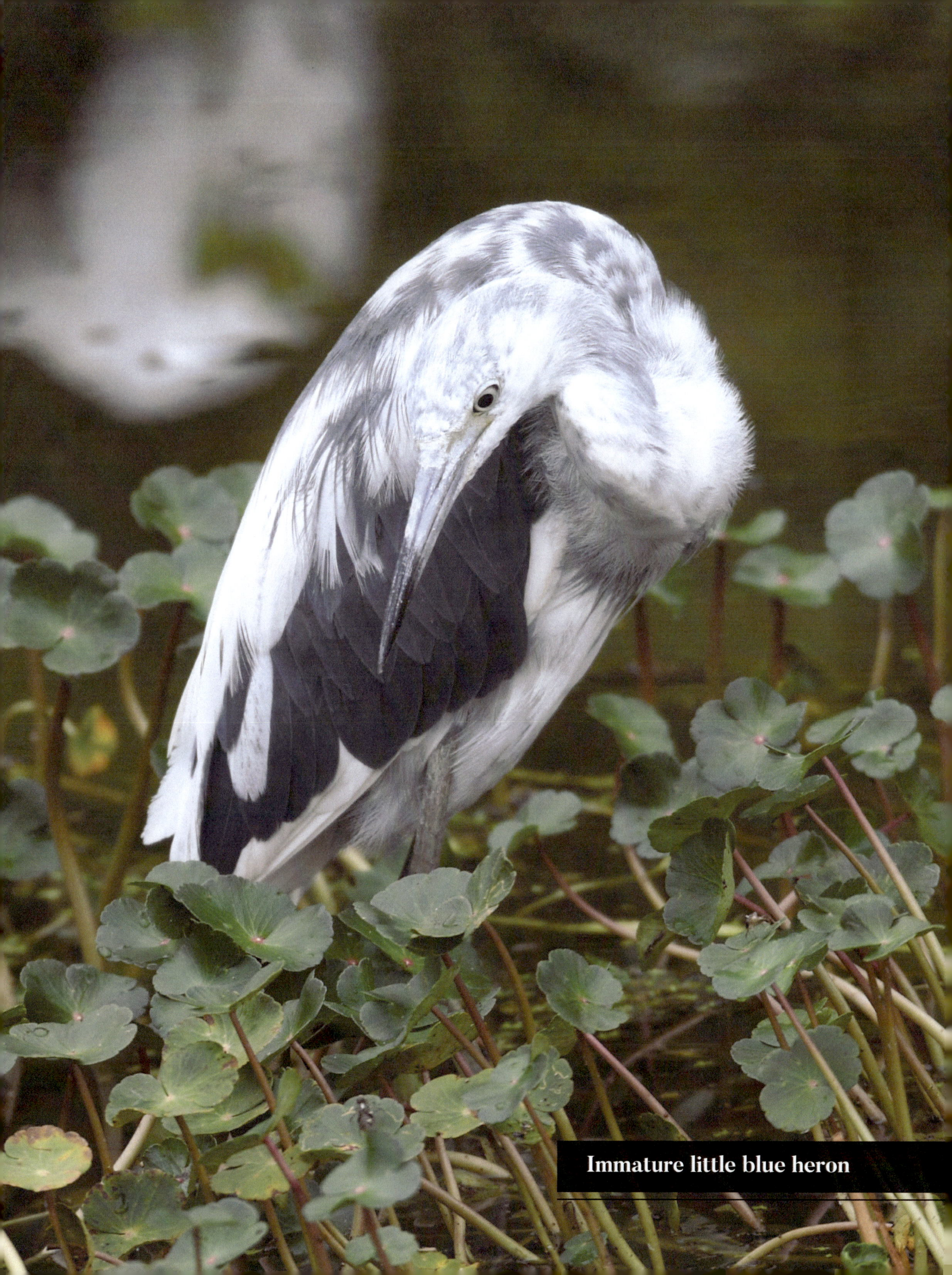

Immature little blue heron

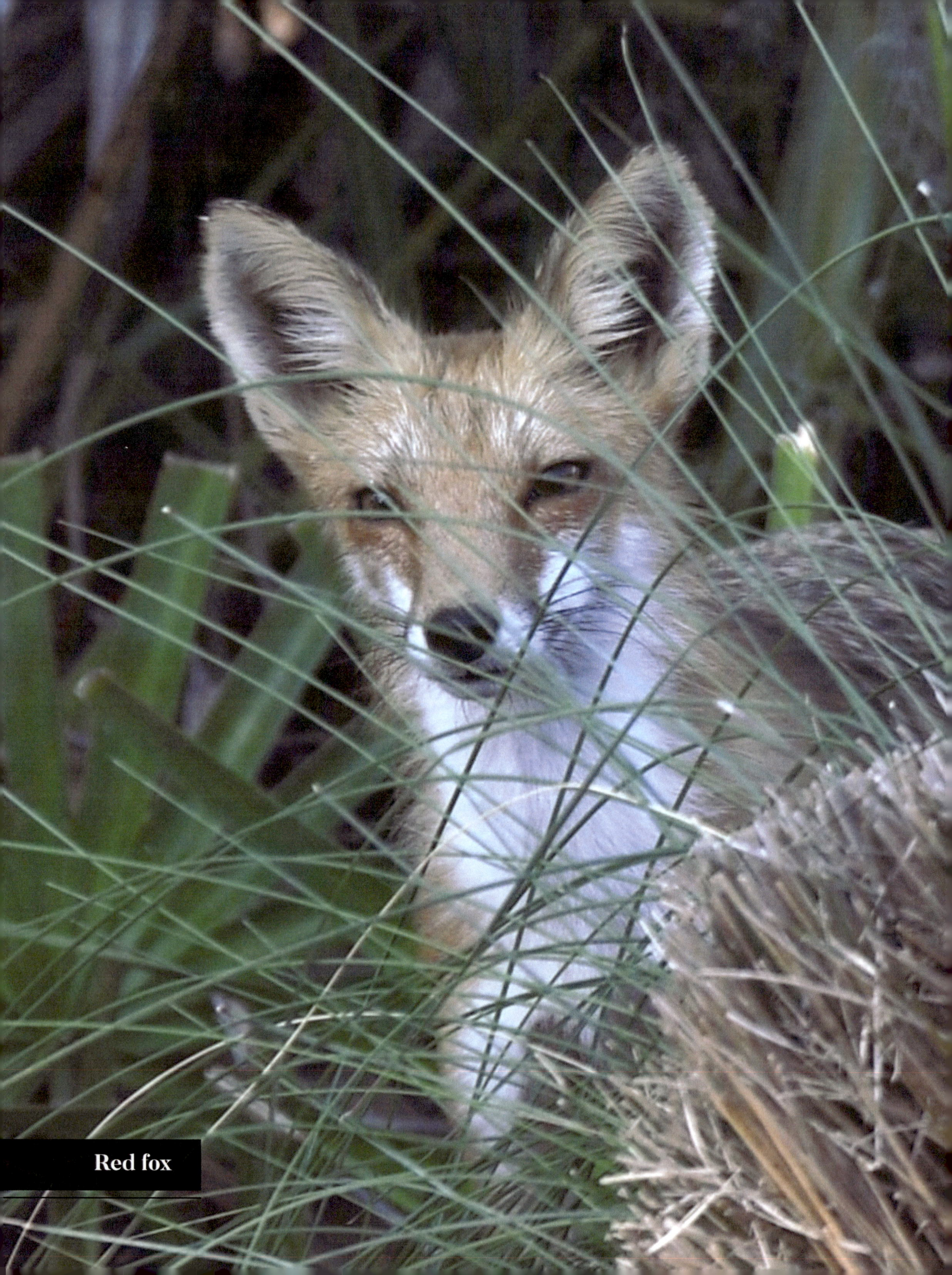

Red fox

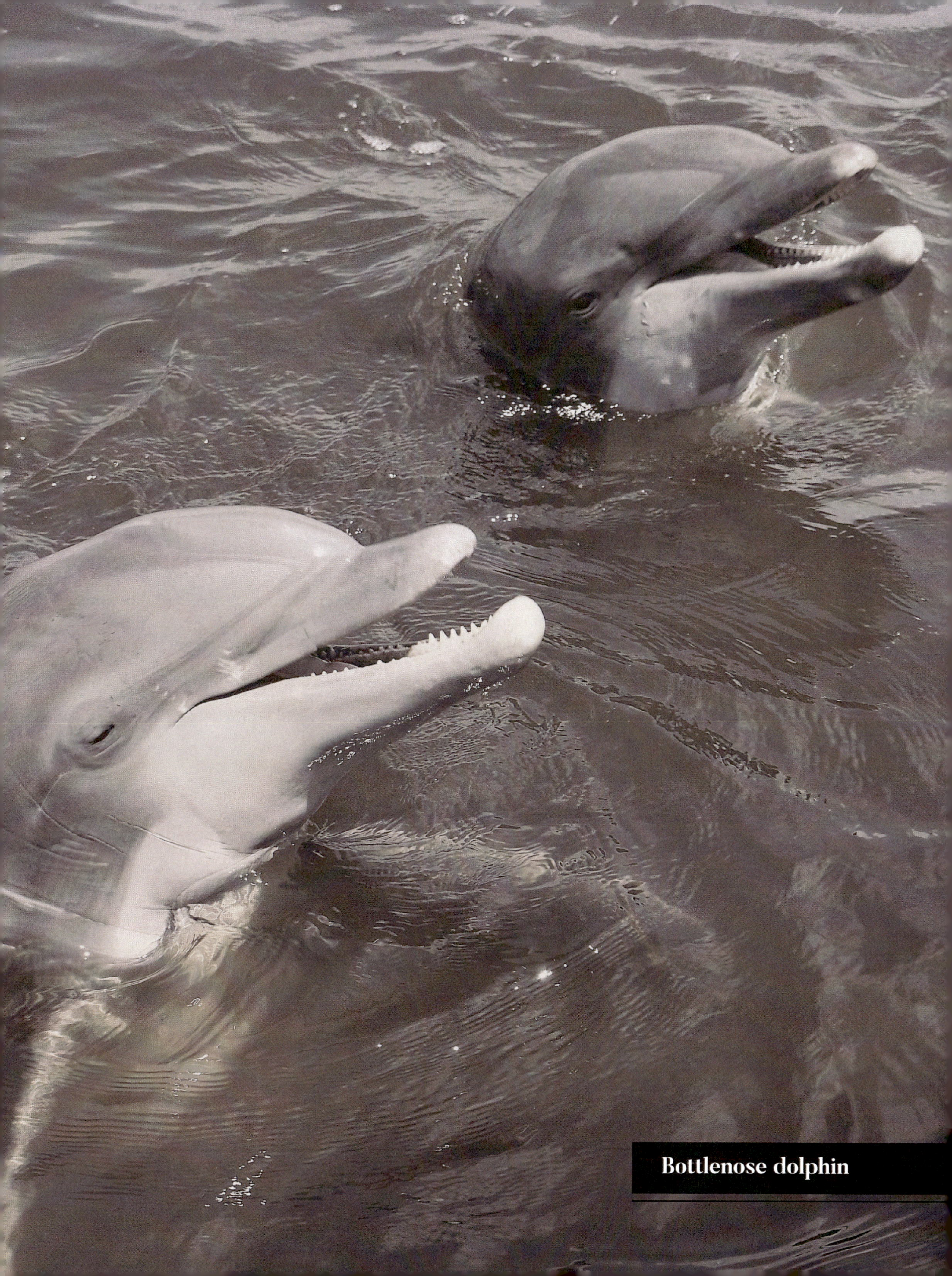

Bottlenose dolphin

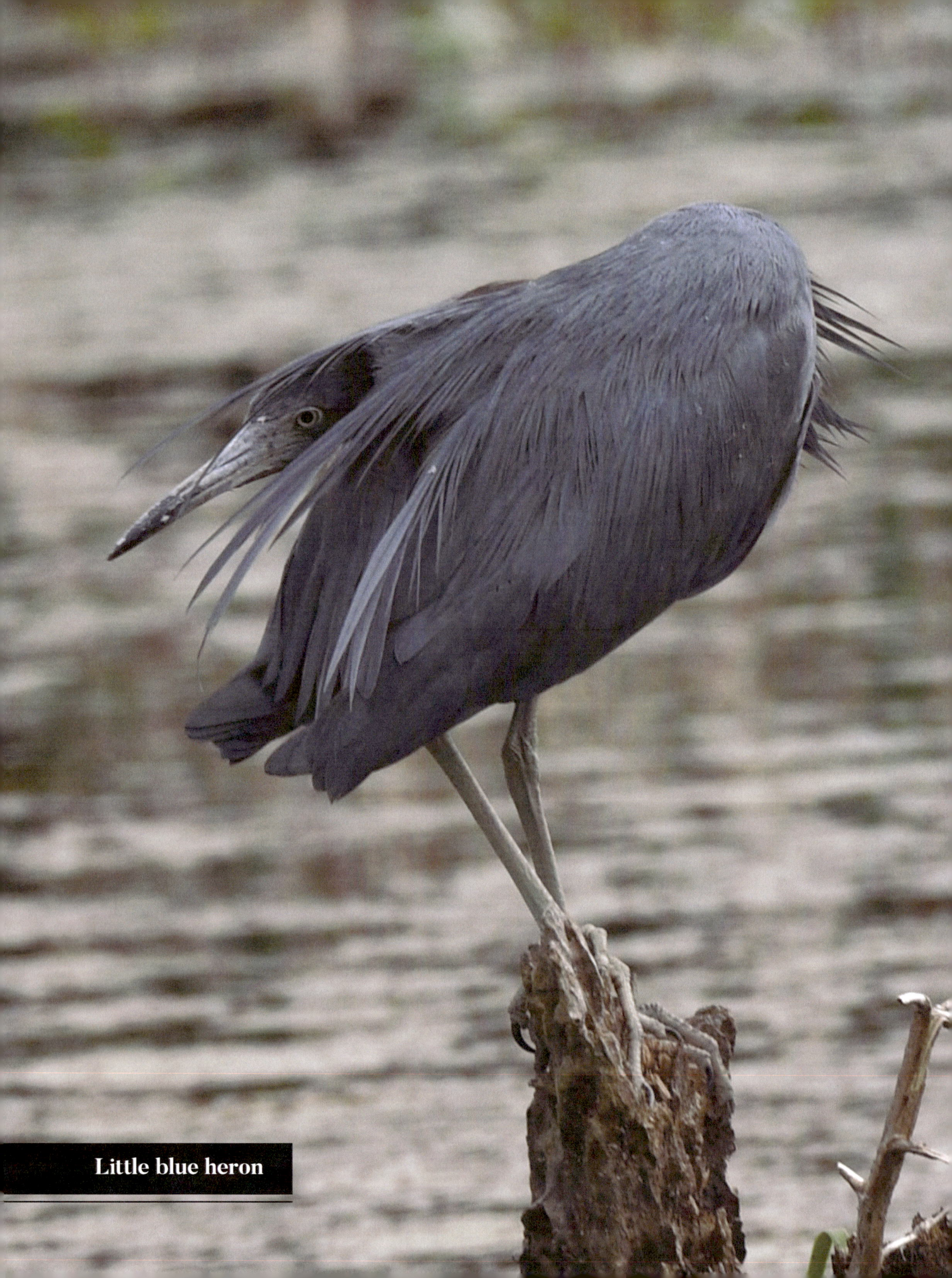

Little blue heron

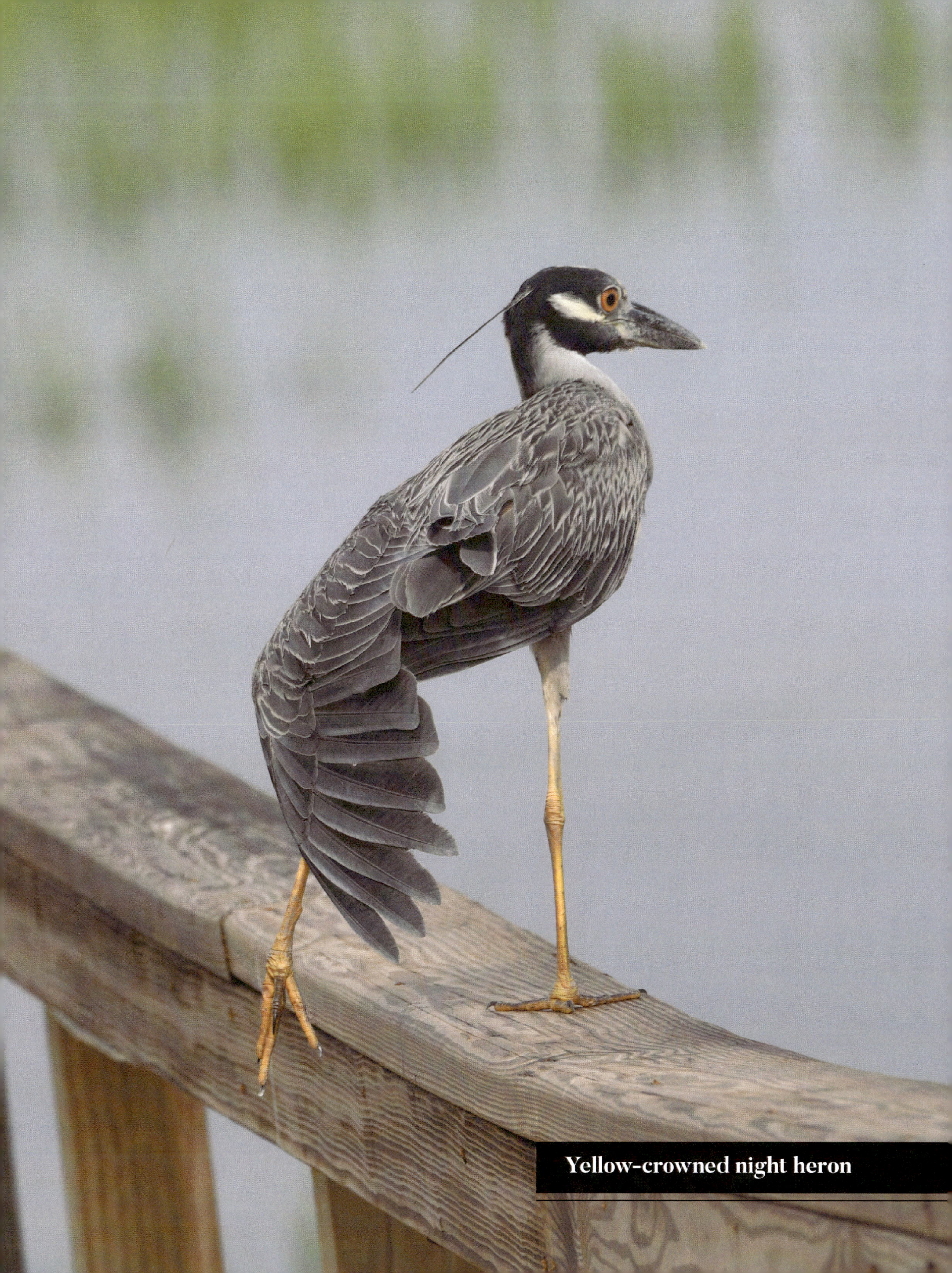

Yellow-crowned night heron

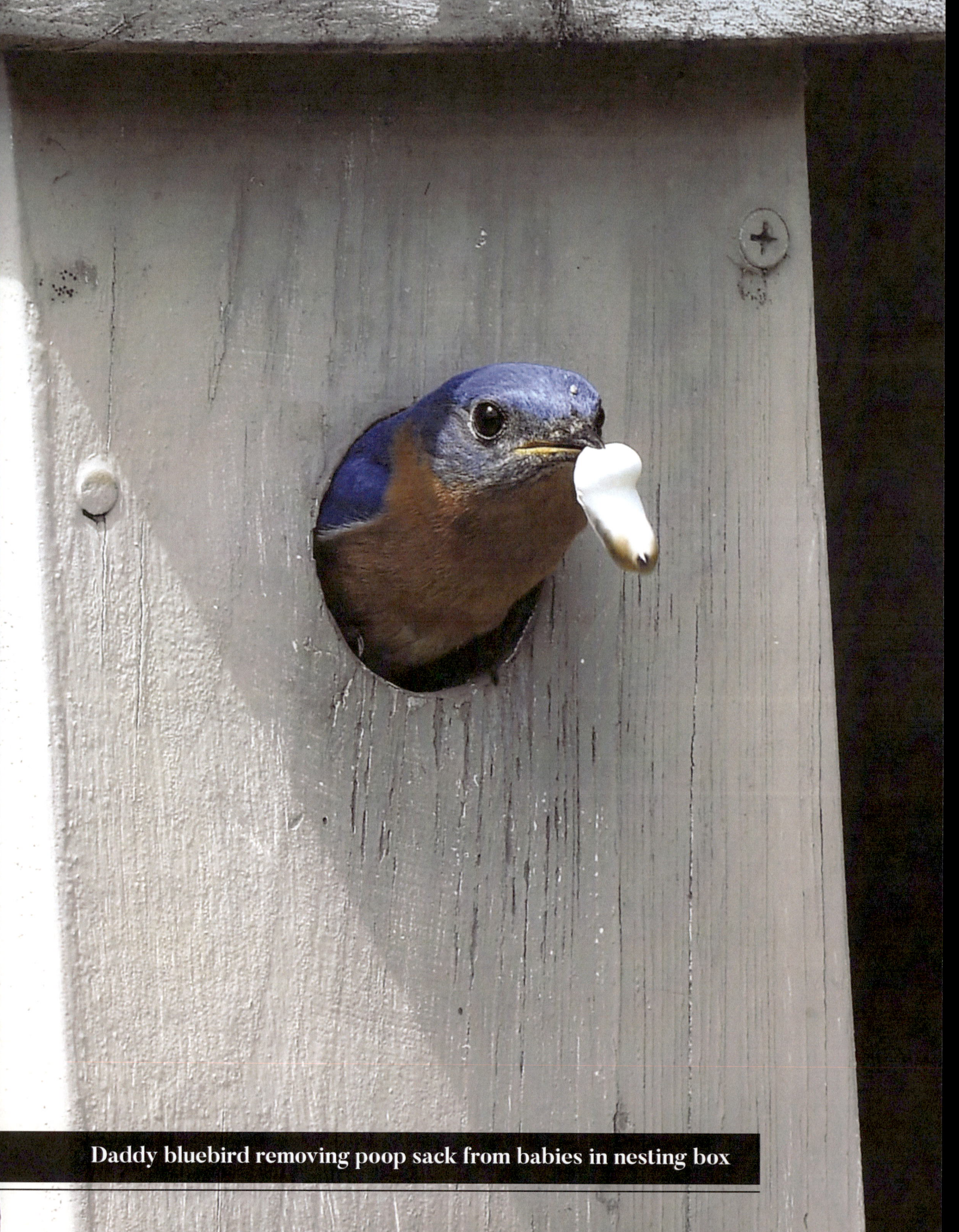

Daddy bluebird removing poop sack from babies in nesting box

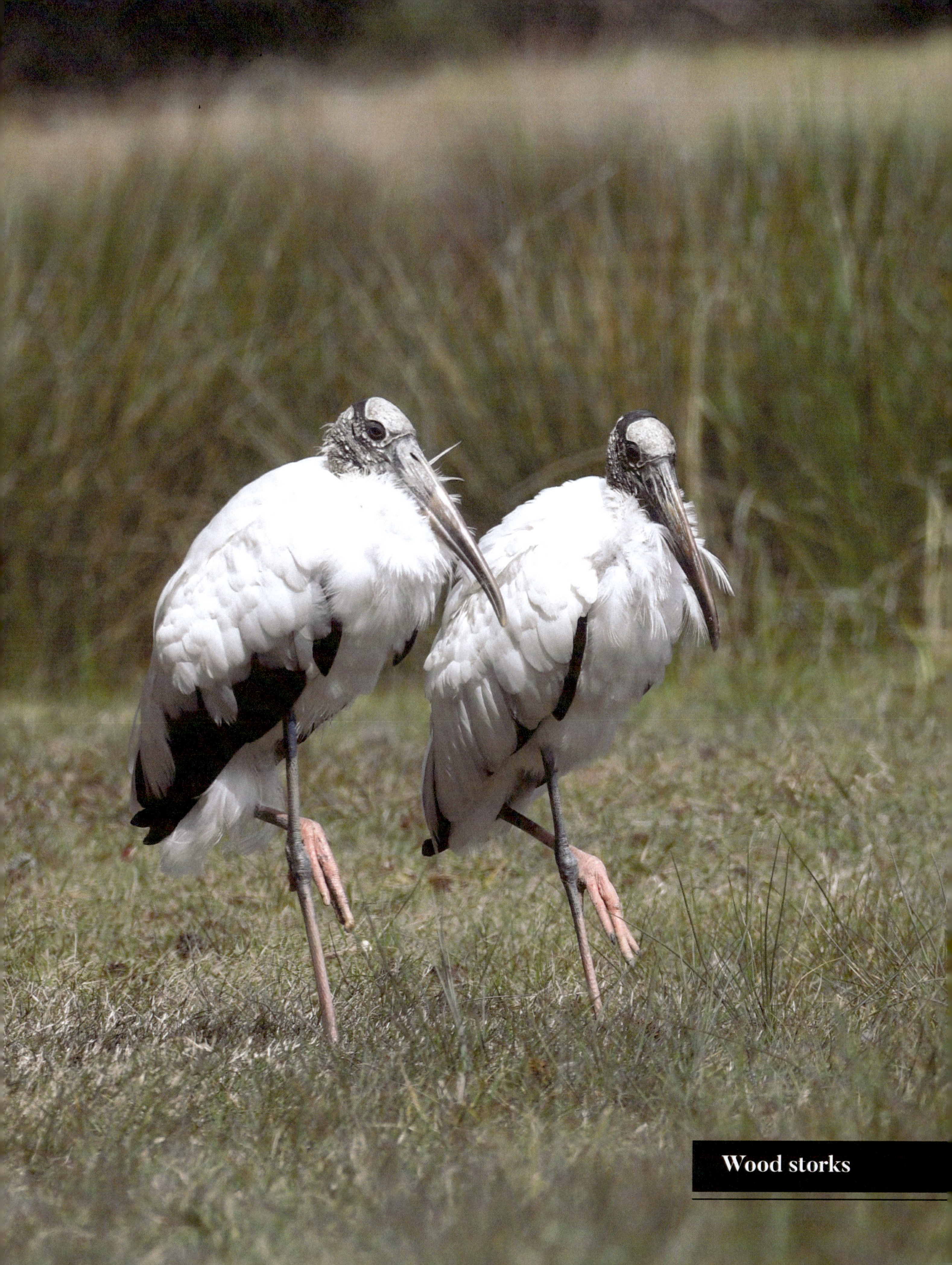

Wood storks

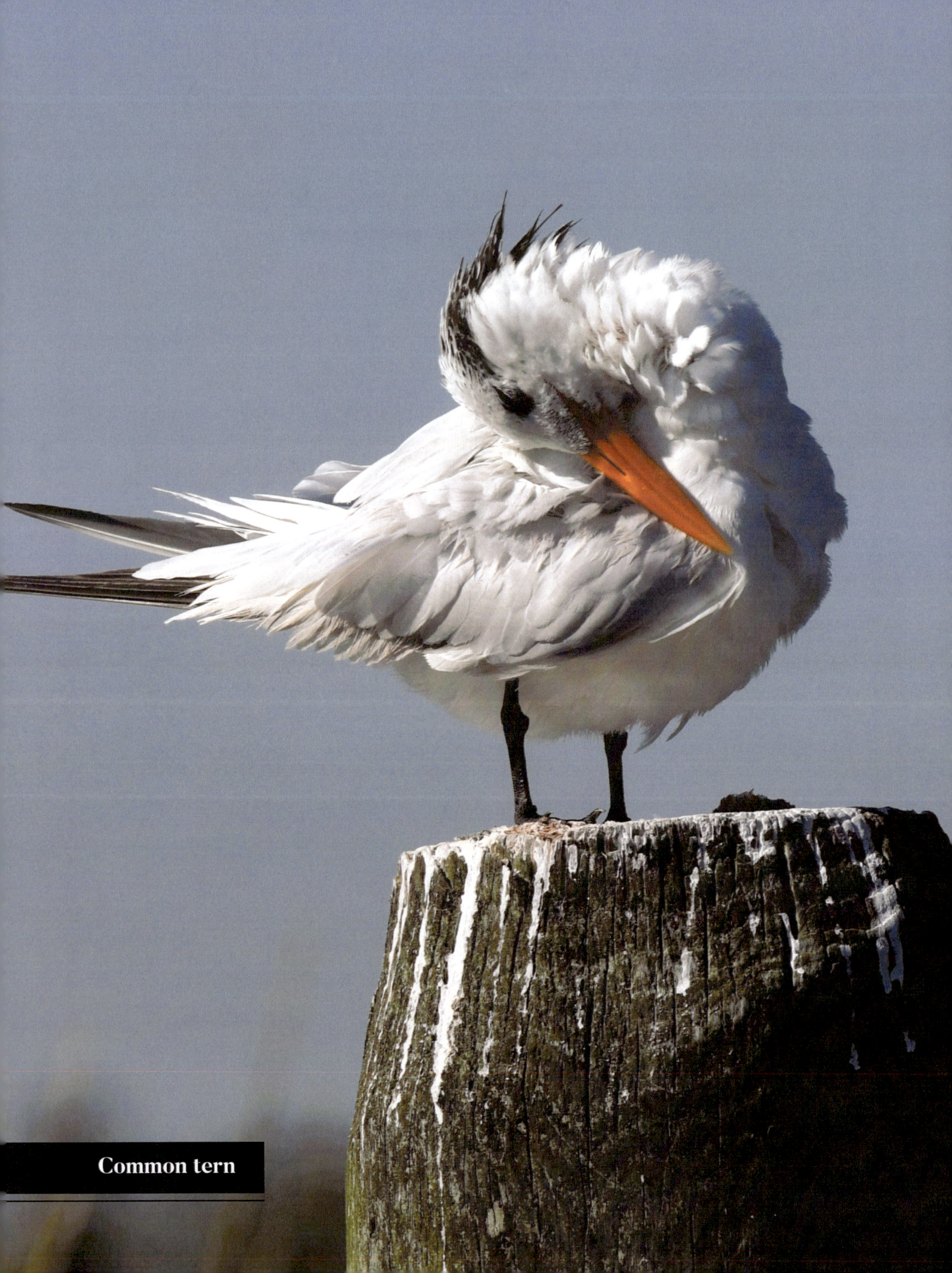

Common tern

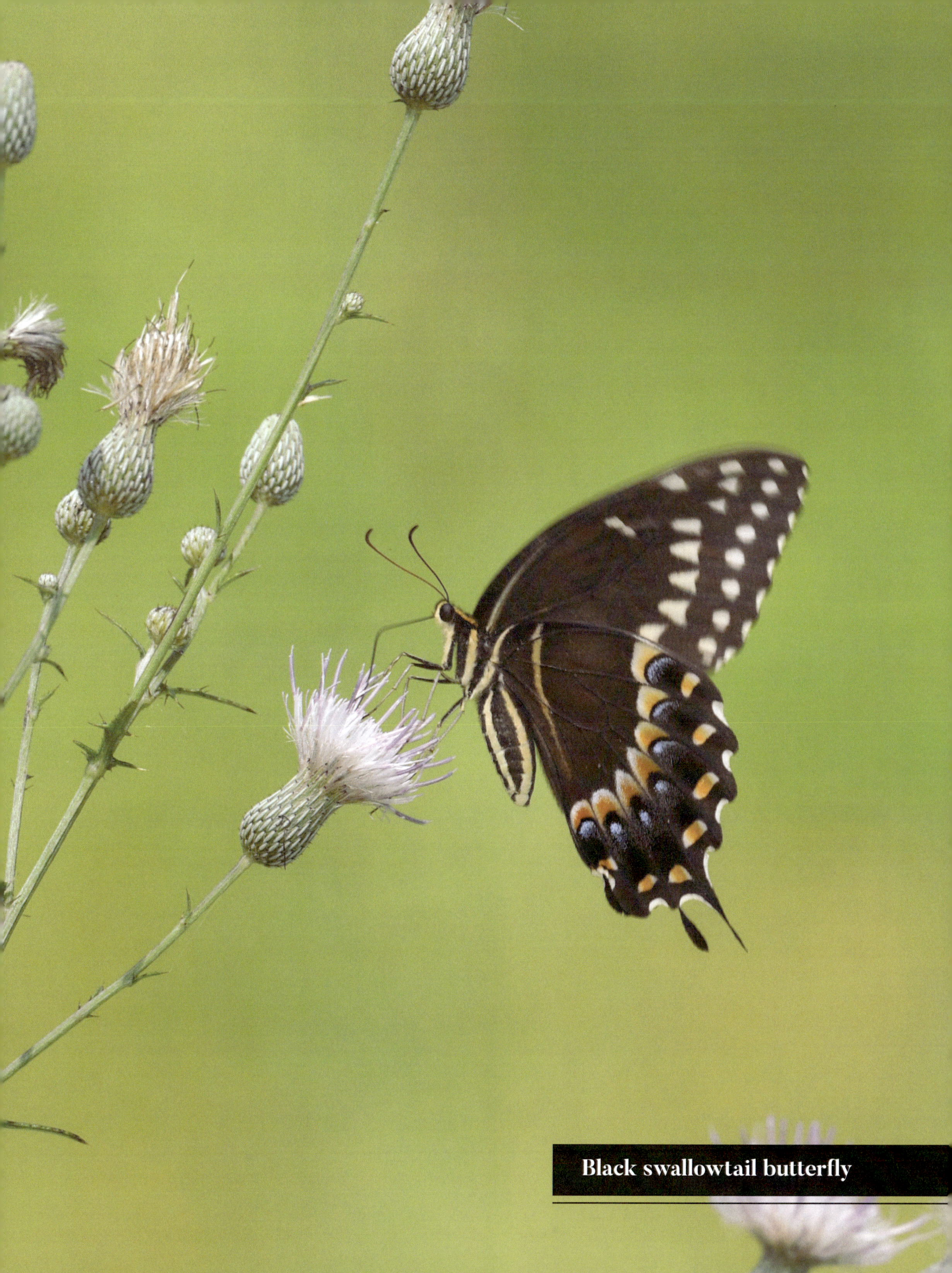

Black swallowtail butterfly

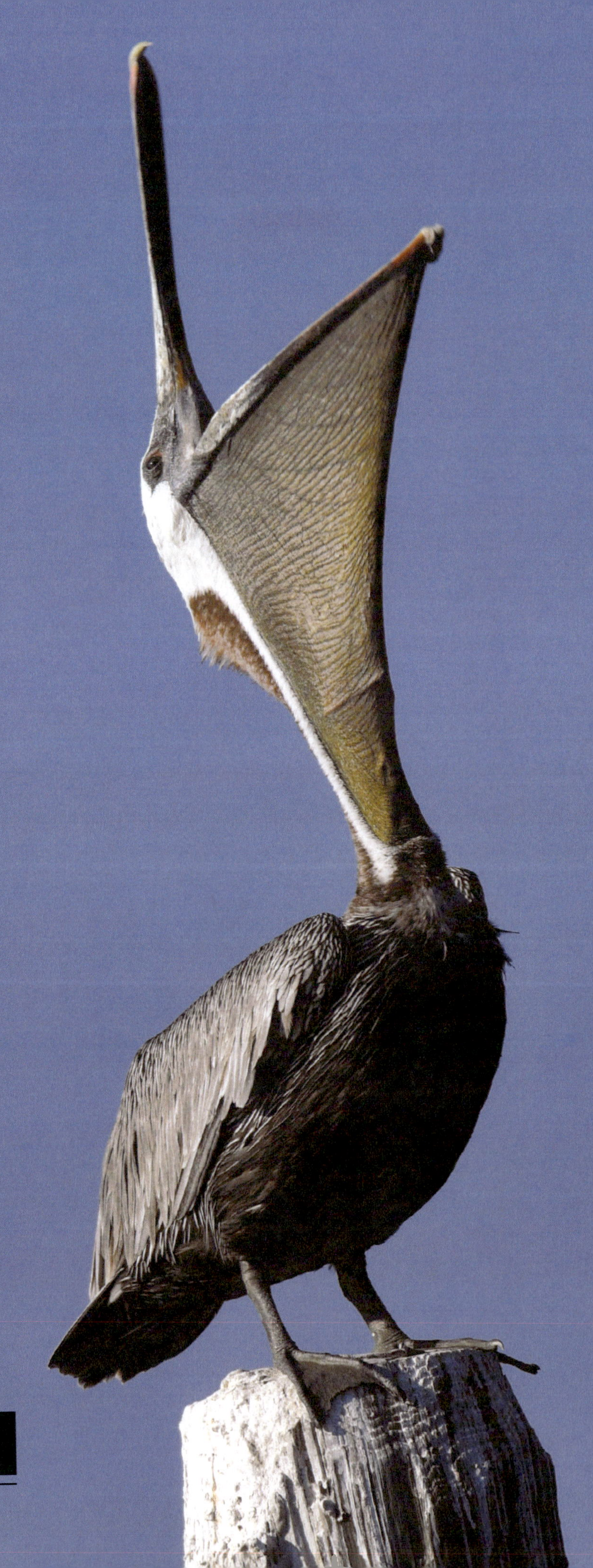

Brown pelican

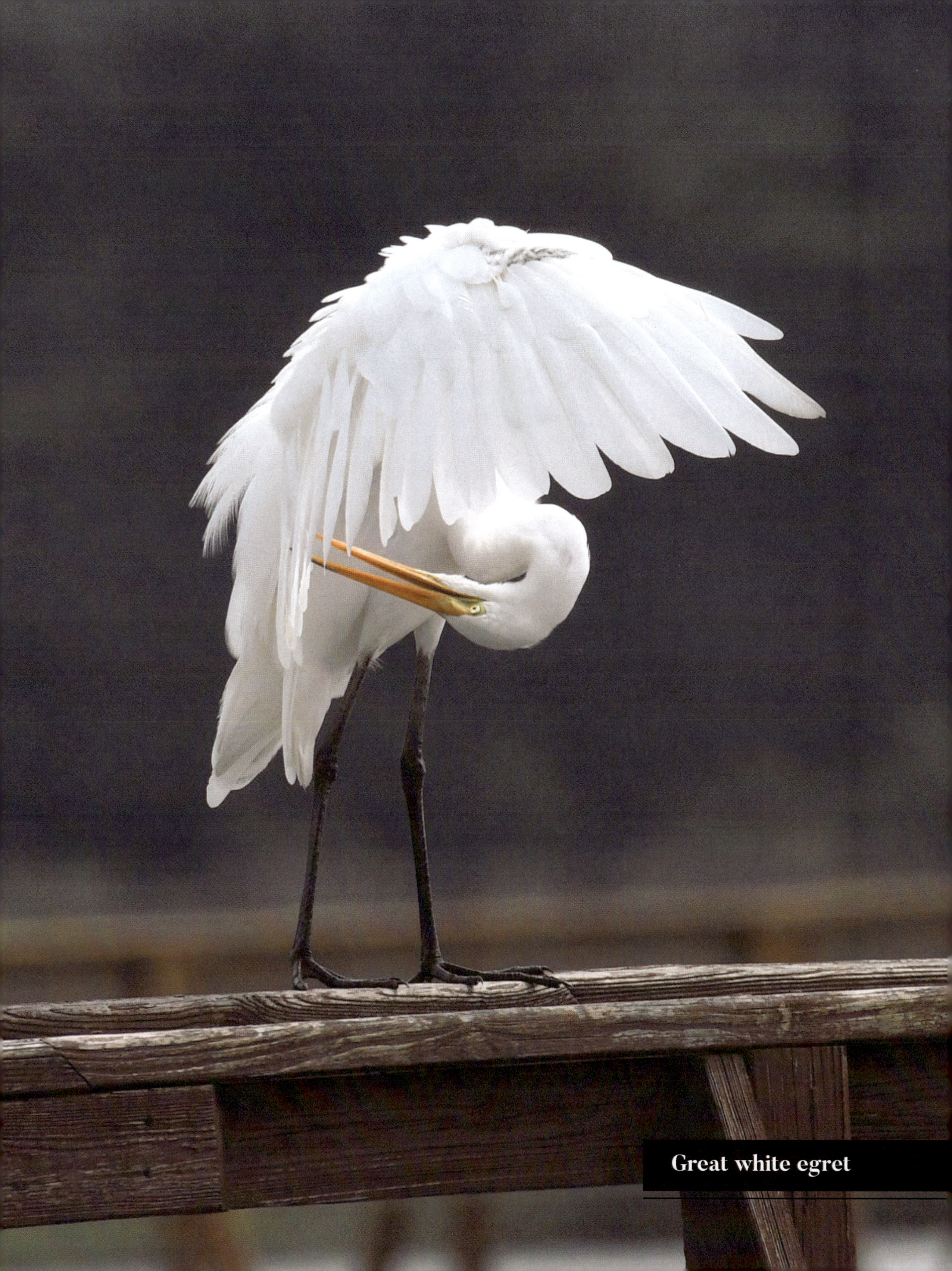
Great white egret

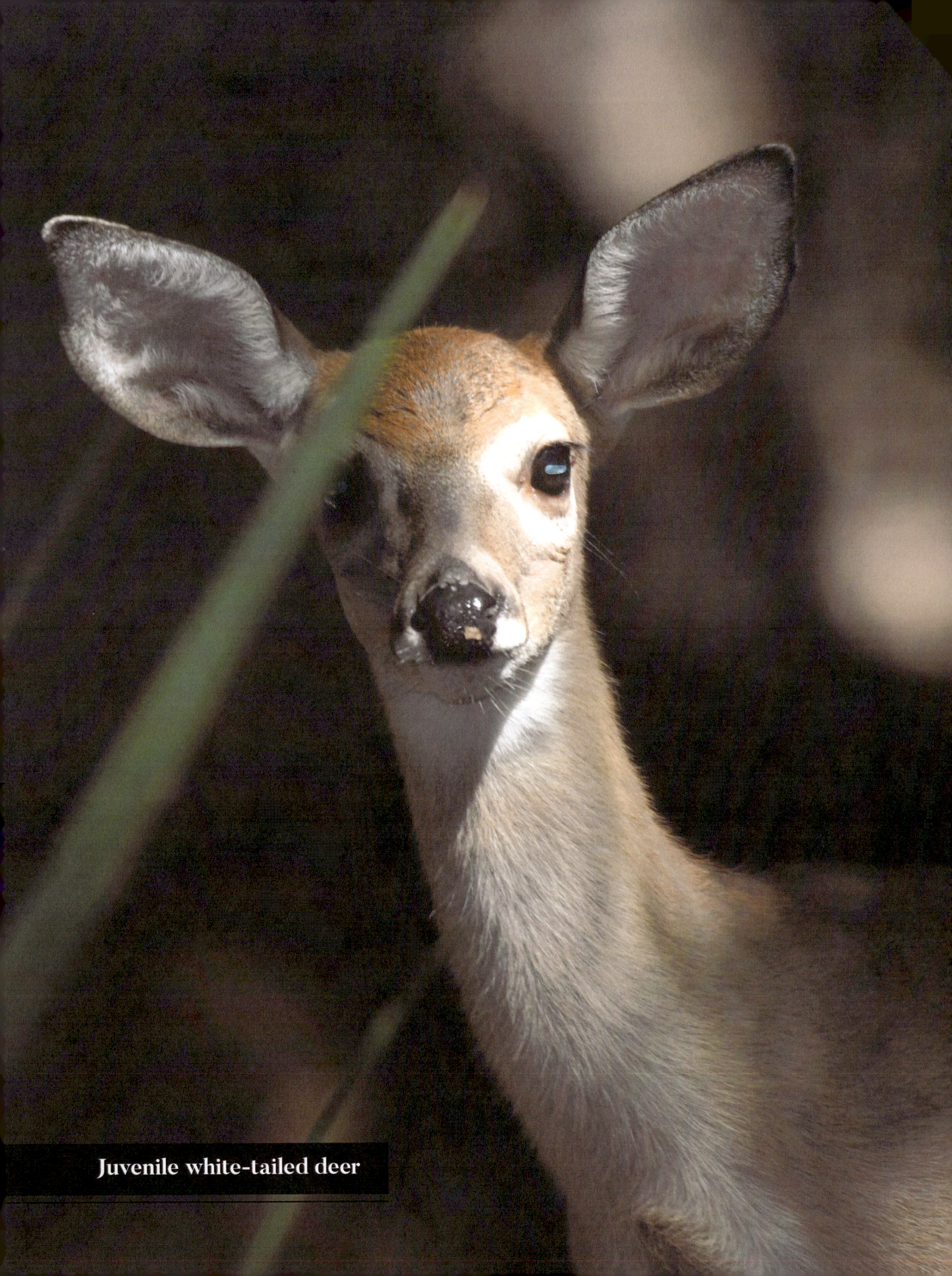

Juvenile white-tailed deer

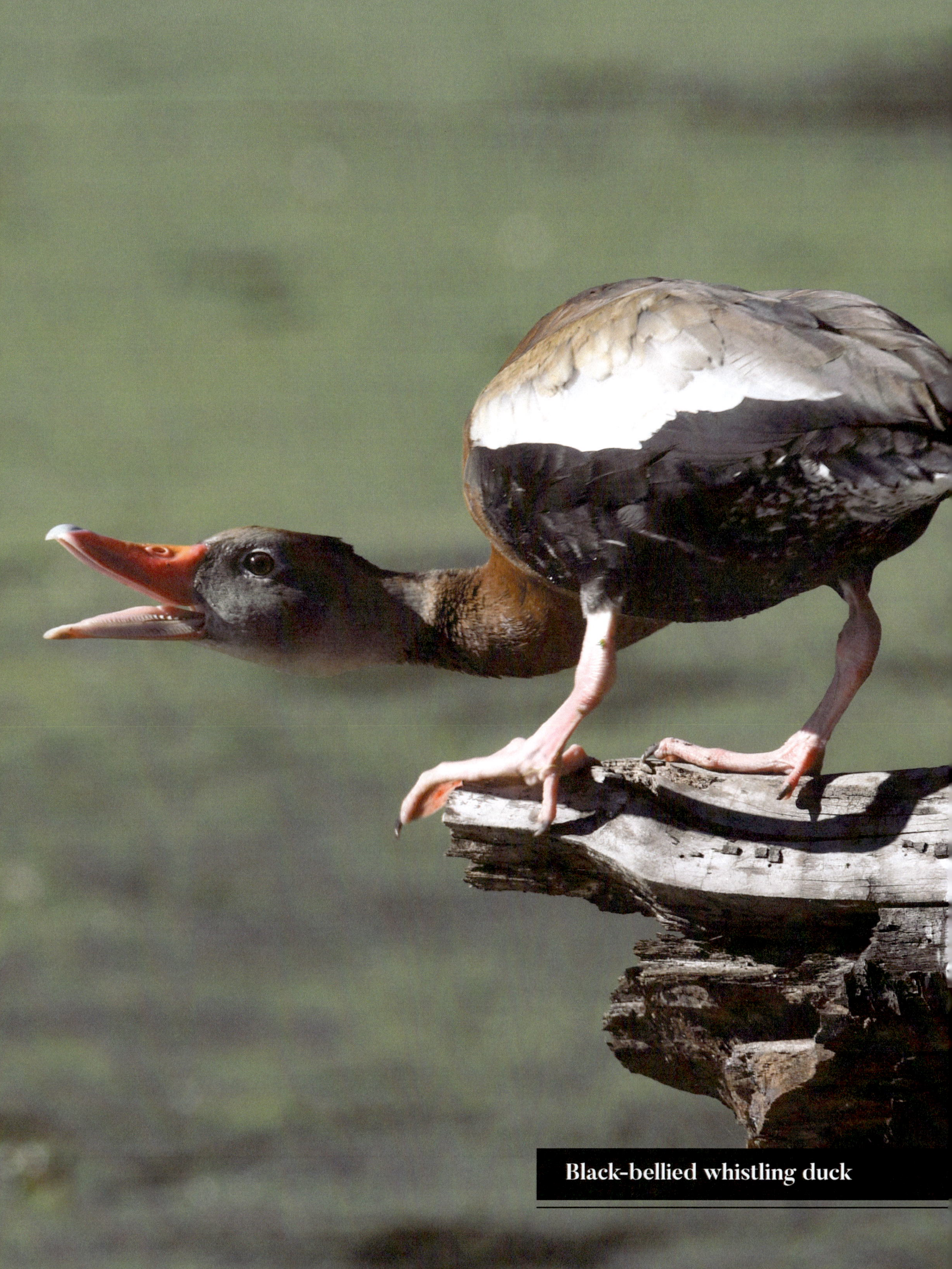
Black-bellied whistling duck

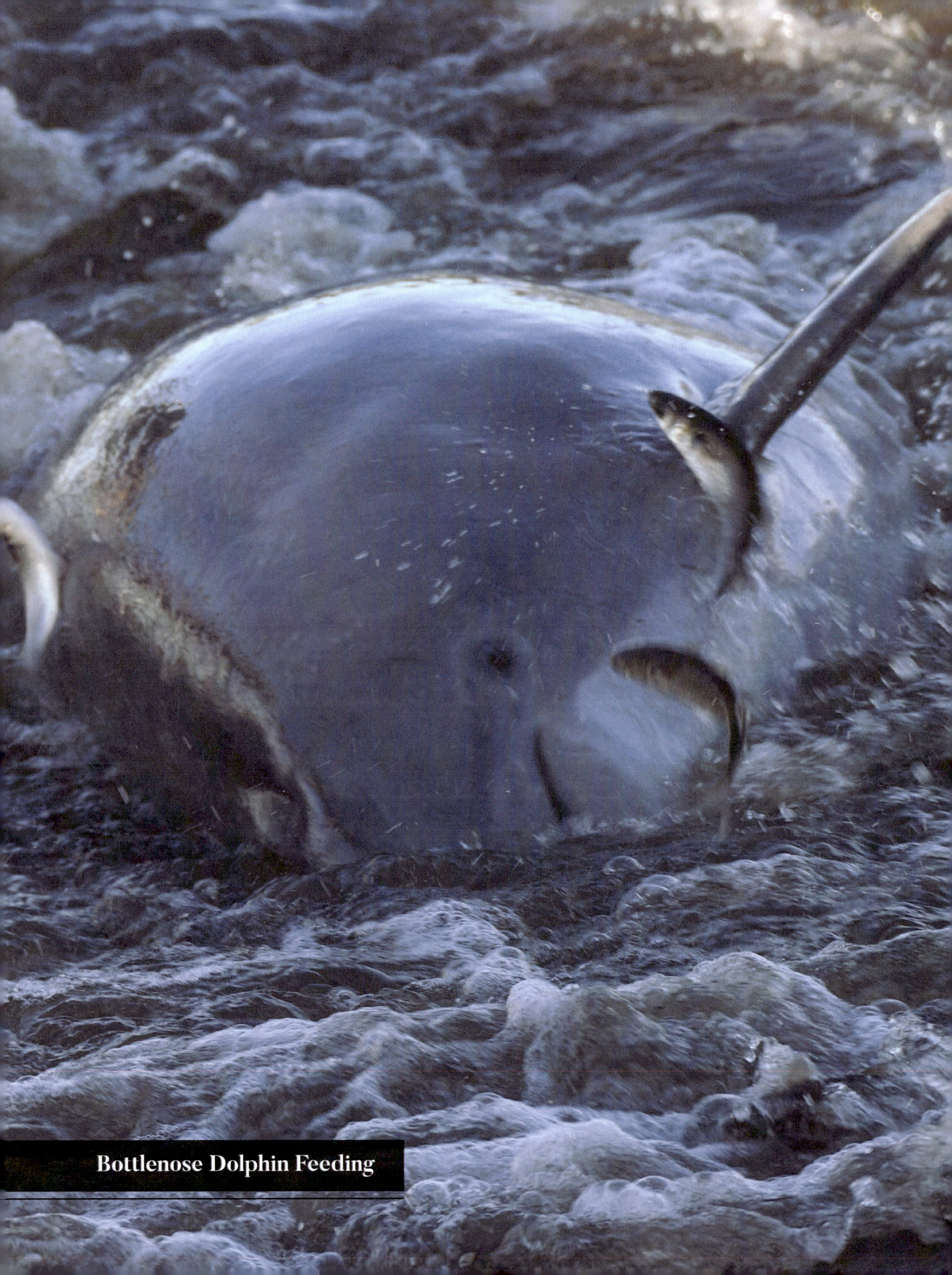

Bottlenose Dolphin Feeding

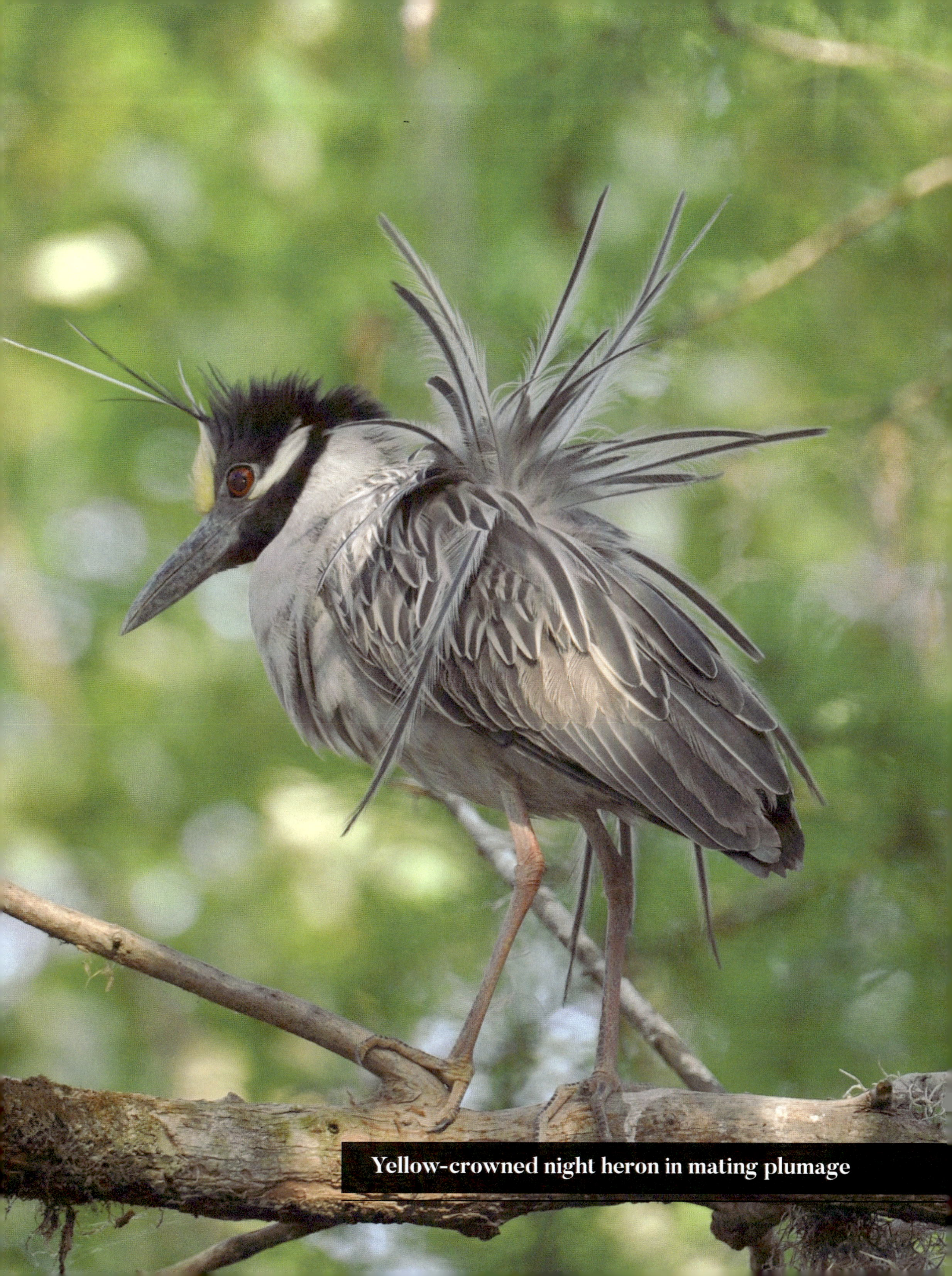

Yellow-crowned night heron in mating plumage

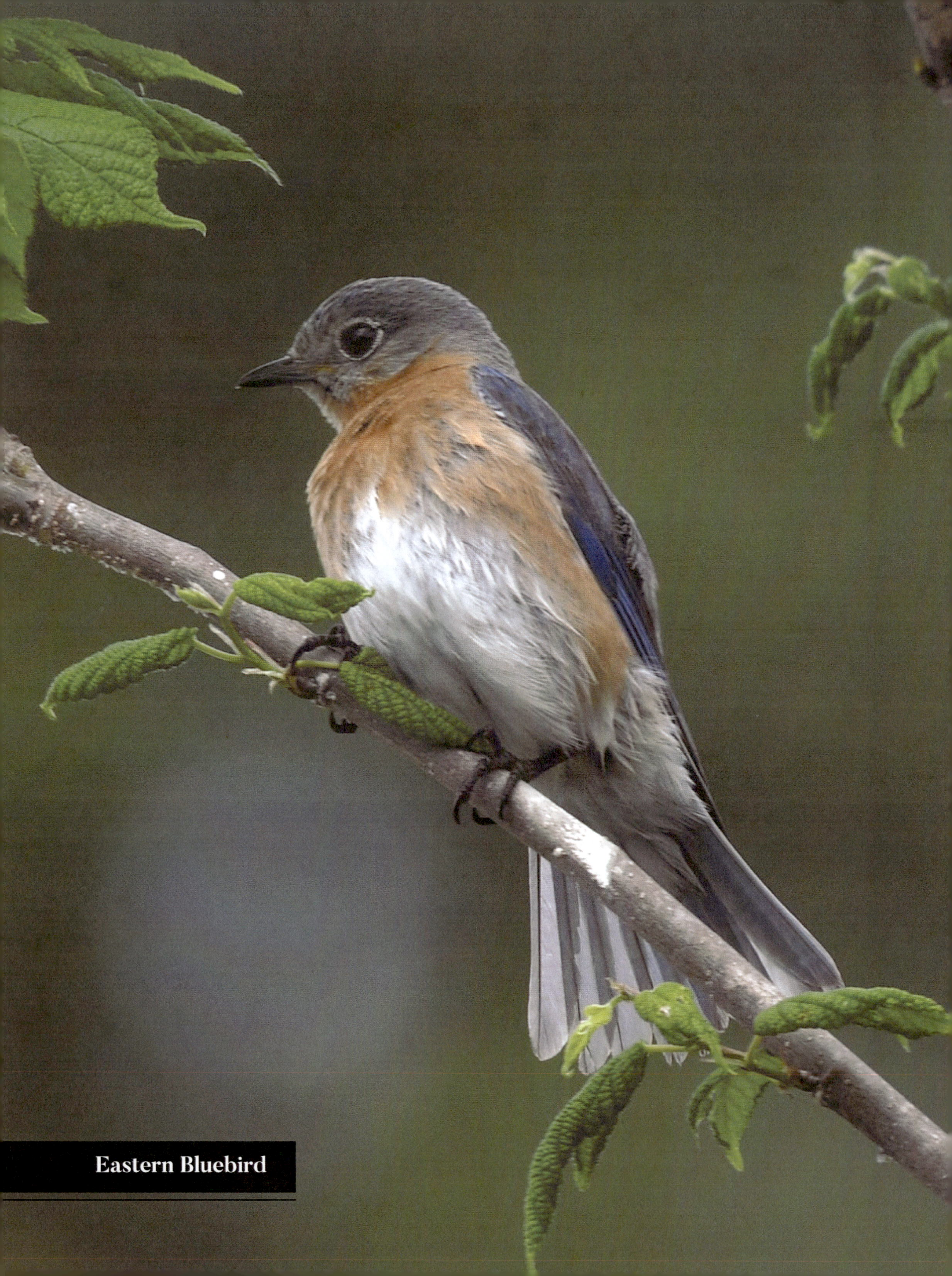

Eastern Bluebird

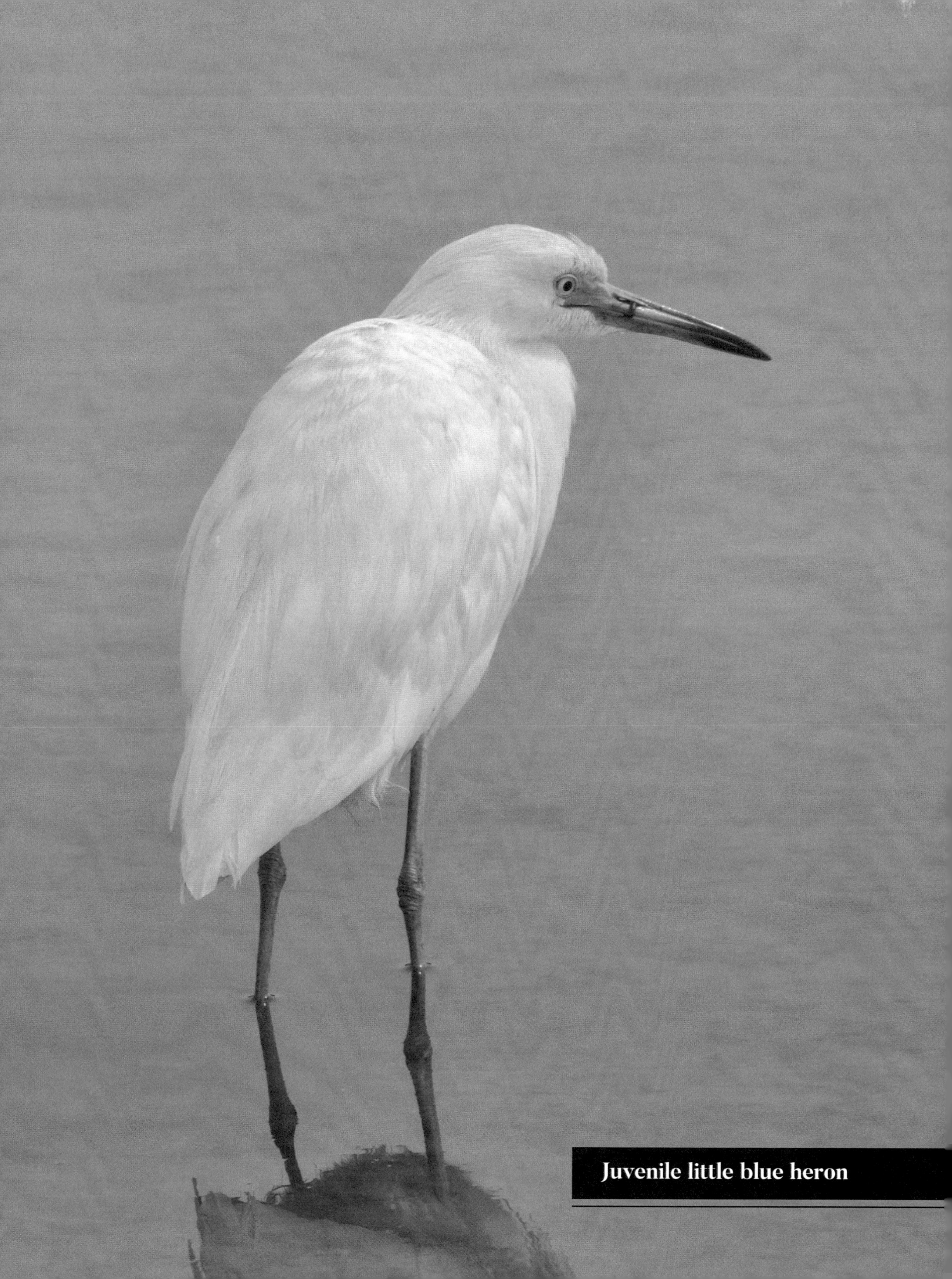

Juvenile little blue heron

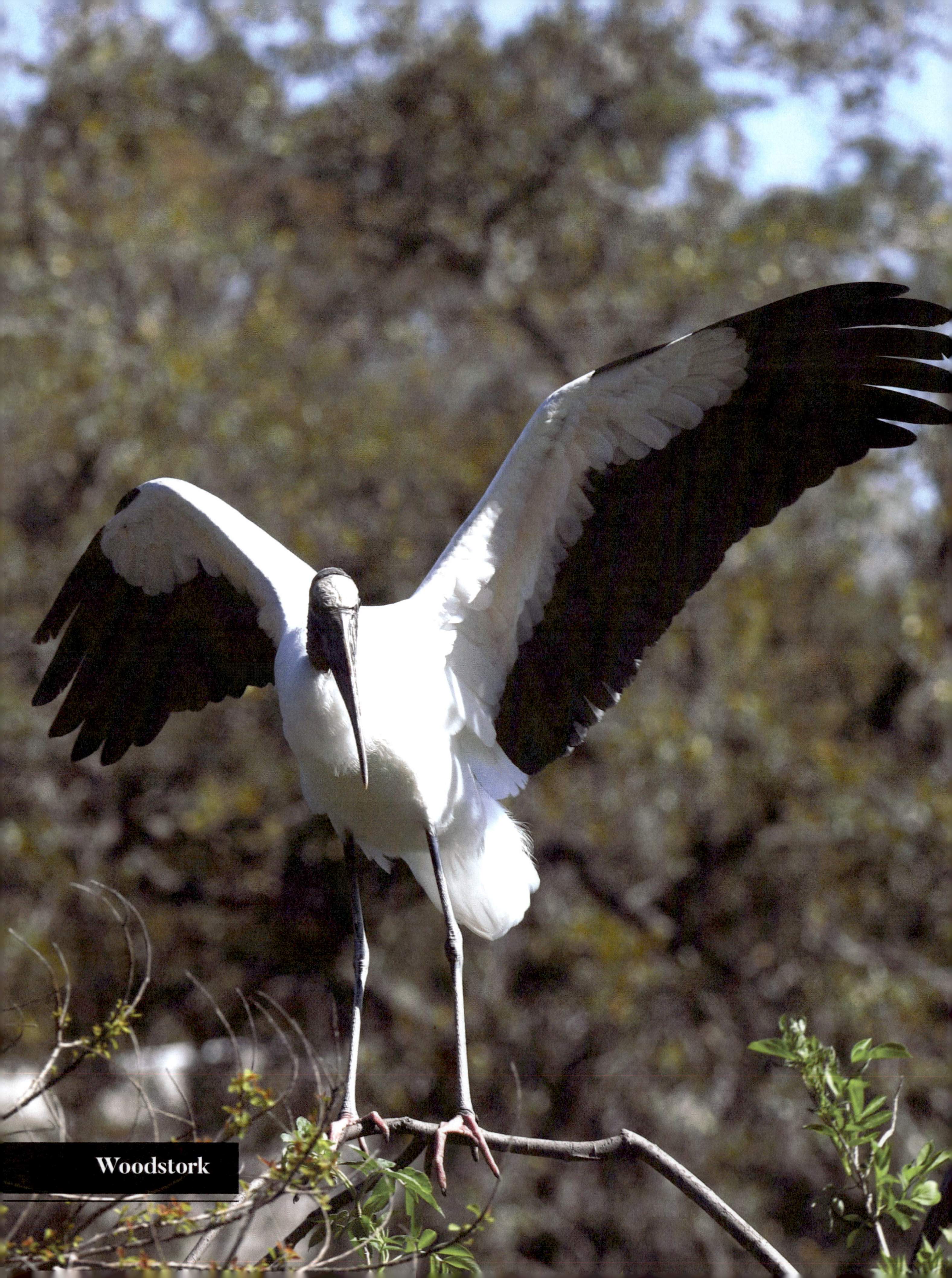

Woodstork

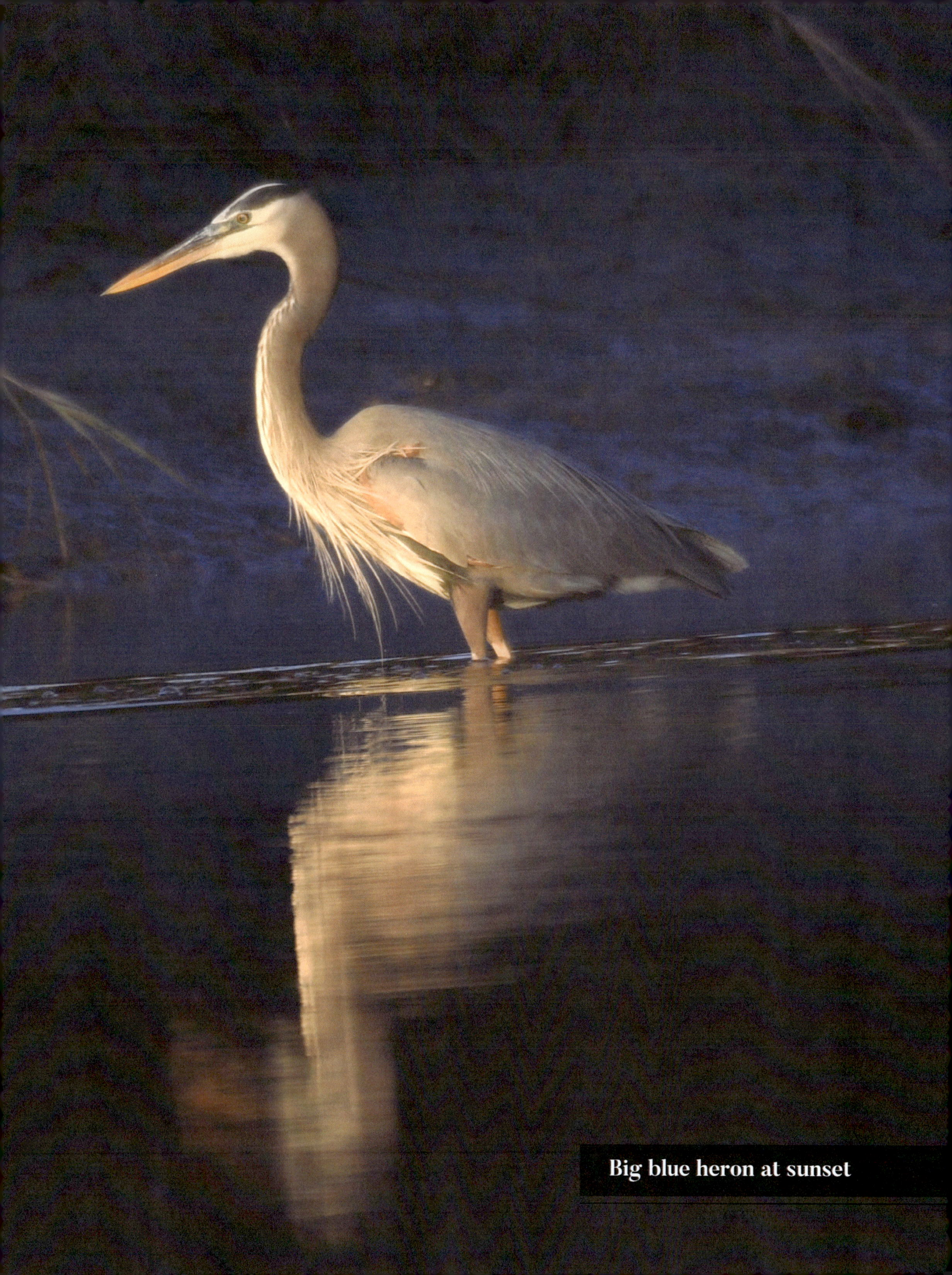
Big blue heron at sunset

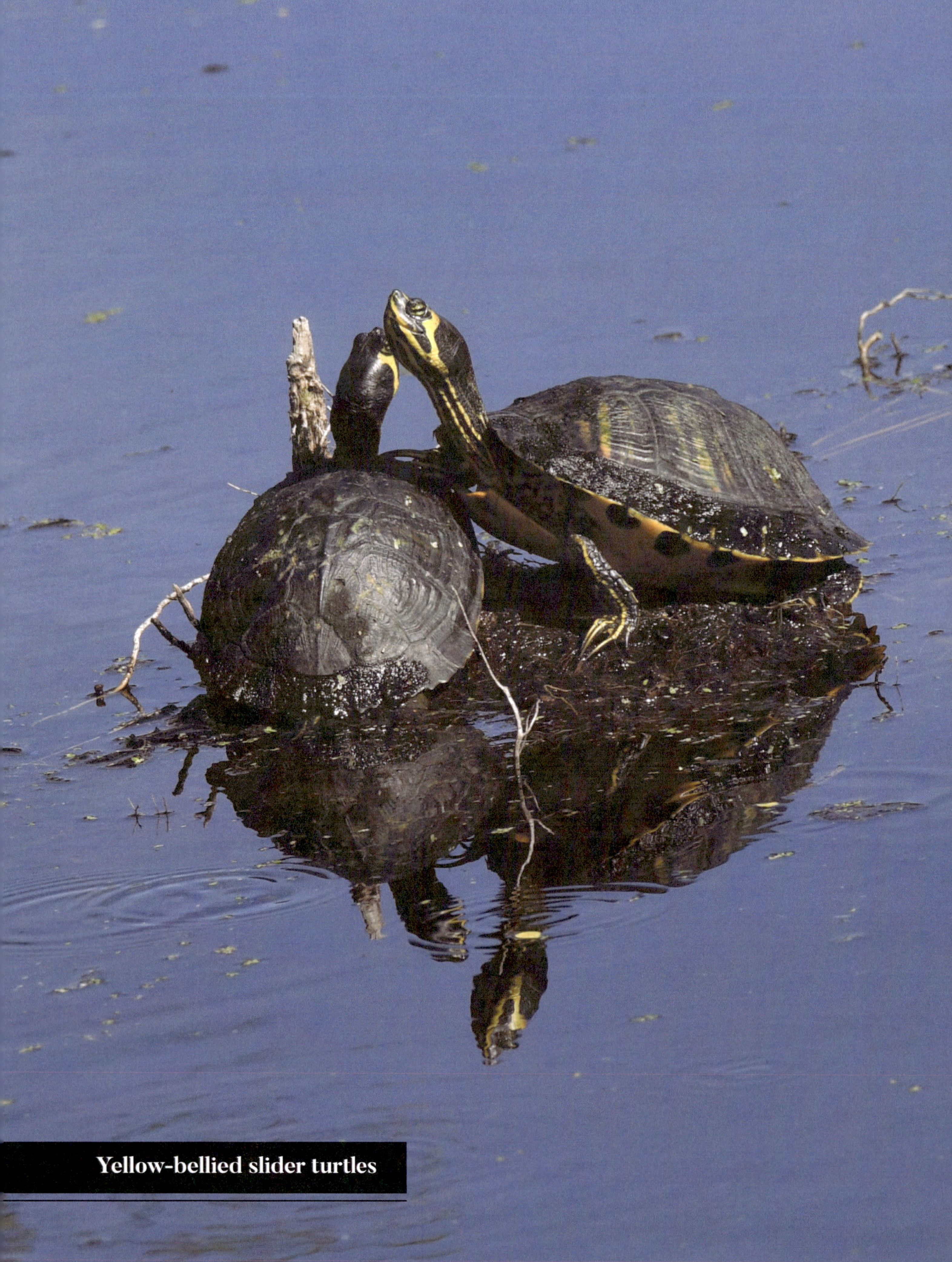

Yellow-bellied slider turtles

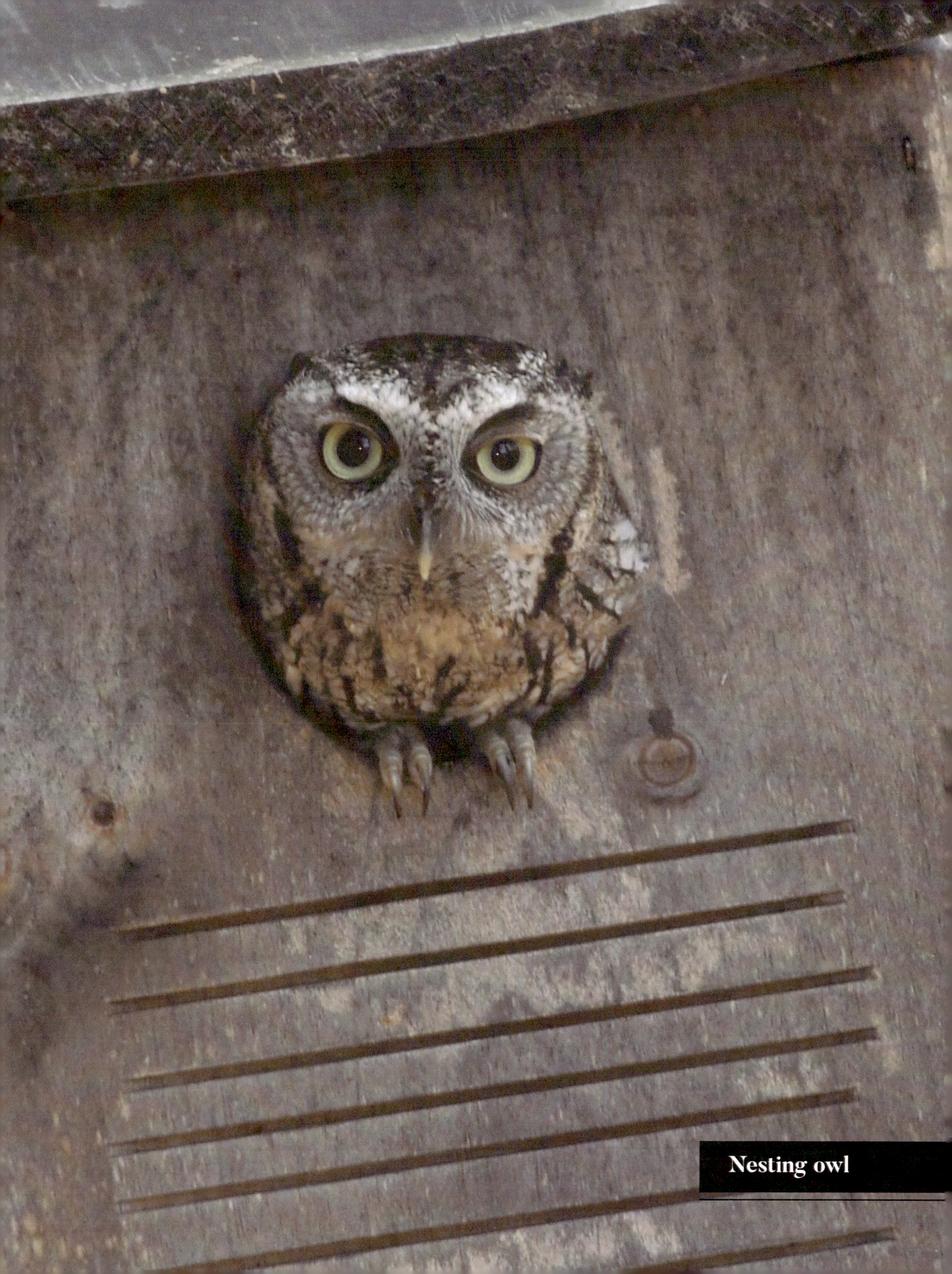

Nesting owl

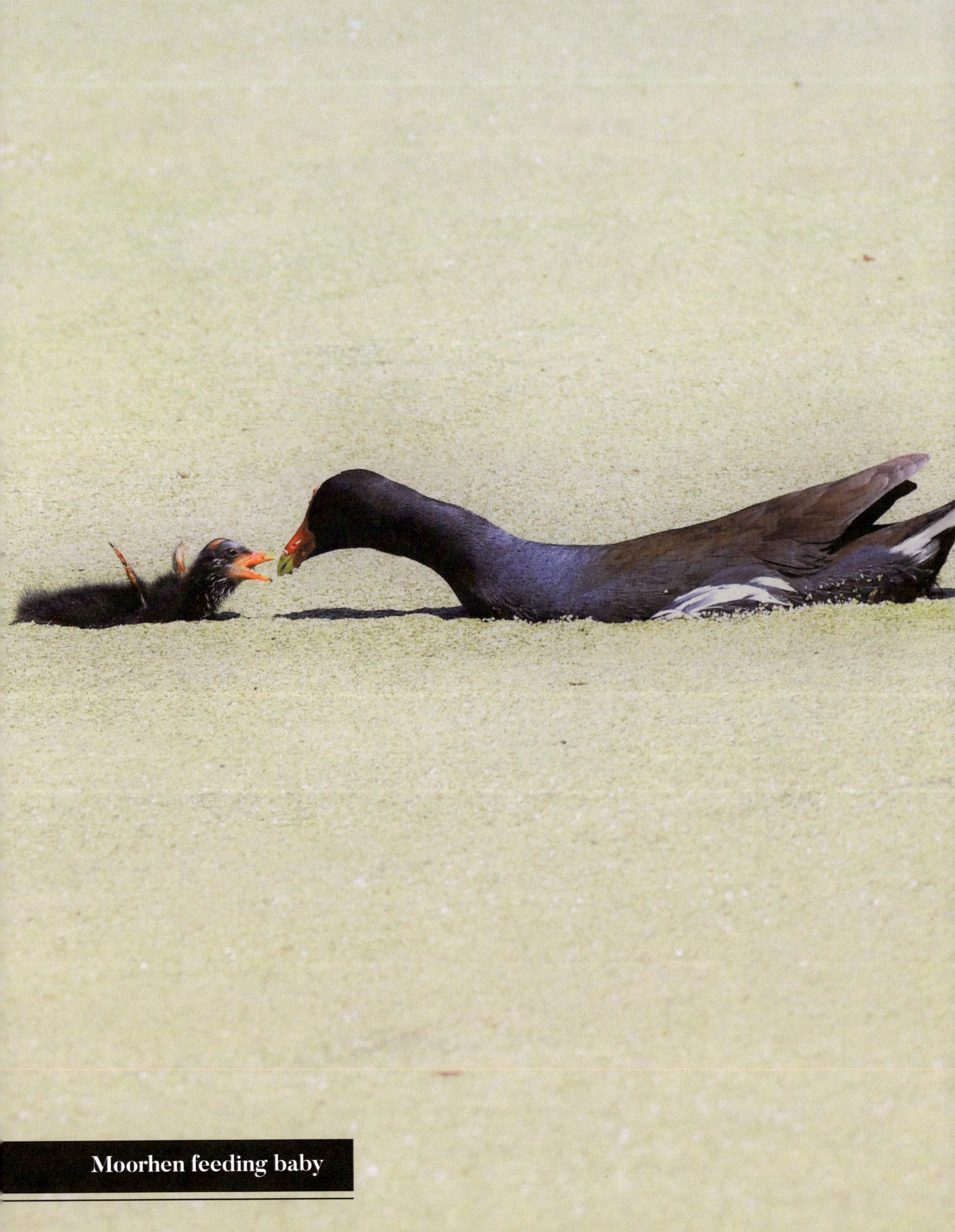

Moorhen feeding baby

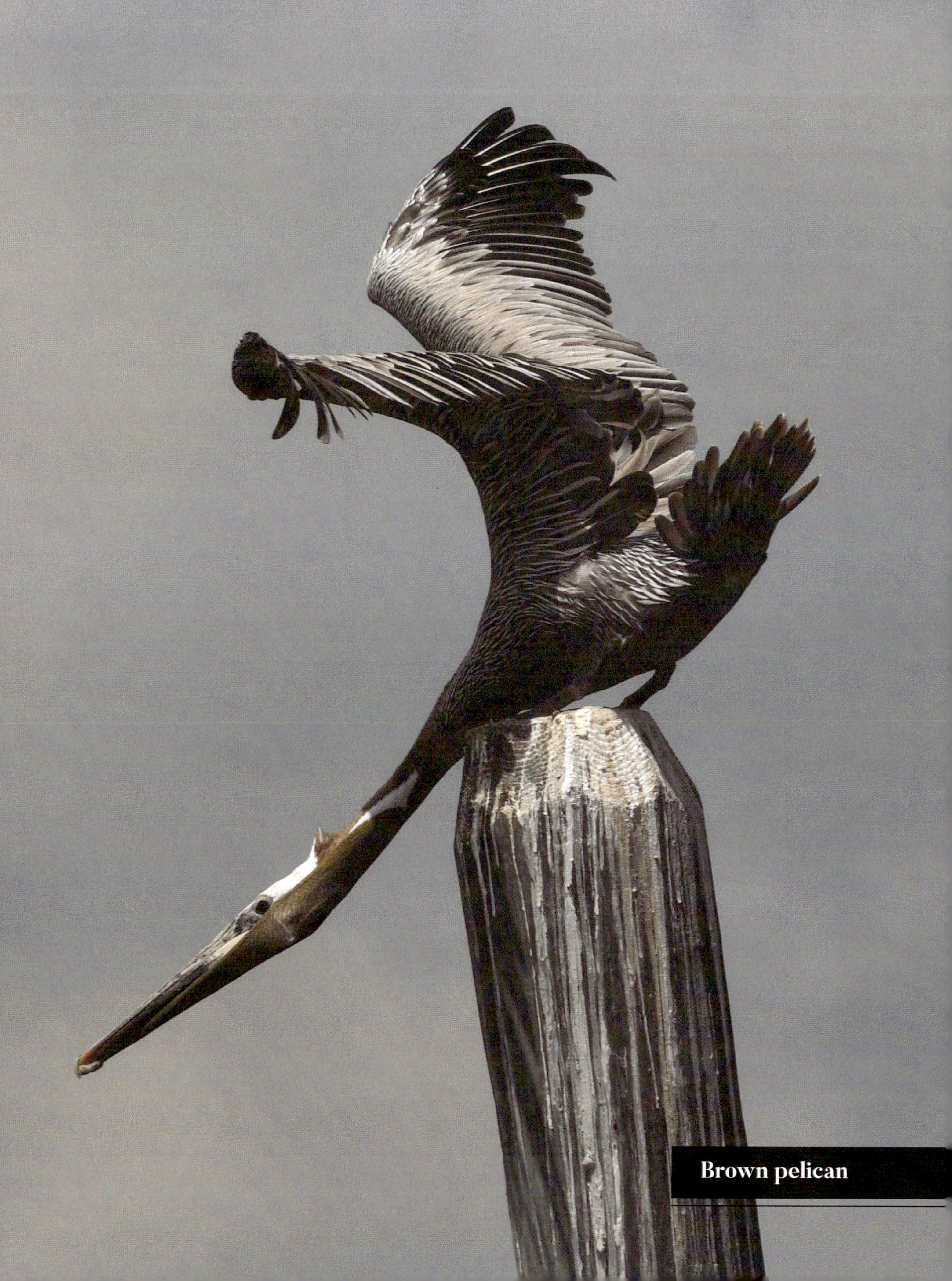
Brown pelican

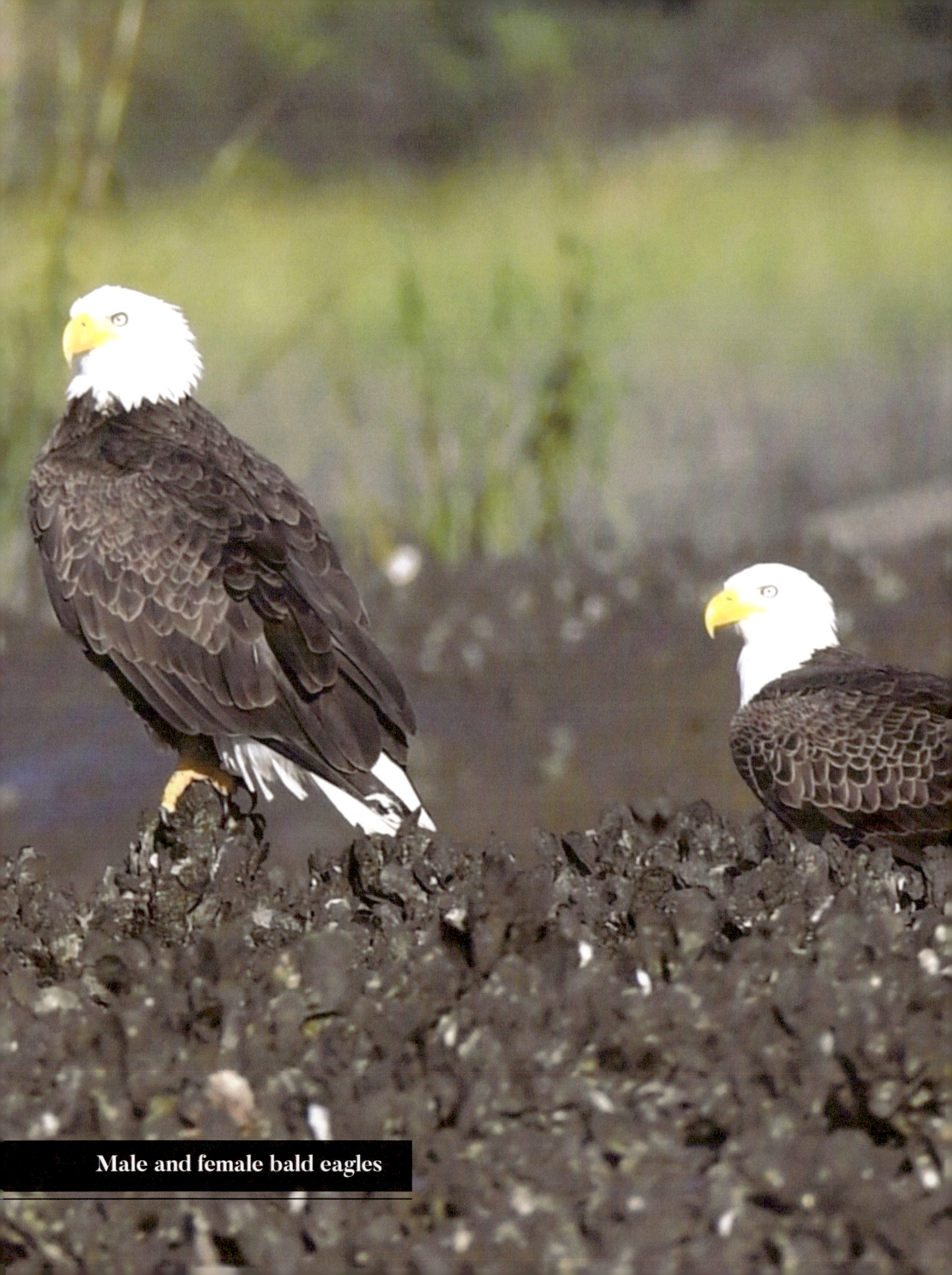

Male and female bald eagles

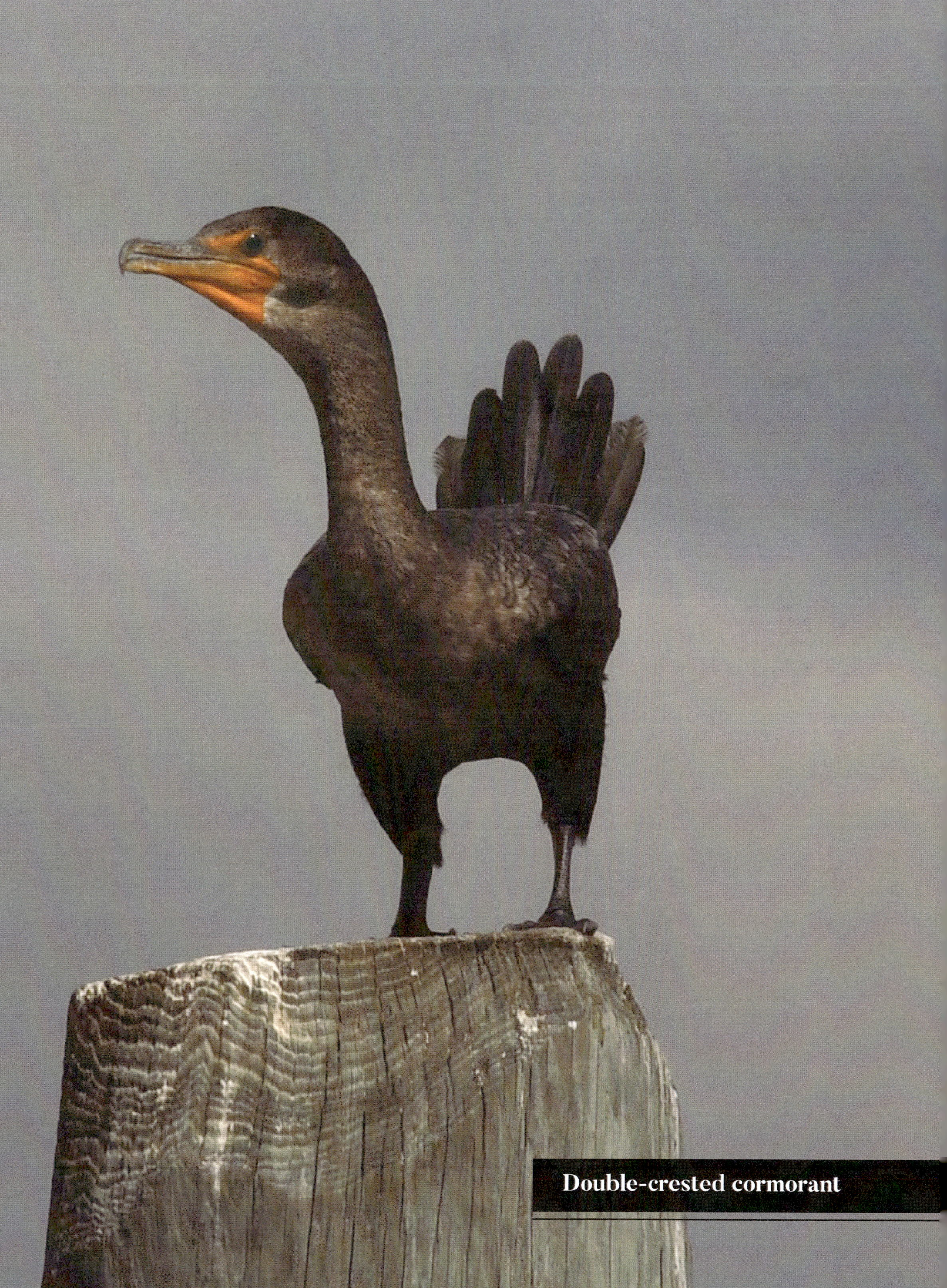
Double-crested cormorant

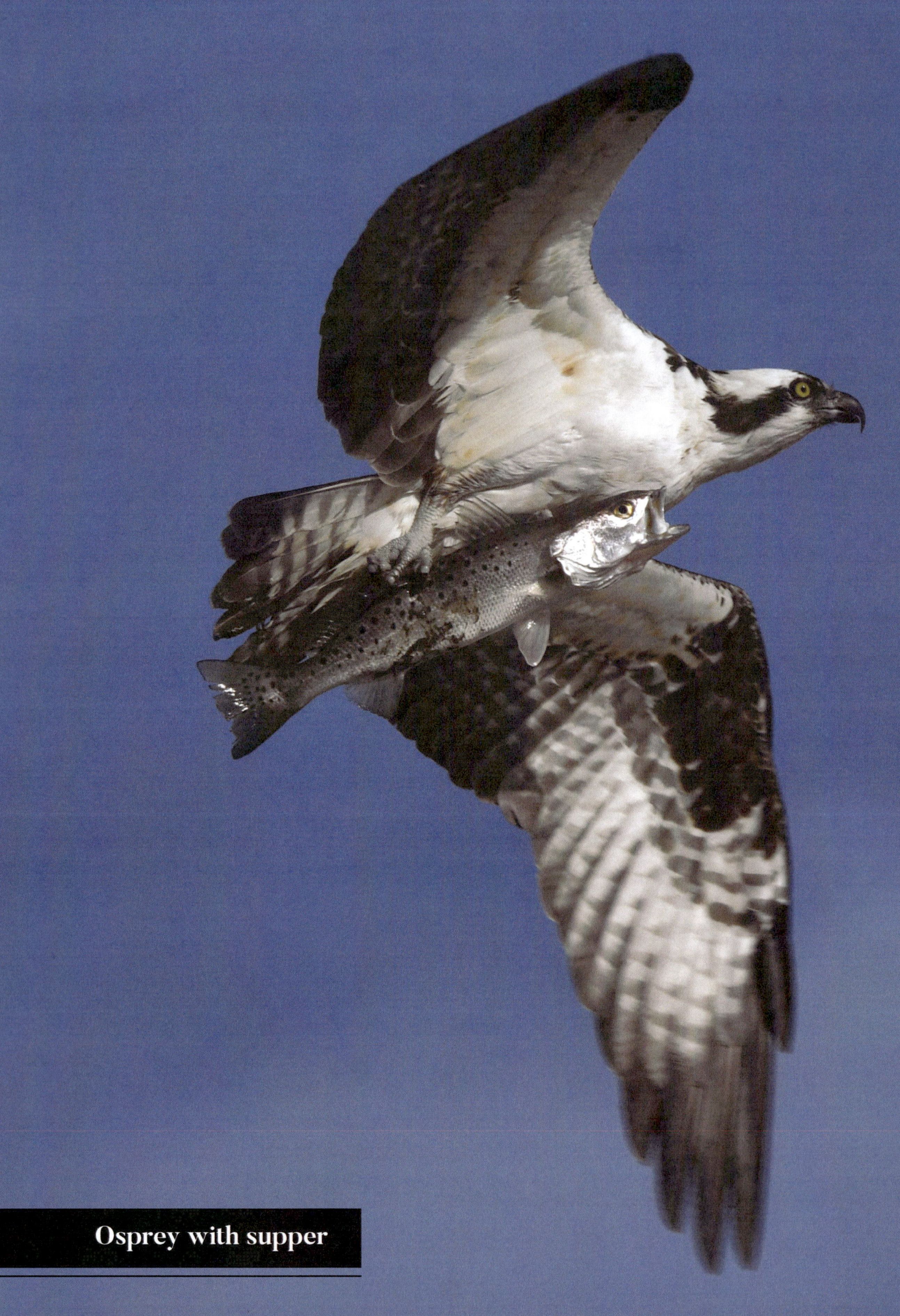

Osprey with supper

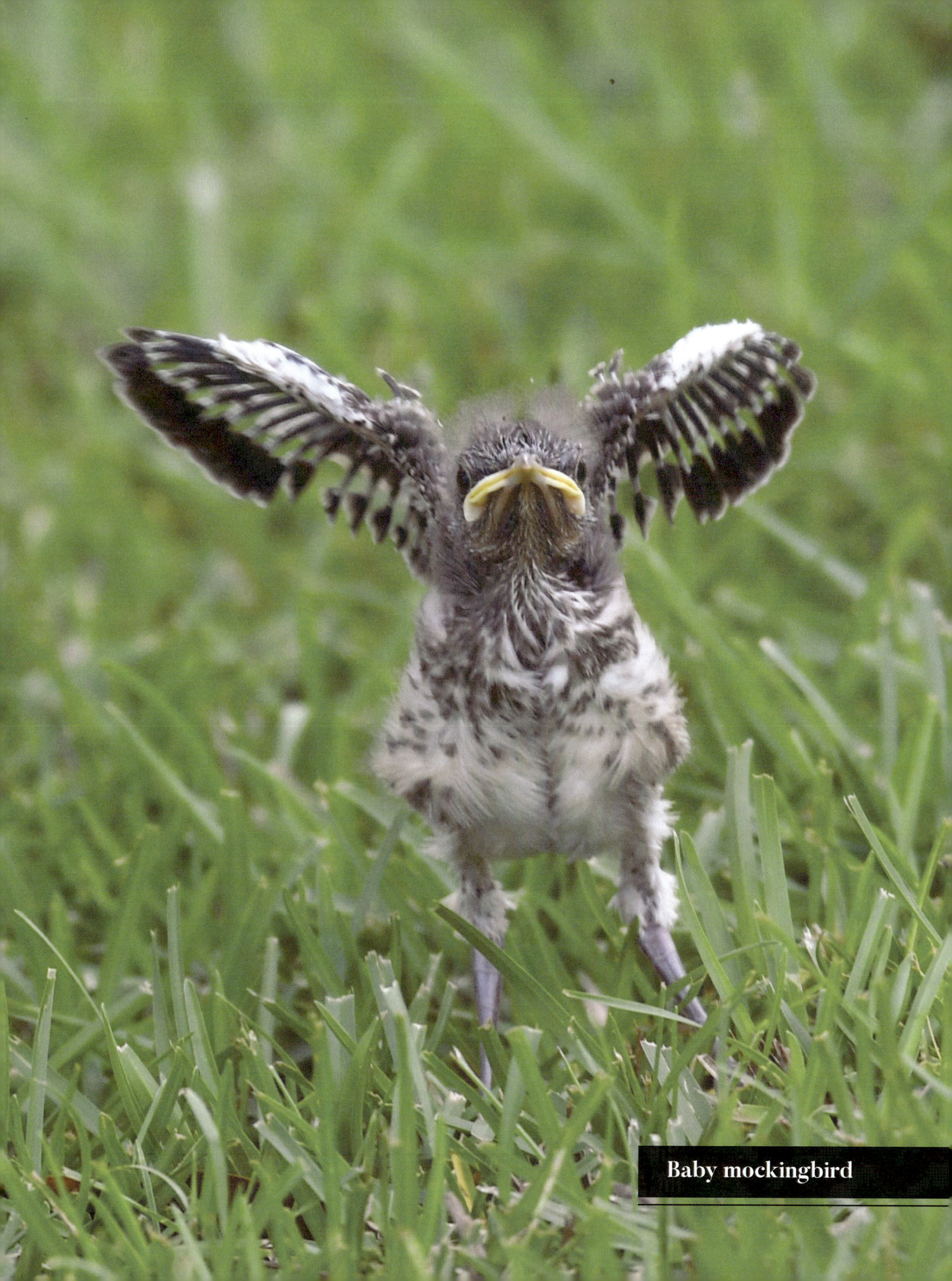

Baby mockingbird

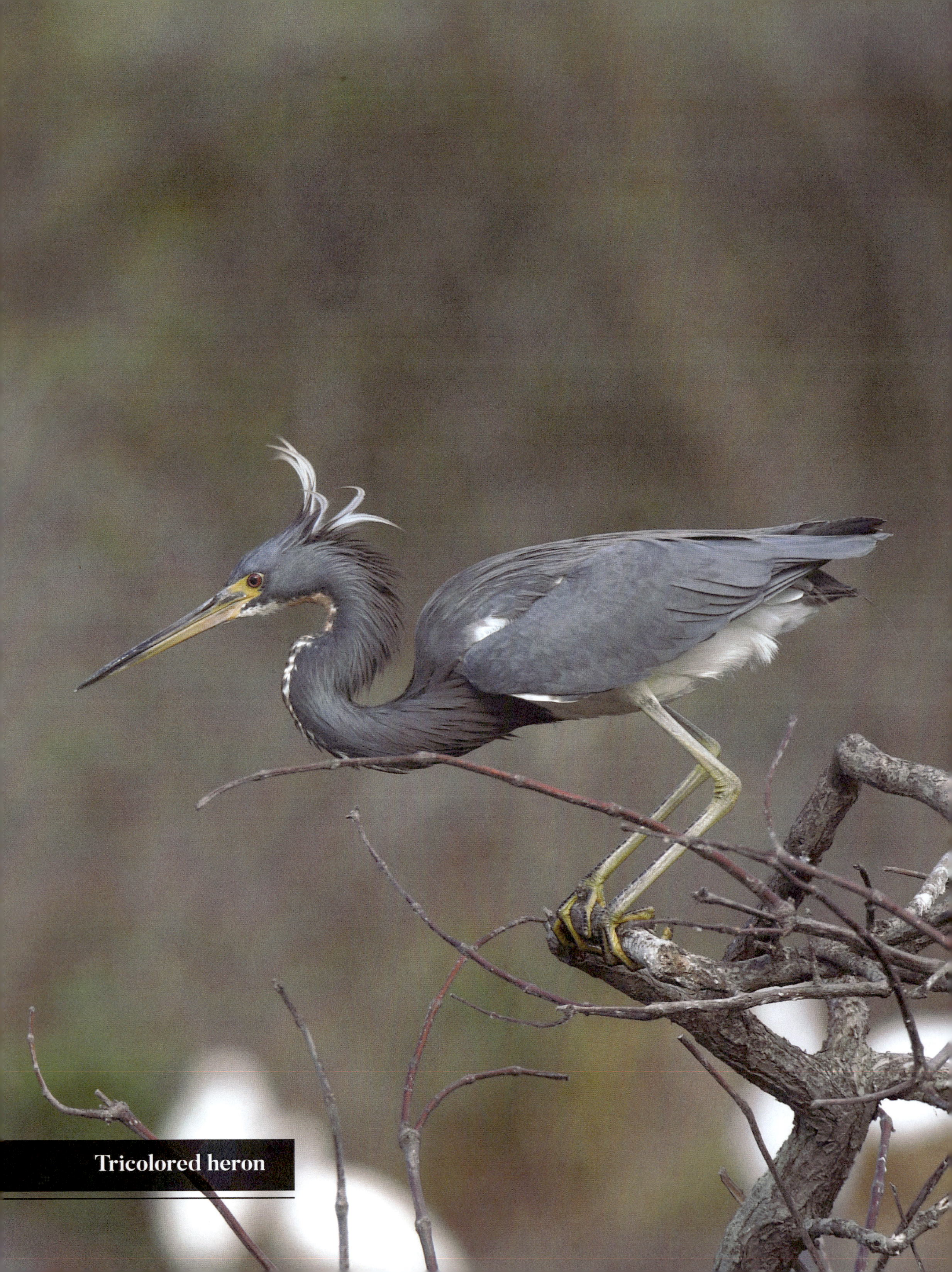

Tricolored heron

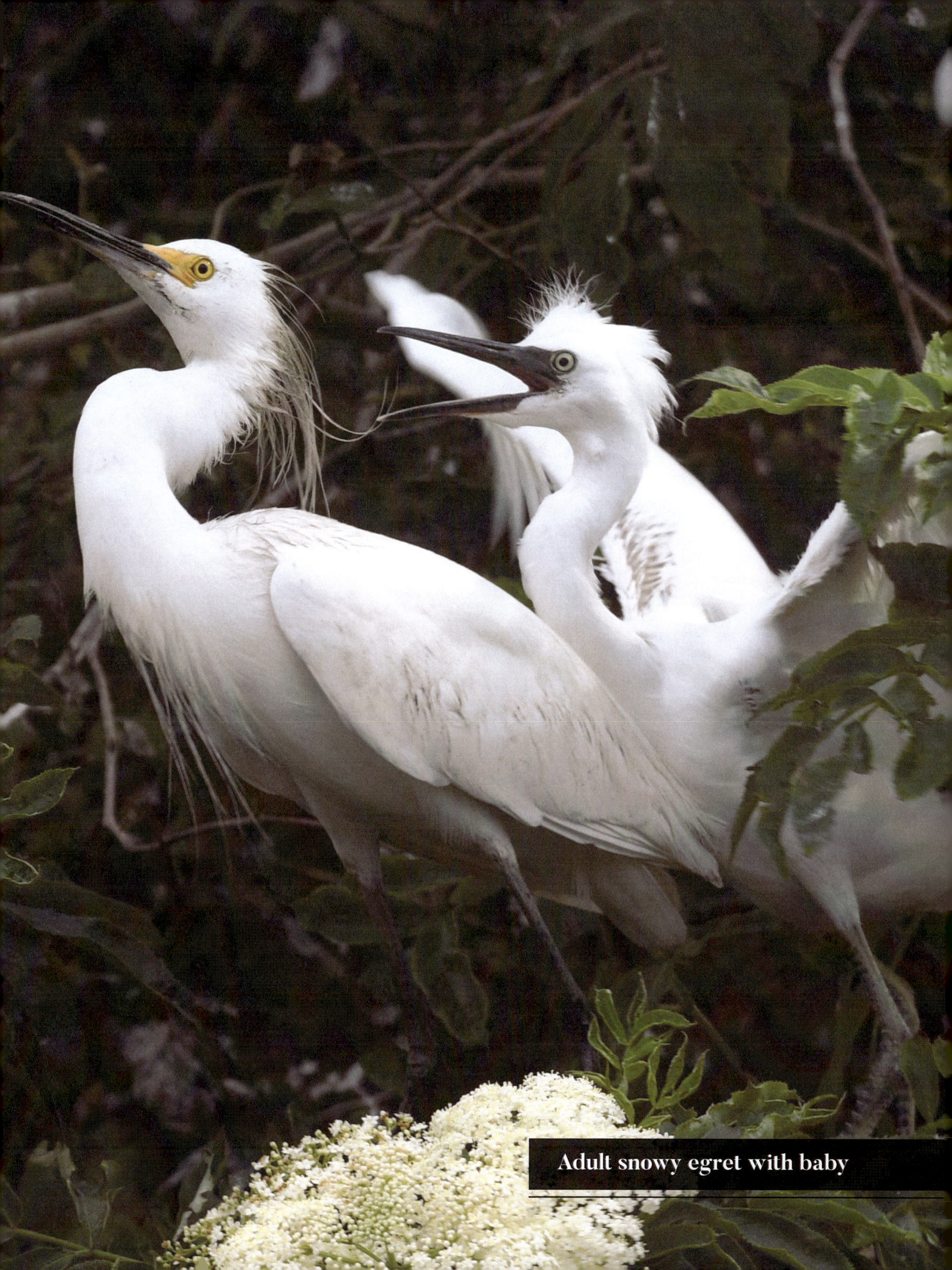

Adult snowy egret with baby

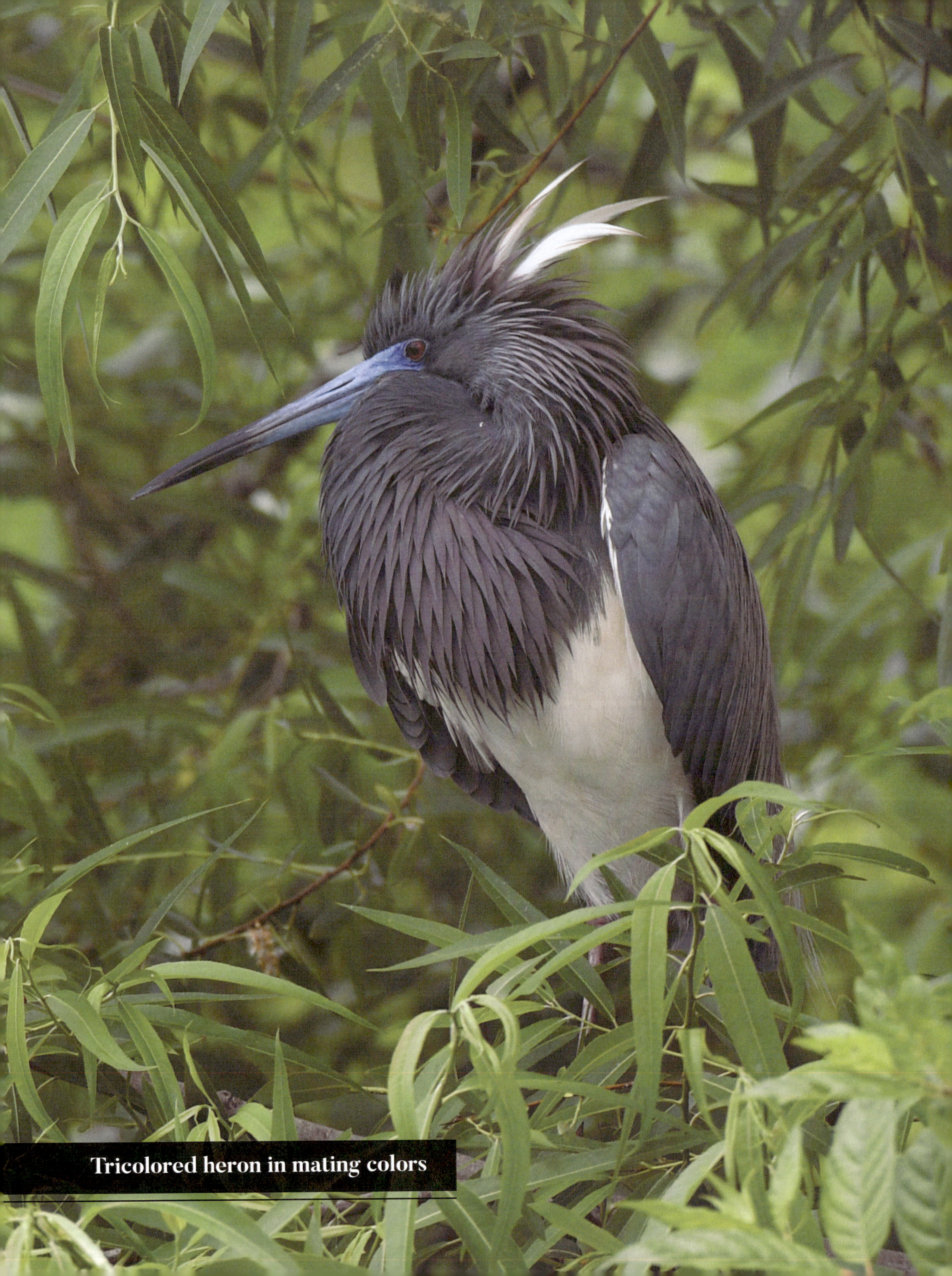

Tricolored heron in mating colors

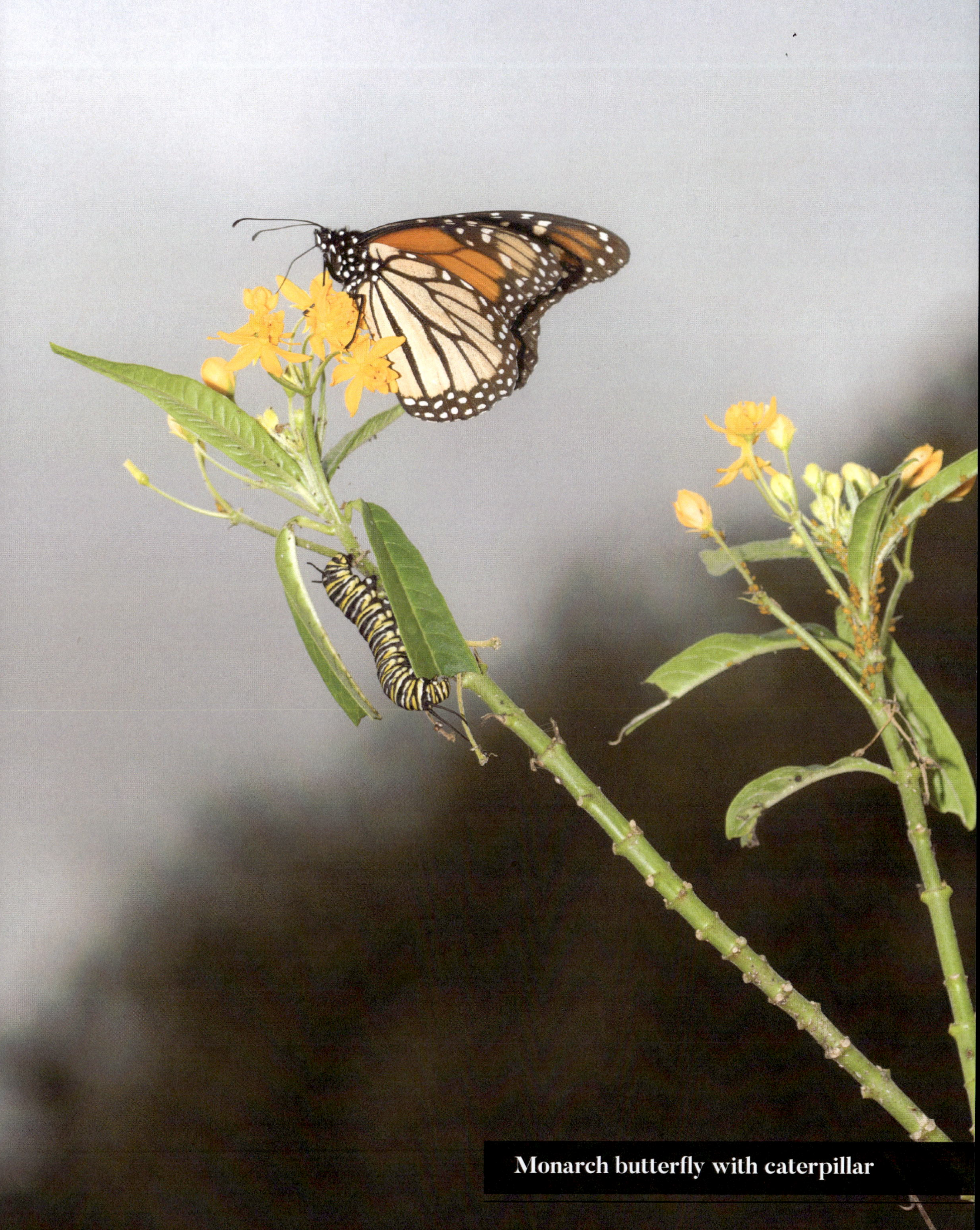

Monarch butterfly with caterpillar

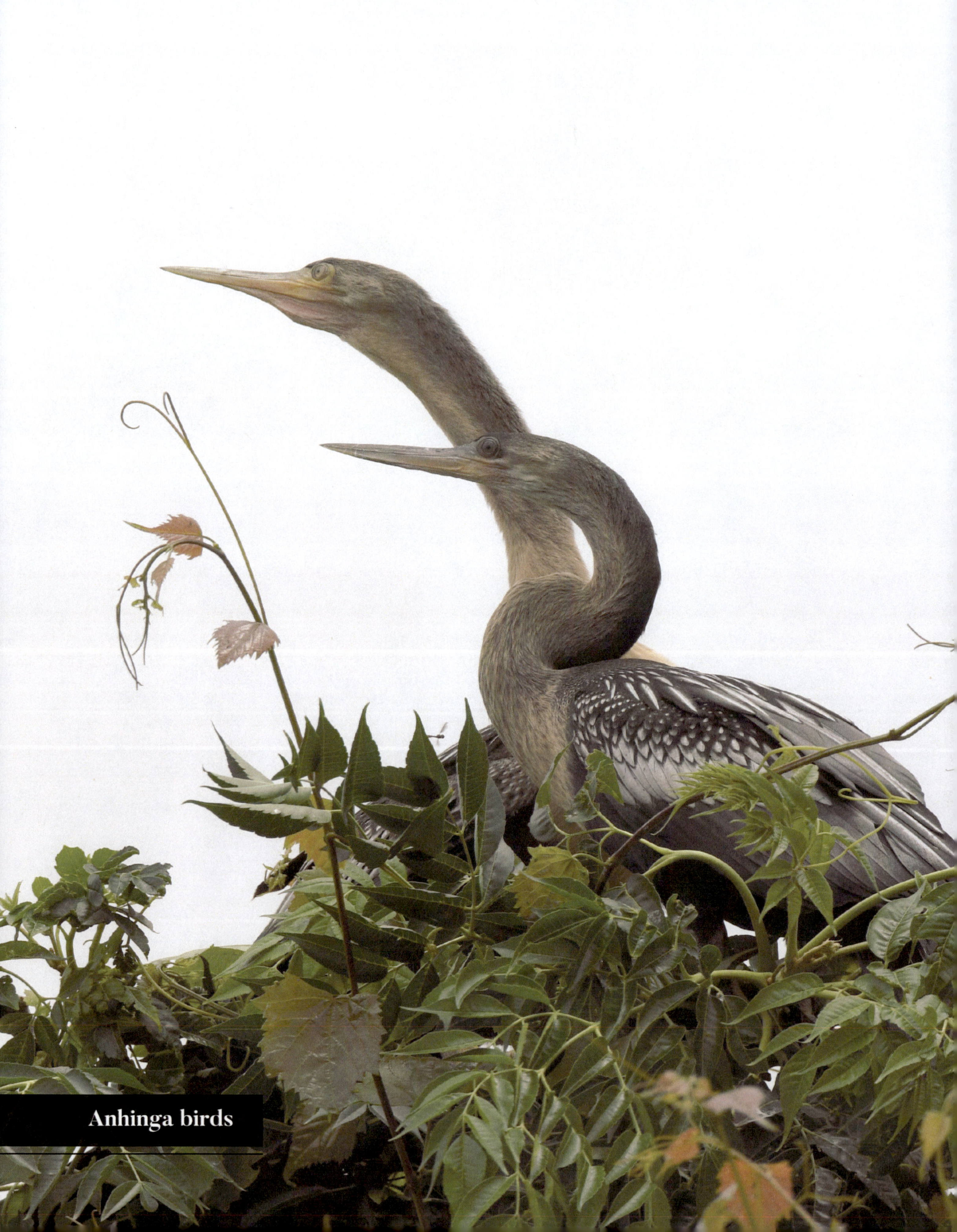

Anhinga birds

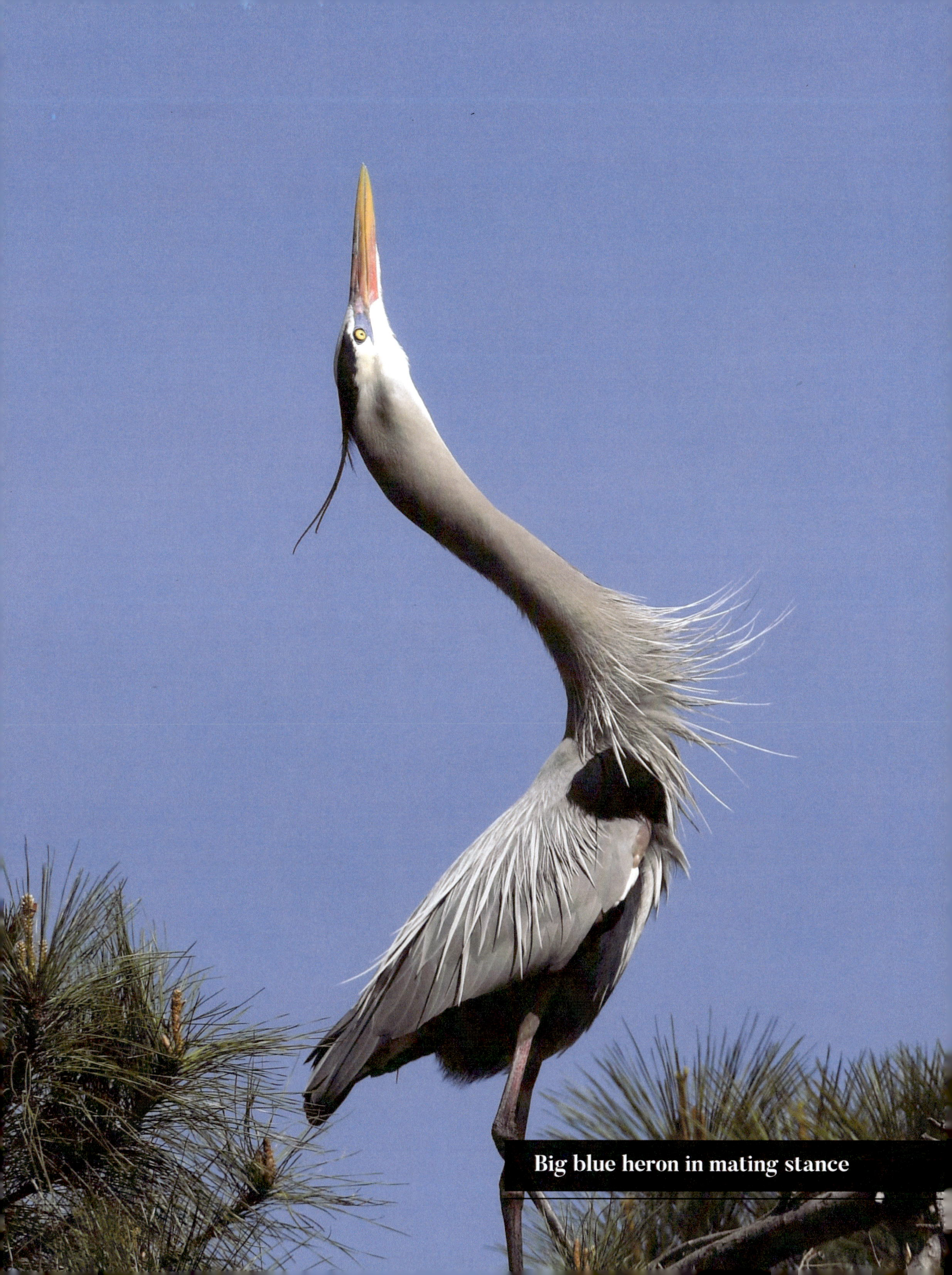
Big blue heron in mating stance

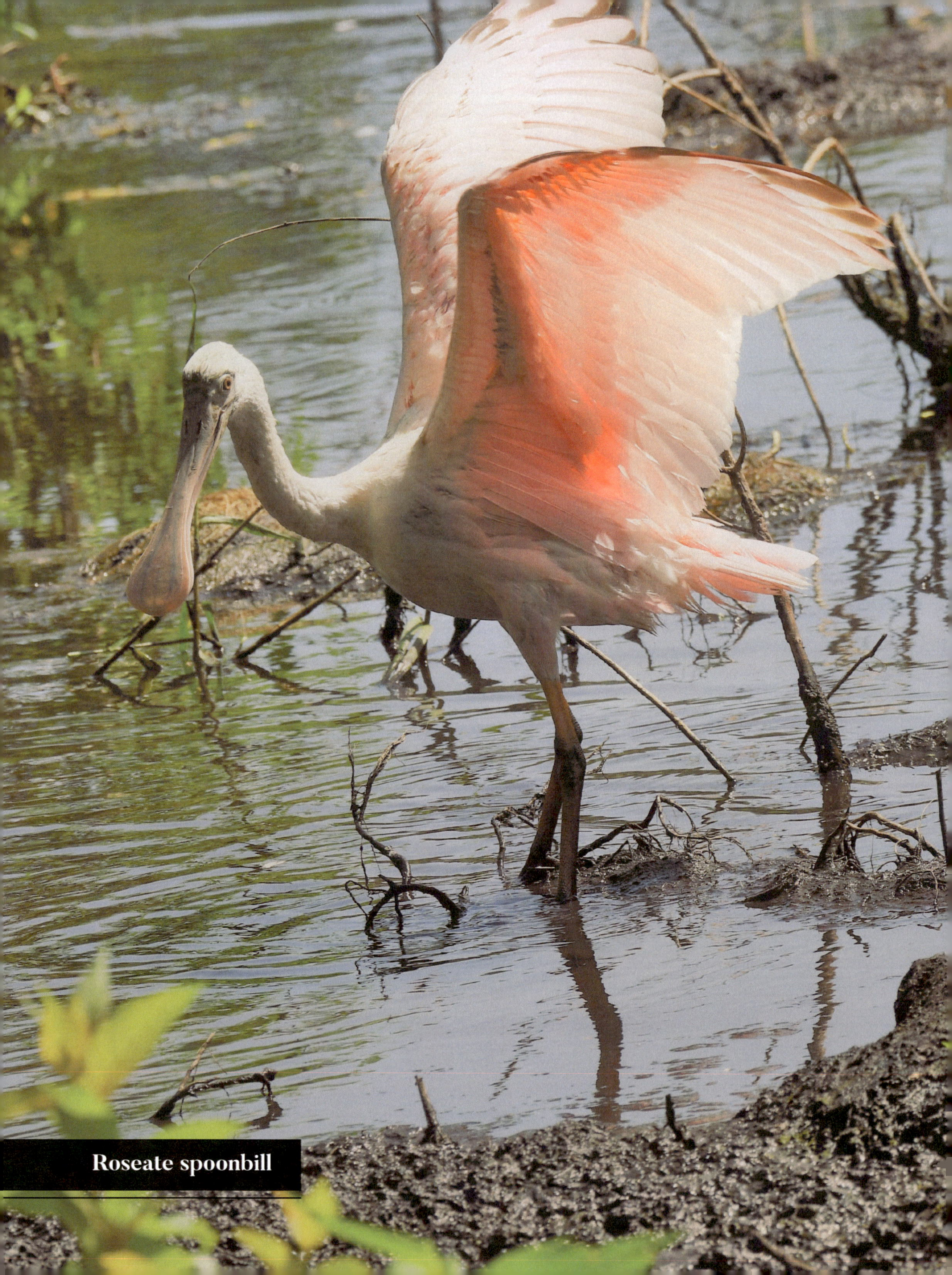

Roseate spoonbill

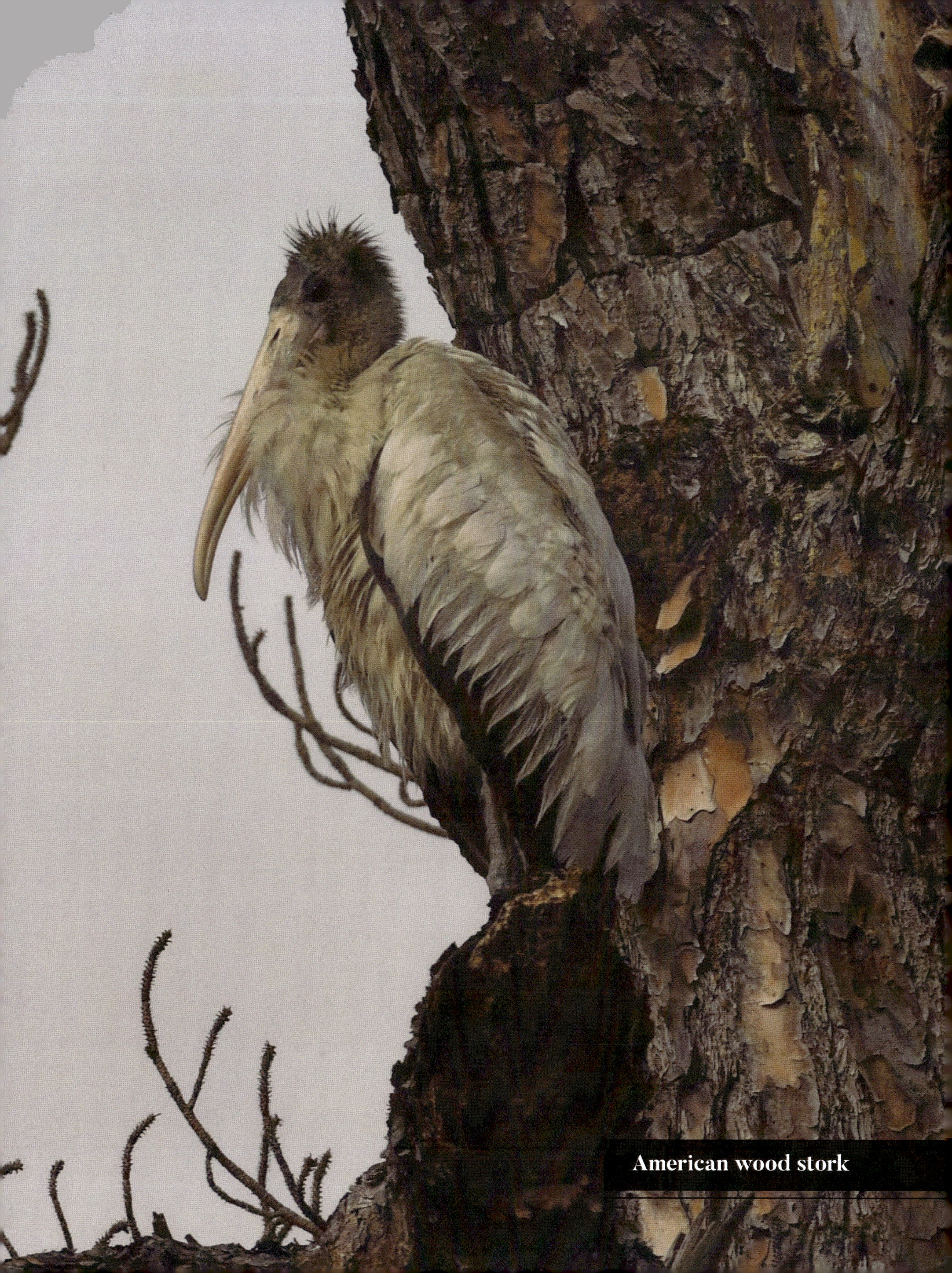

American wood stork

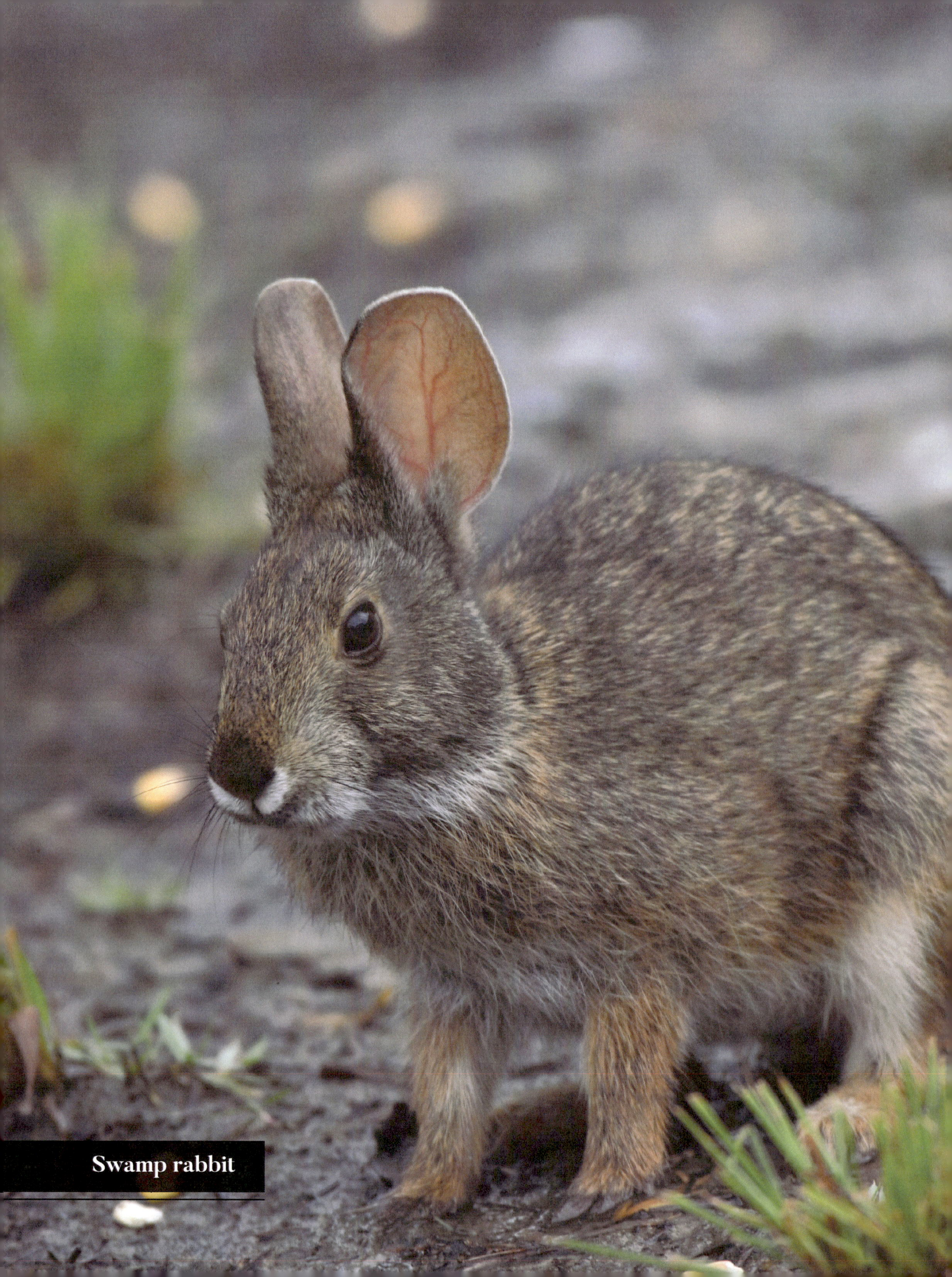

Swamp rabbit

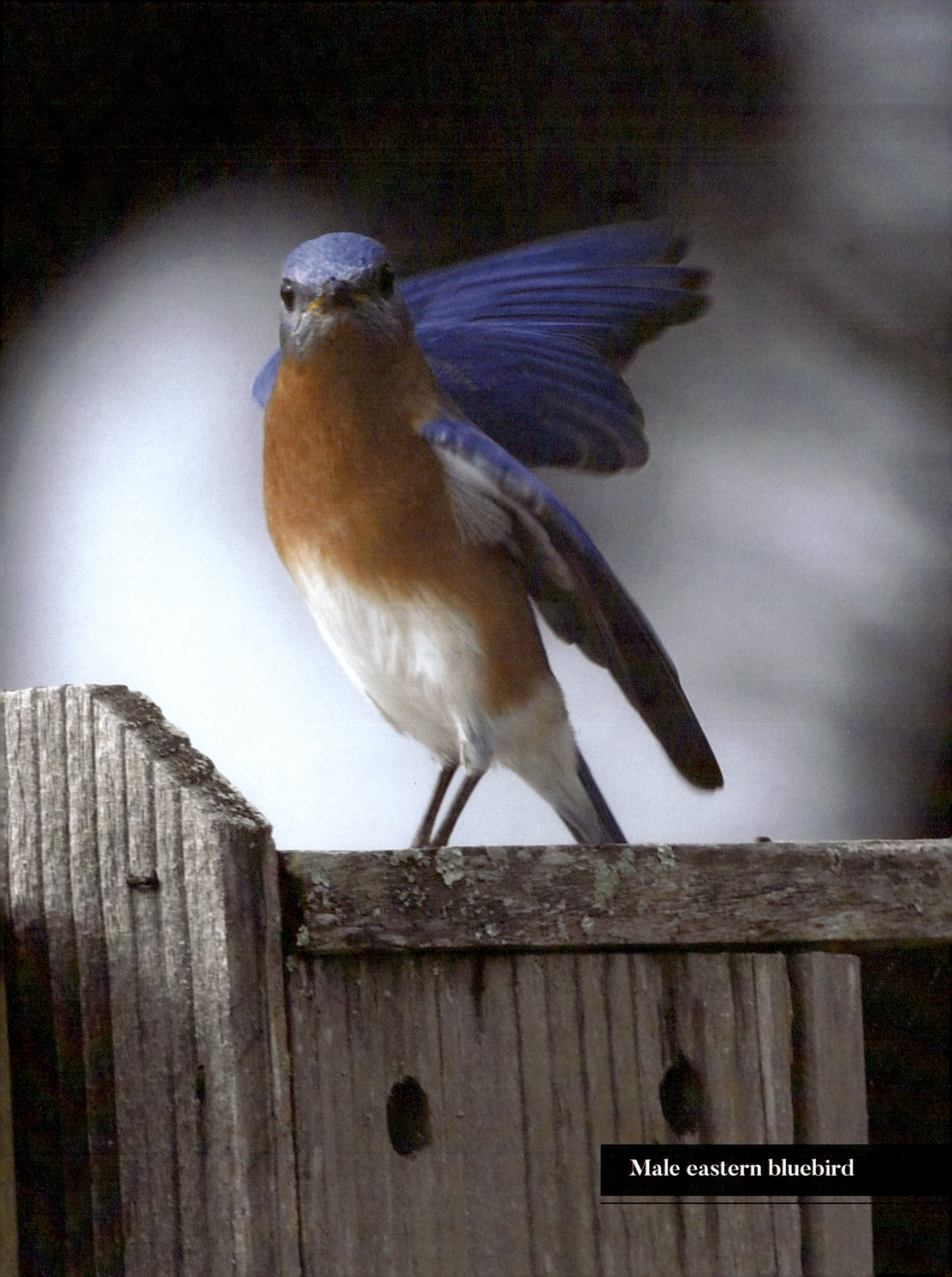

Male eastern bluebird

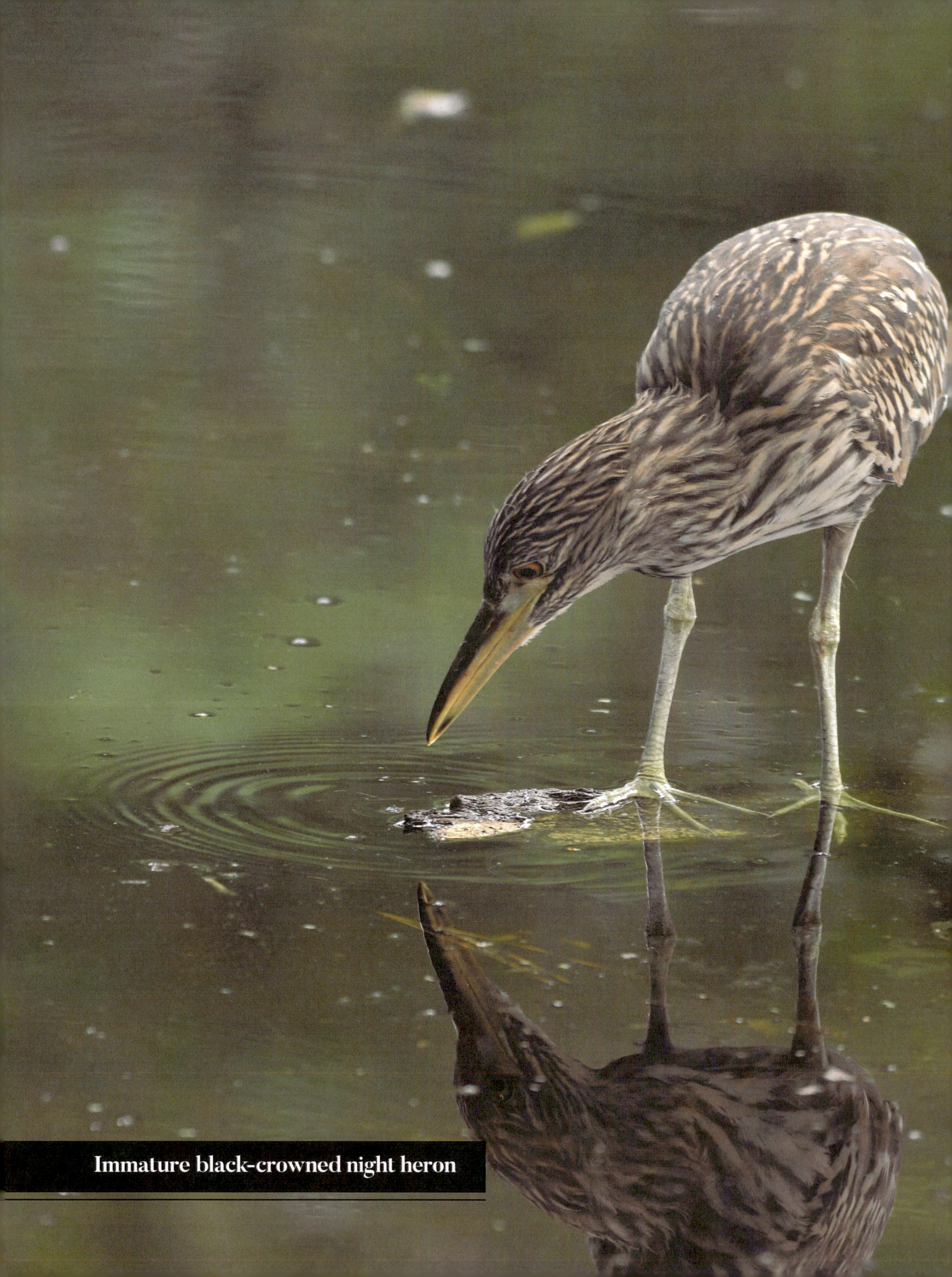

Immature black-crowned night heron

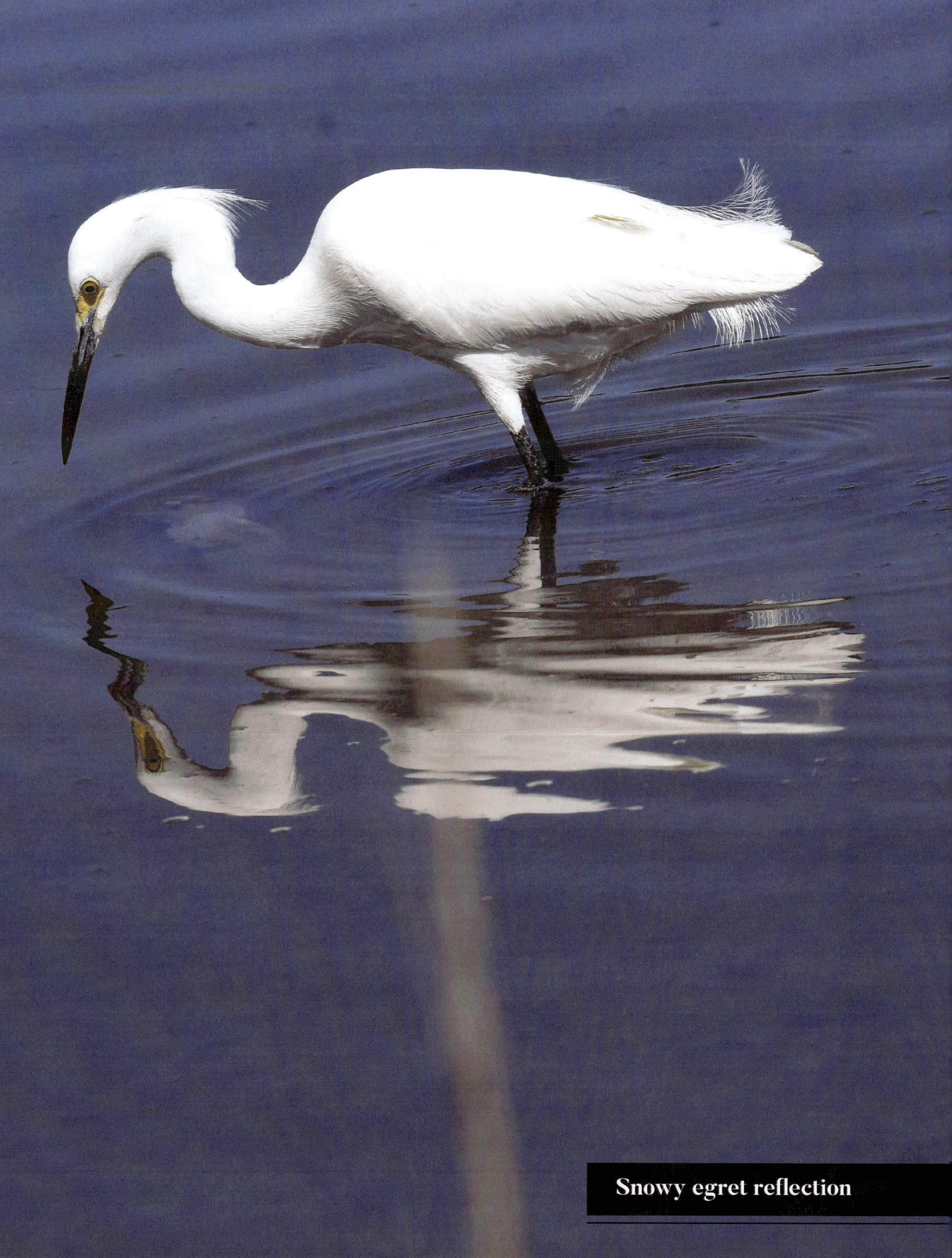

Snowy egret reflection

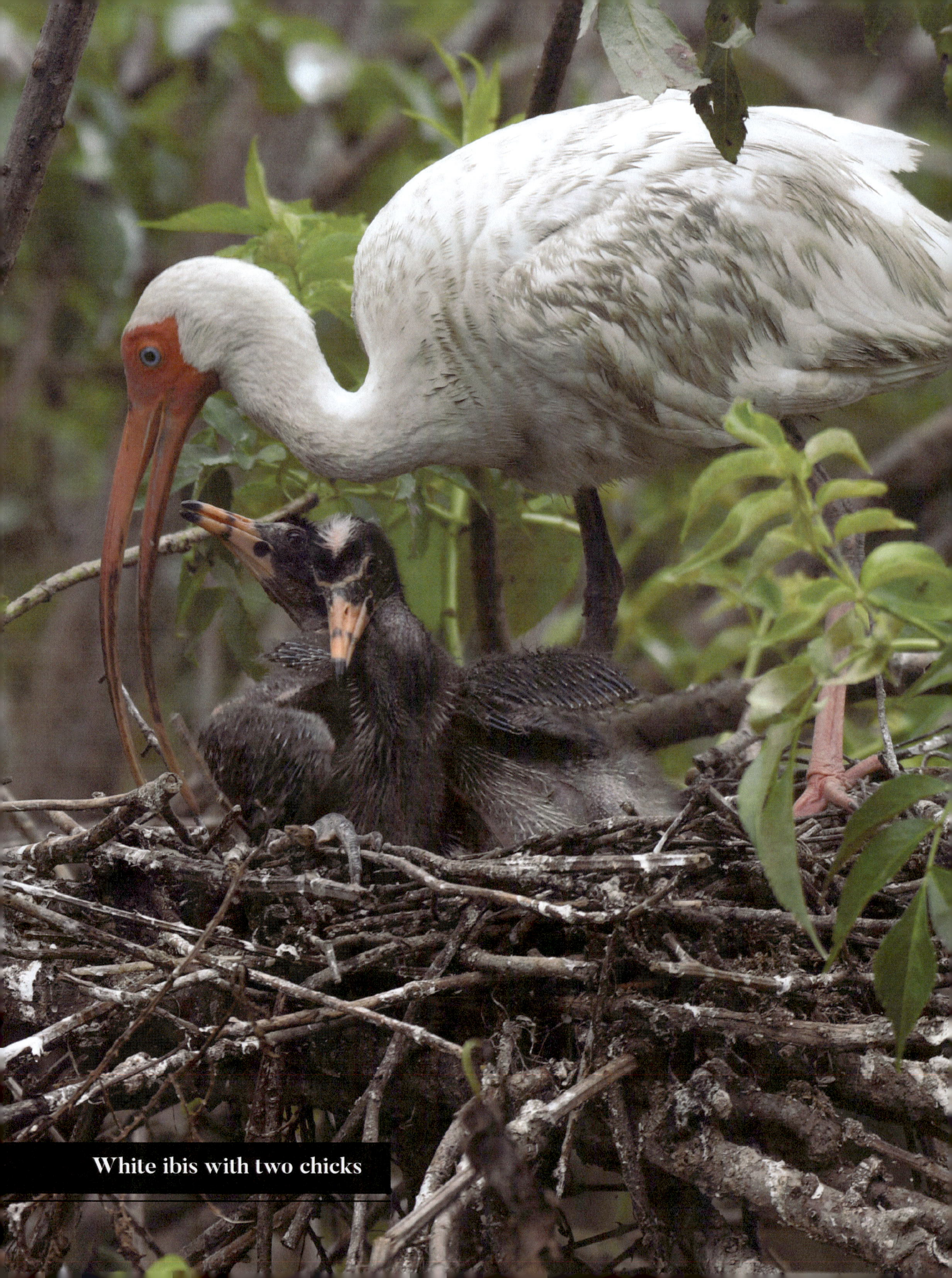

White ibis with two chicks

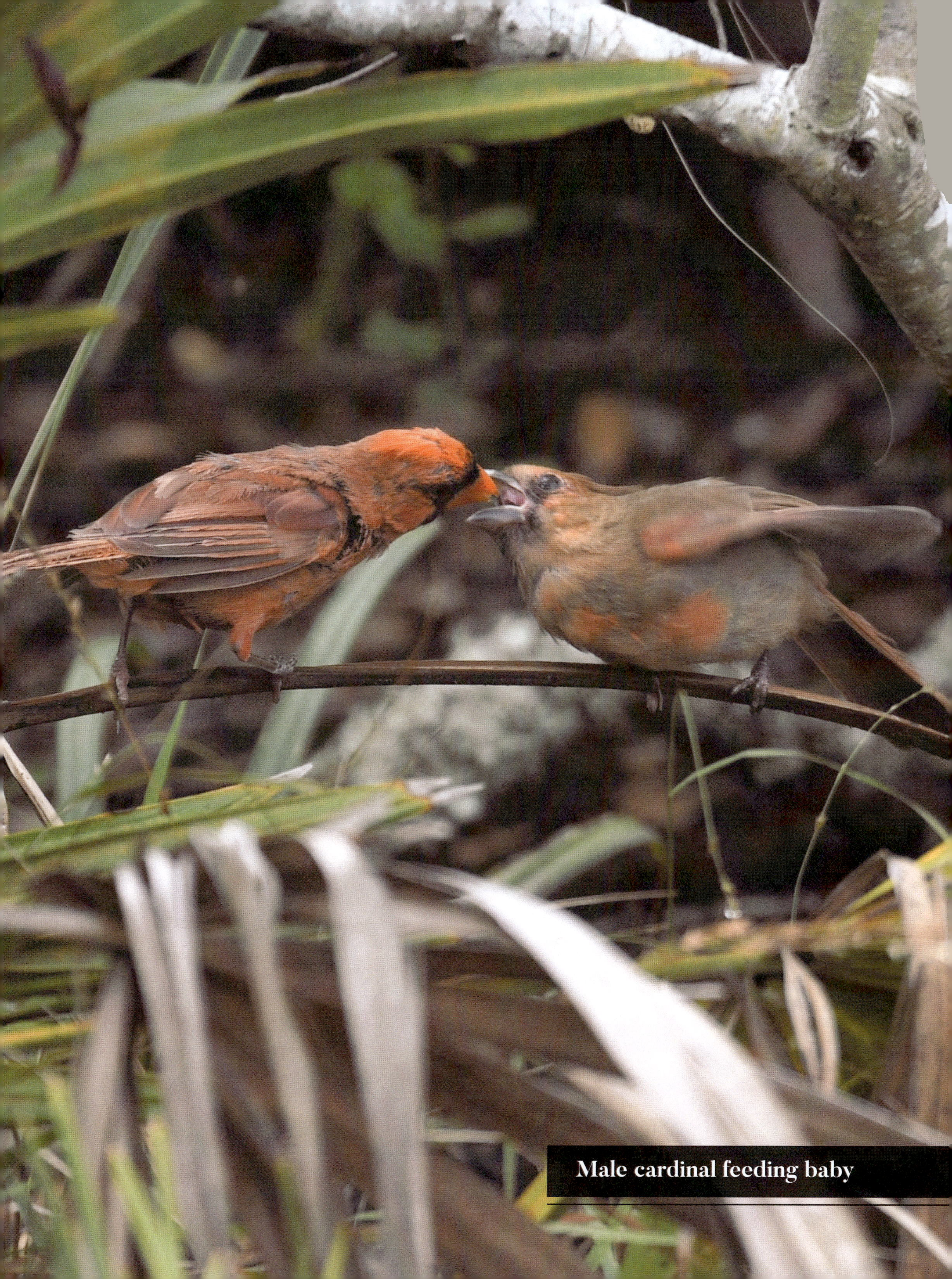

Male cardinal feeding baby

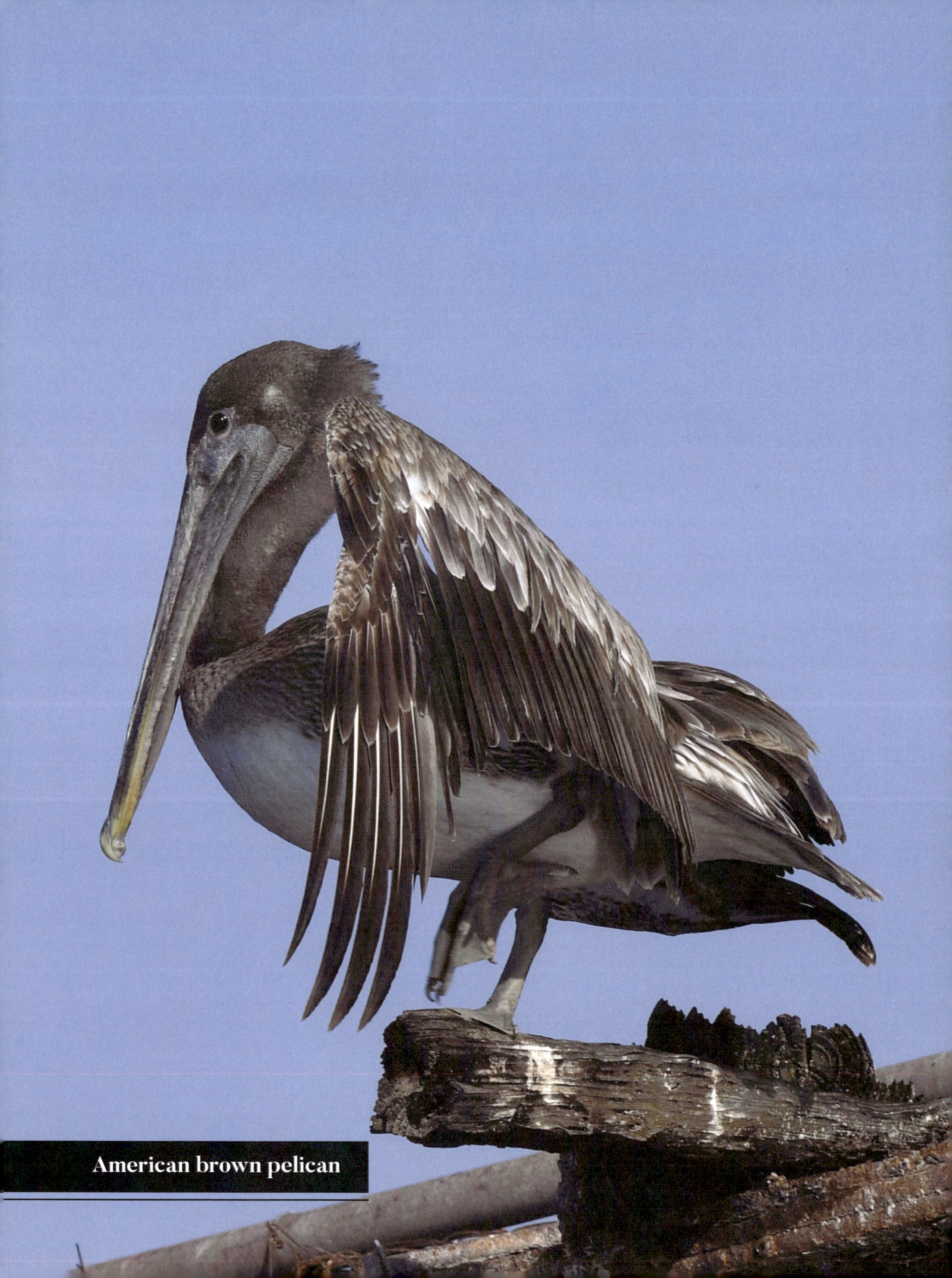

American brown pelican

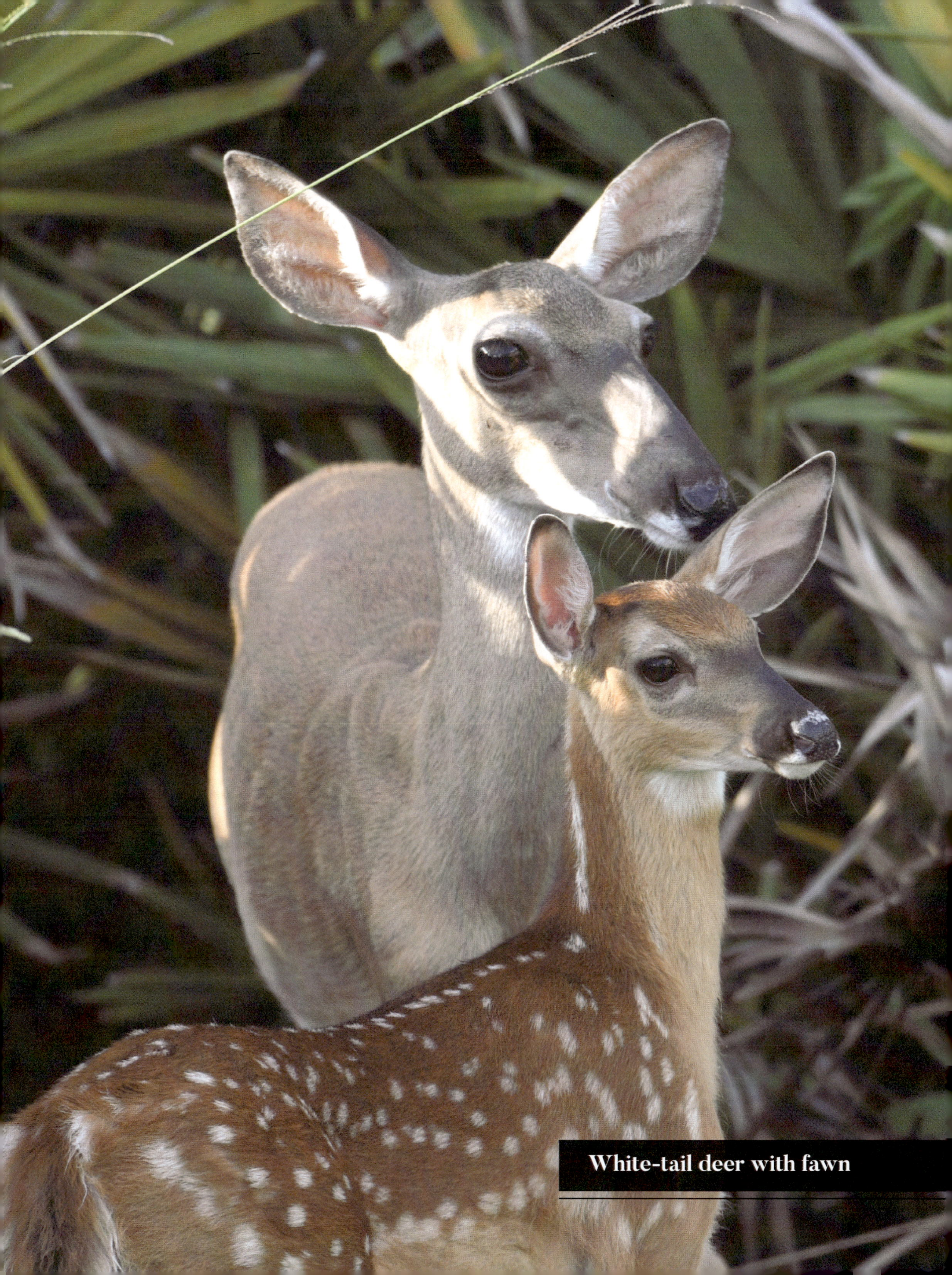

White-tail deer with fawn

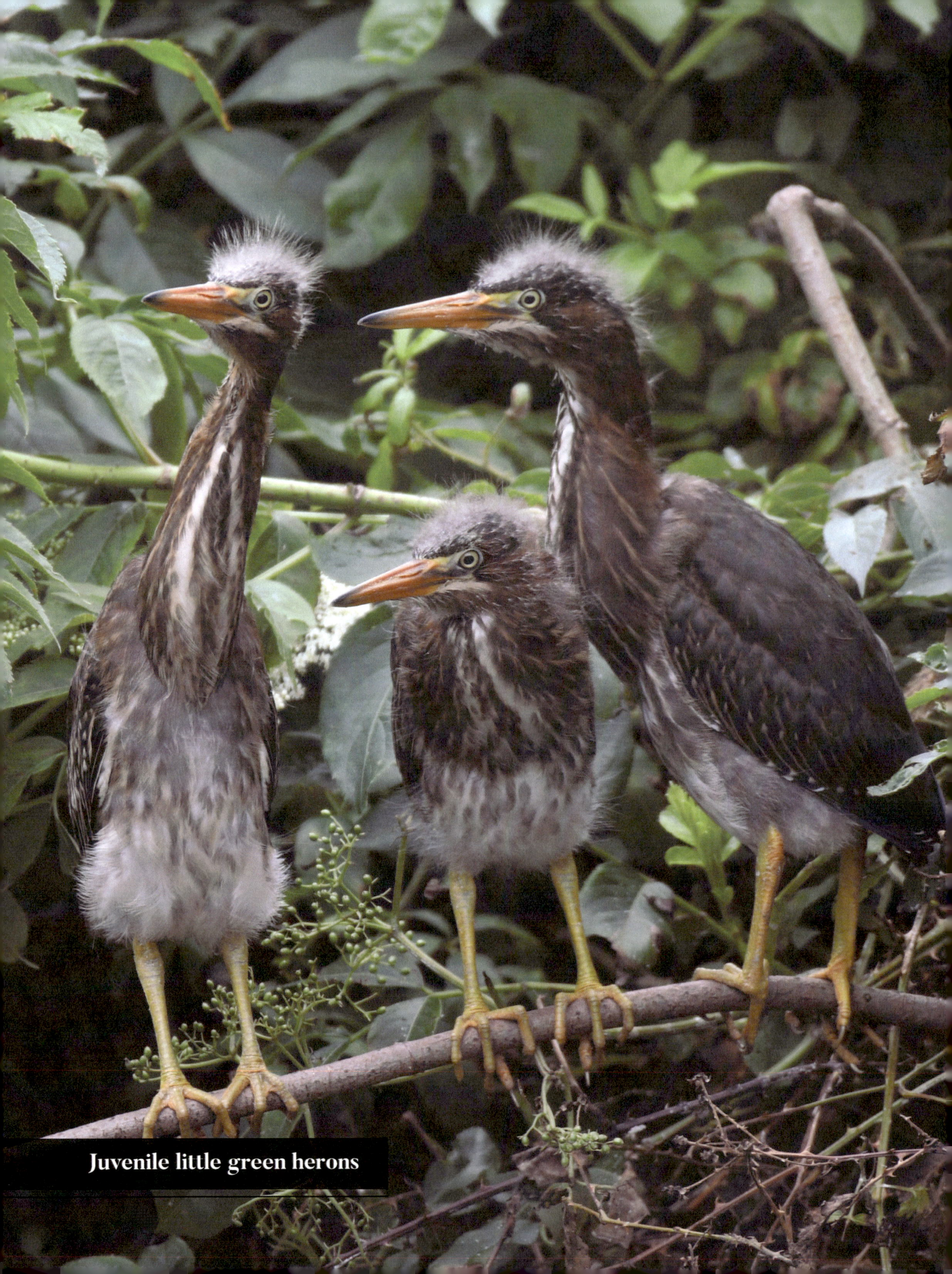

Juvenile little green herons

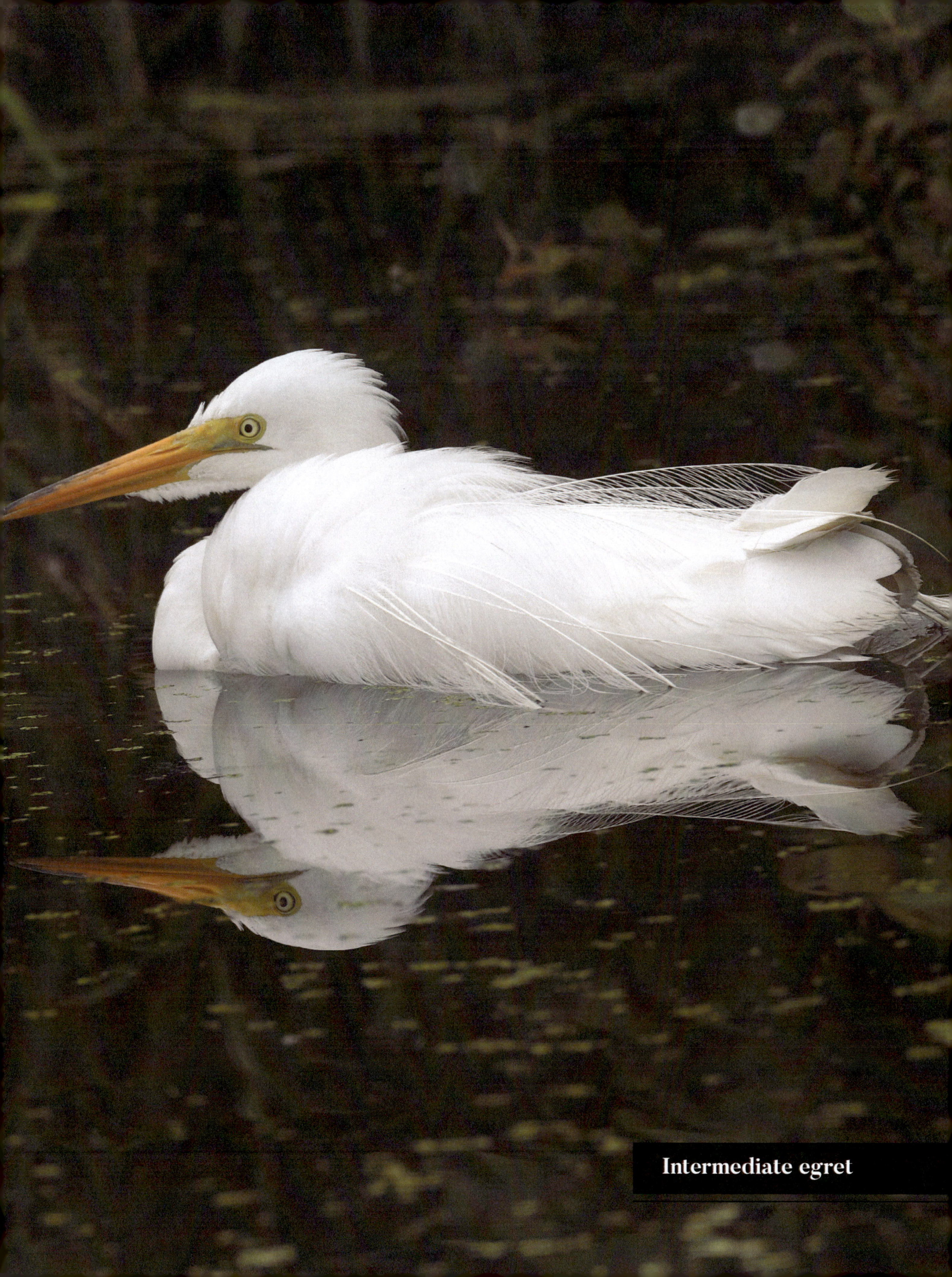
Intermediate egret

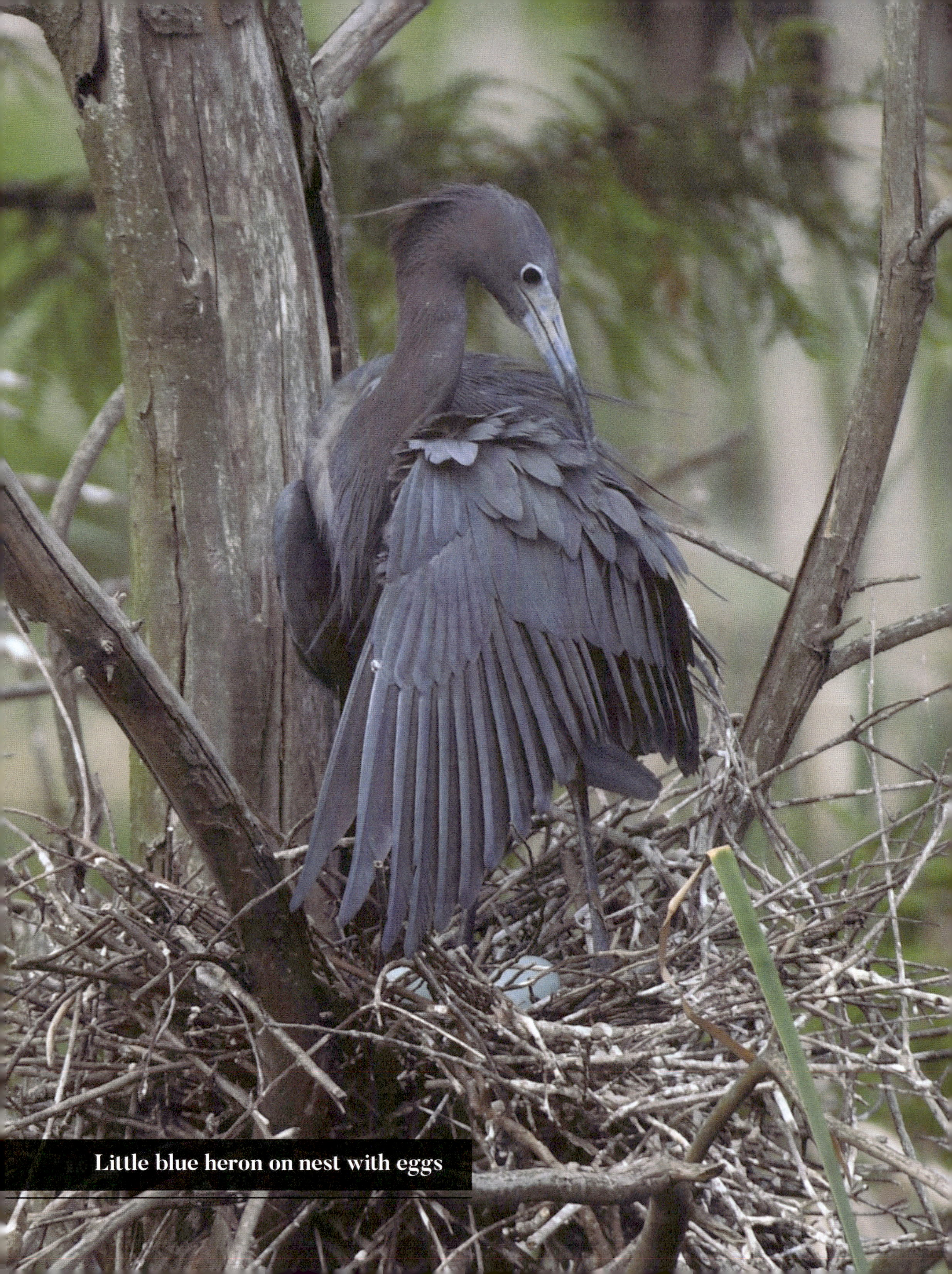

Little blue heron on nest with eggs

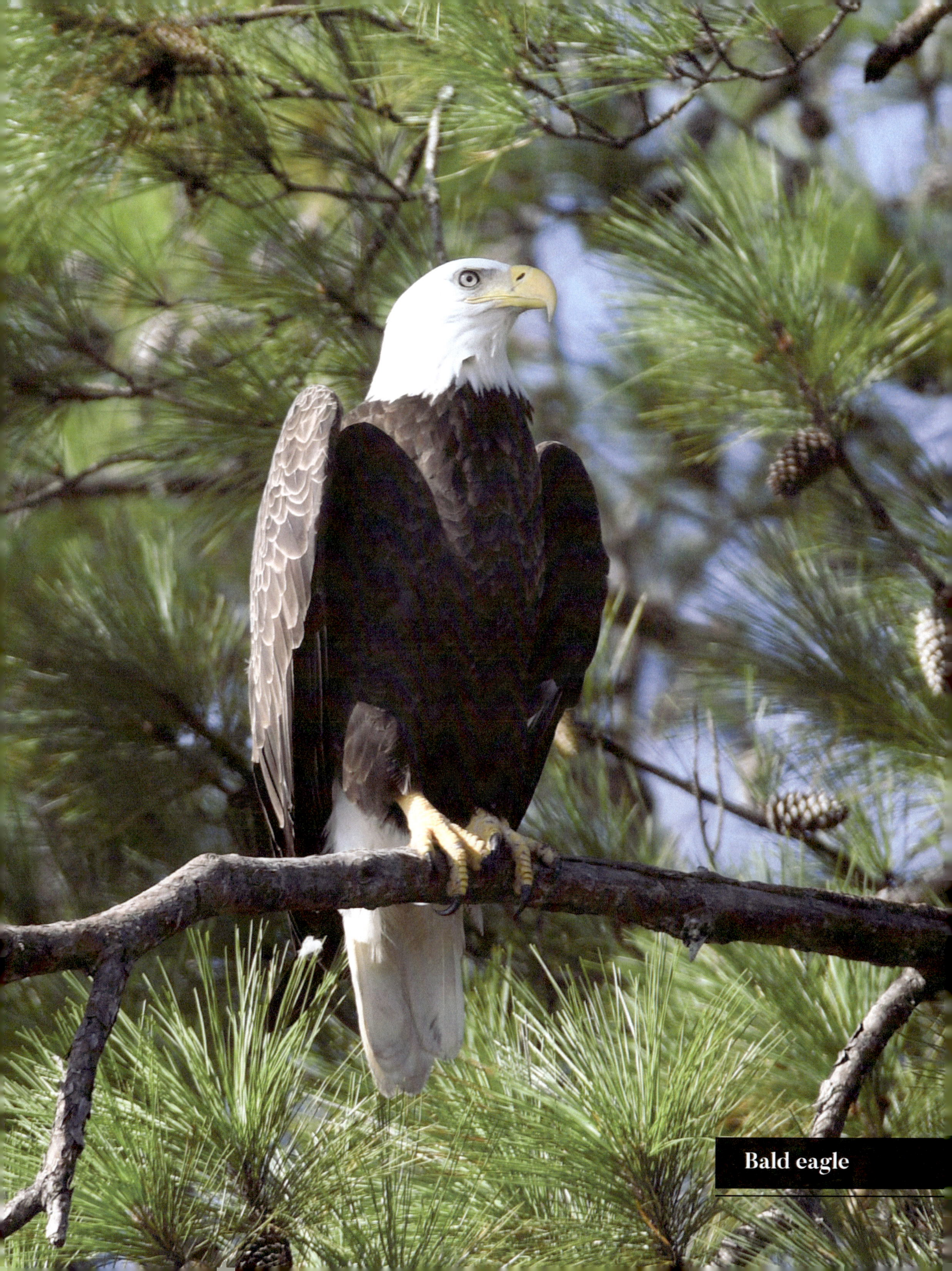

Bald eagle

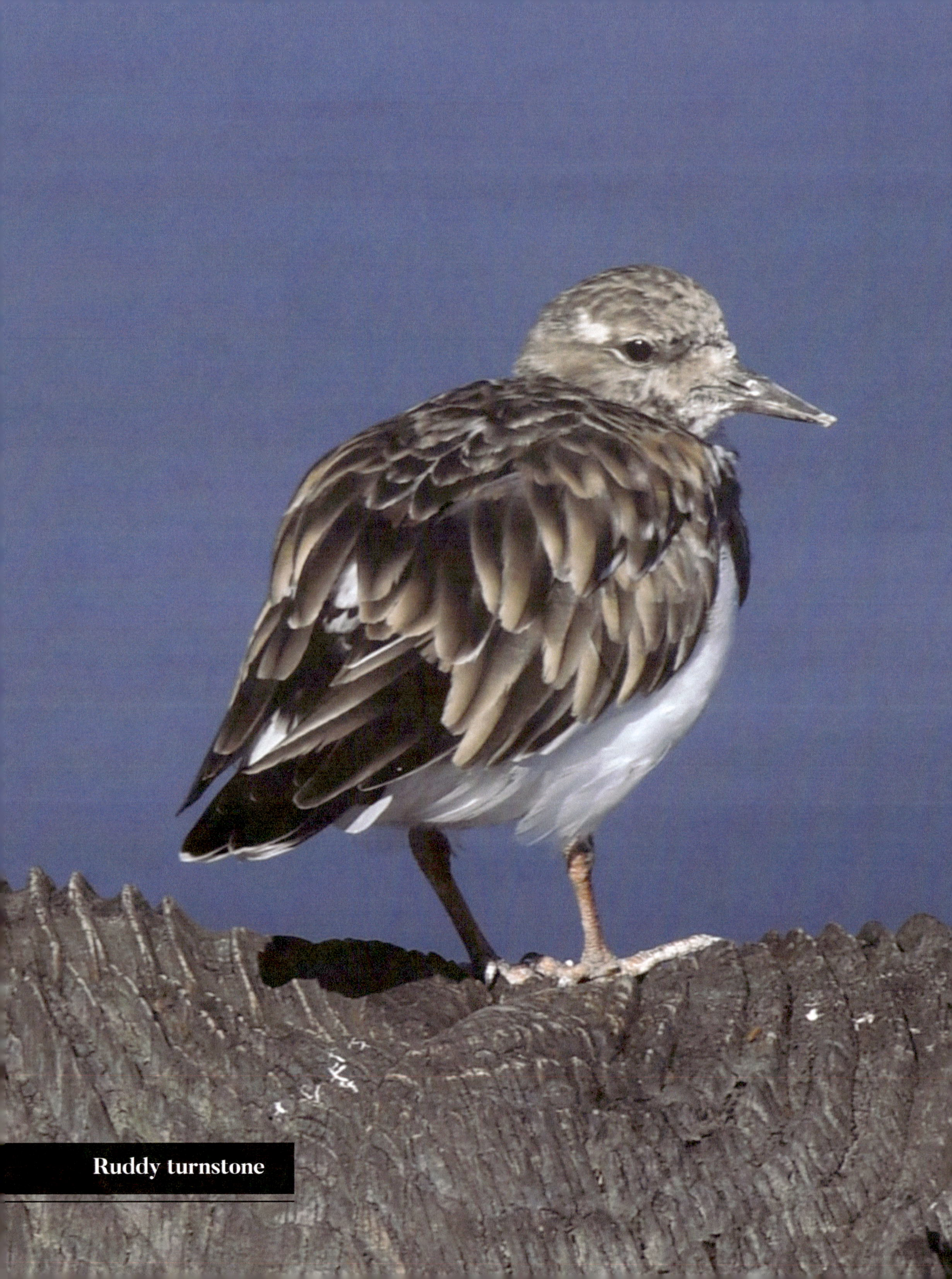

Ruddy turnstone

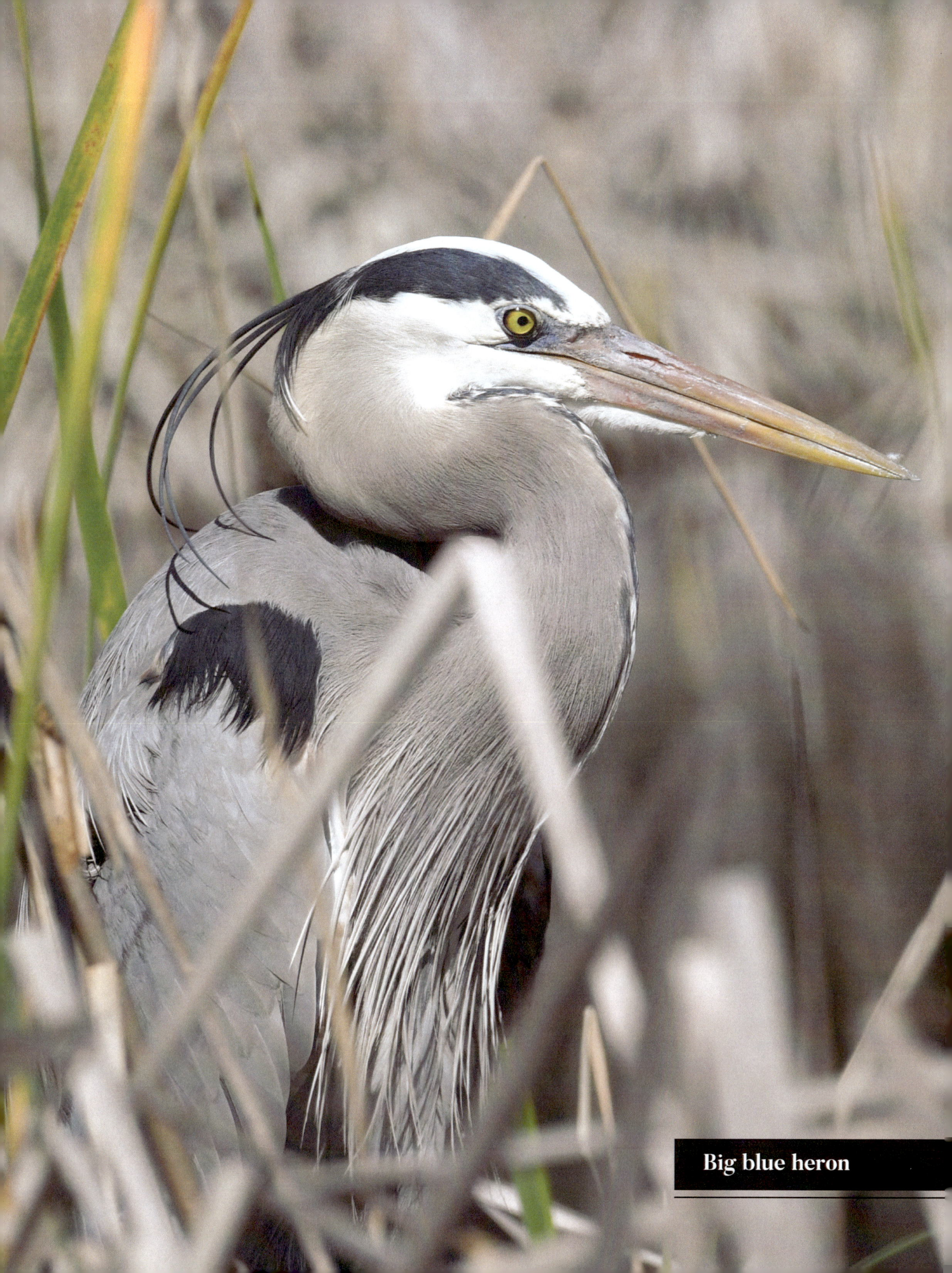

Big blue heron

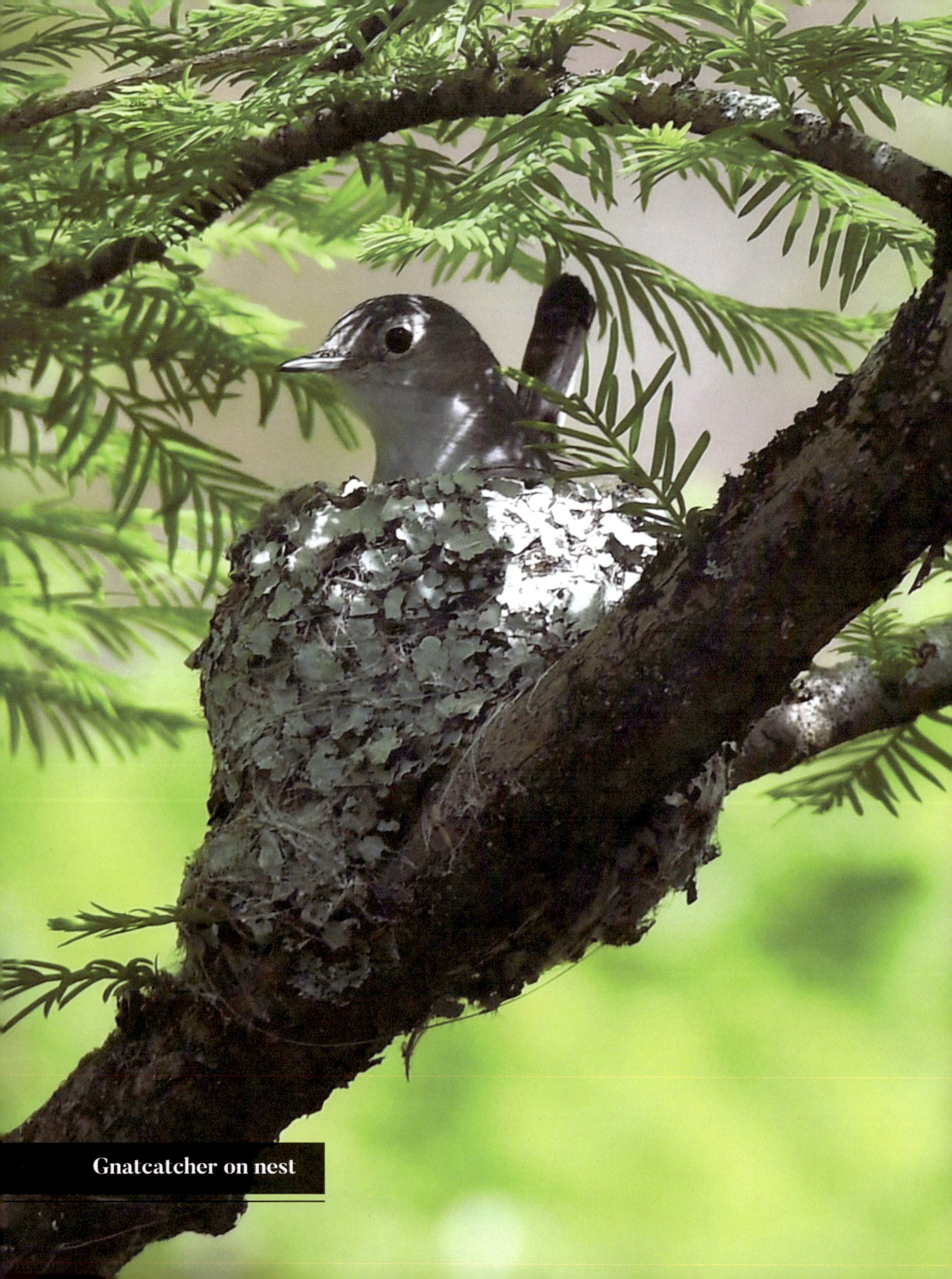

Gnatcatcher on nest

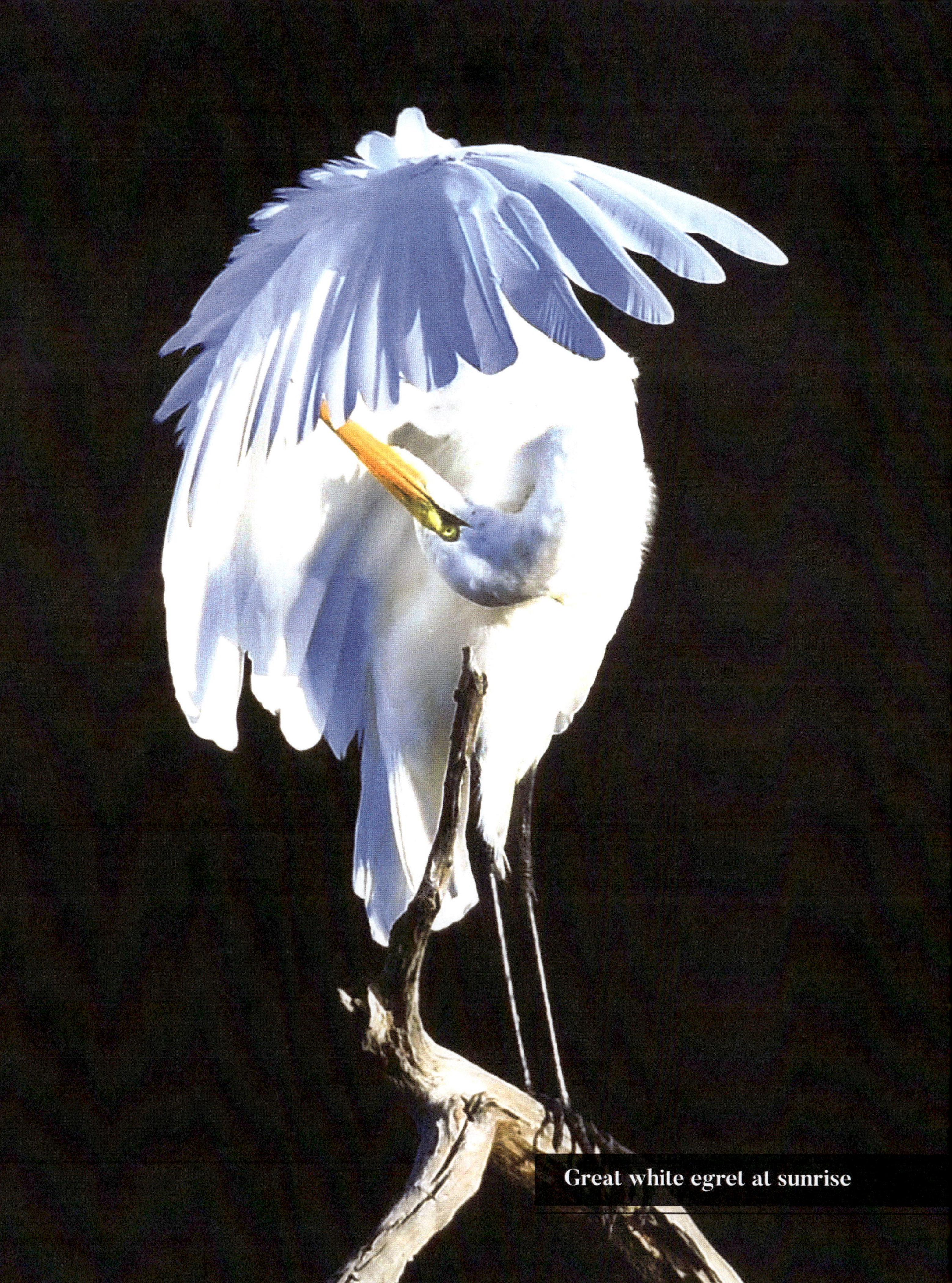

Great white egret at sunrise

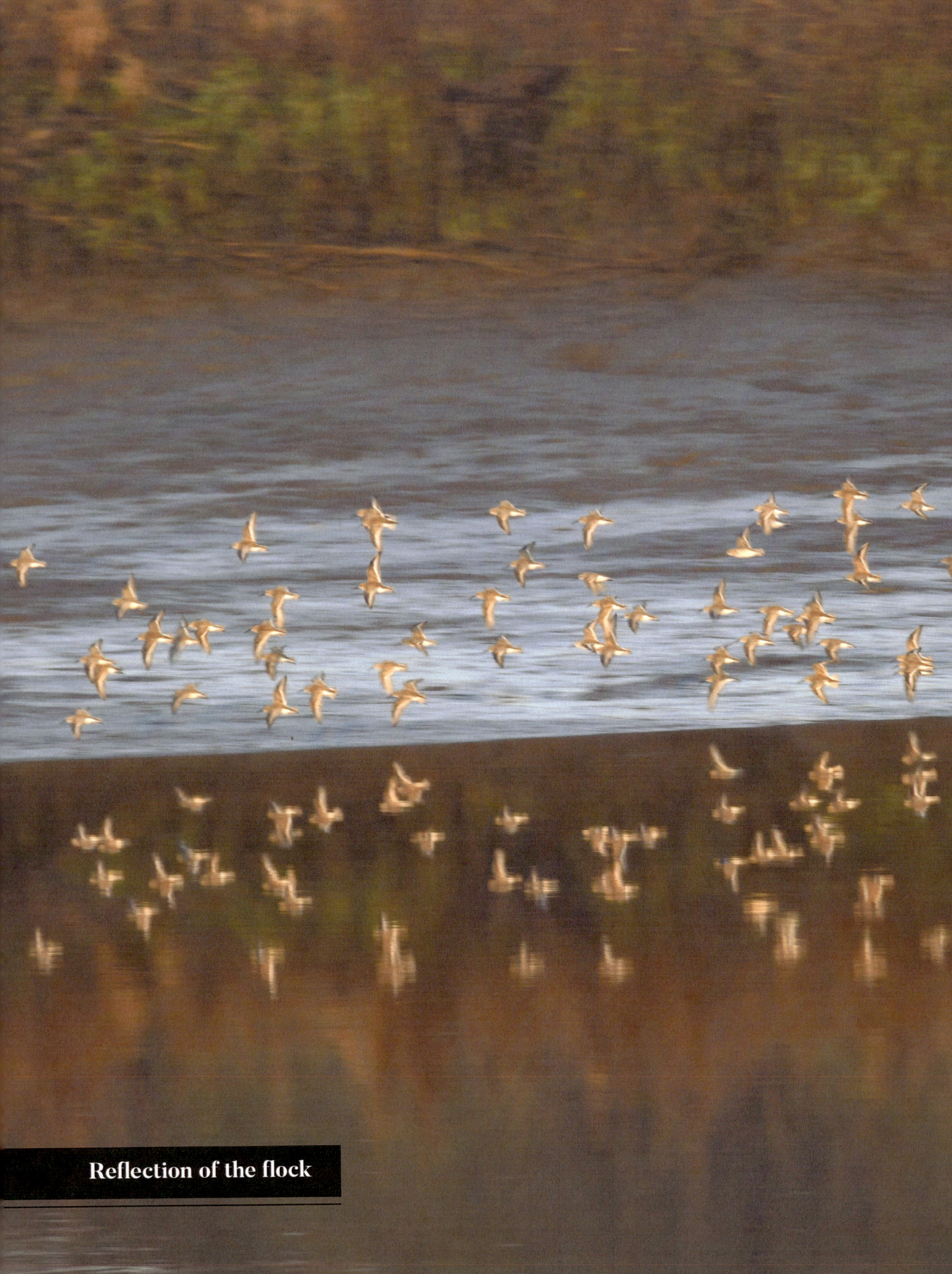

Reflection of the flock

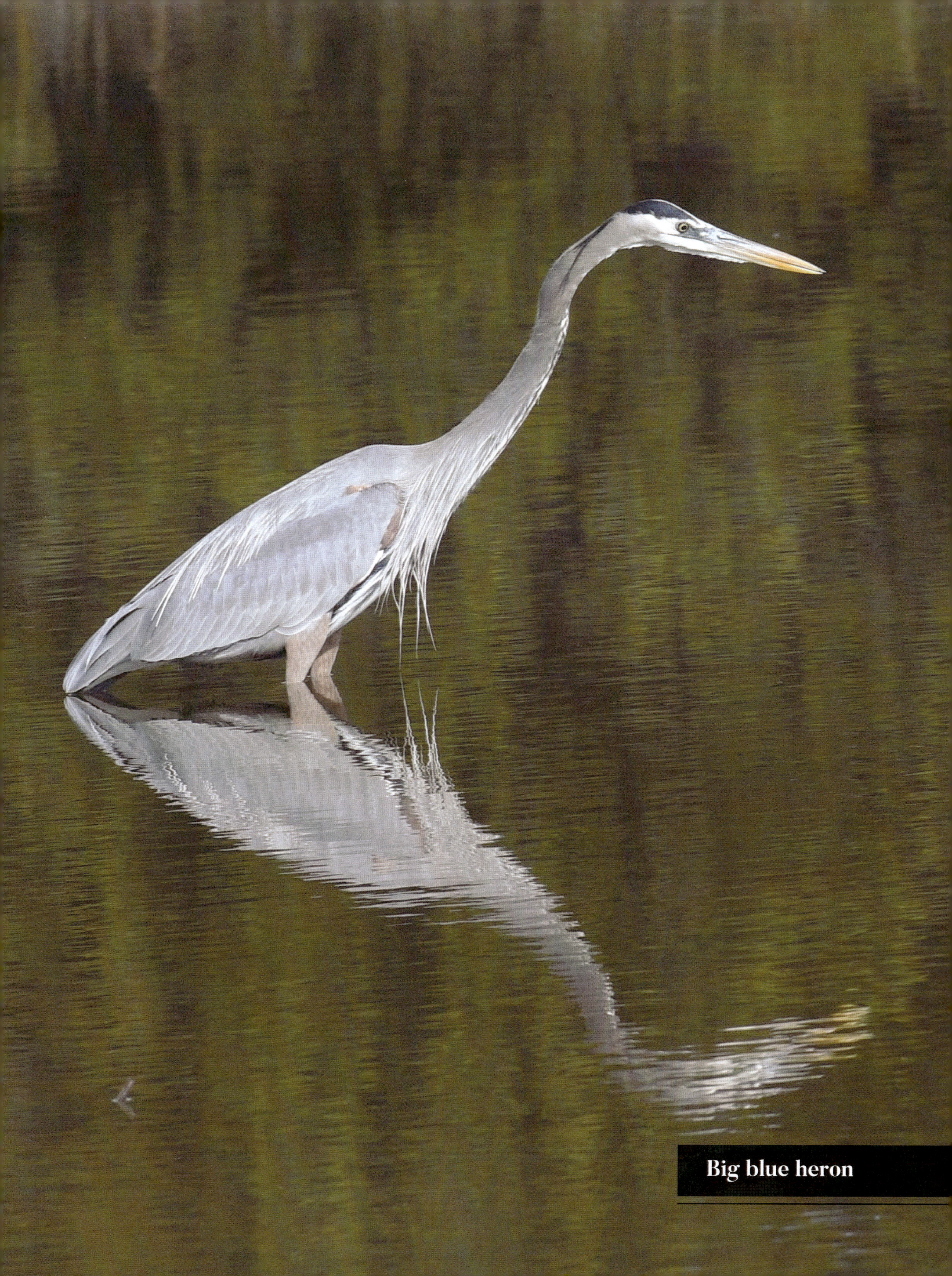

Big blue heron

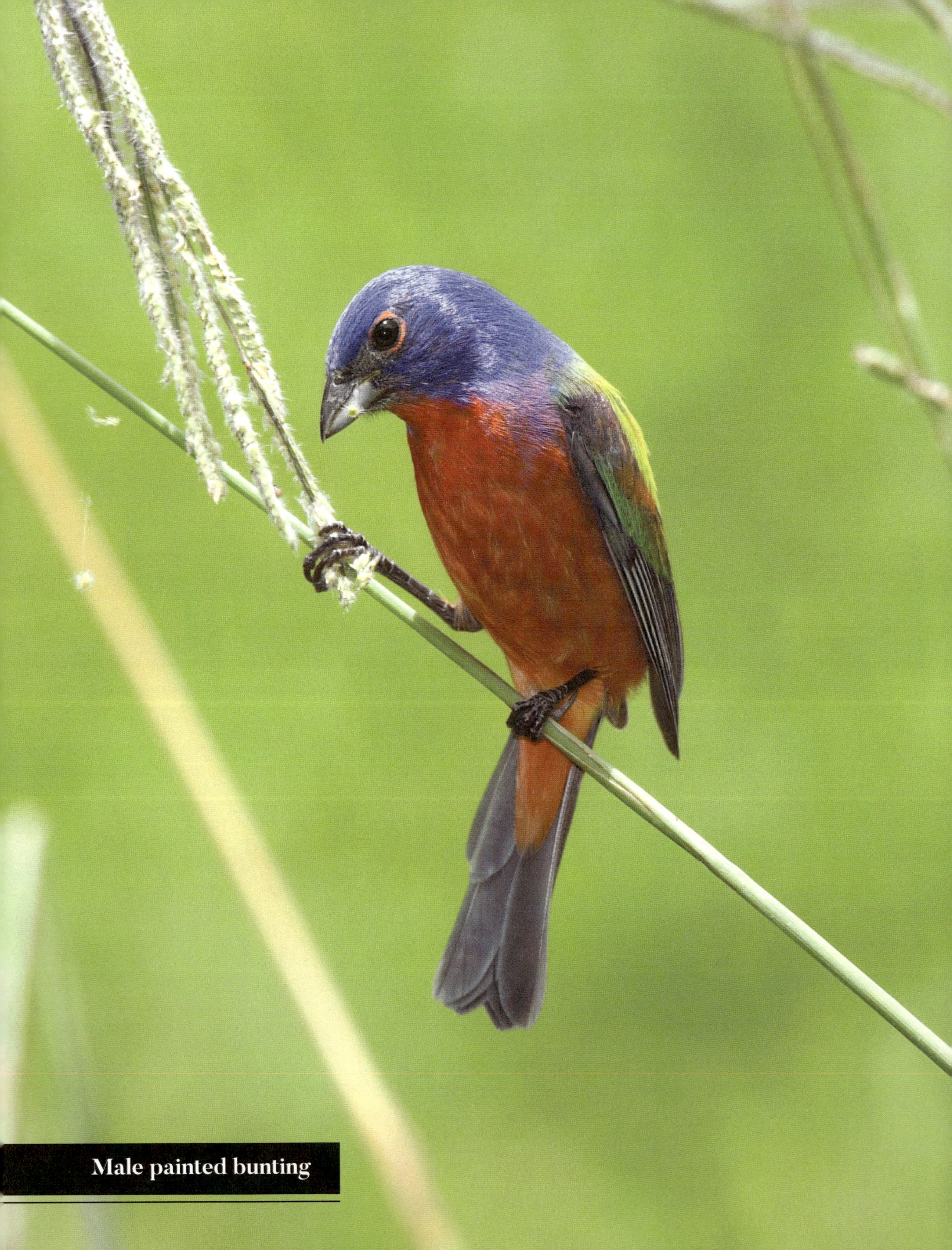

Male painted bunting

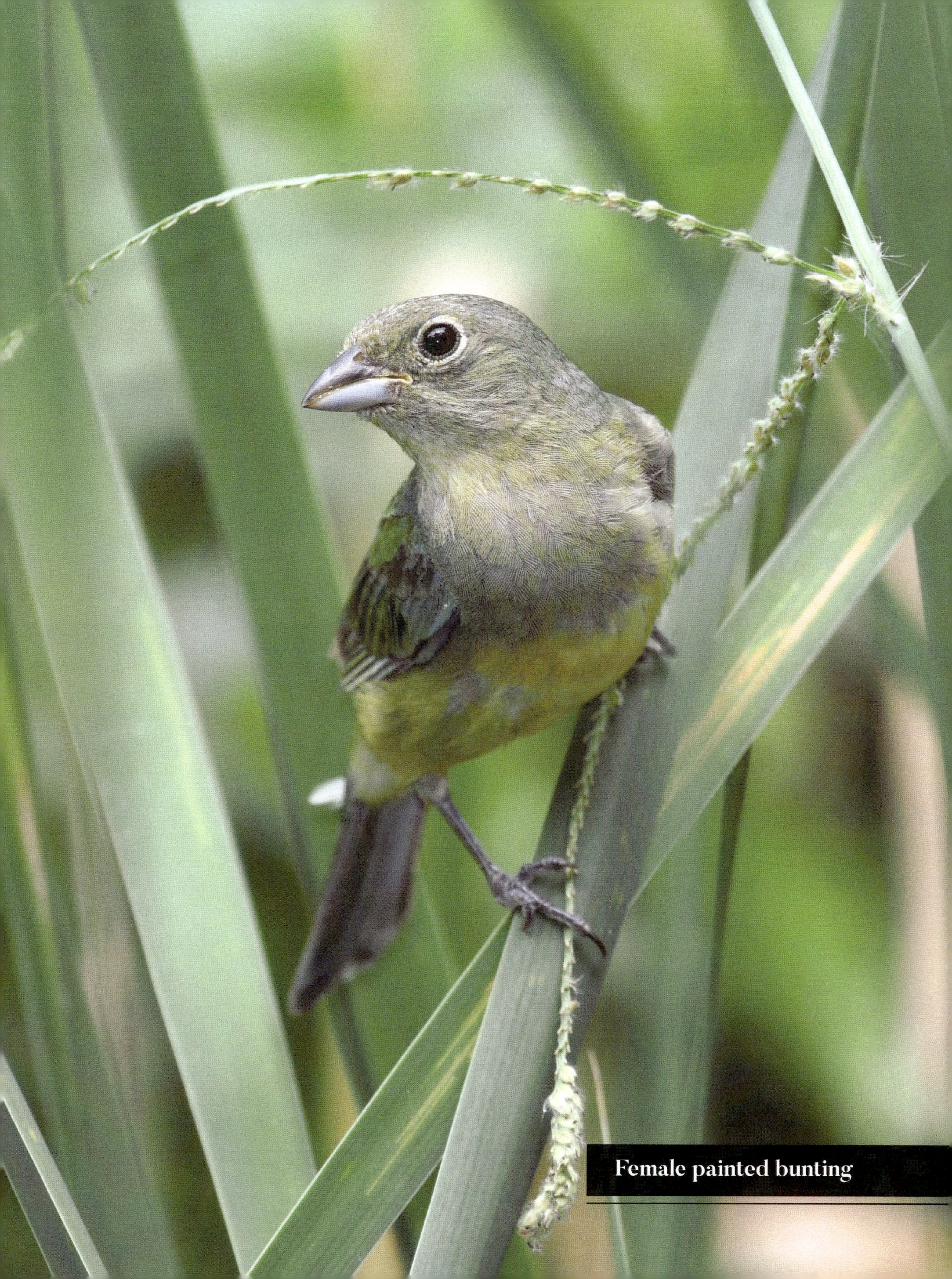

Female painted bunting

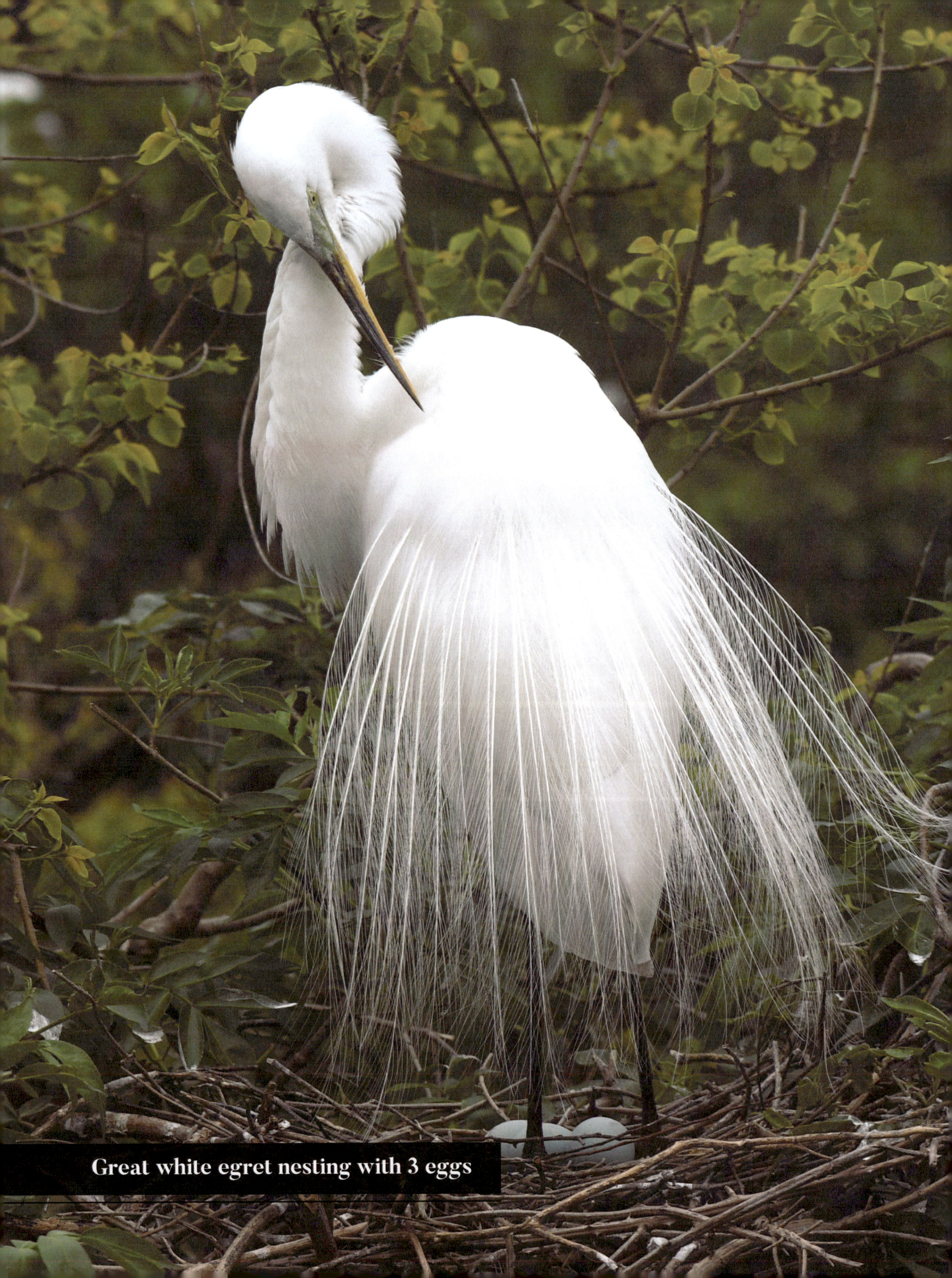

Great white egret nesting with 3 eggs

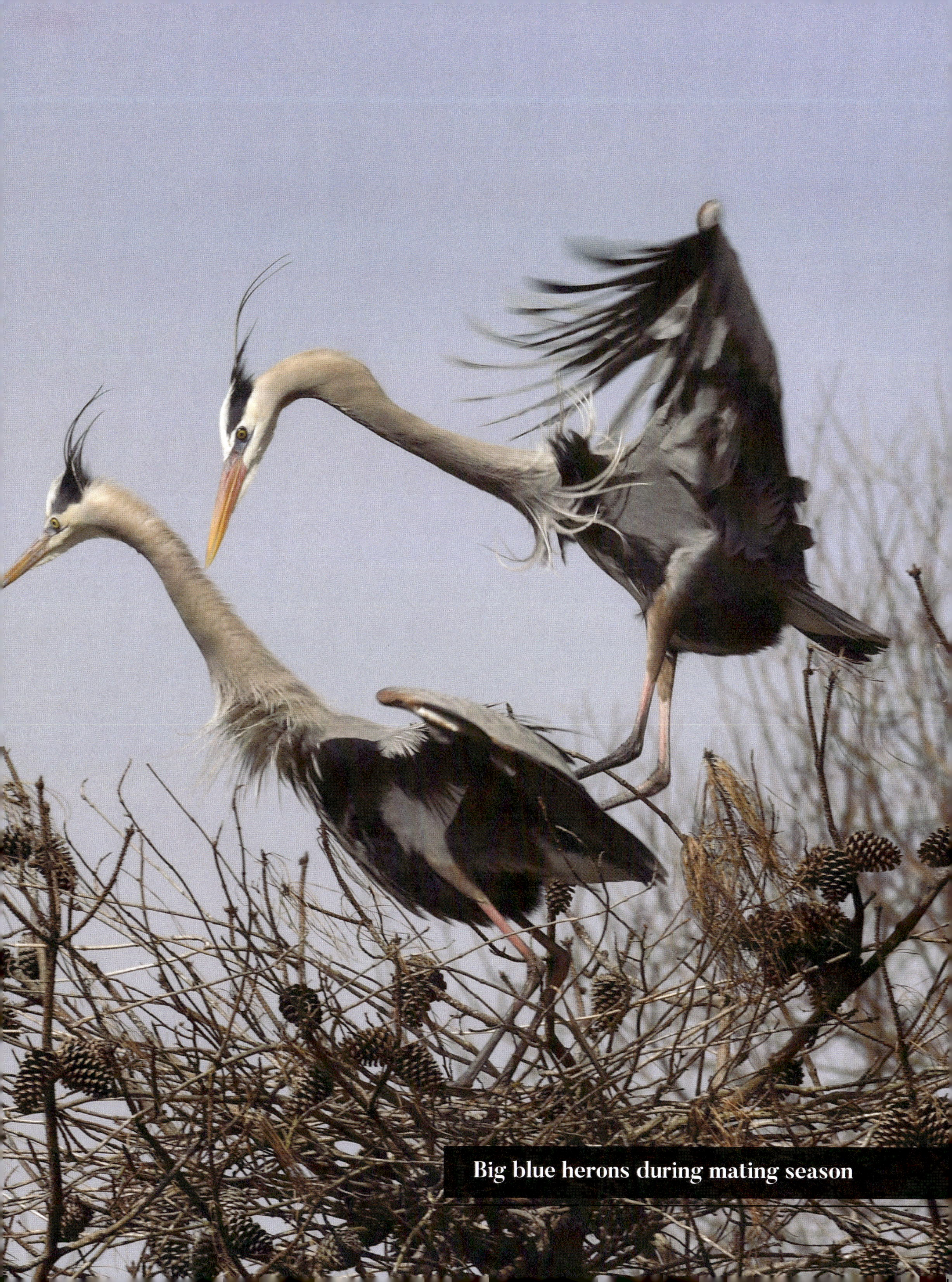

Big blue herons during mating season

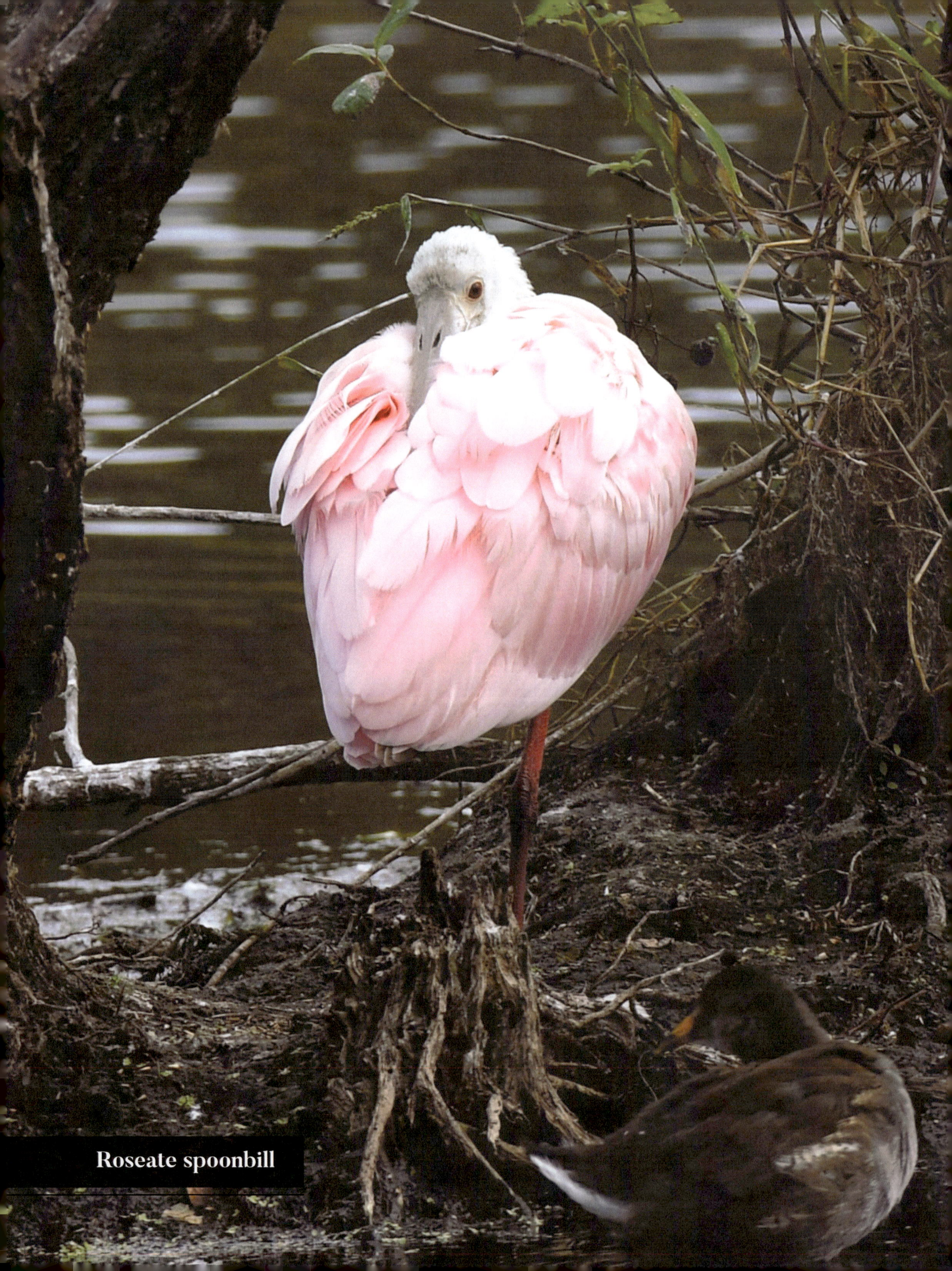

Roseate spoonbill

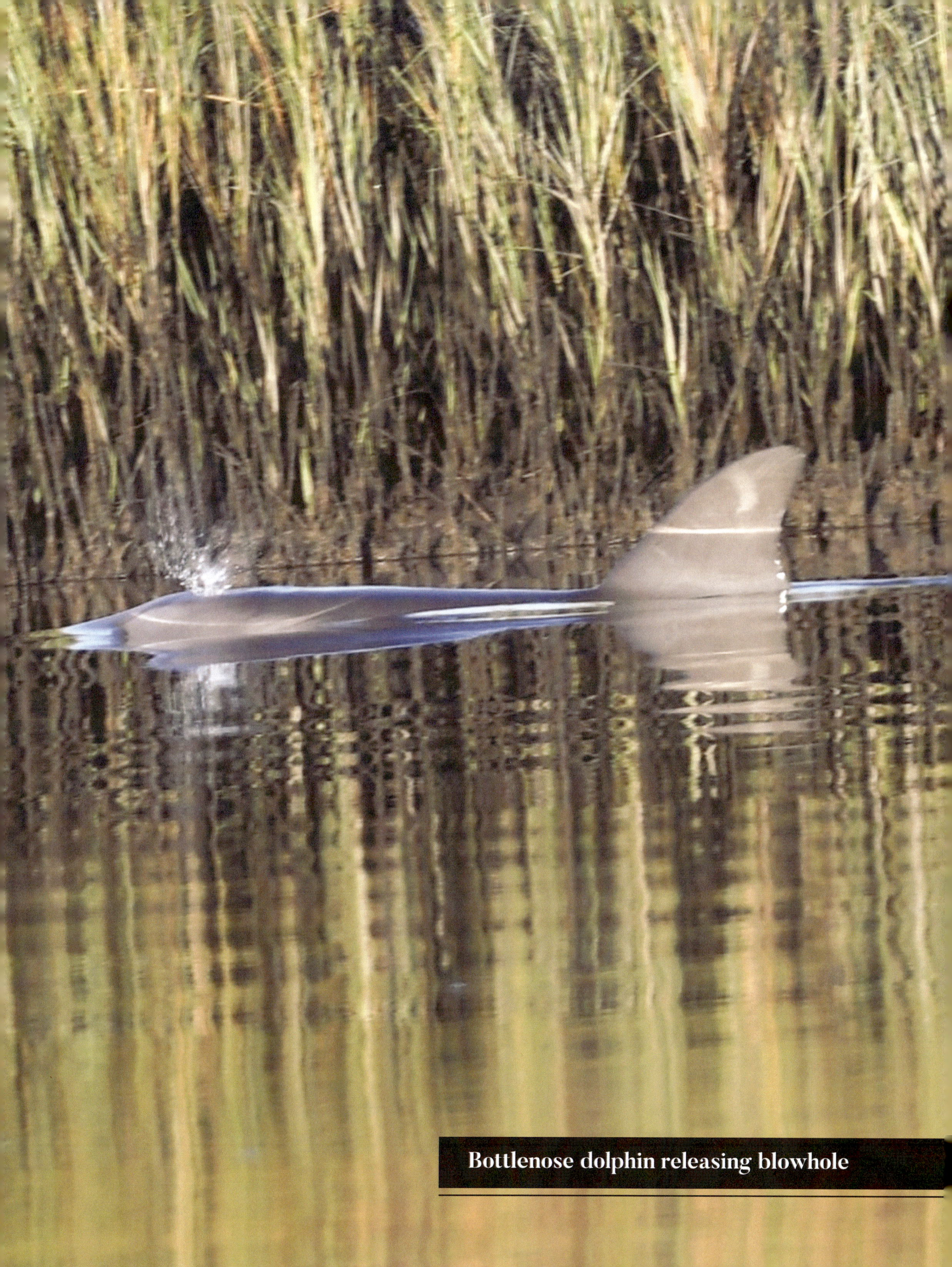

Bottlenose dolphin releasing blowhole

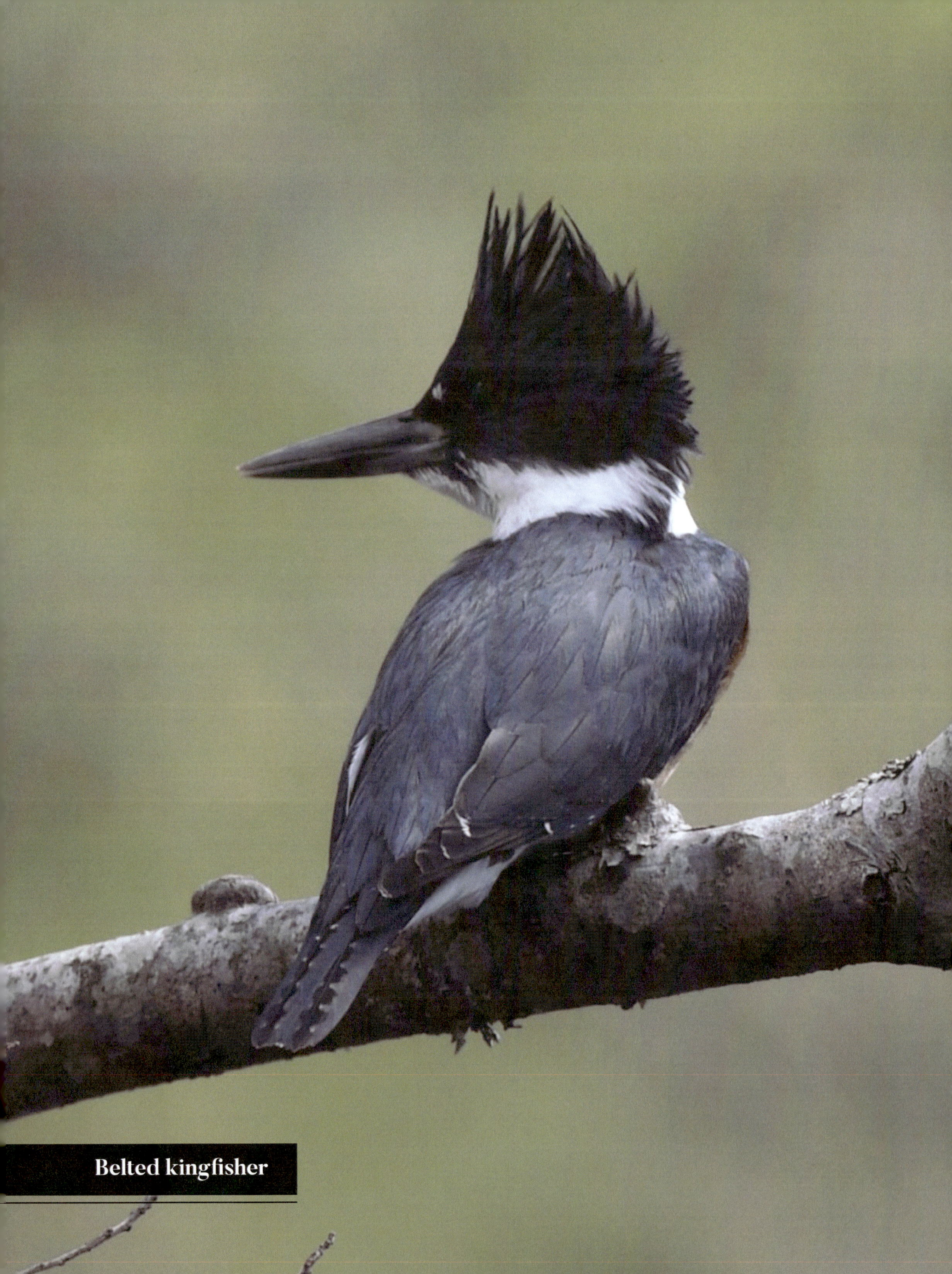

Belted kingfisher

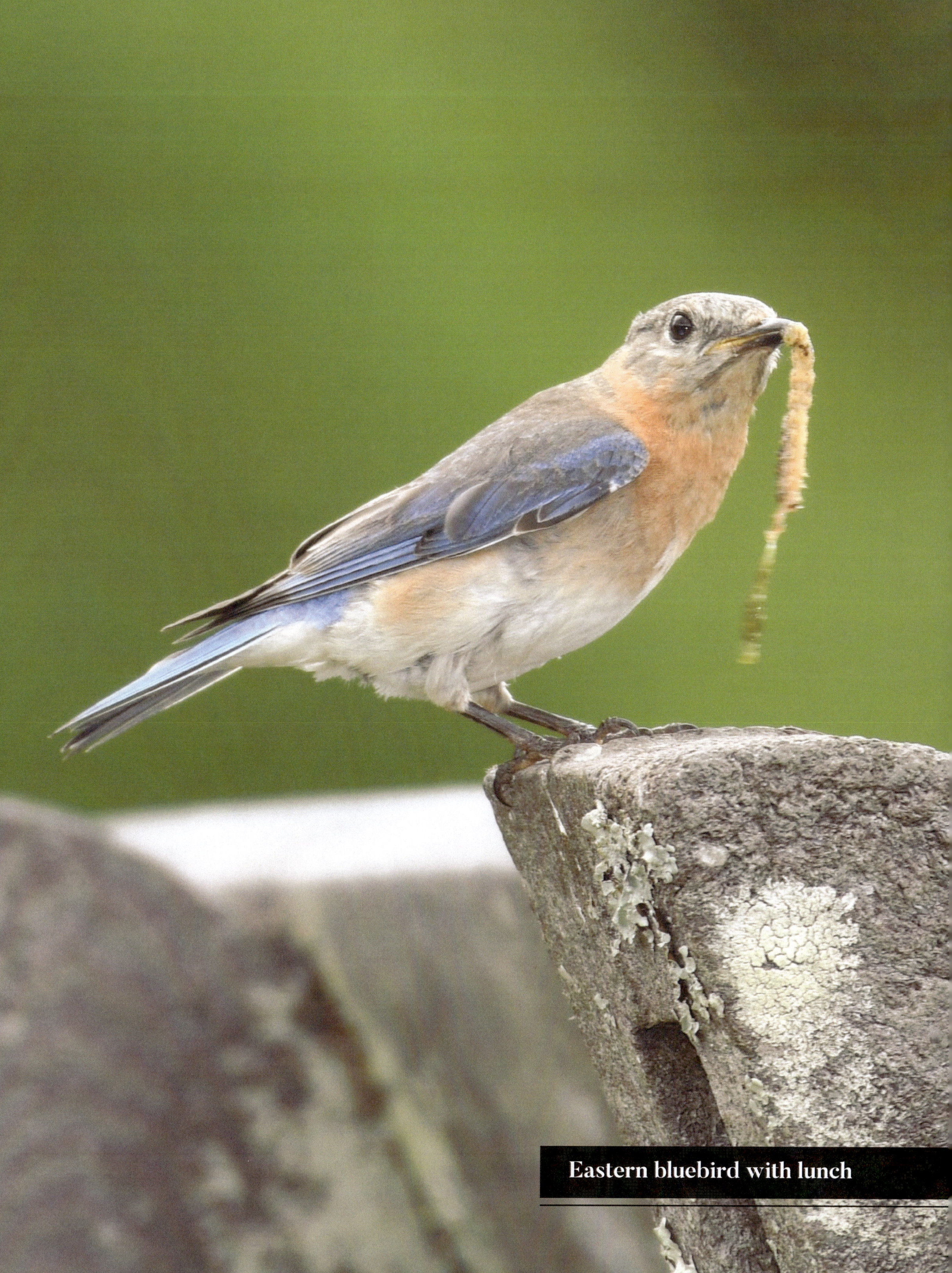

Eastern bluebird with lunch

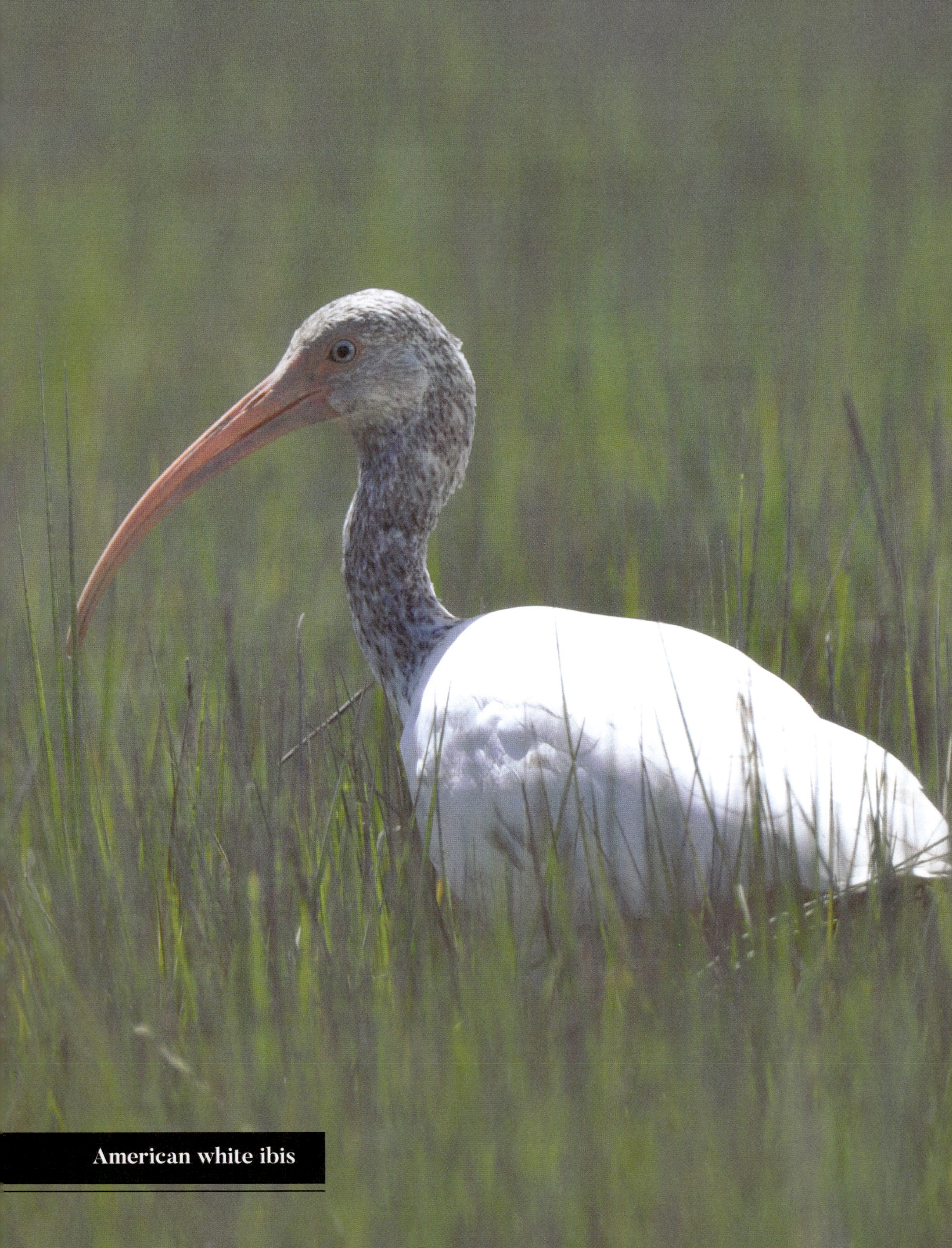

American white ibis

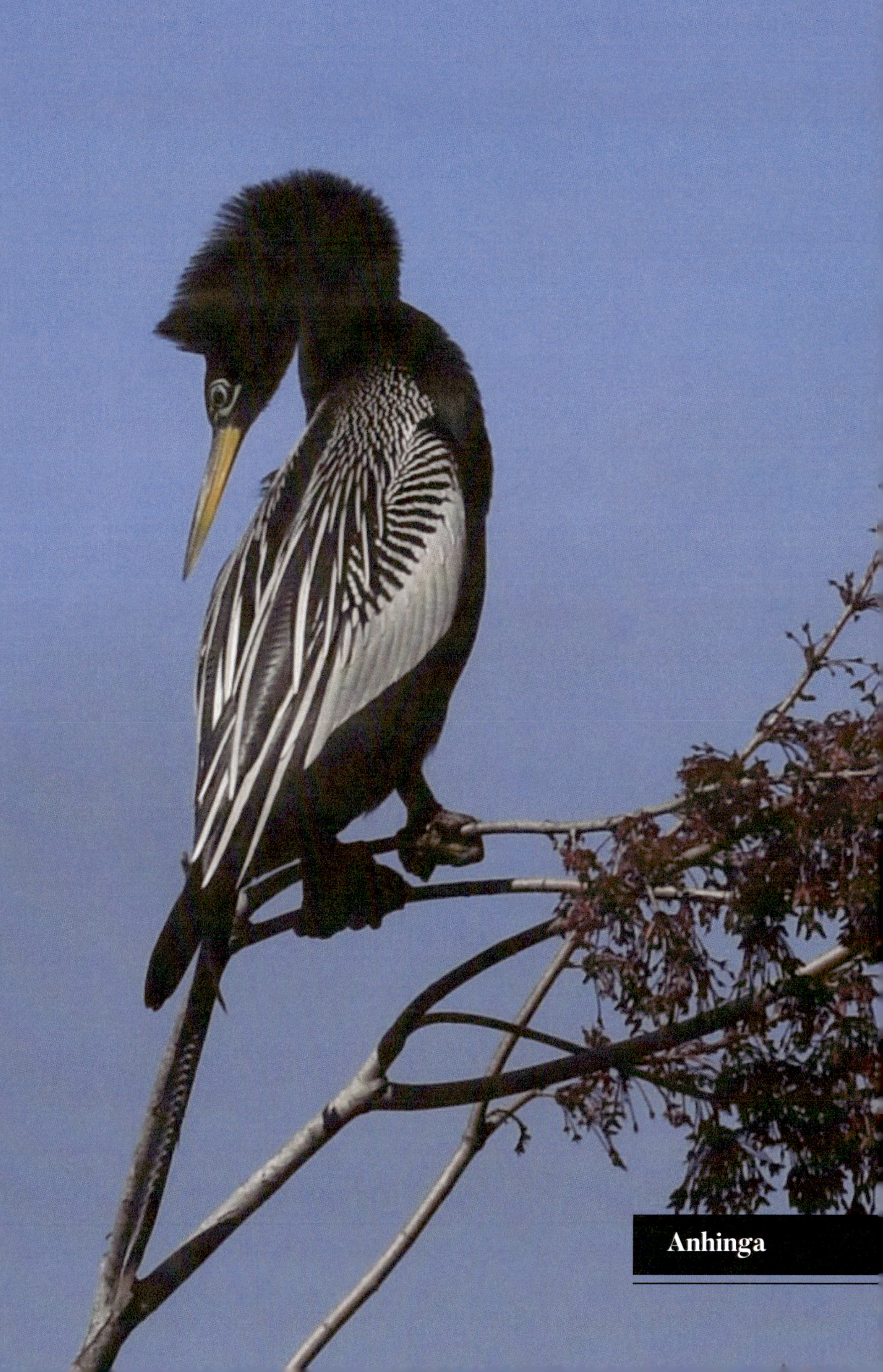

Anhinga

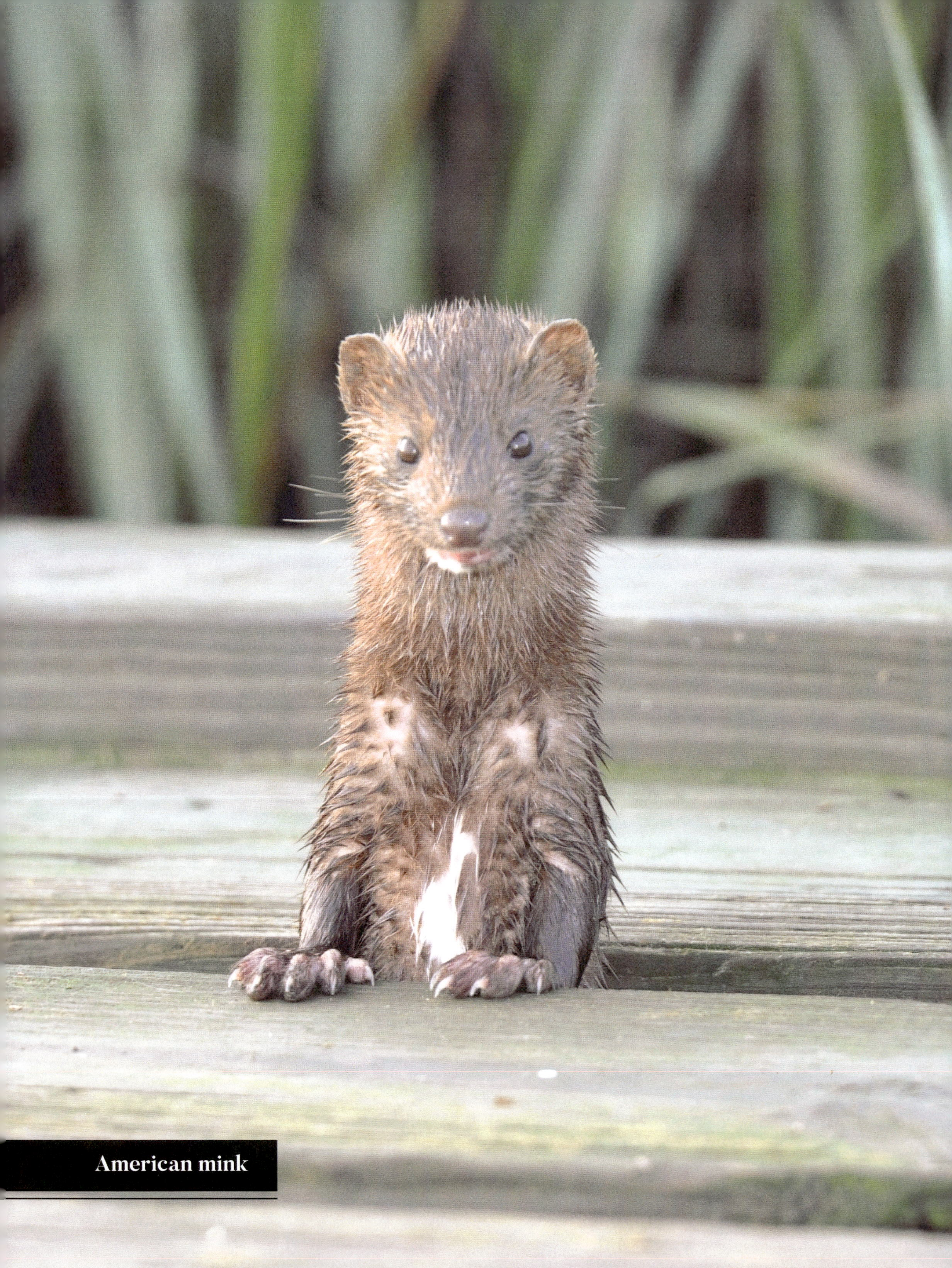

American mink

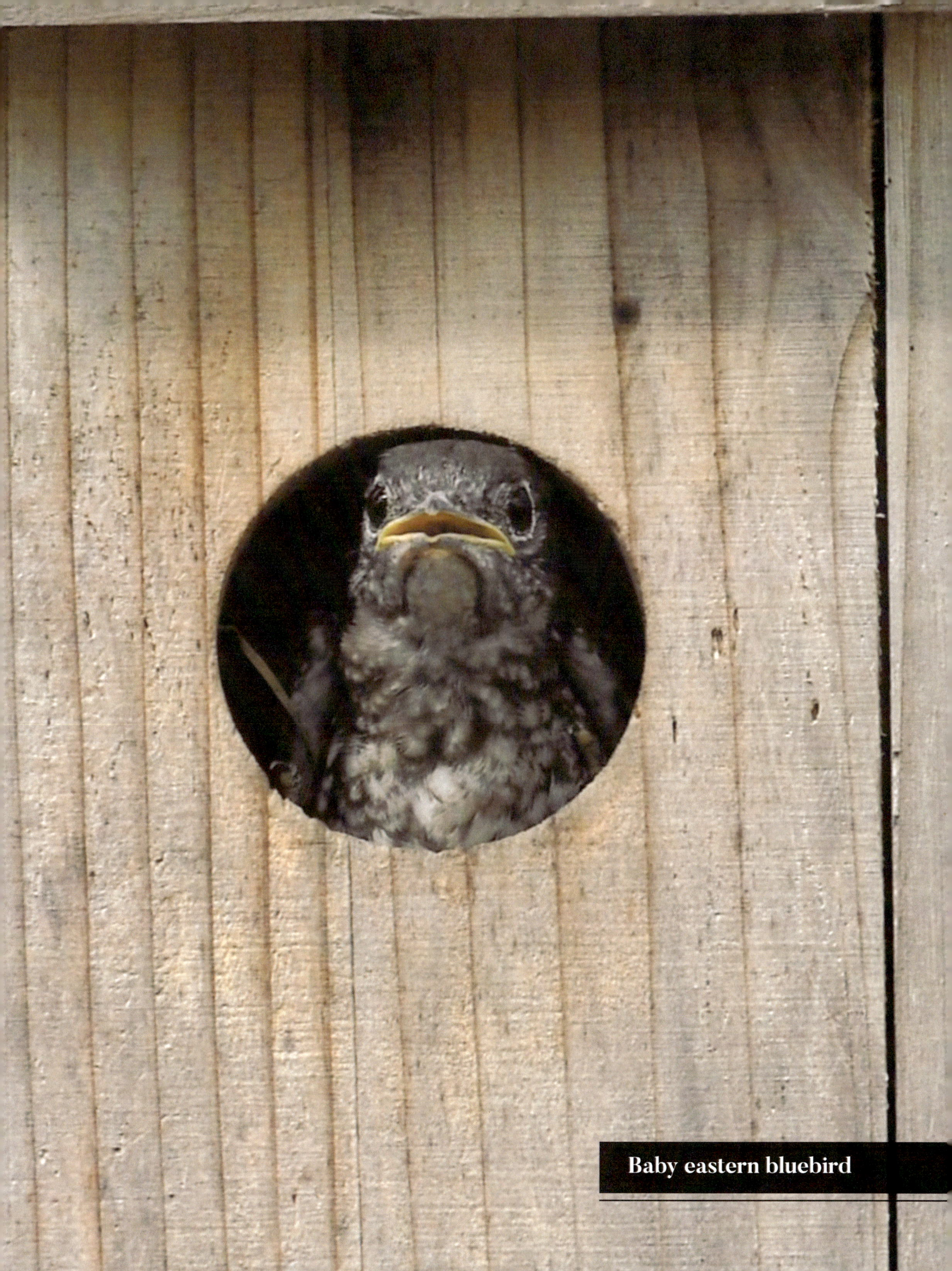

Baby eastern bluebird

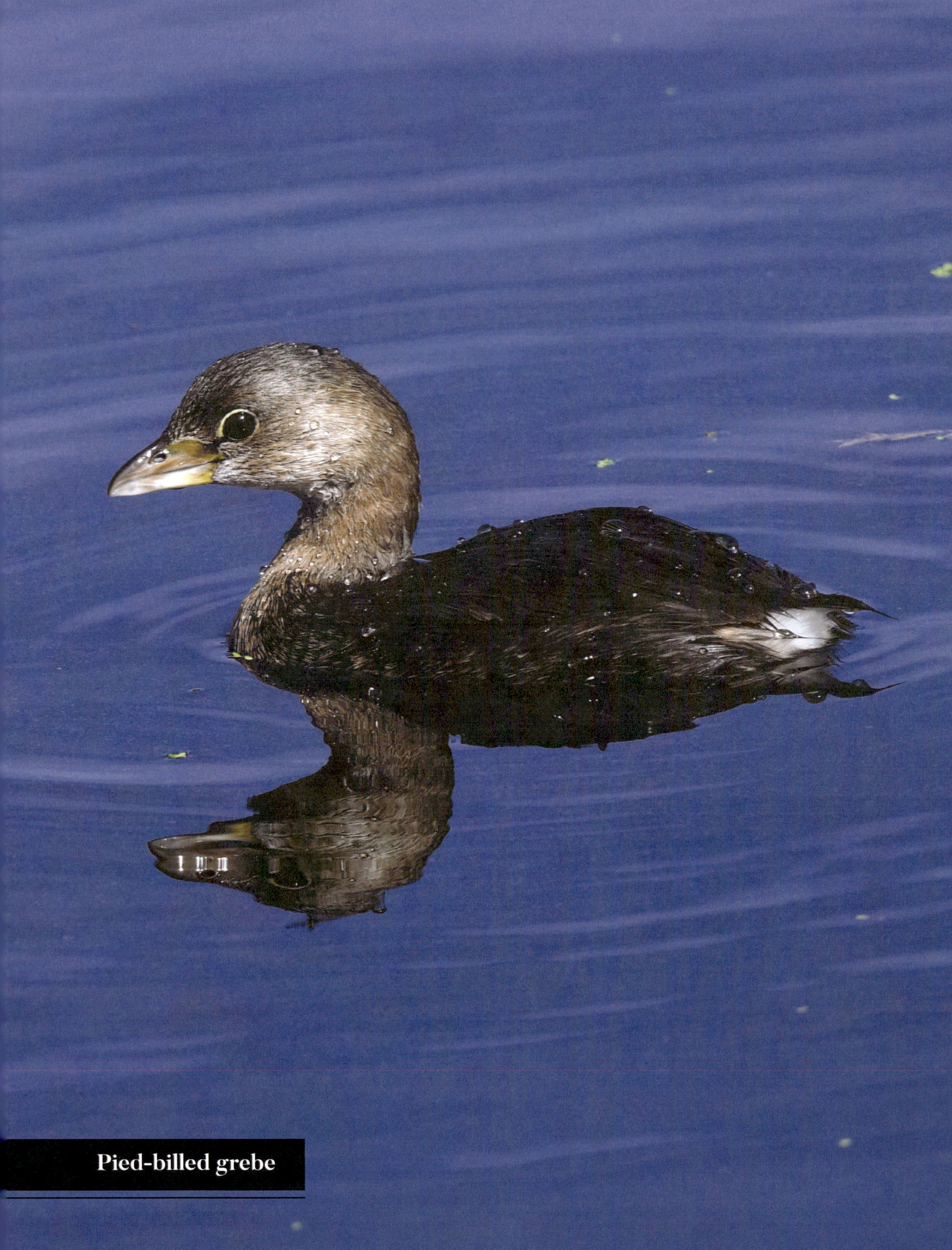

Pied-billed grebe

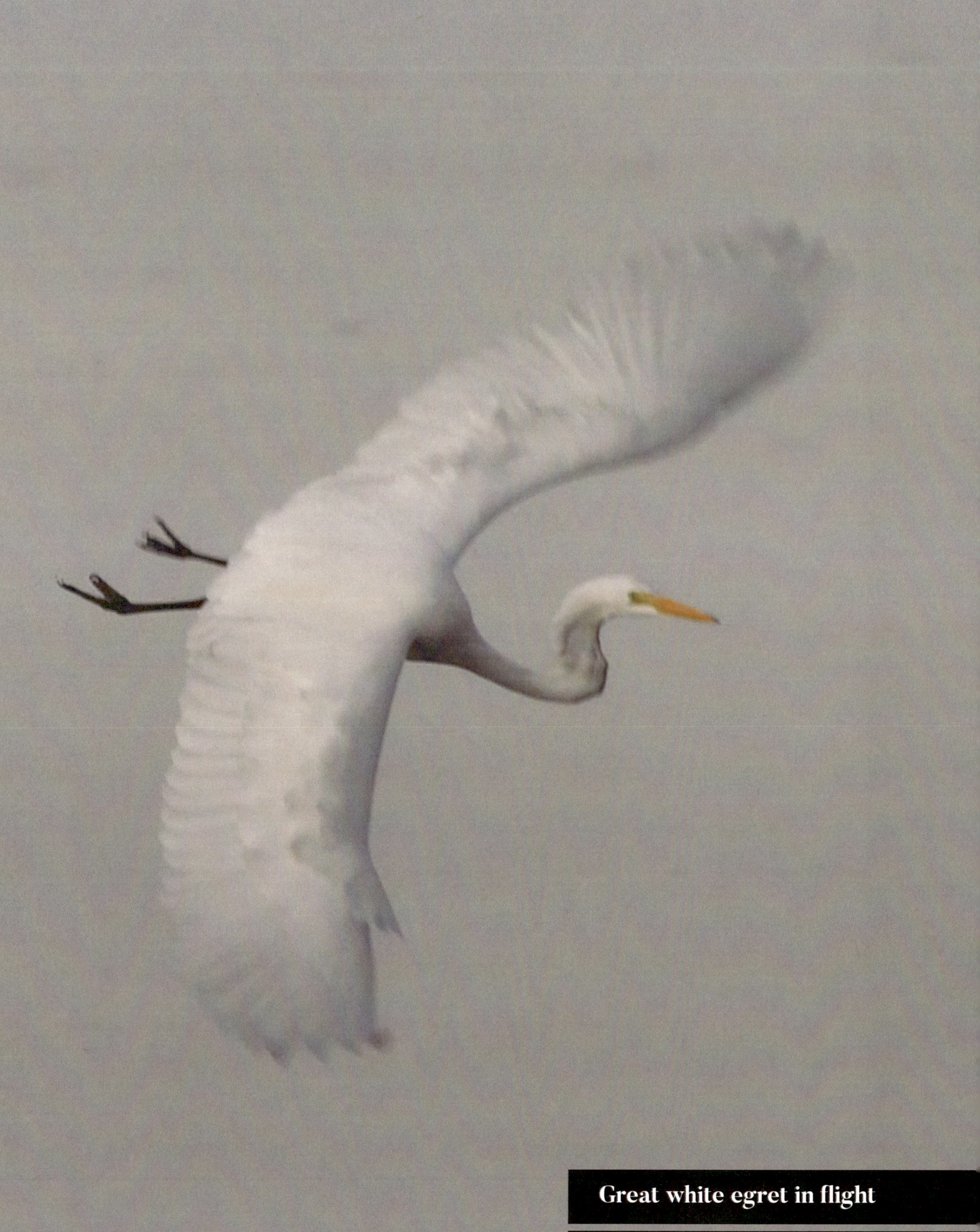

Great white egret in flight

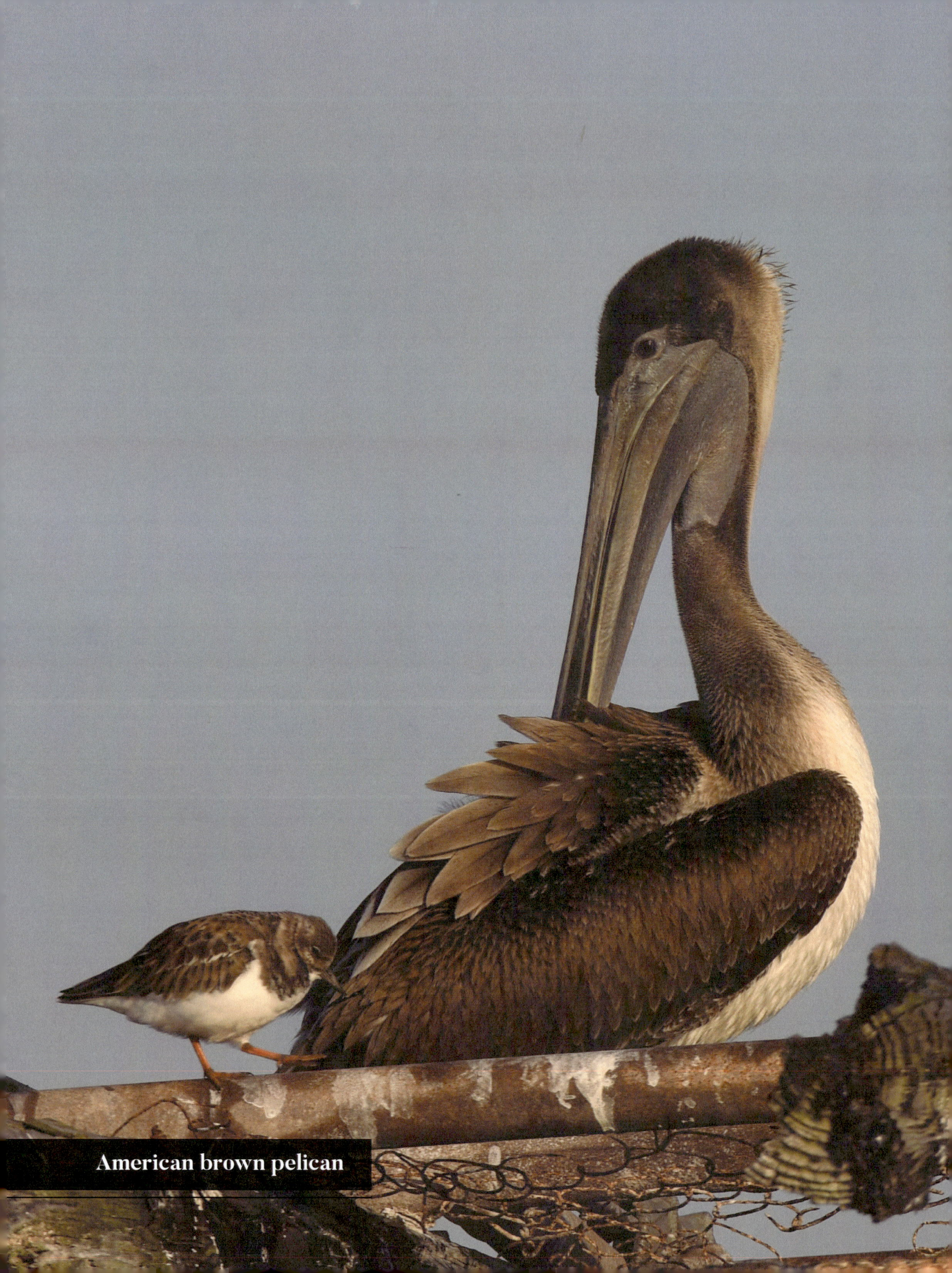

American brown pelican

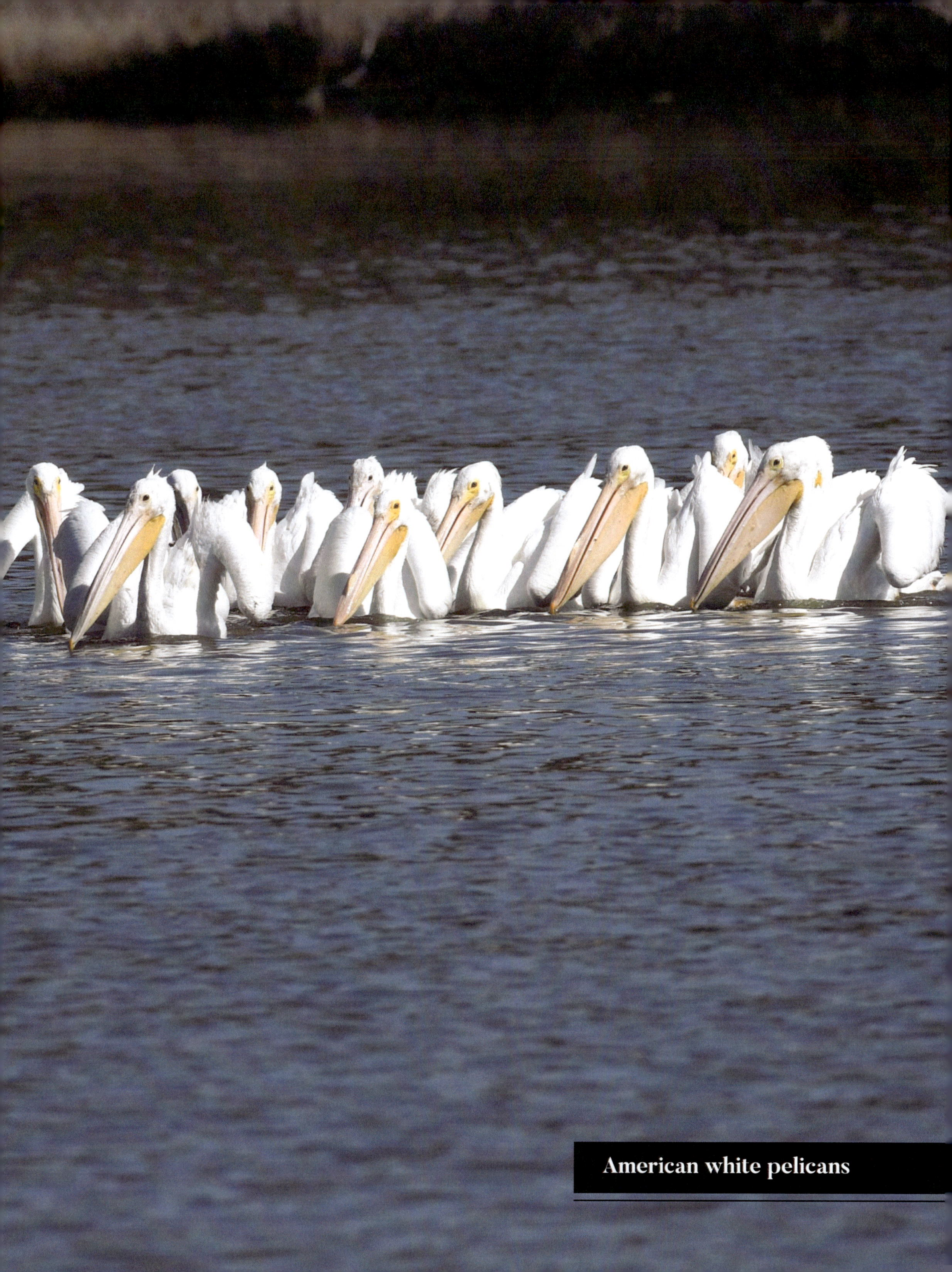

American white pelicans

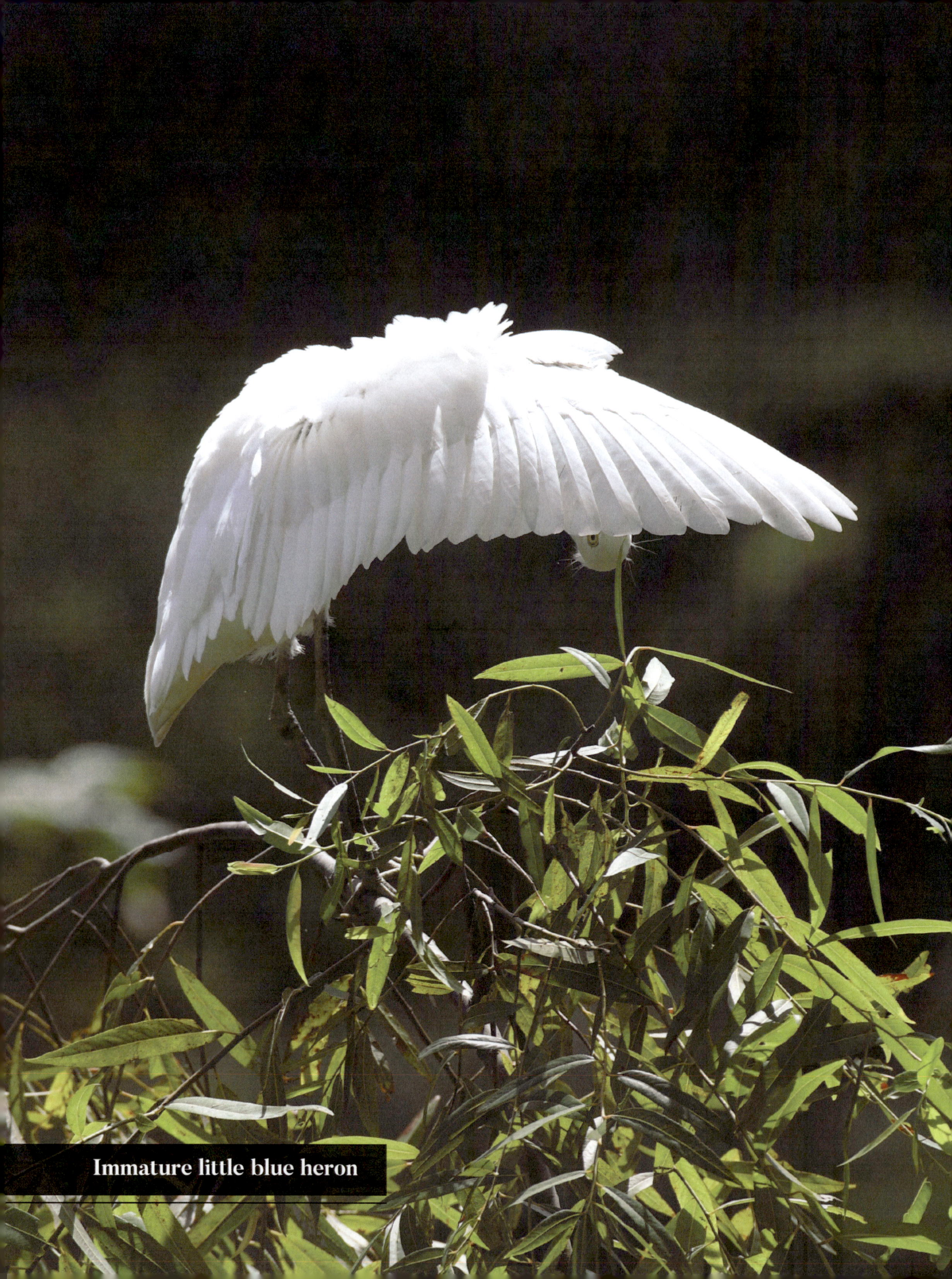

Immature little blue heron

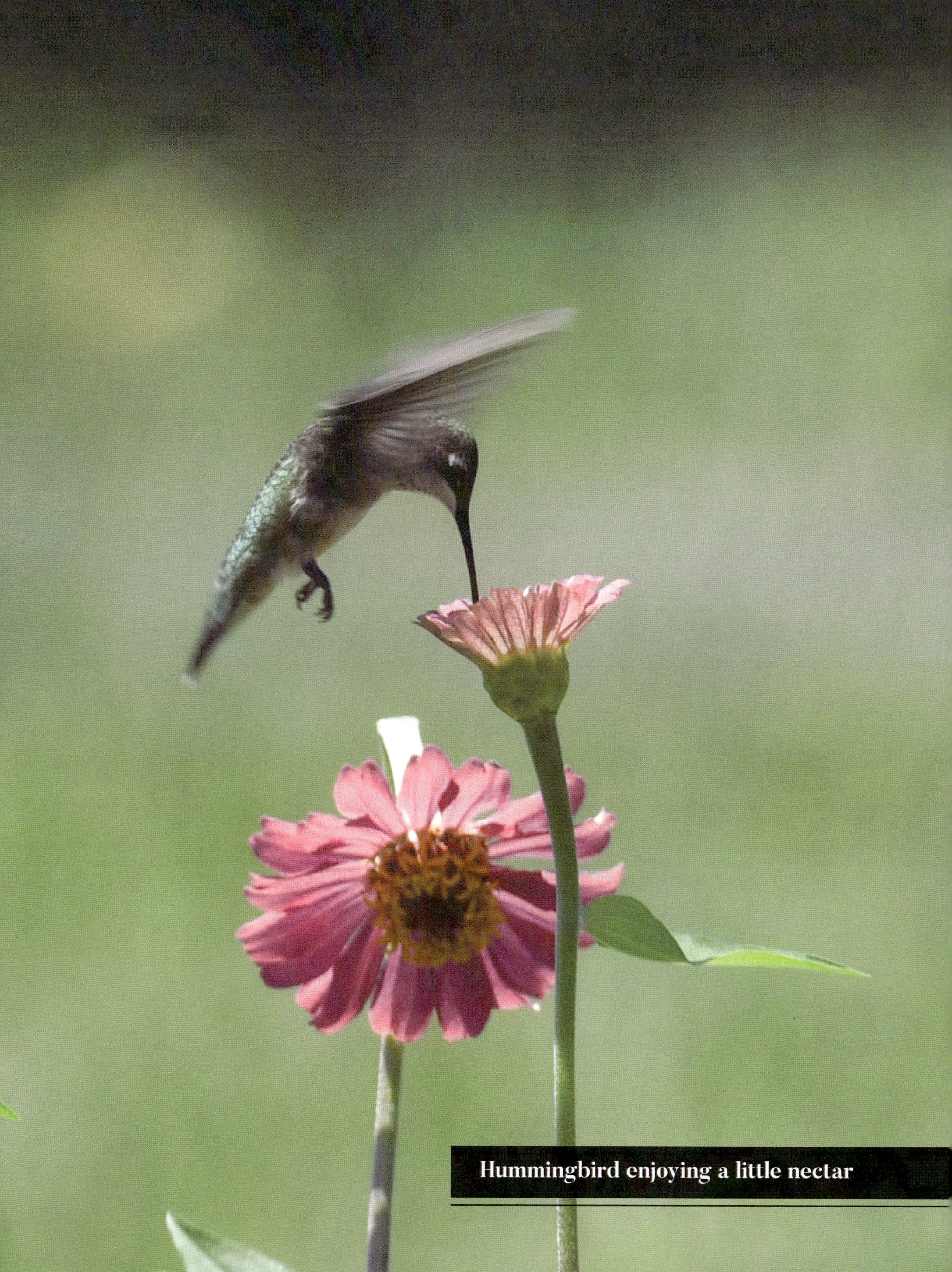

Hummingbird enjoying a little nectar

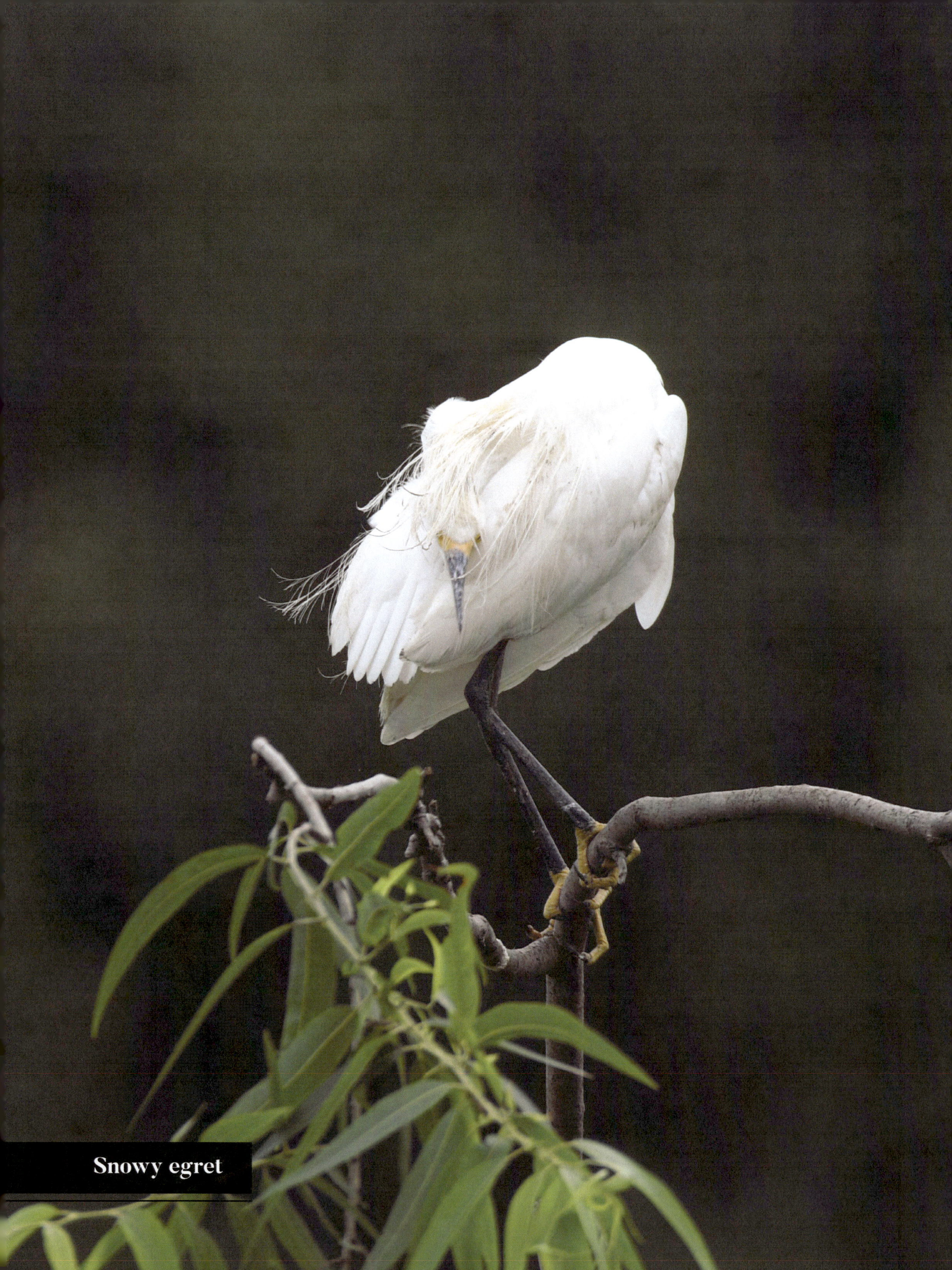

Snowy egret

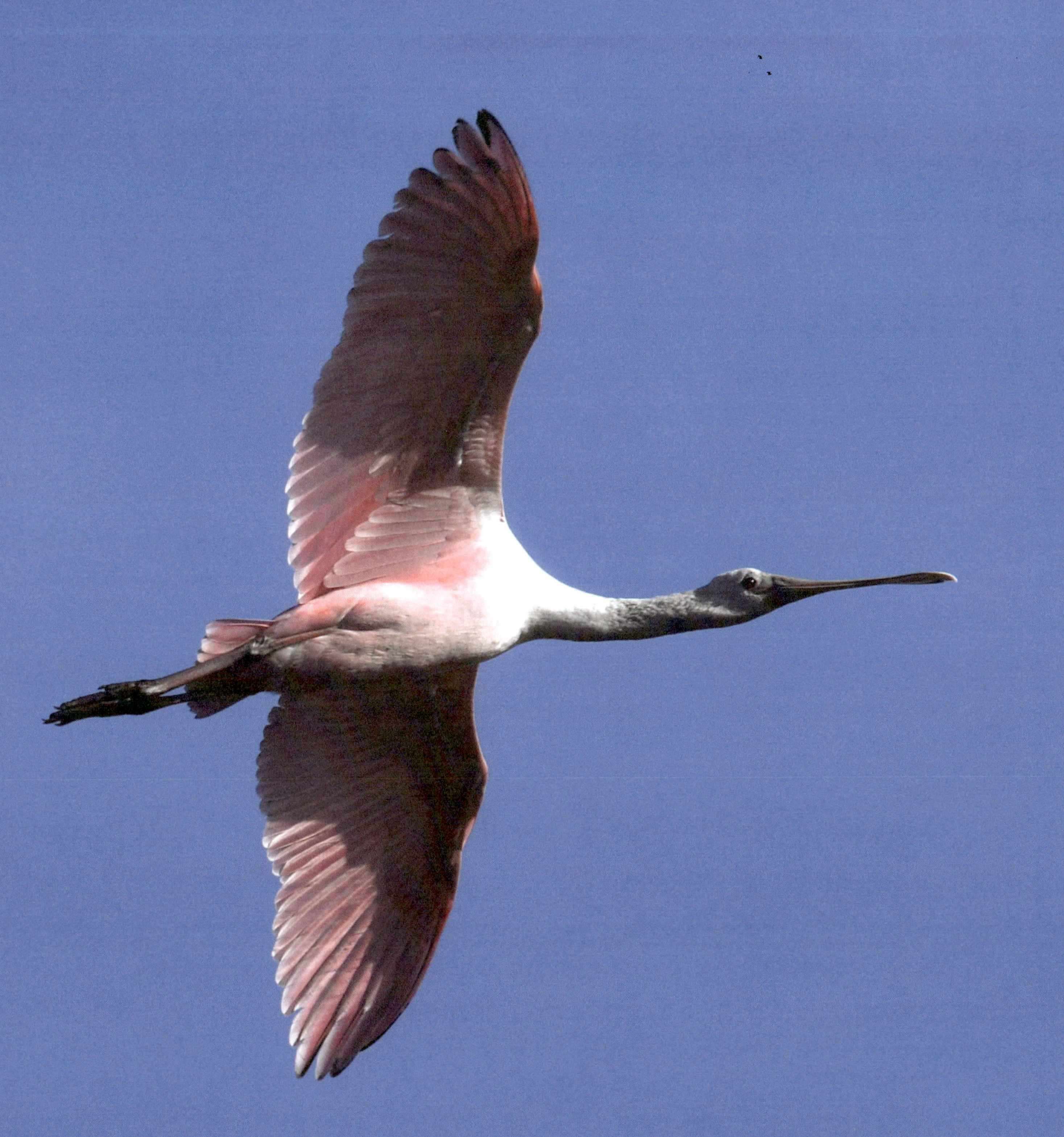

Roseate spoonbill in flight

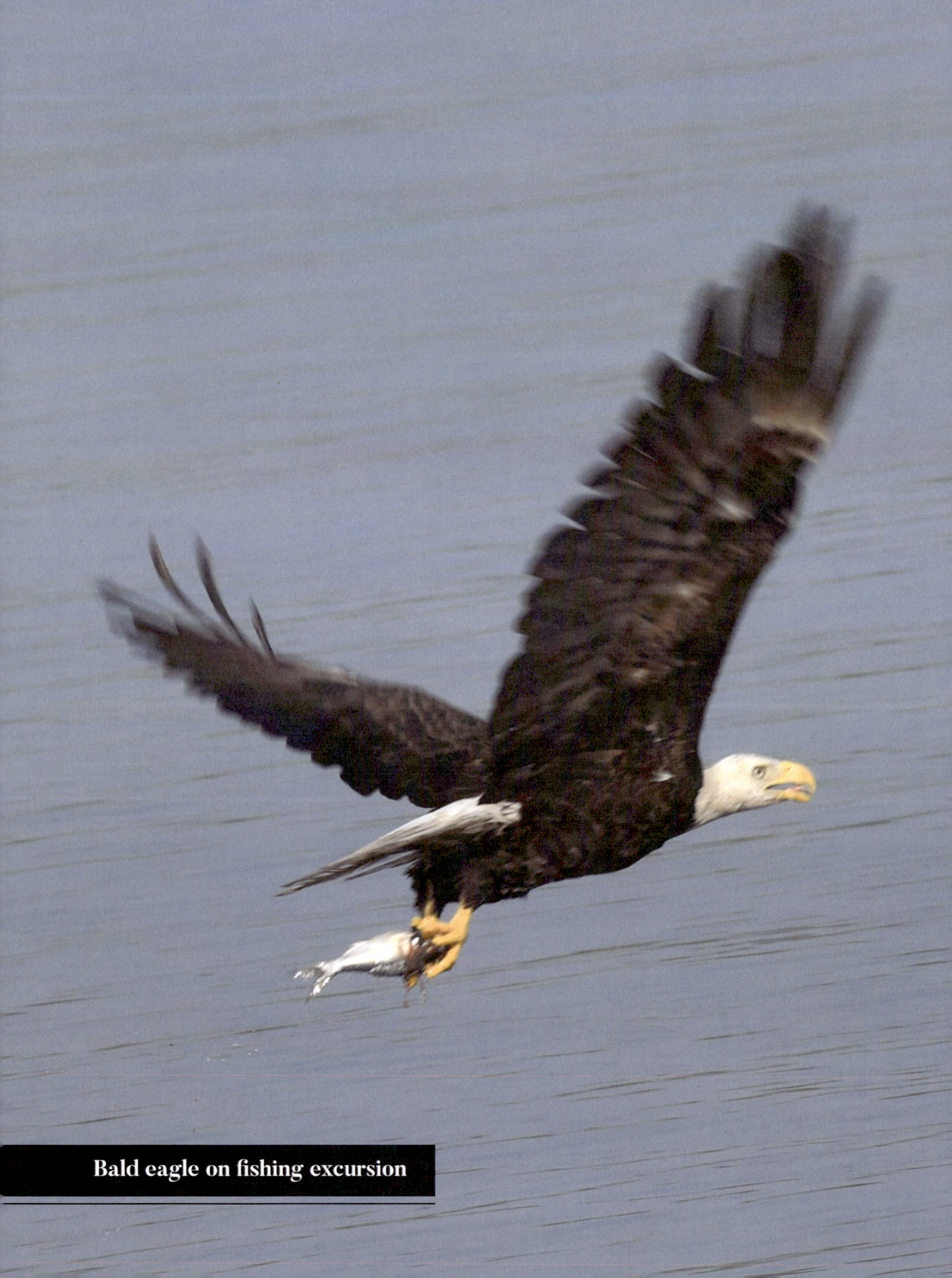

Bald eagle on fishing excursion

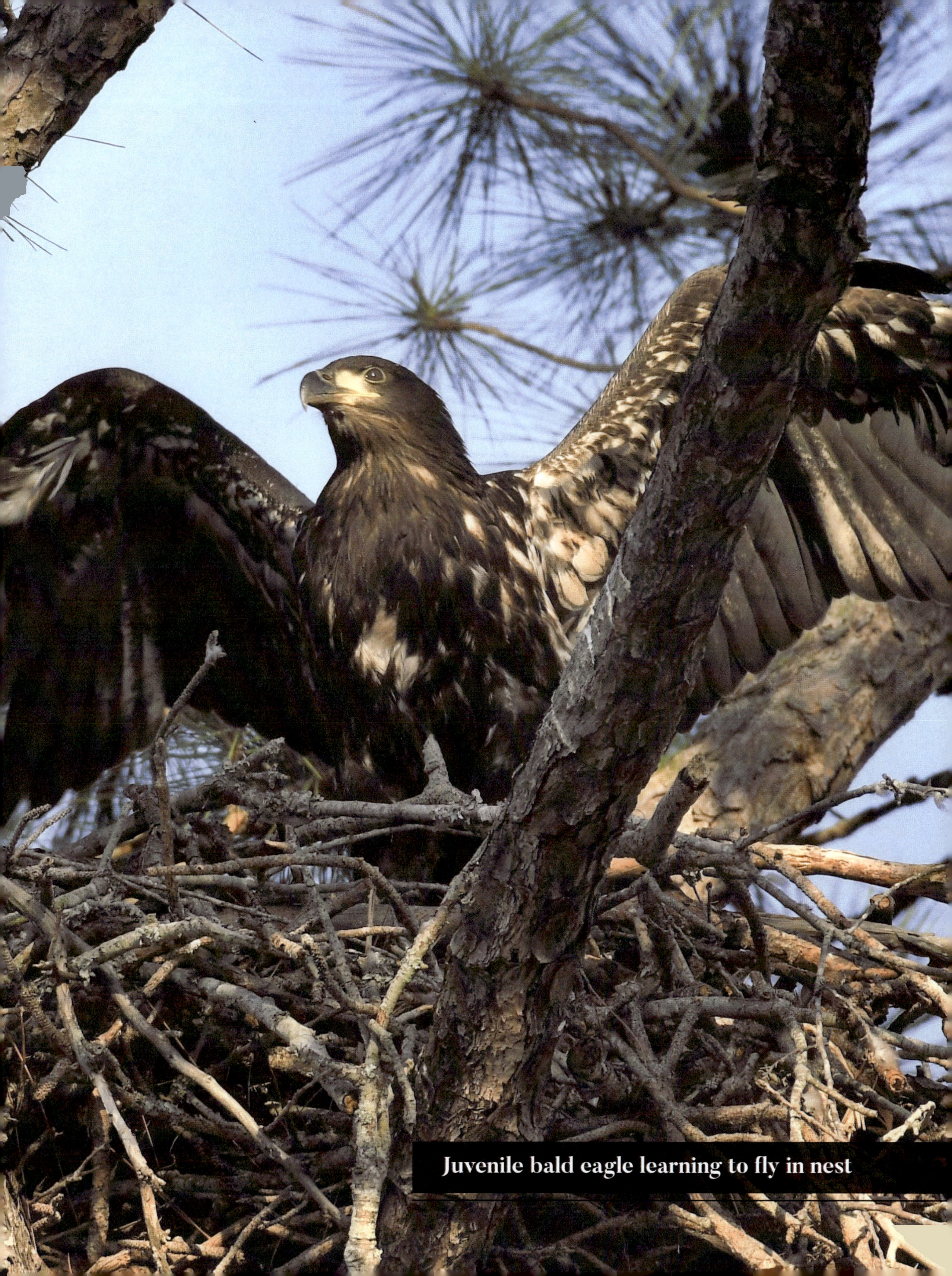

Juvenile bald eagle learning to fly in nest

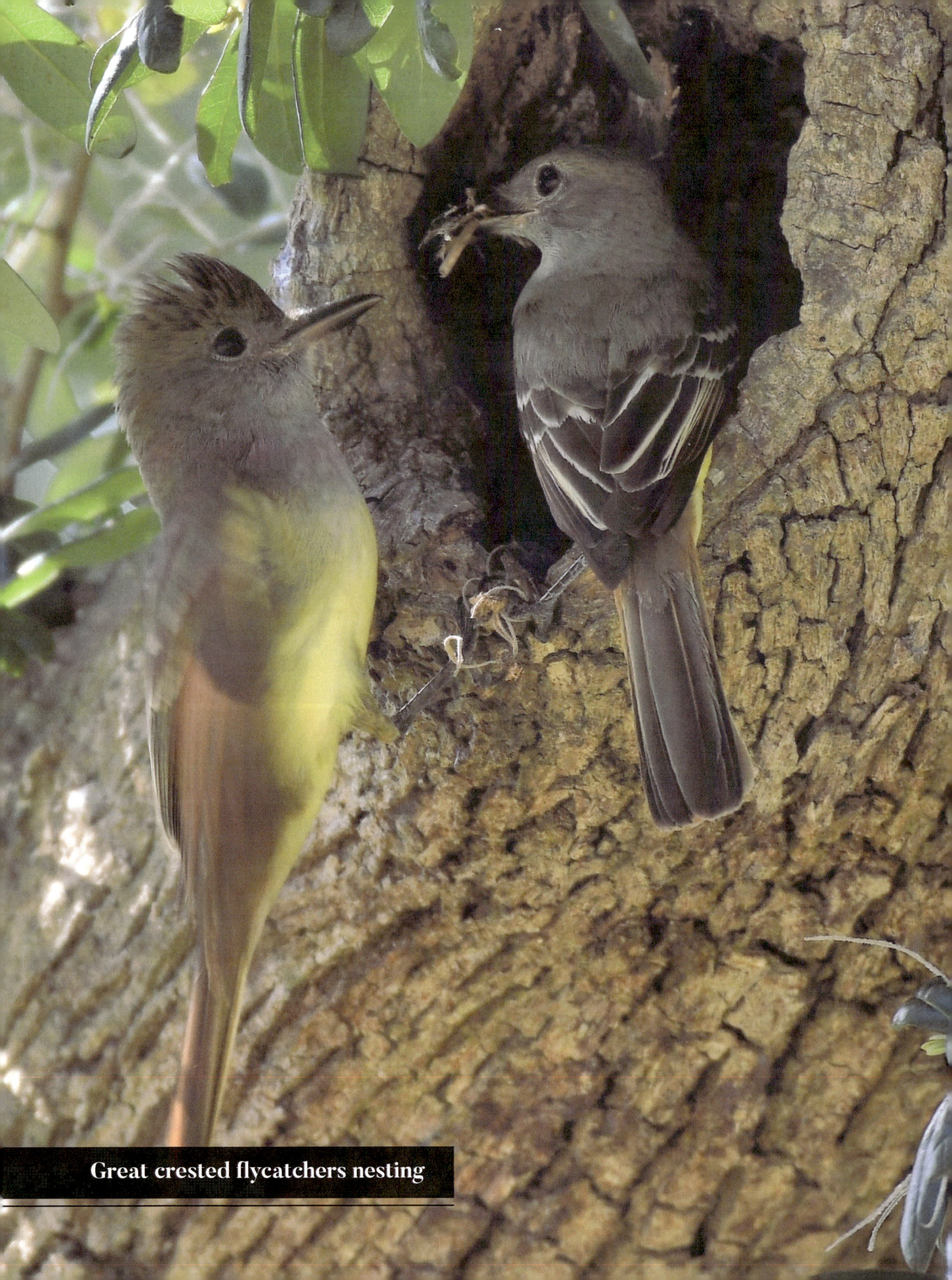

Great crested flycatchers nesting

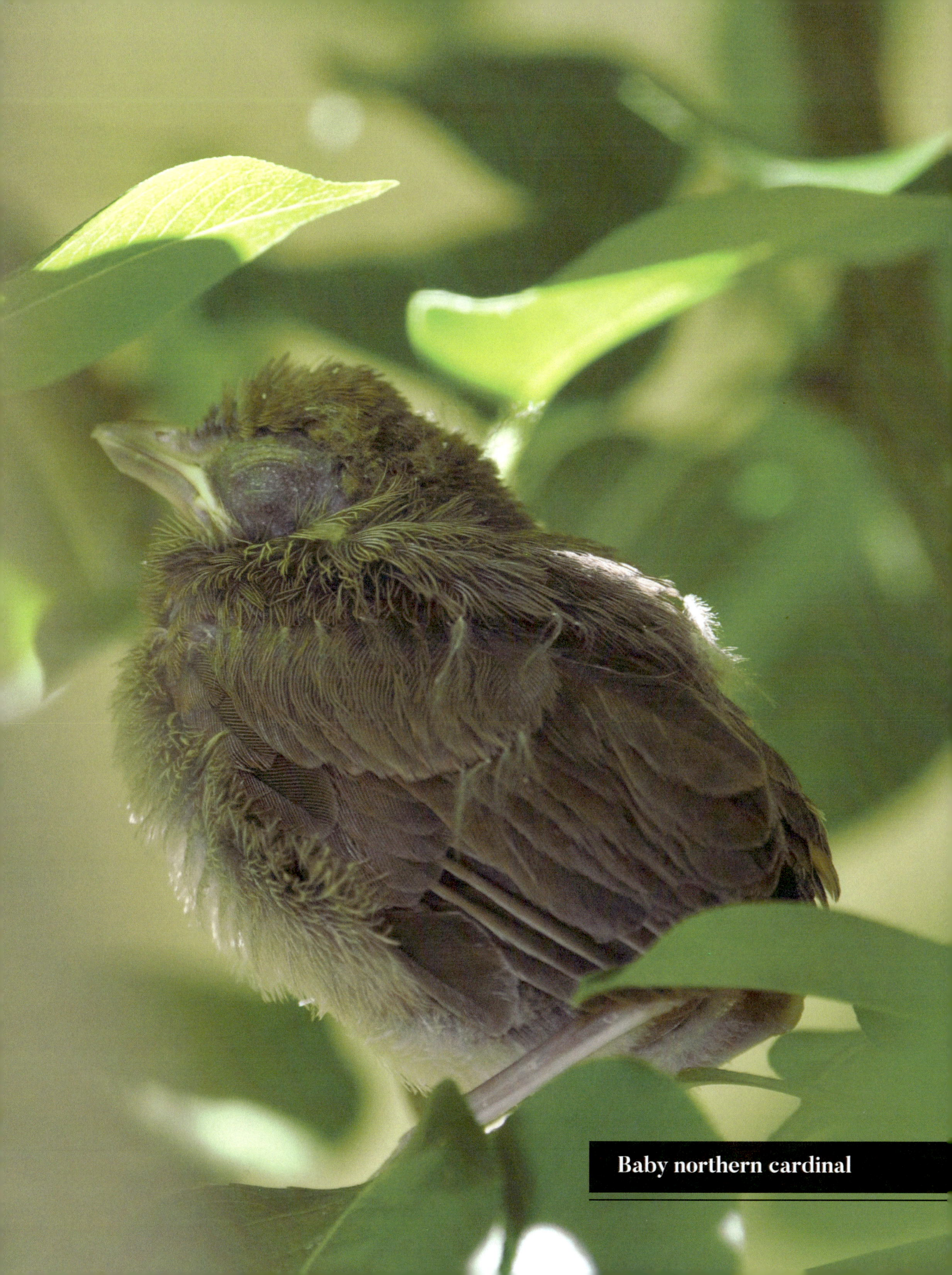

Baby northern cardinal

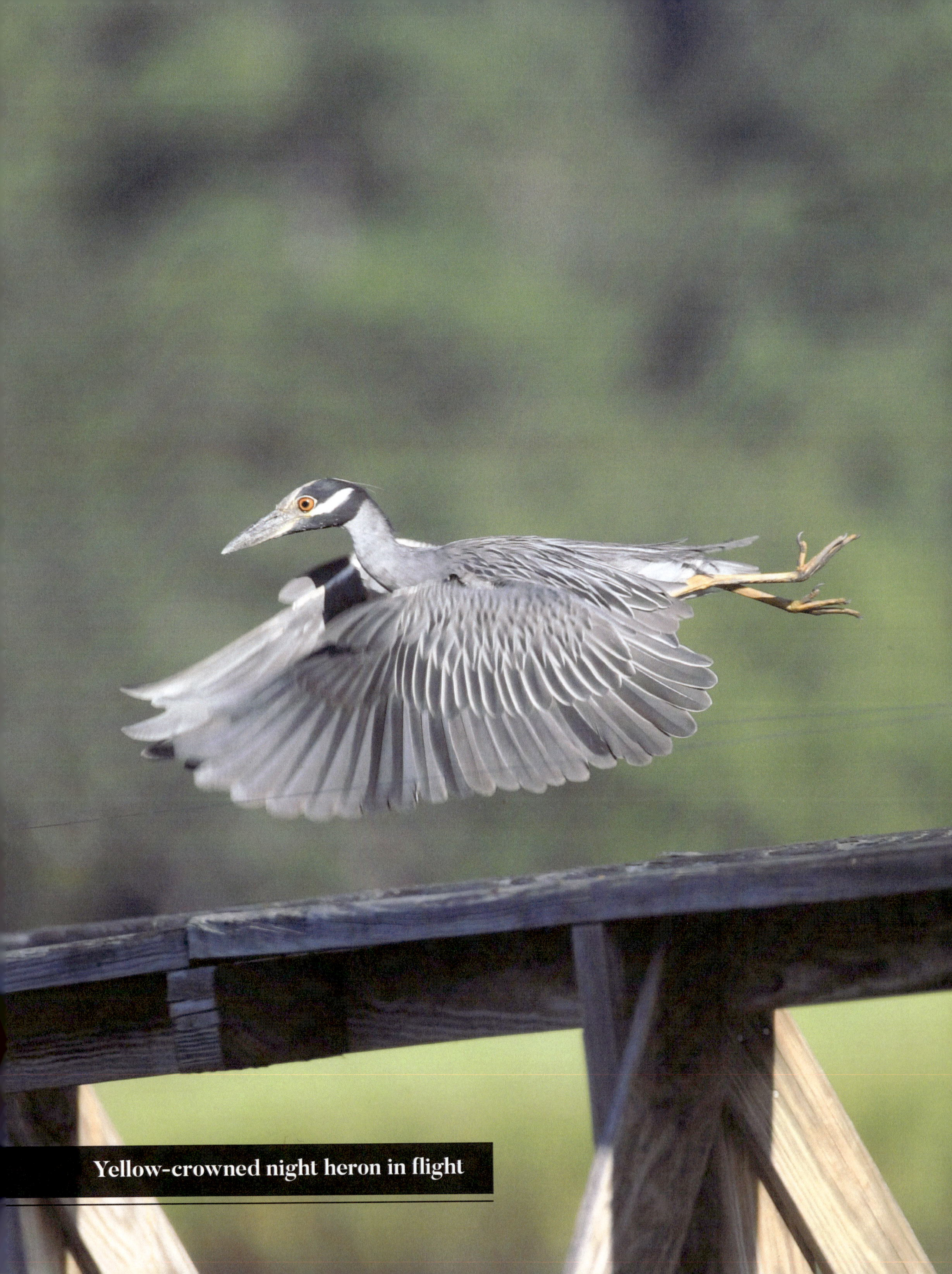

Yellow-crowned night heron in flight

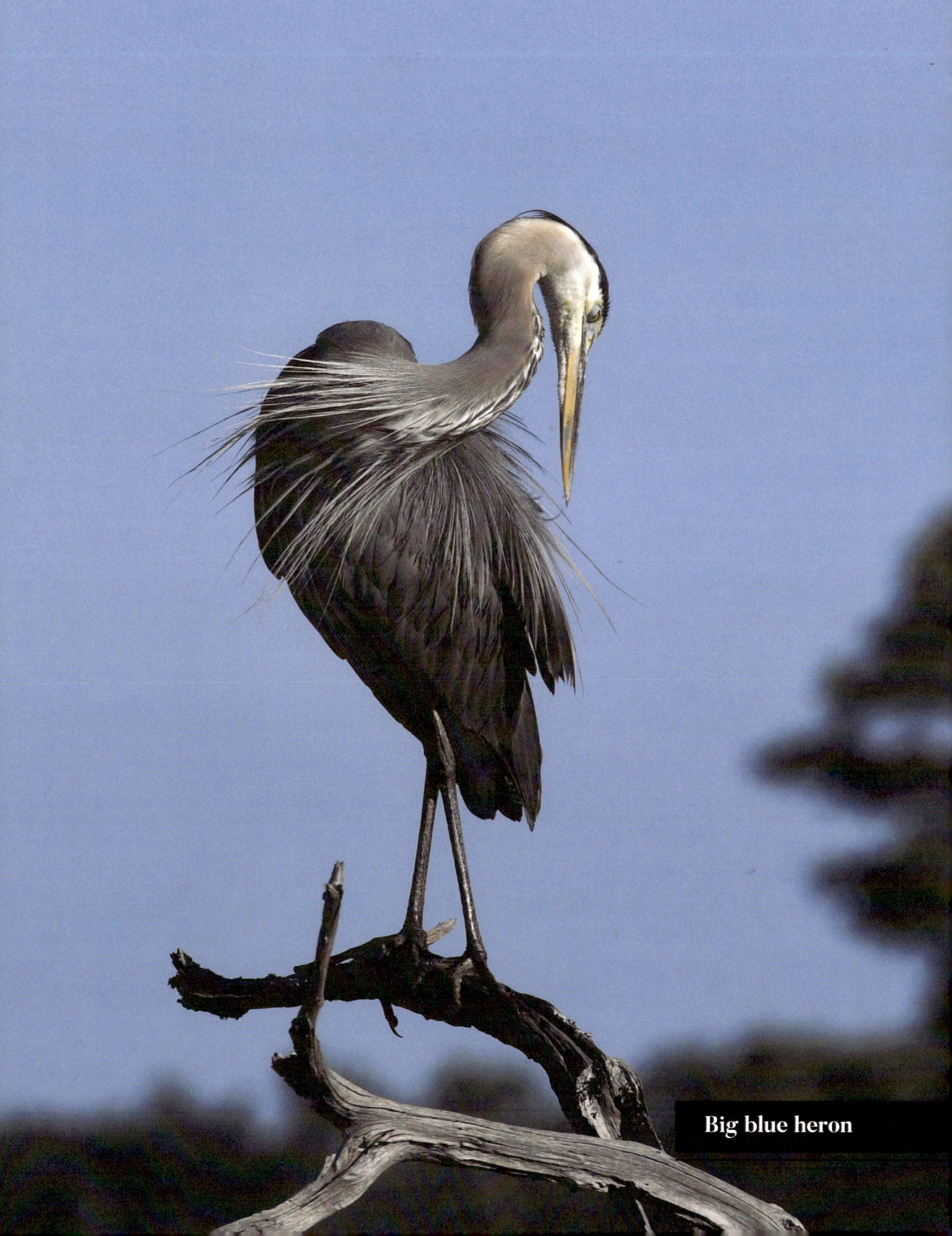

Big blue heron

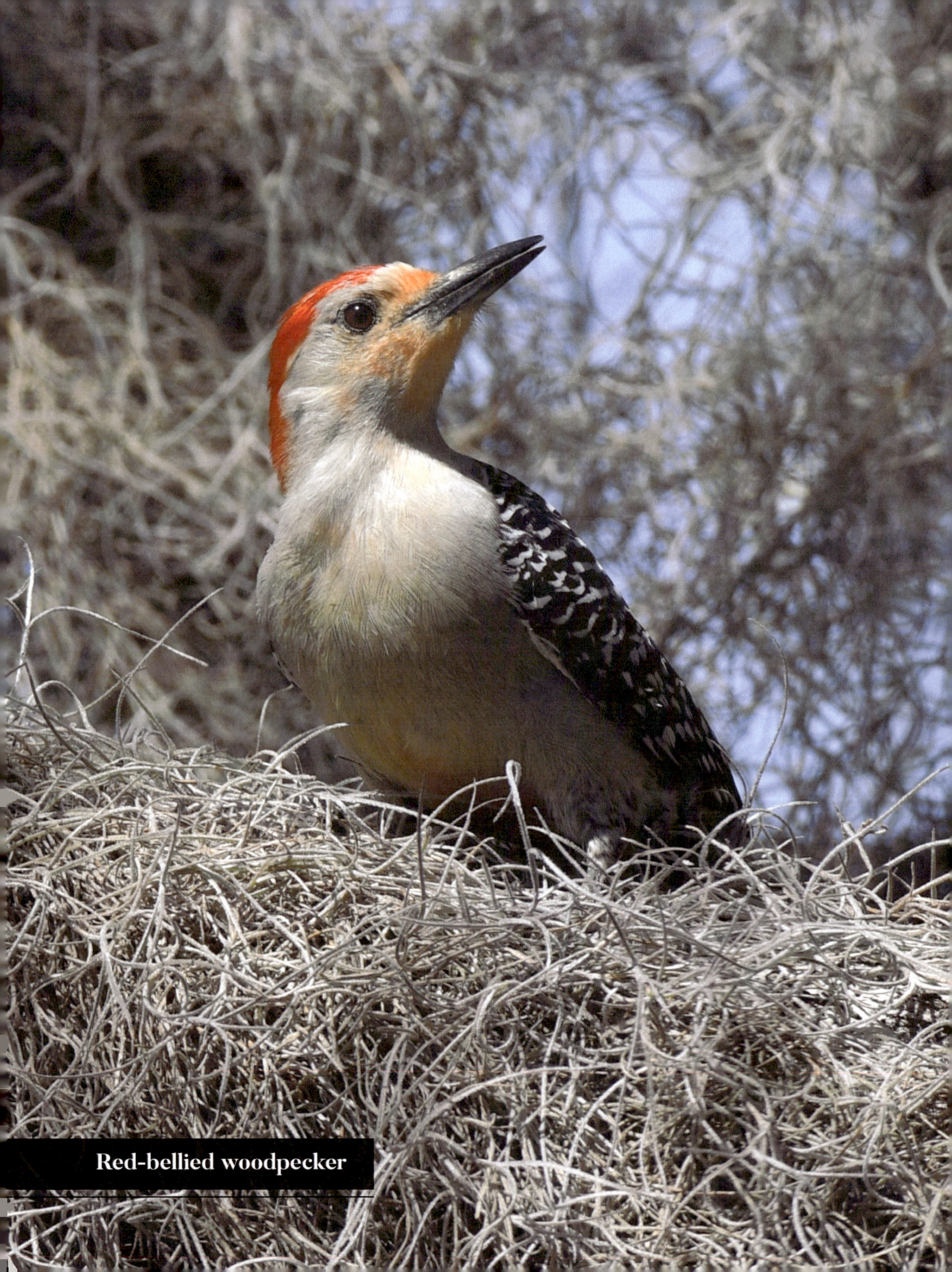

Red-bellied woodpecker

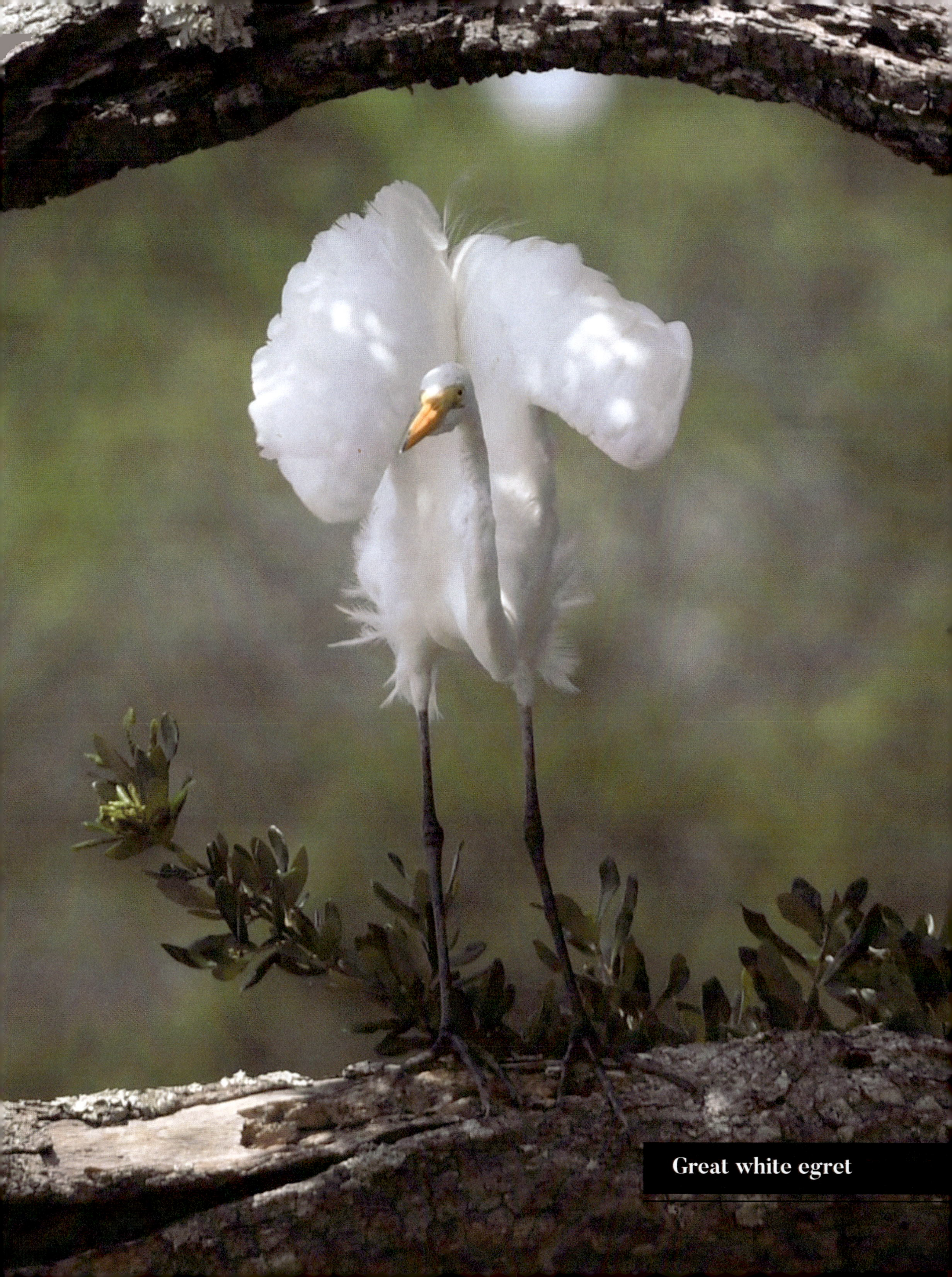

Great white egret

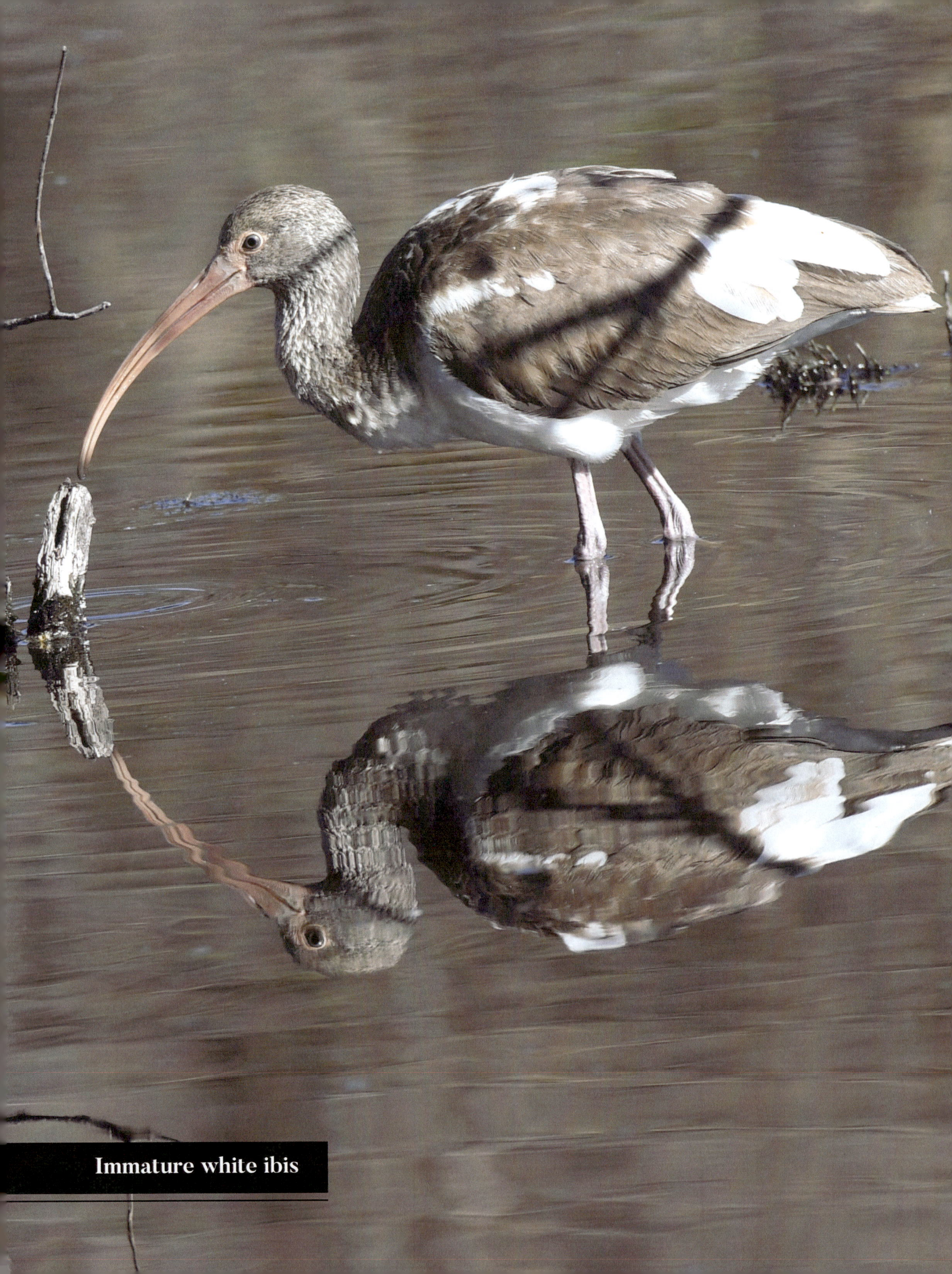

Immature white ibis

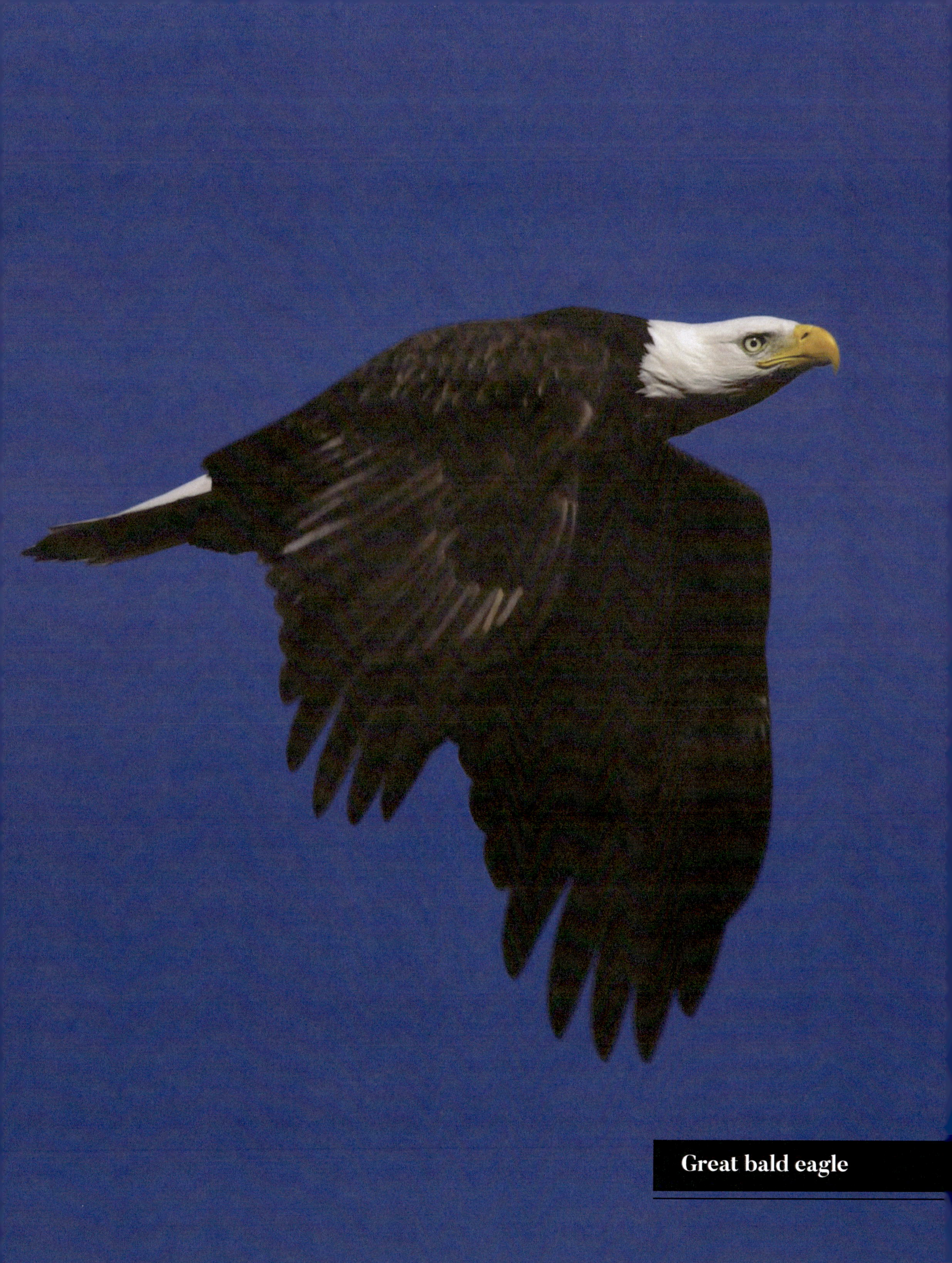

Great bald eagle

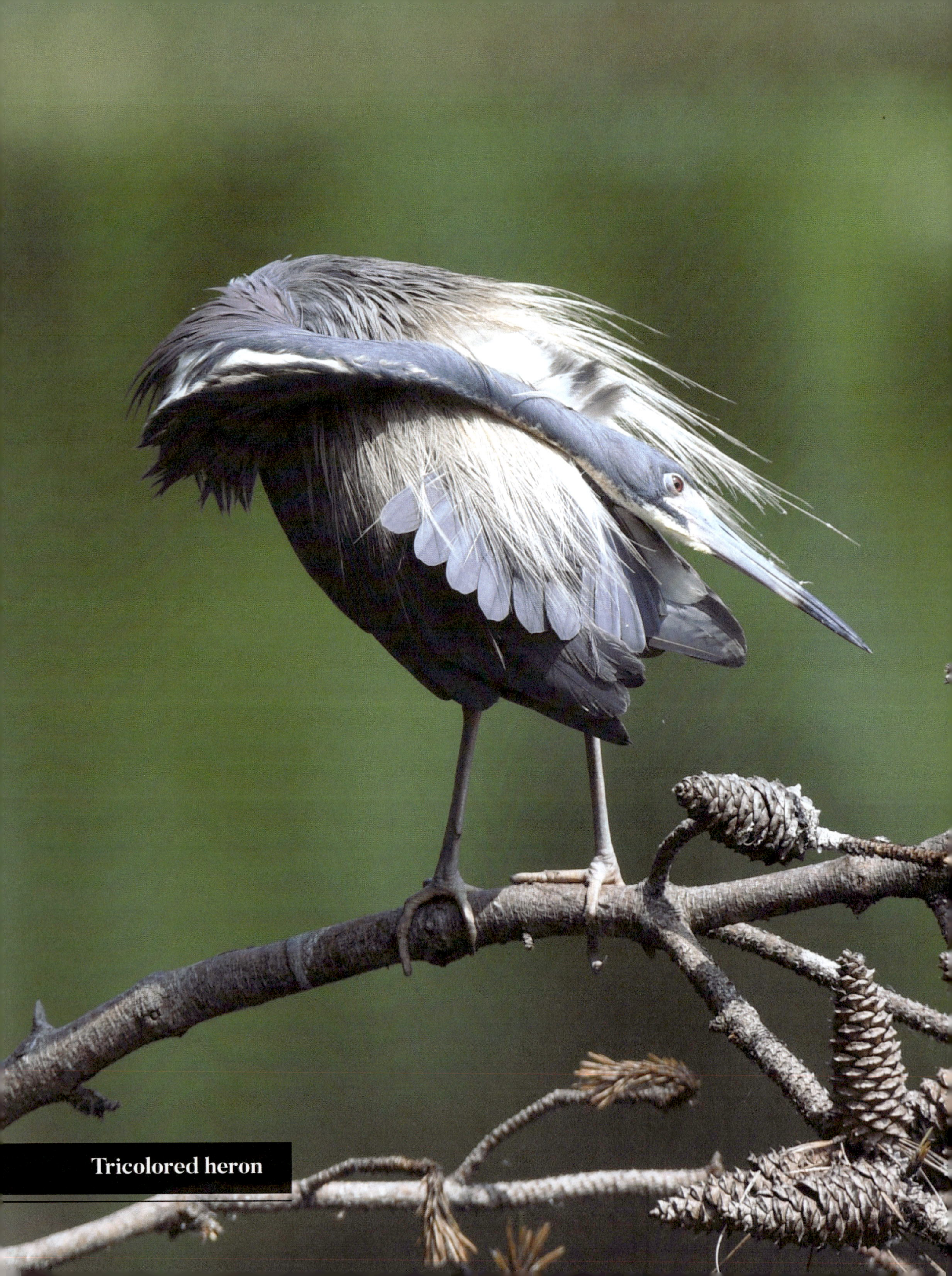

Tricolored heron

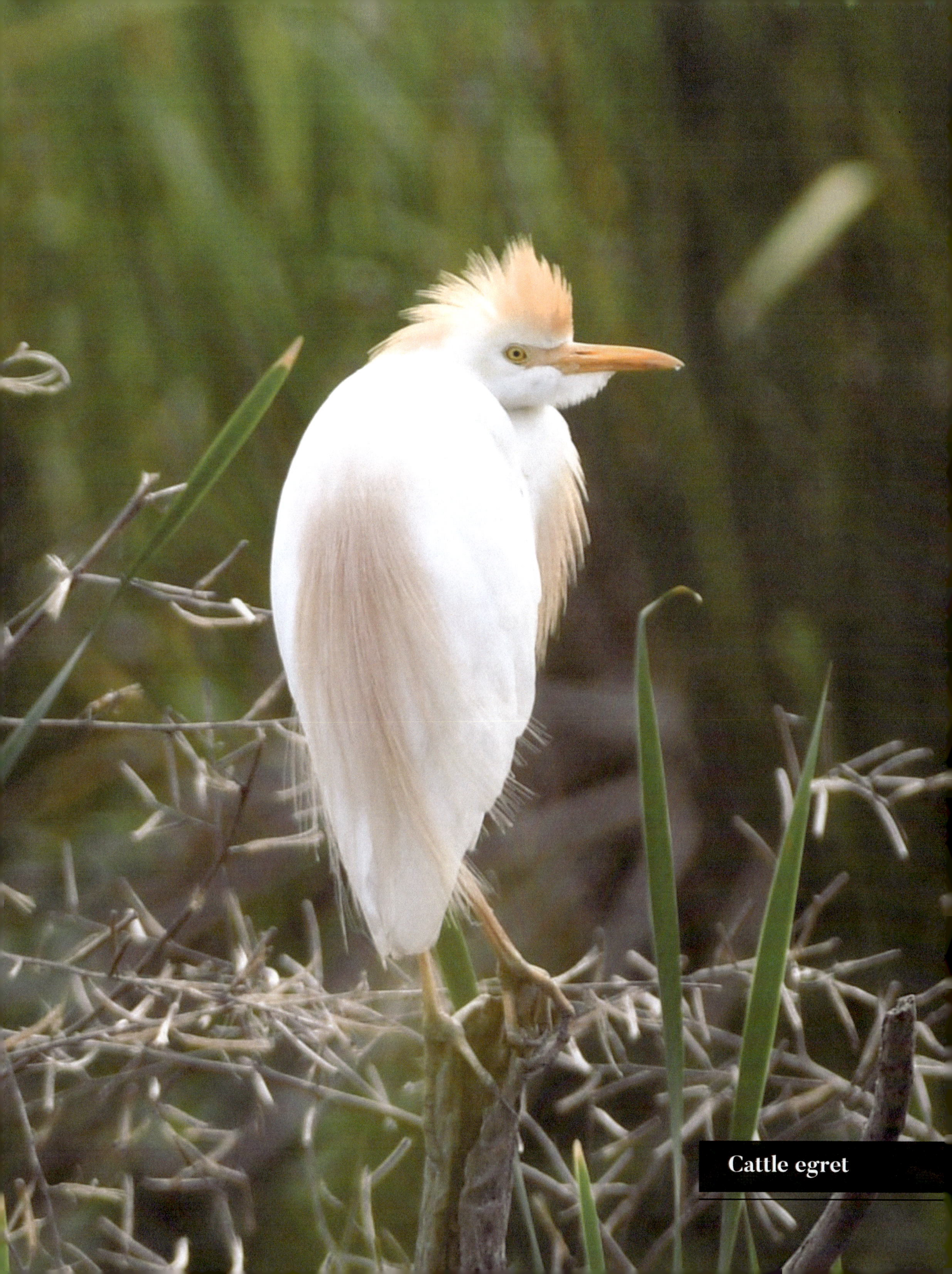

Cattle egret

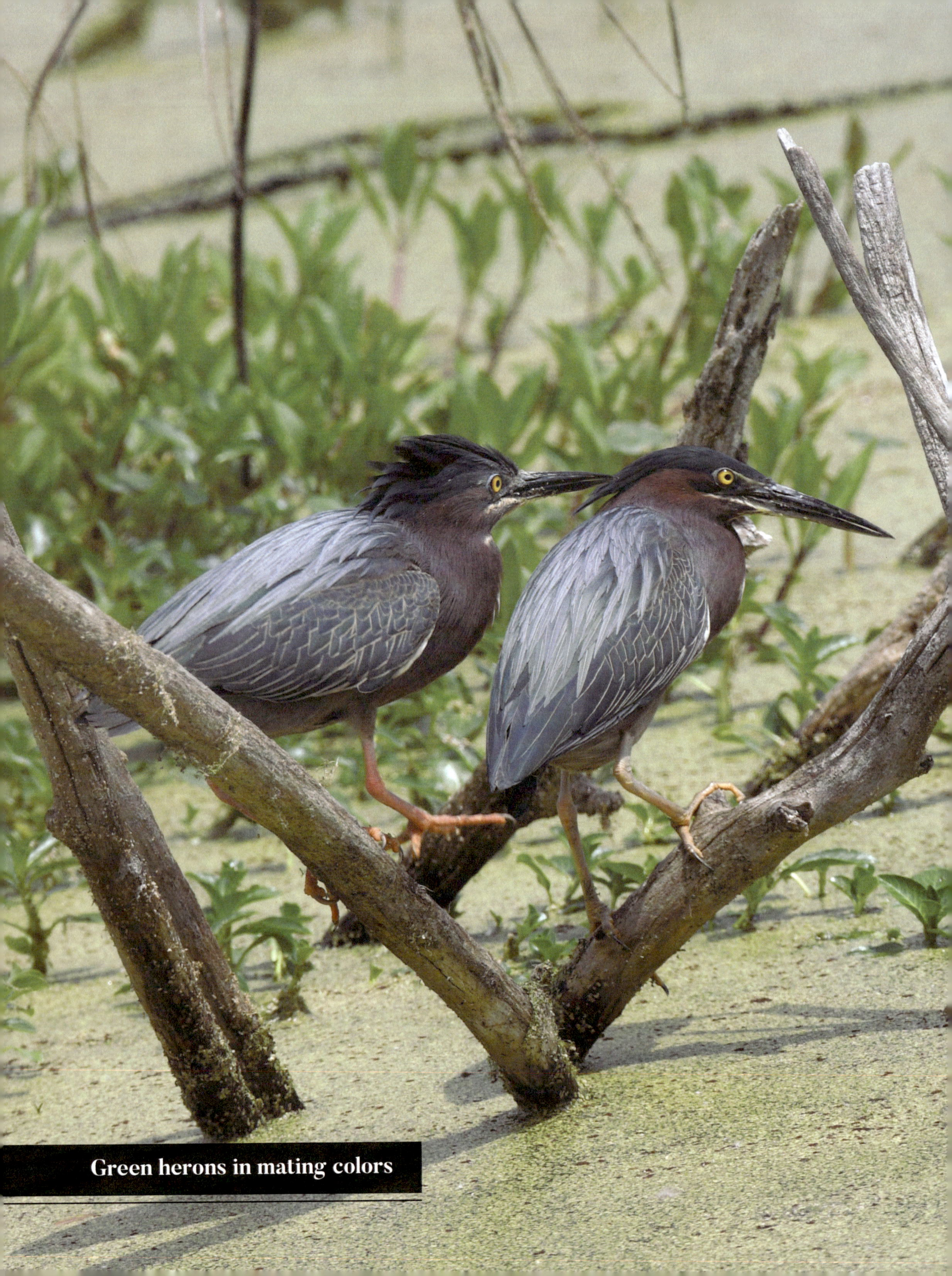

Green herons in mating colors

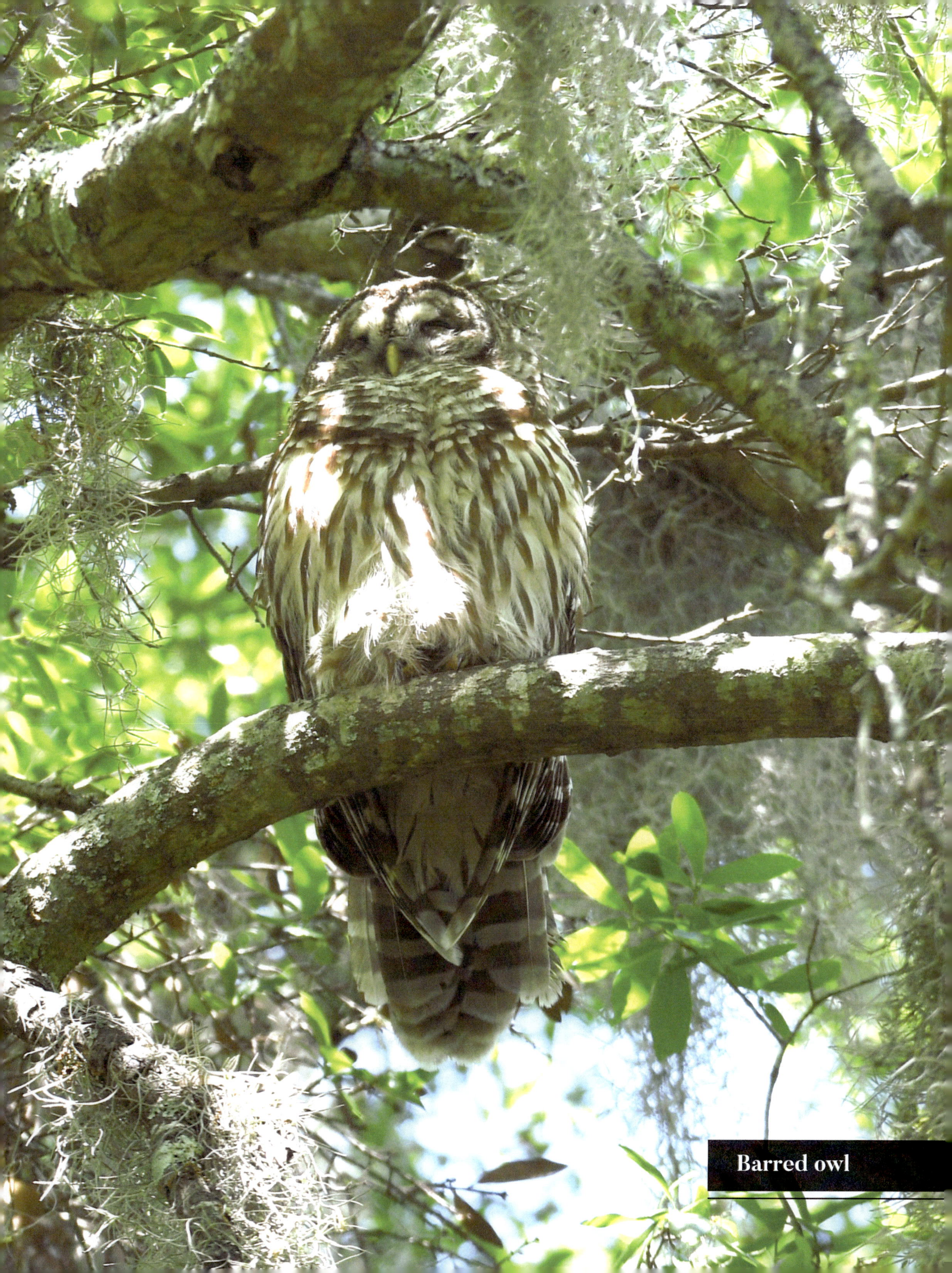
Barred owl

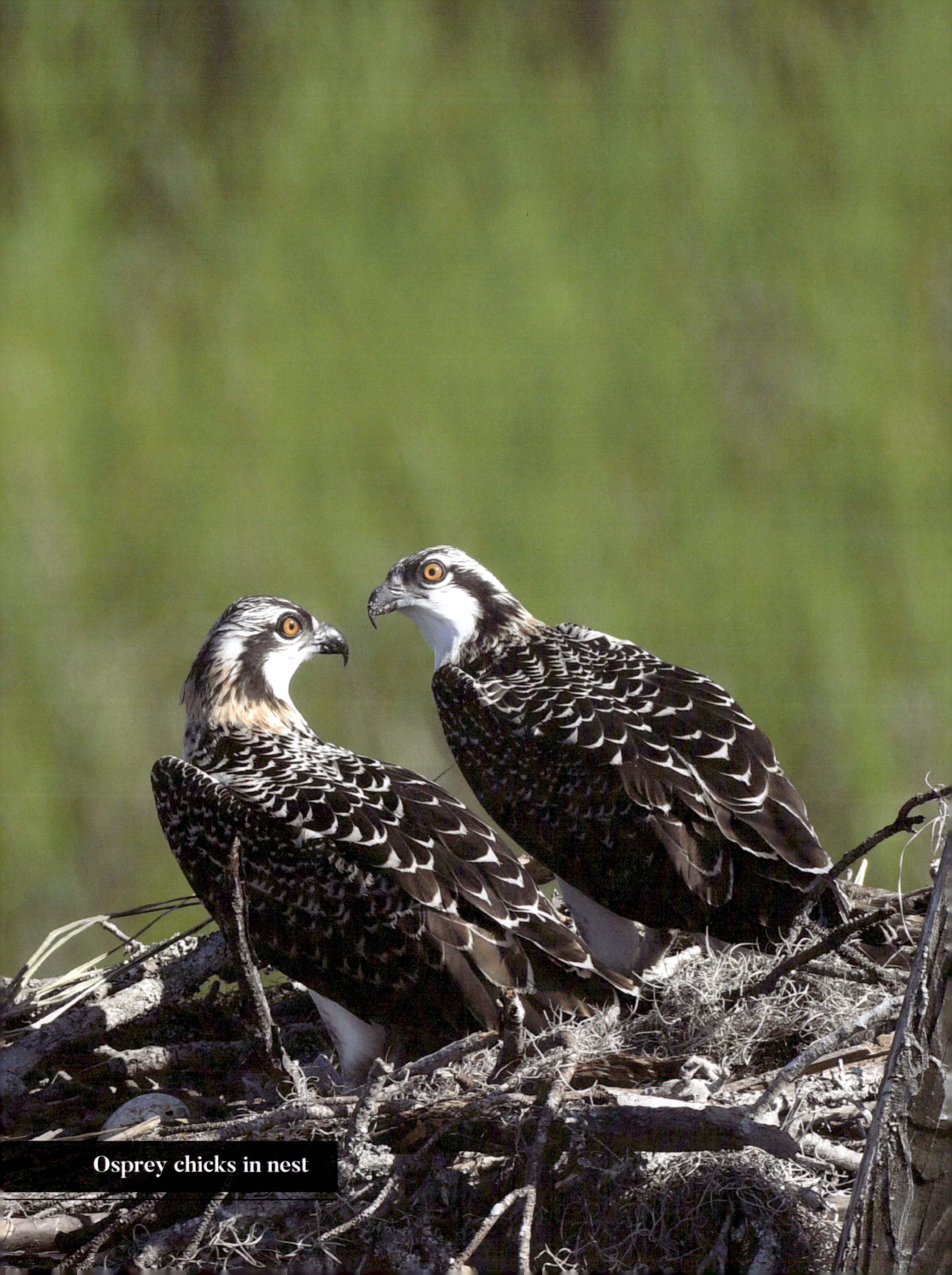

Osprey chicks in nest

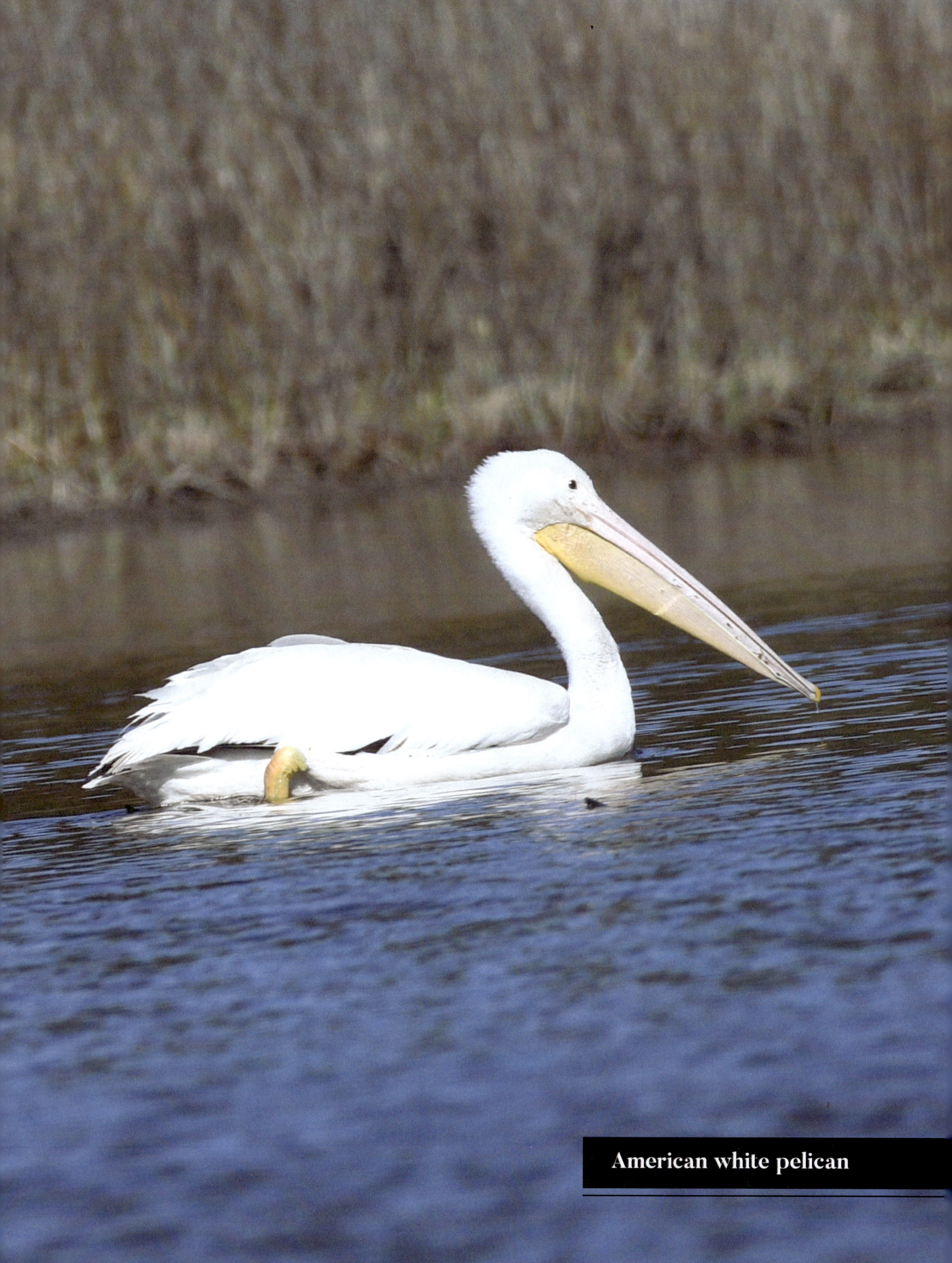

American white pelican

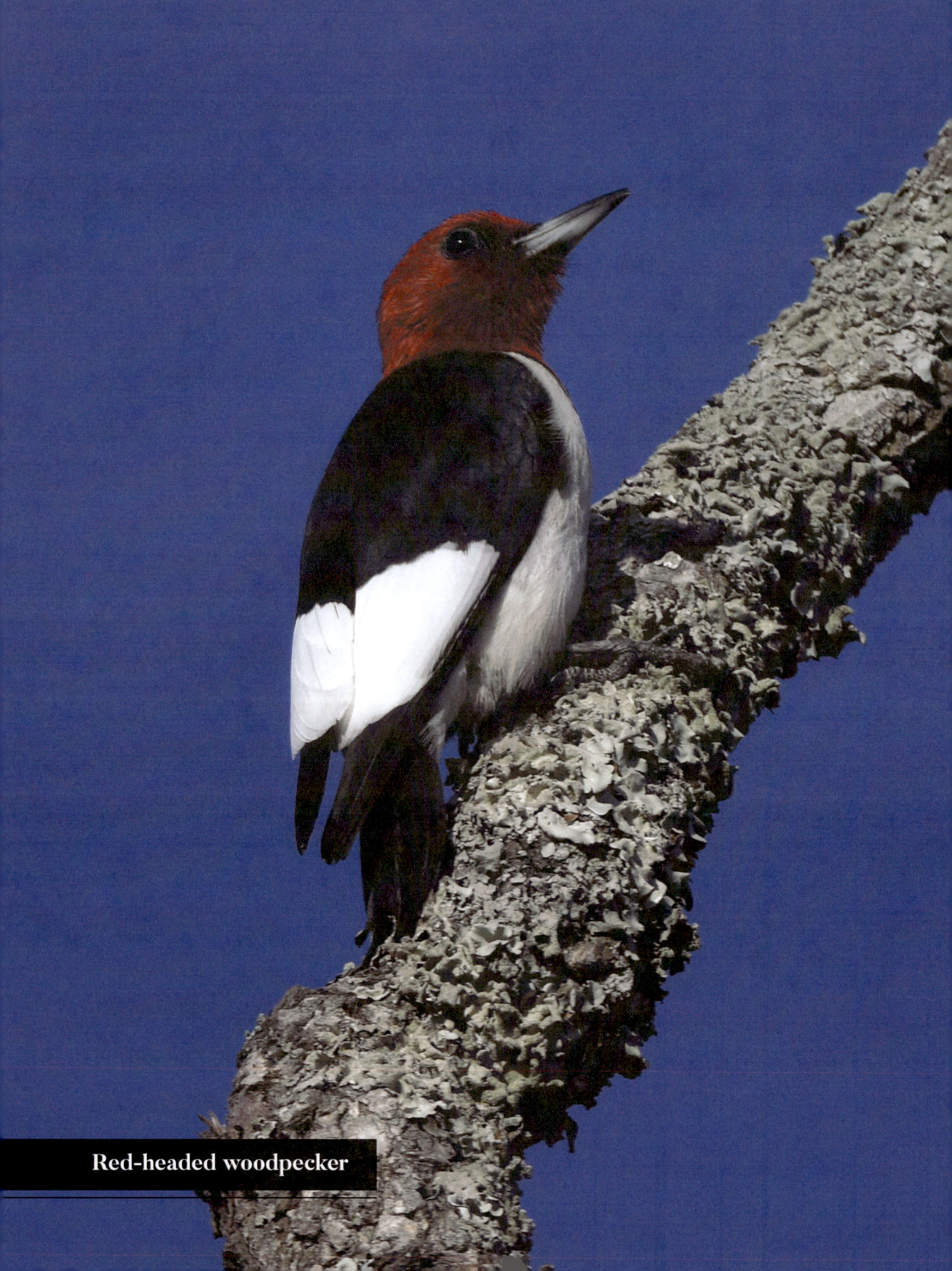

Red-headed woodpecker

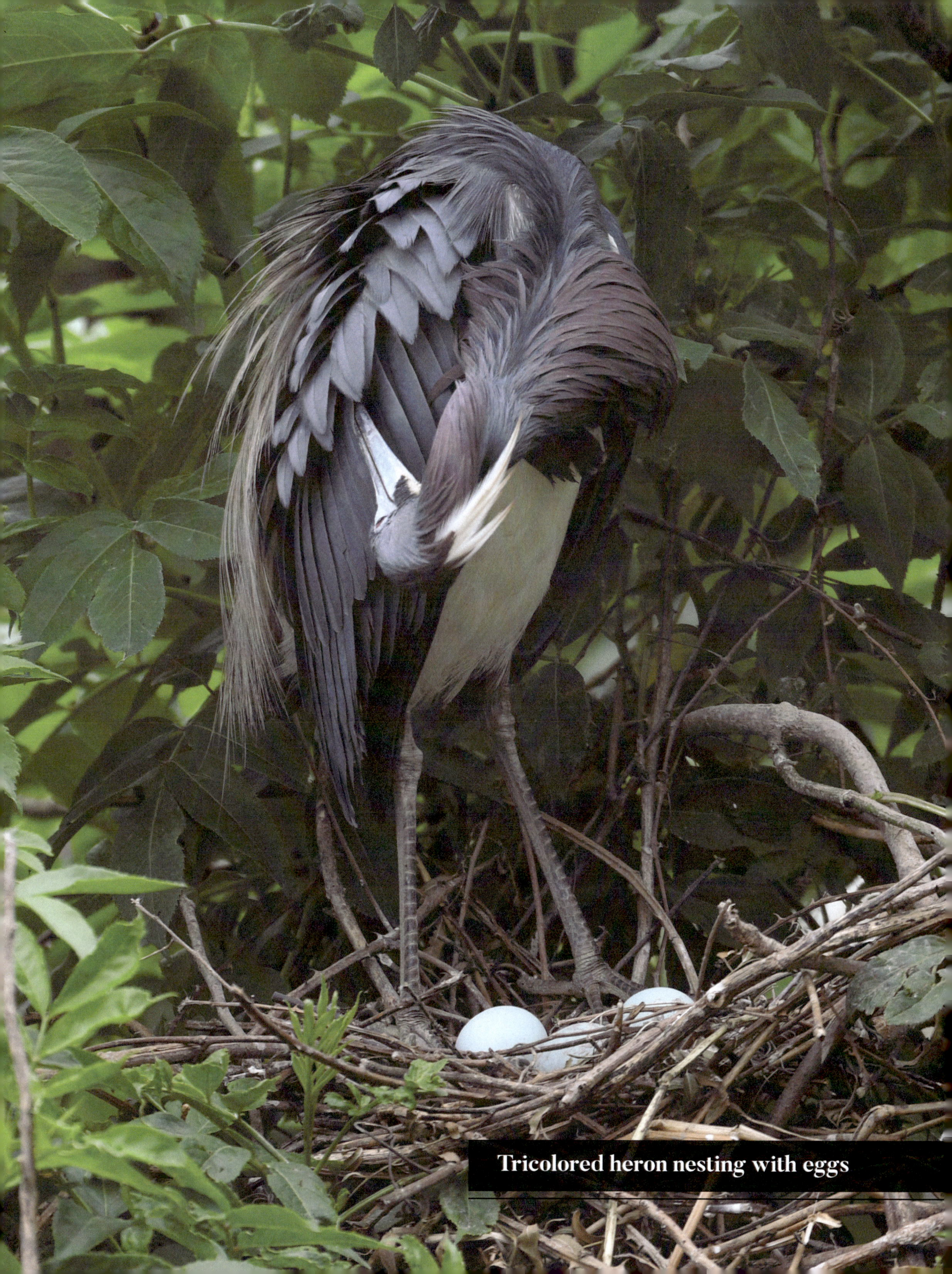

Tricolored heron nesting with eggs

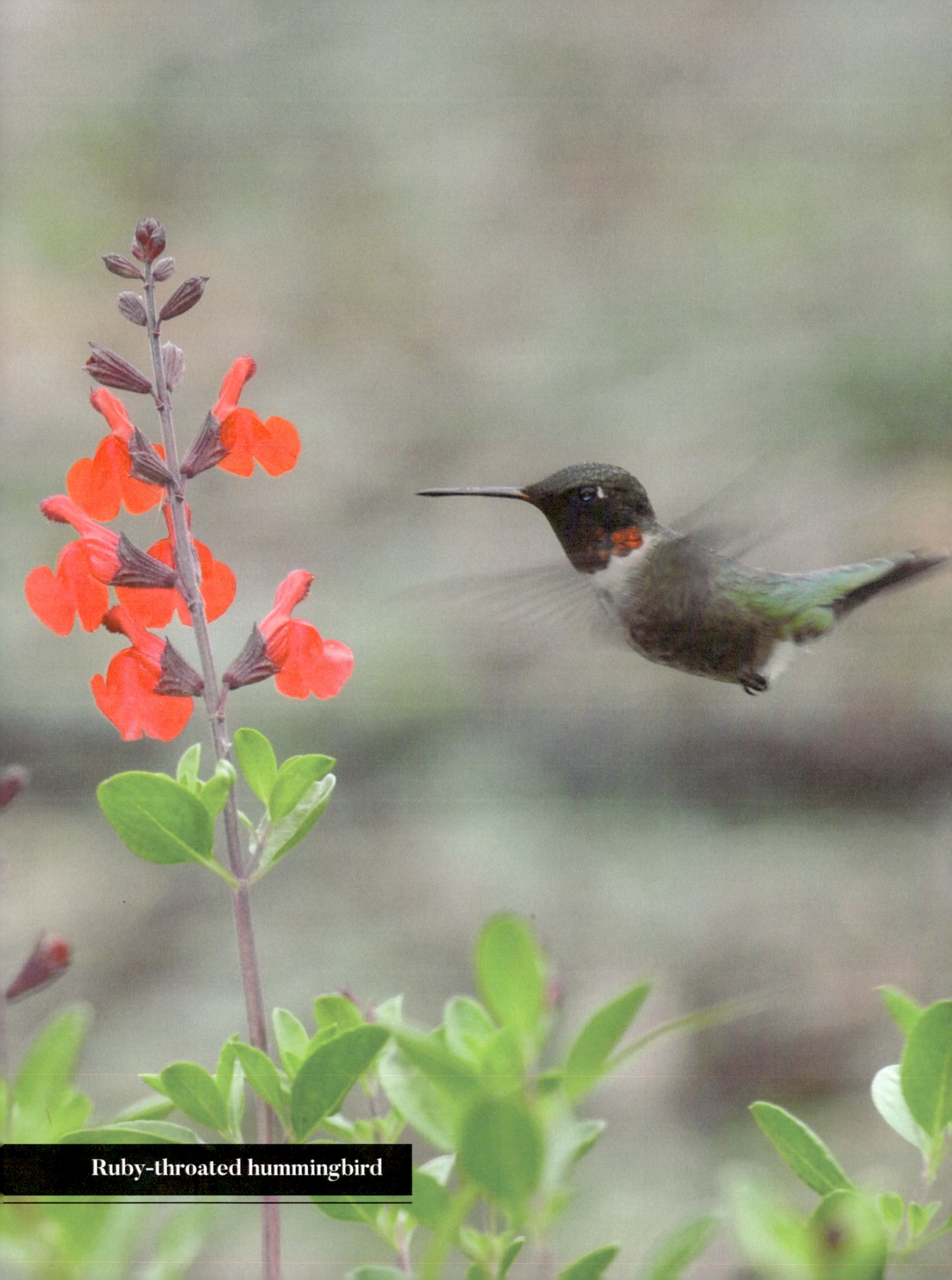

Ruby-throated hummingbird

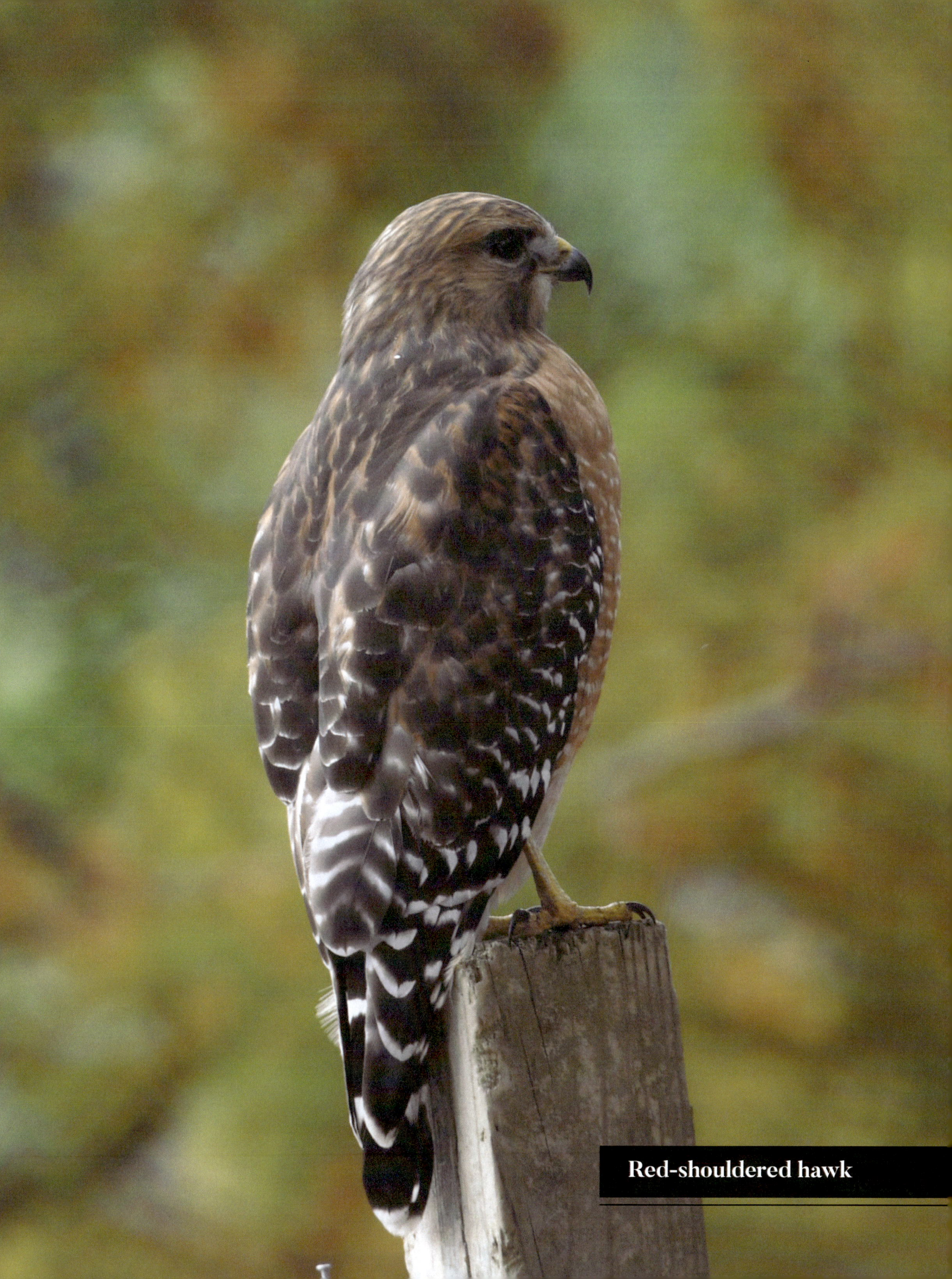

Red-shouldered hawk

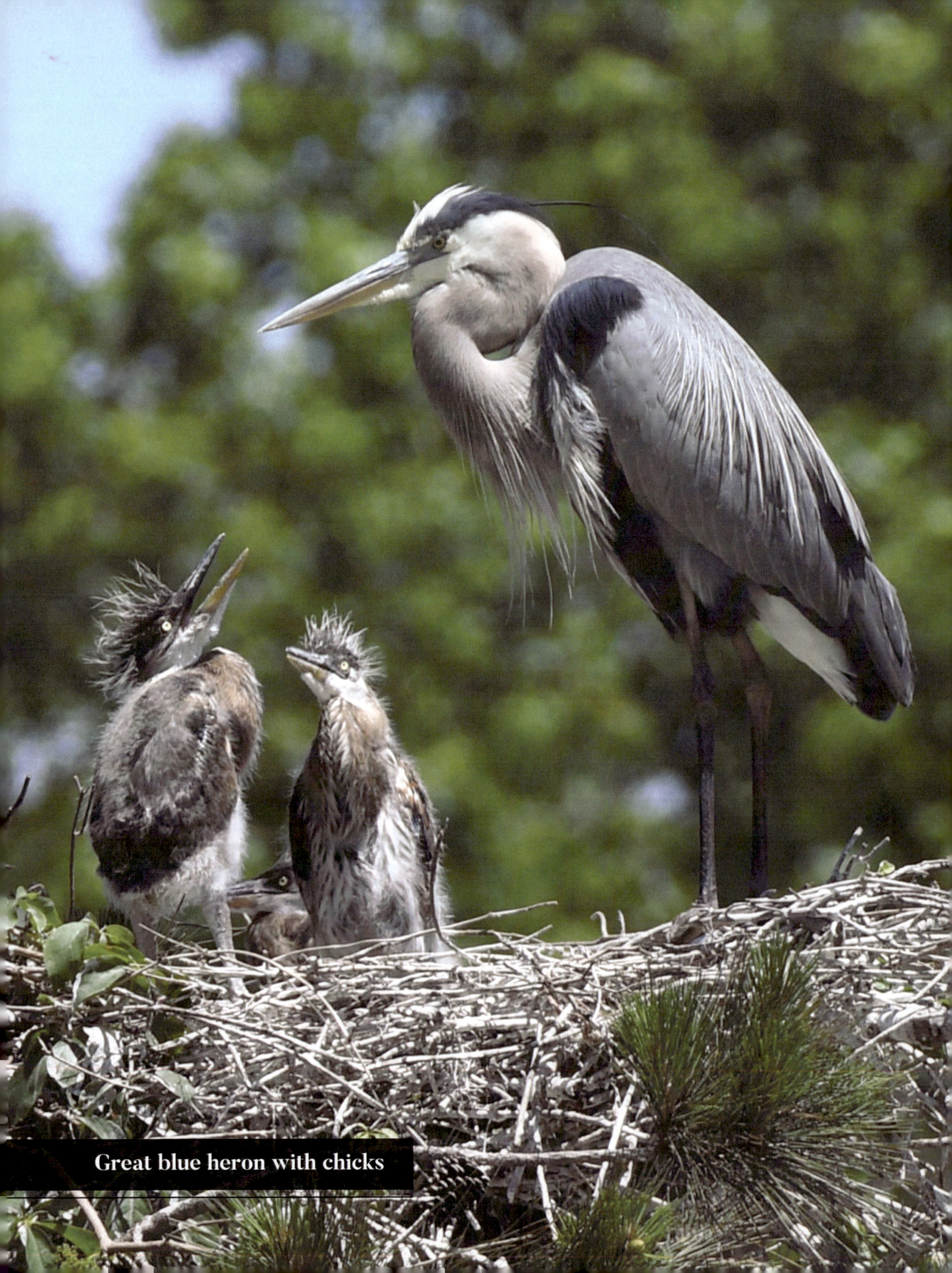

Great blue heron with chicks

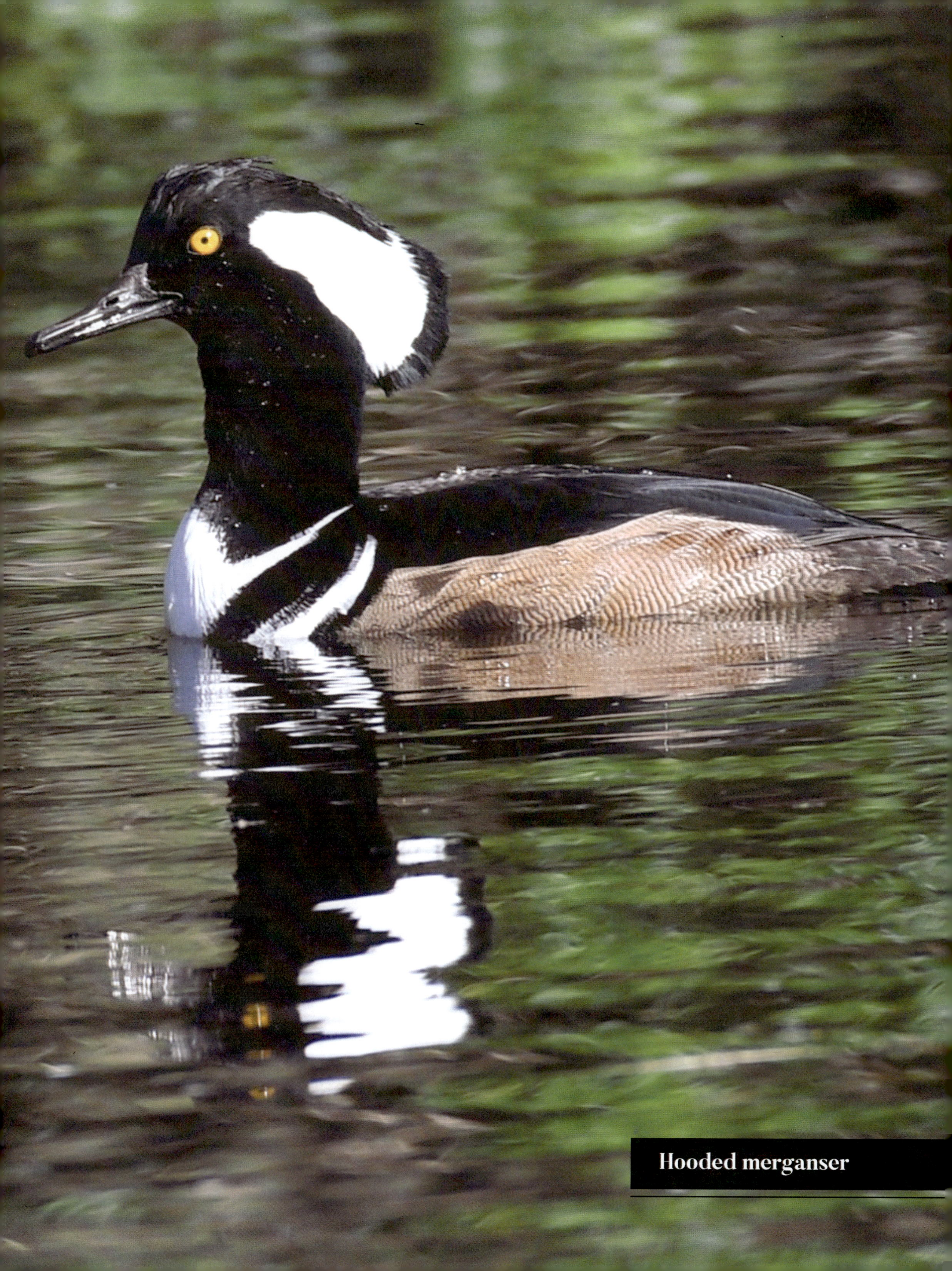

Hooded merganser

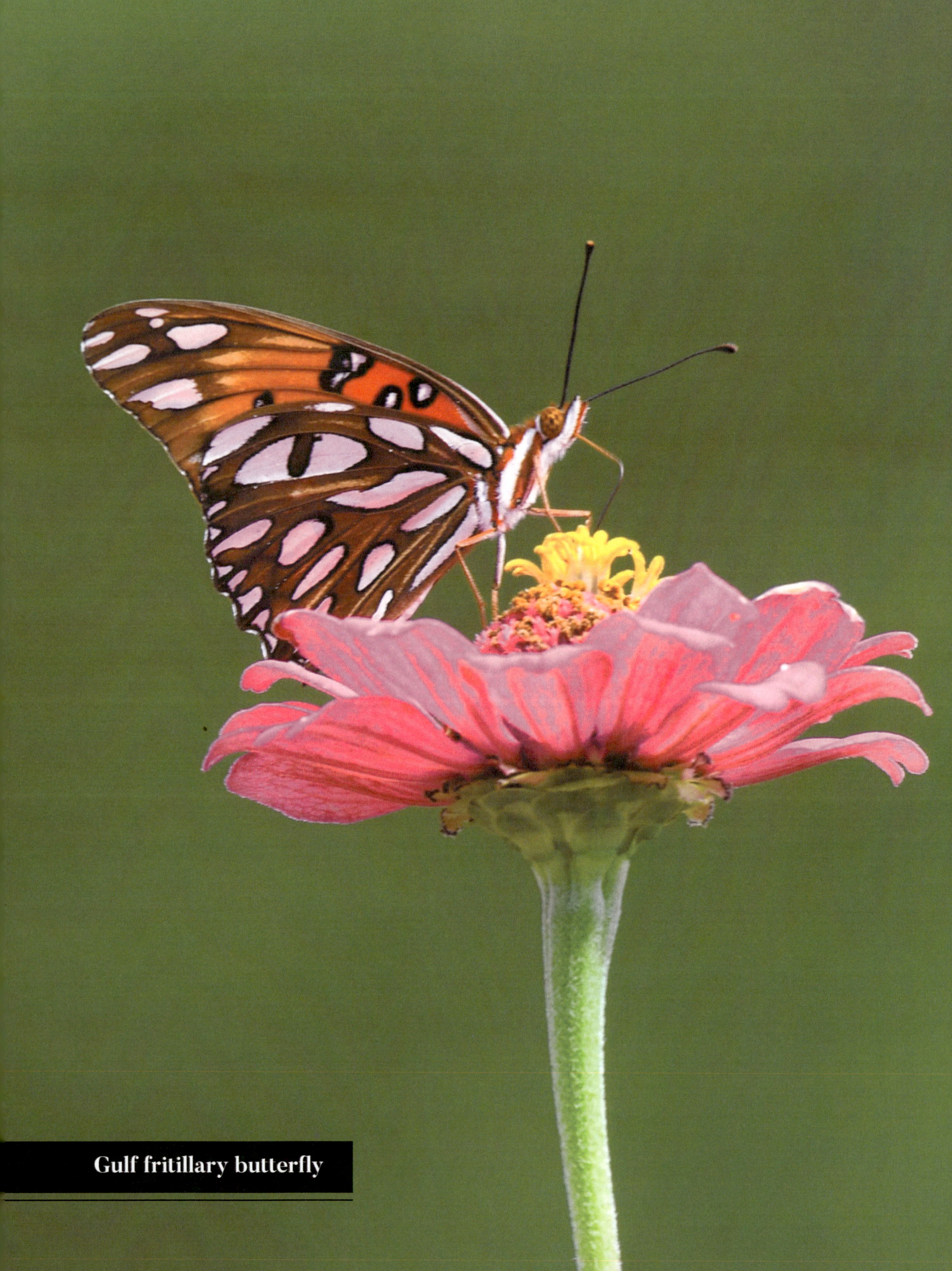

Gulf fritillary butterfly

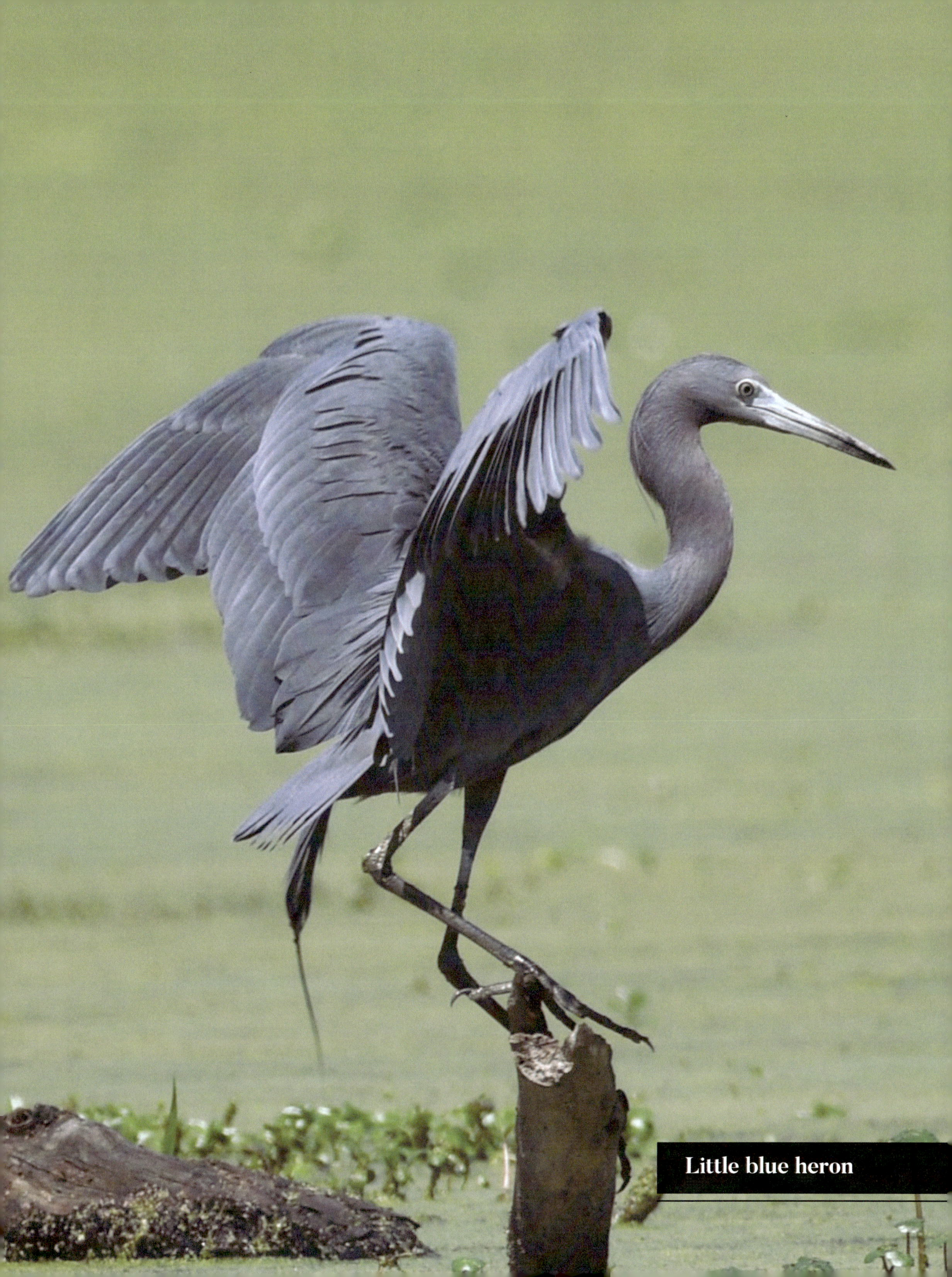

Little blue heron

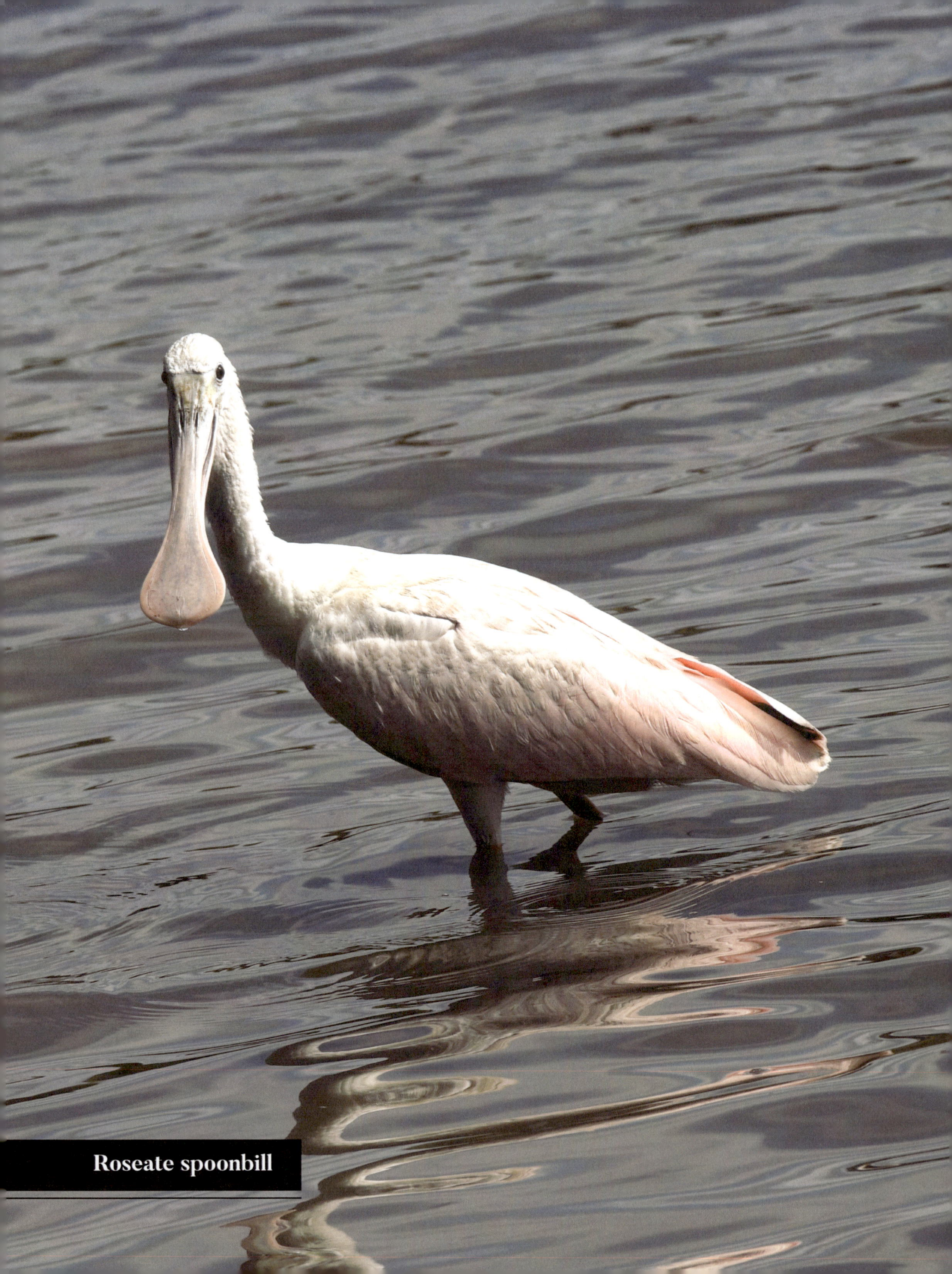

Roseate spoonbill

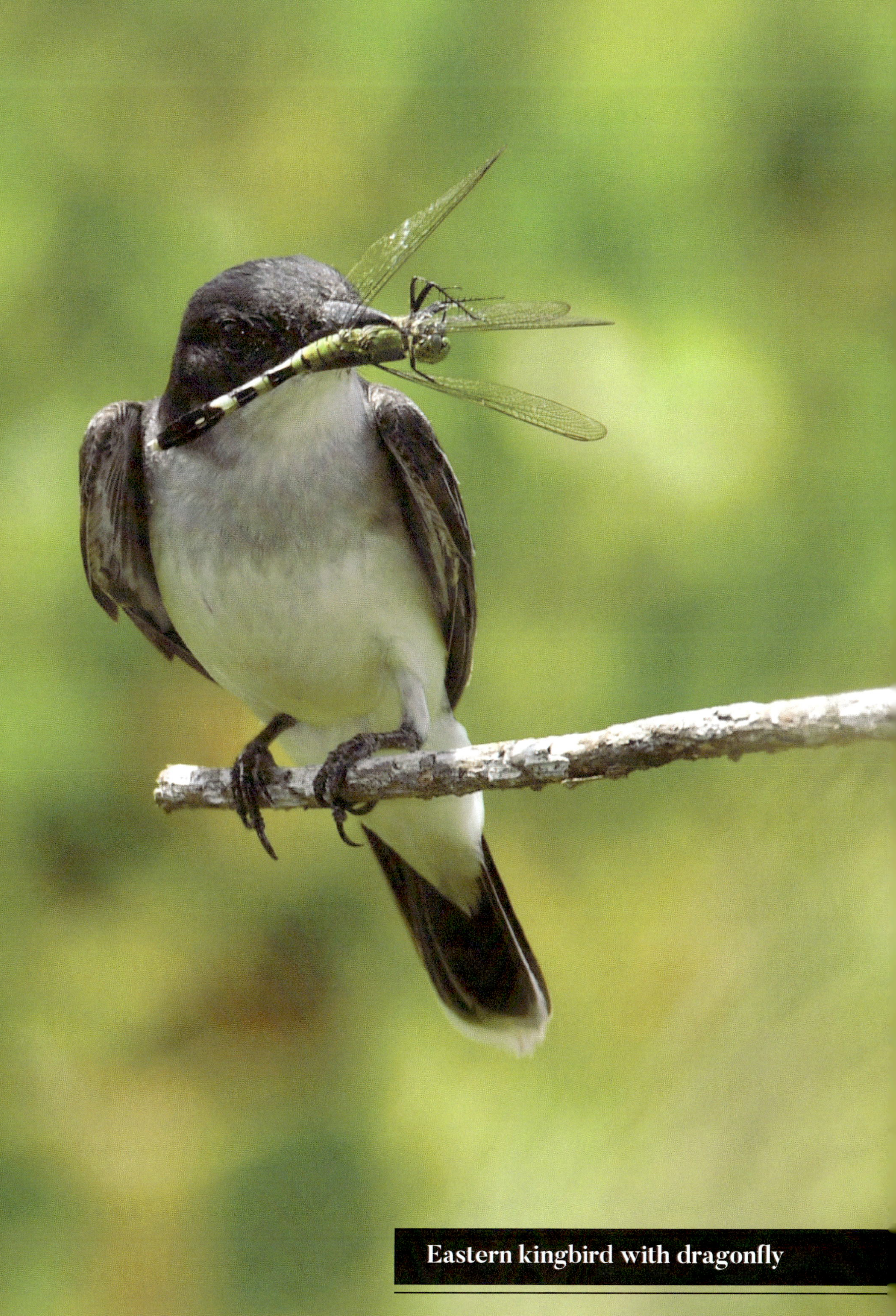

Eastern kingbird with dragonfly

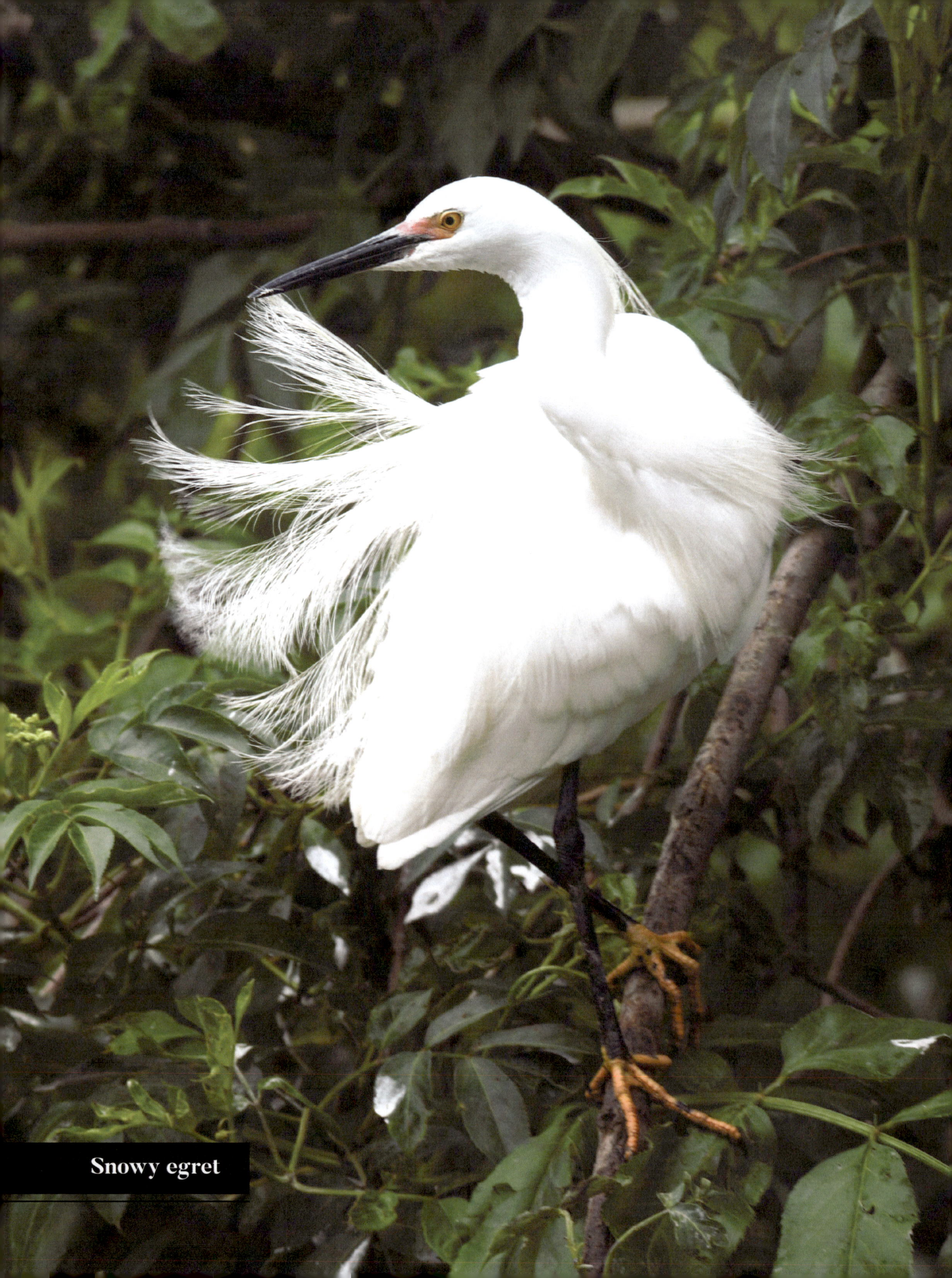

Snowy egret

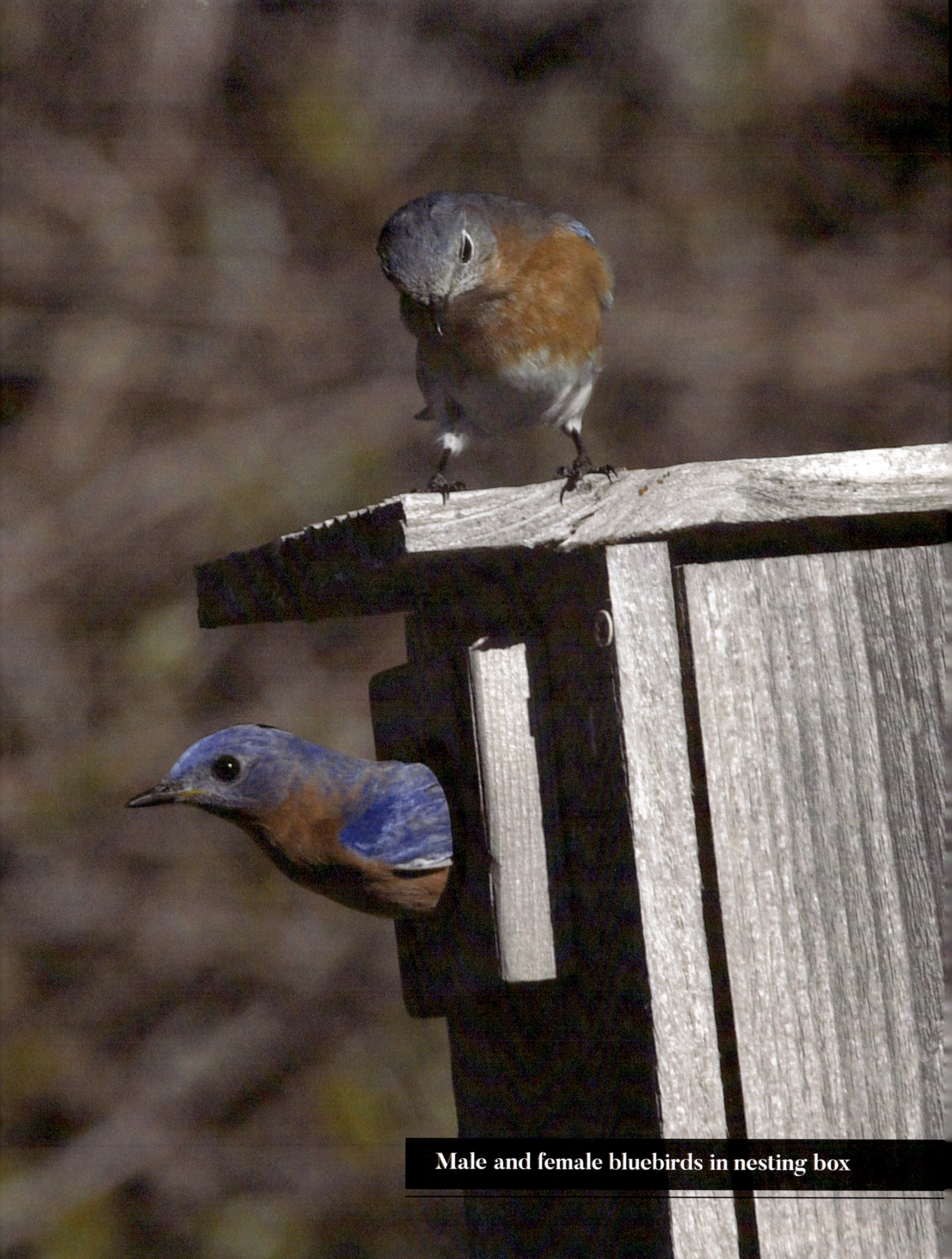

Male and female bluebirds in nesting box

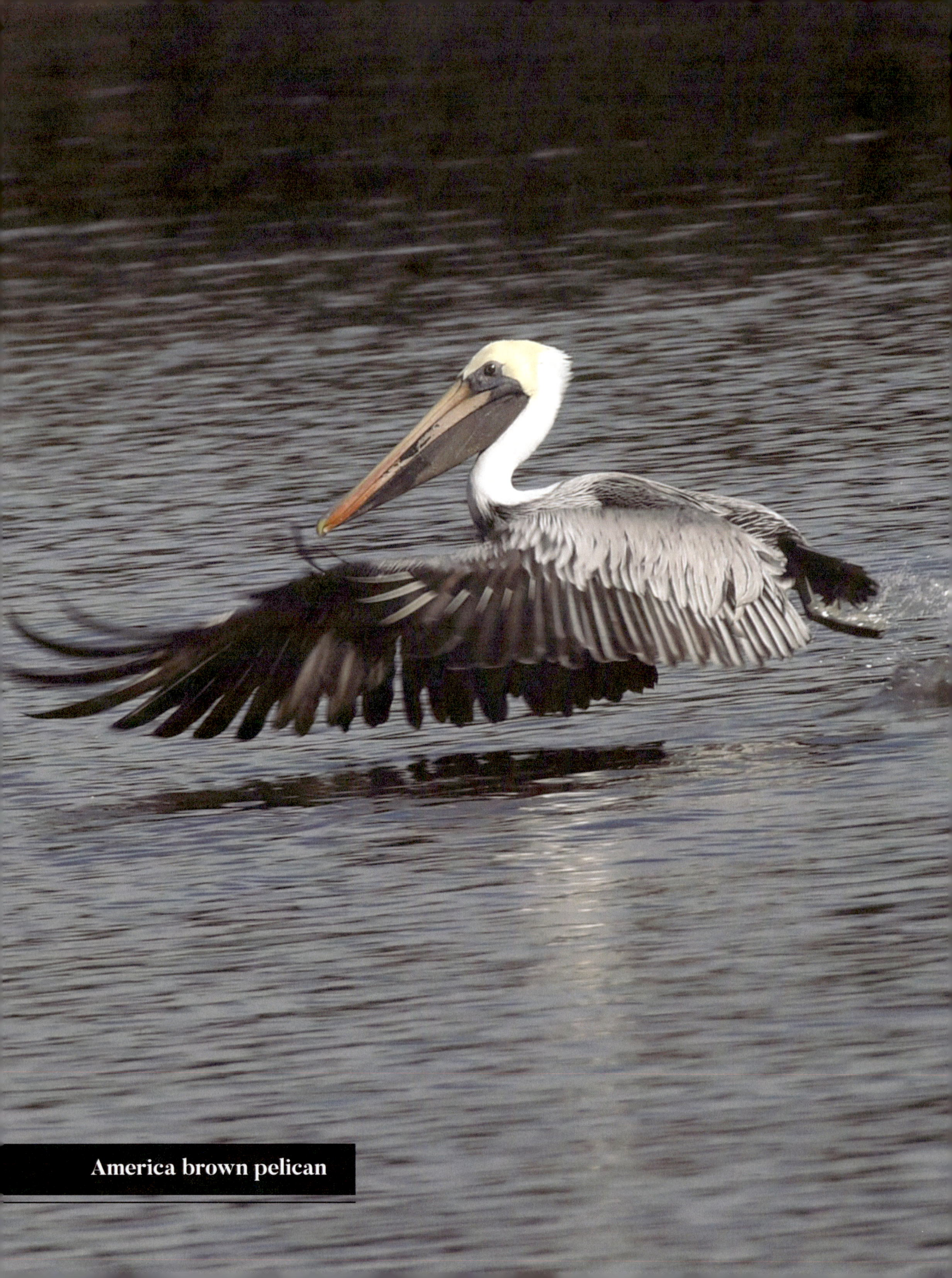

America brown pelican

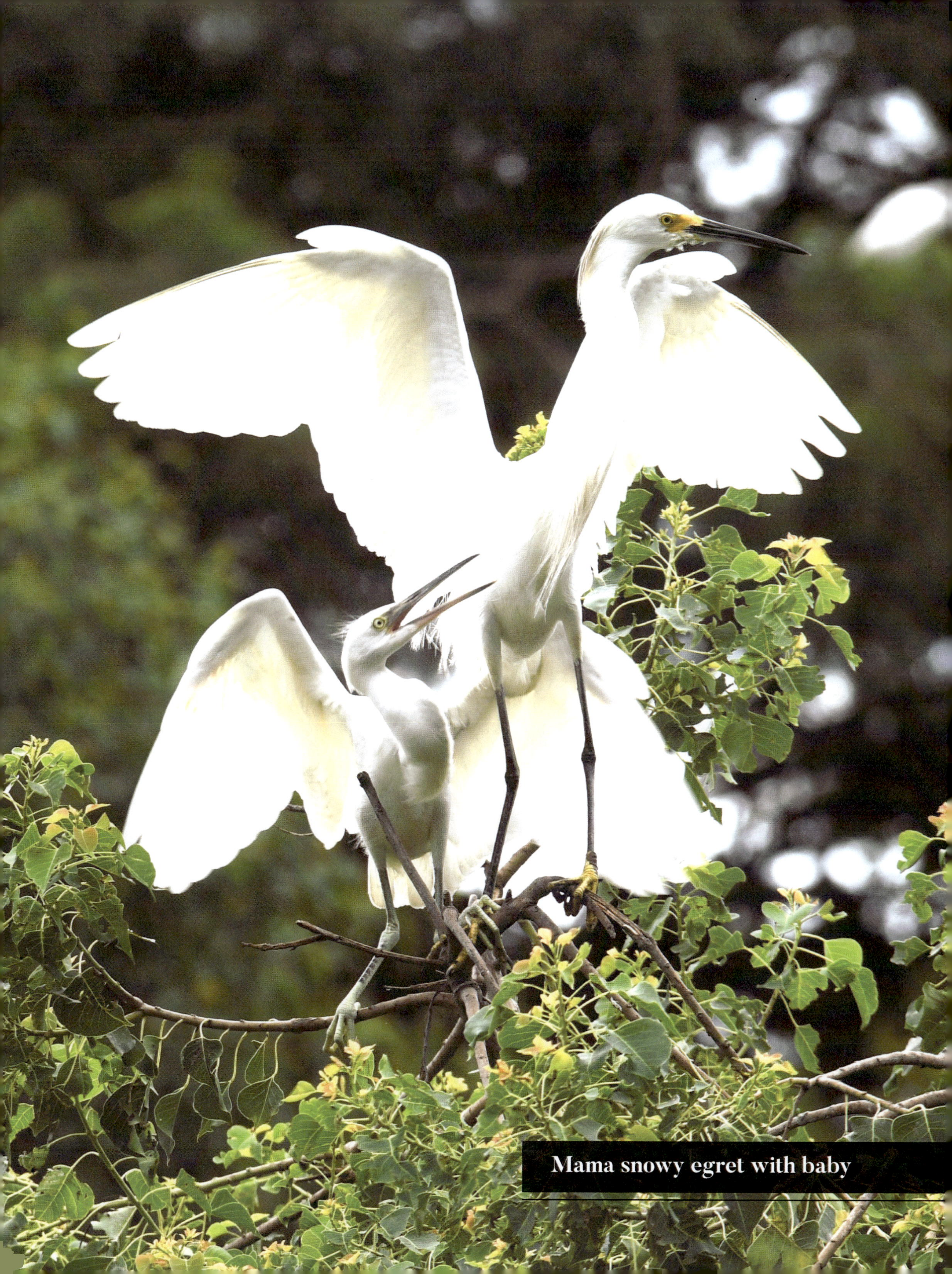

Mama snowy egret with baby

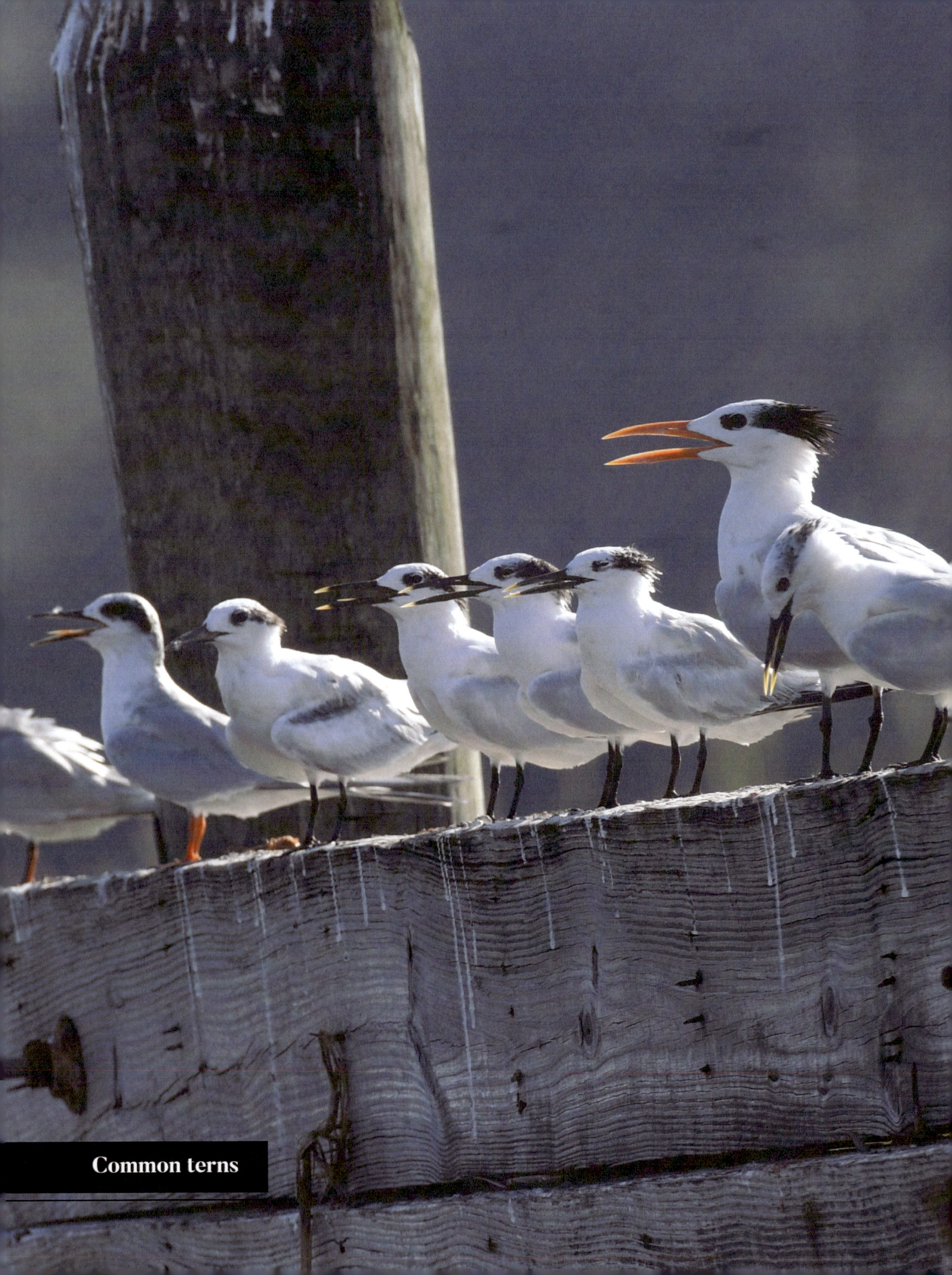
Common terns

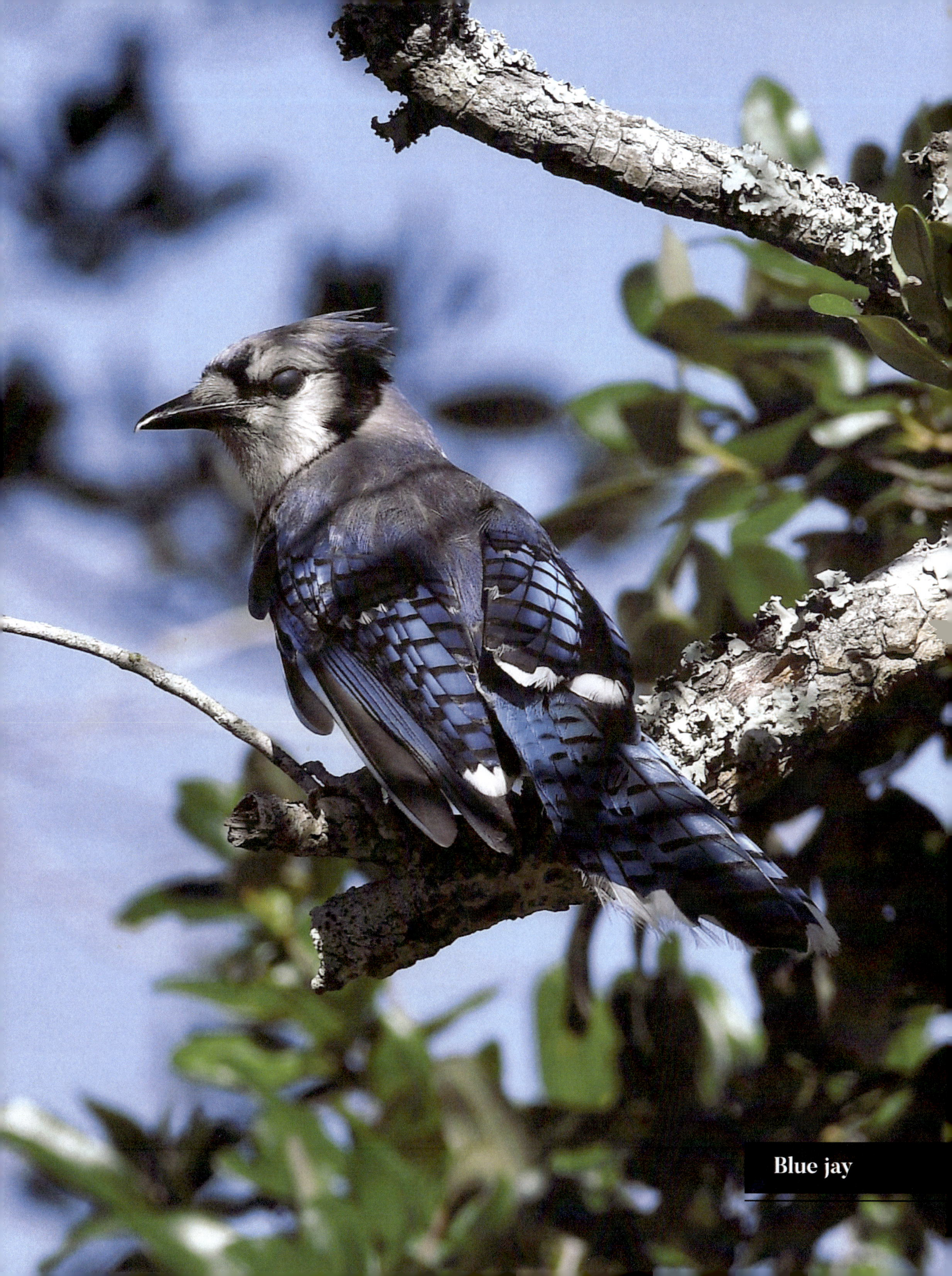

Blue jay

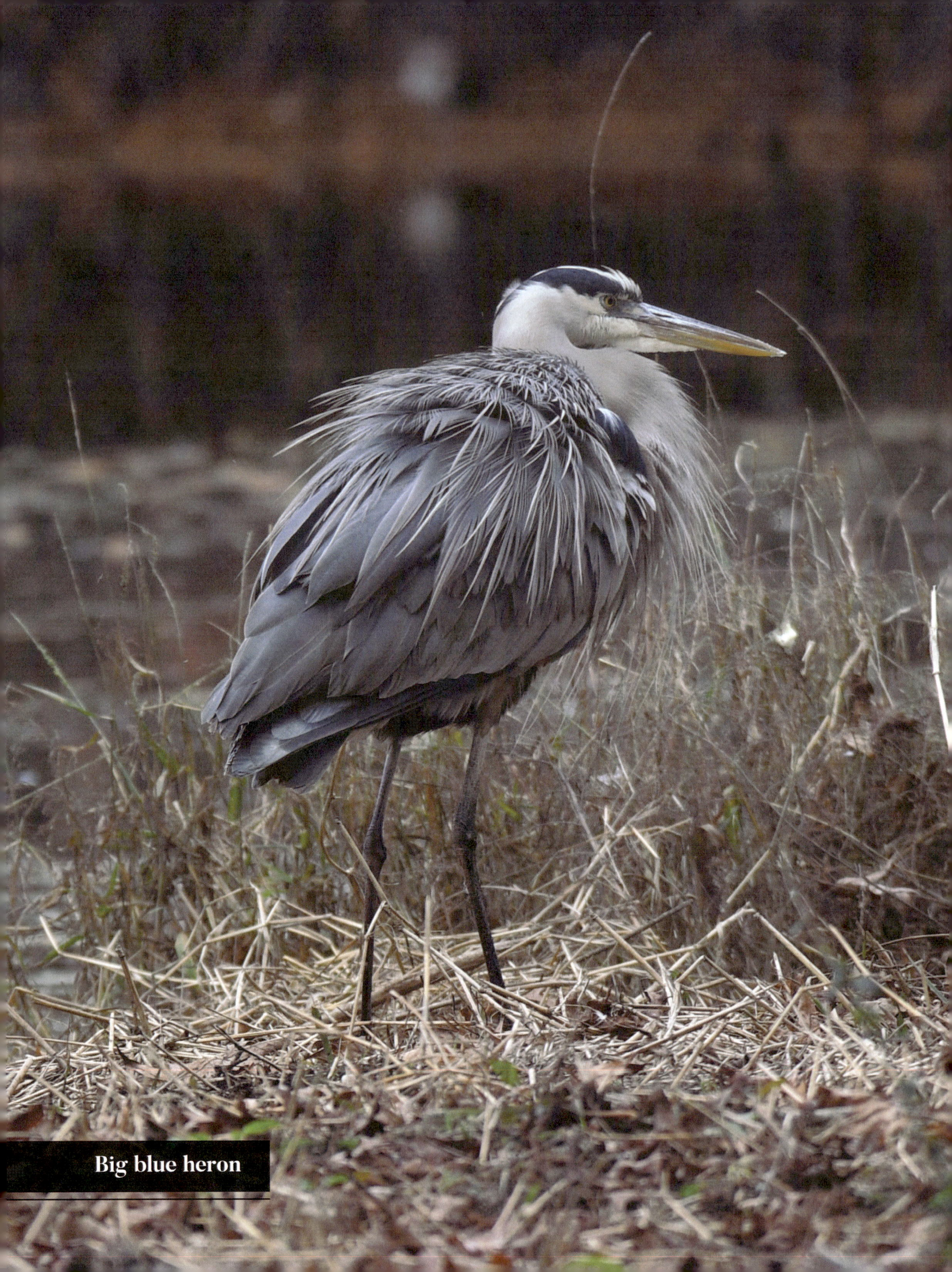

Big blue heron

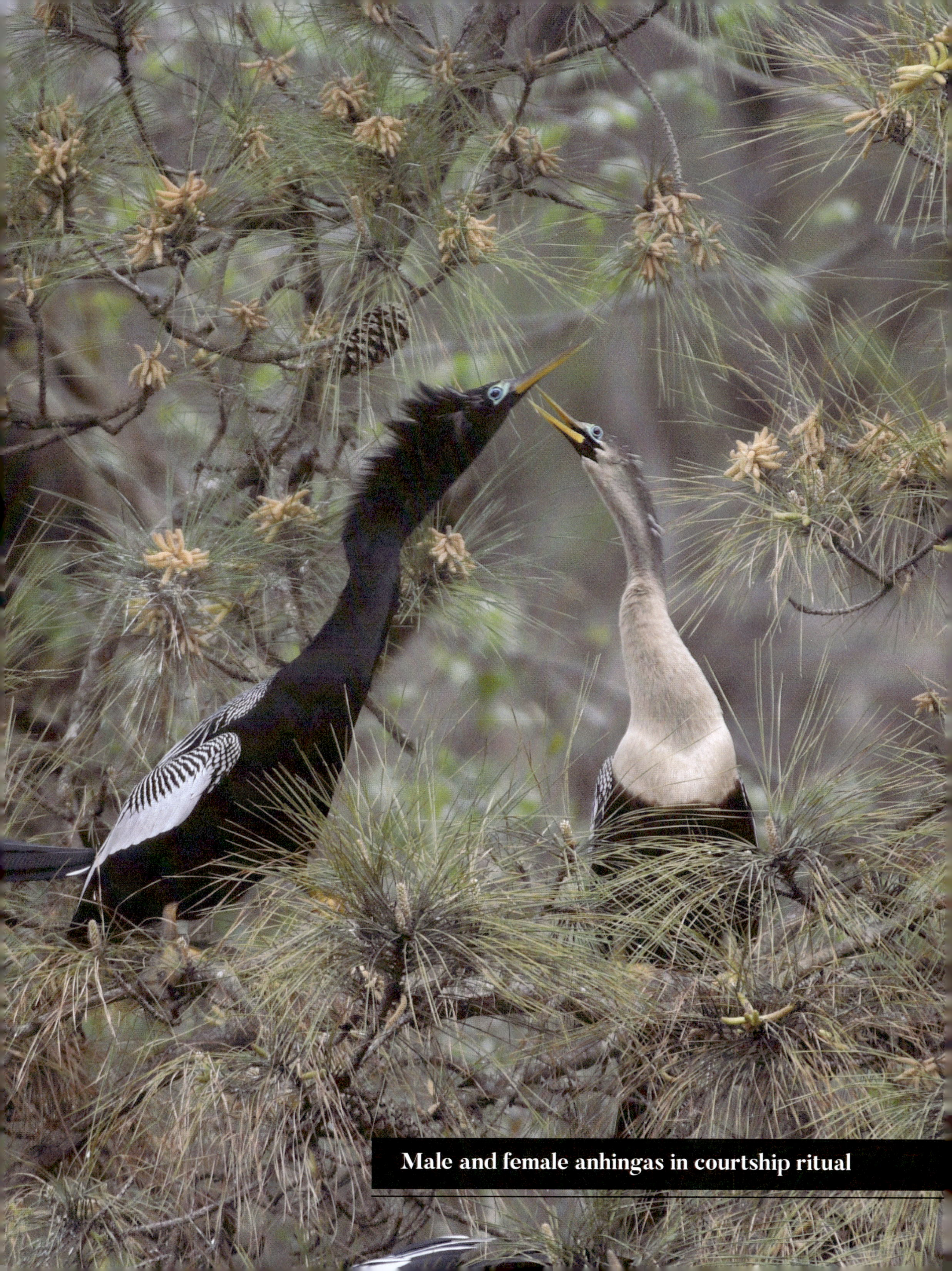

Male and female anhingas in courtship ritual

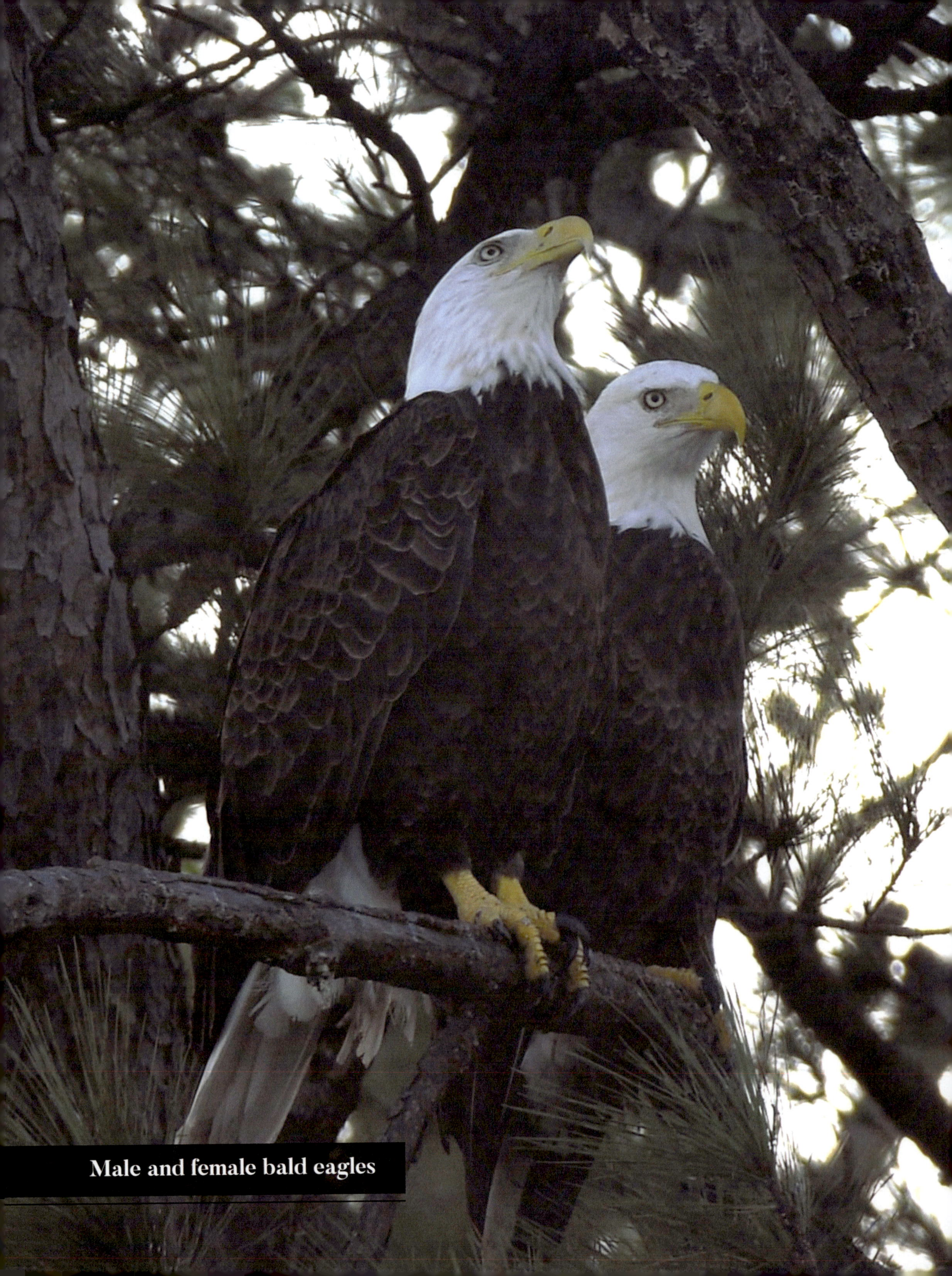

Male and female bald eagles

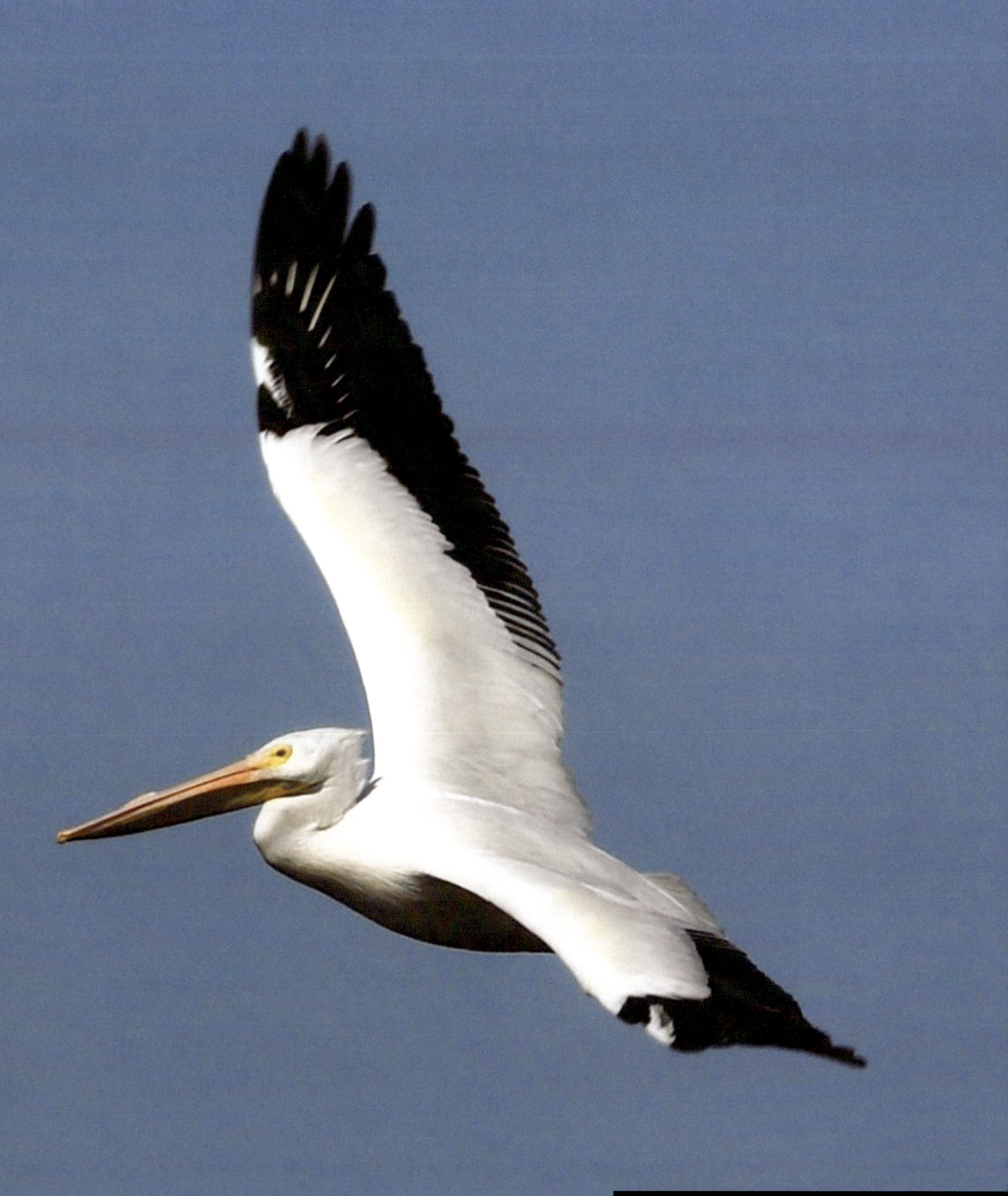
American white pelican

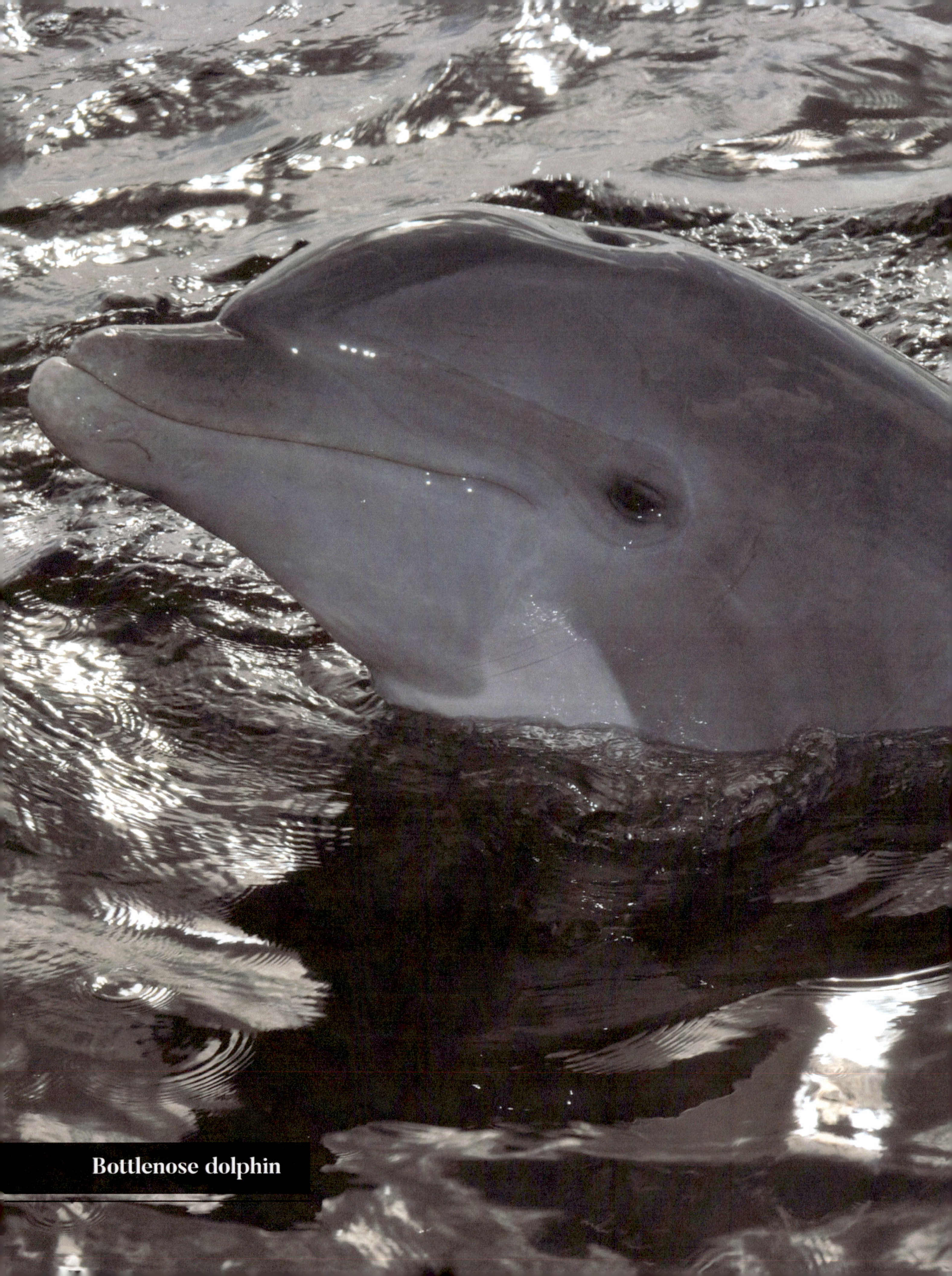

Bottlenose dolphin

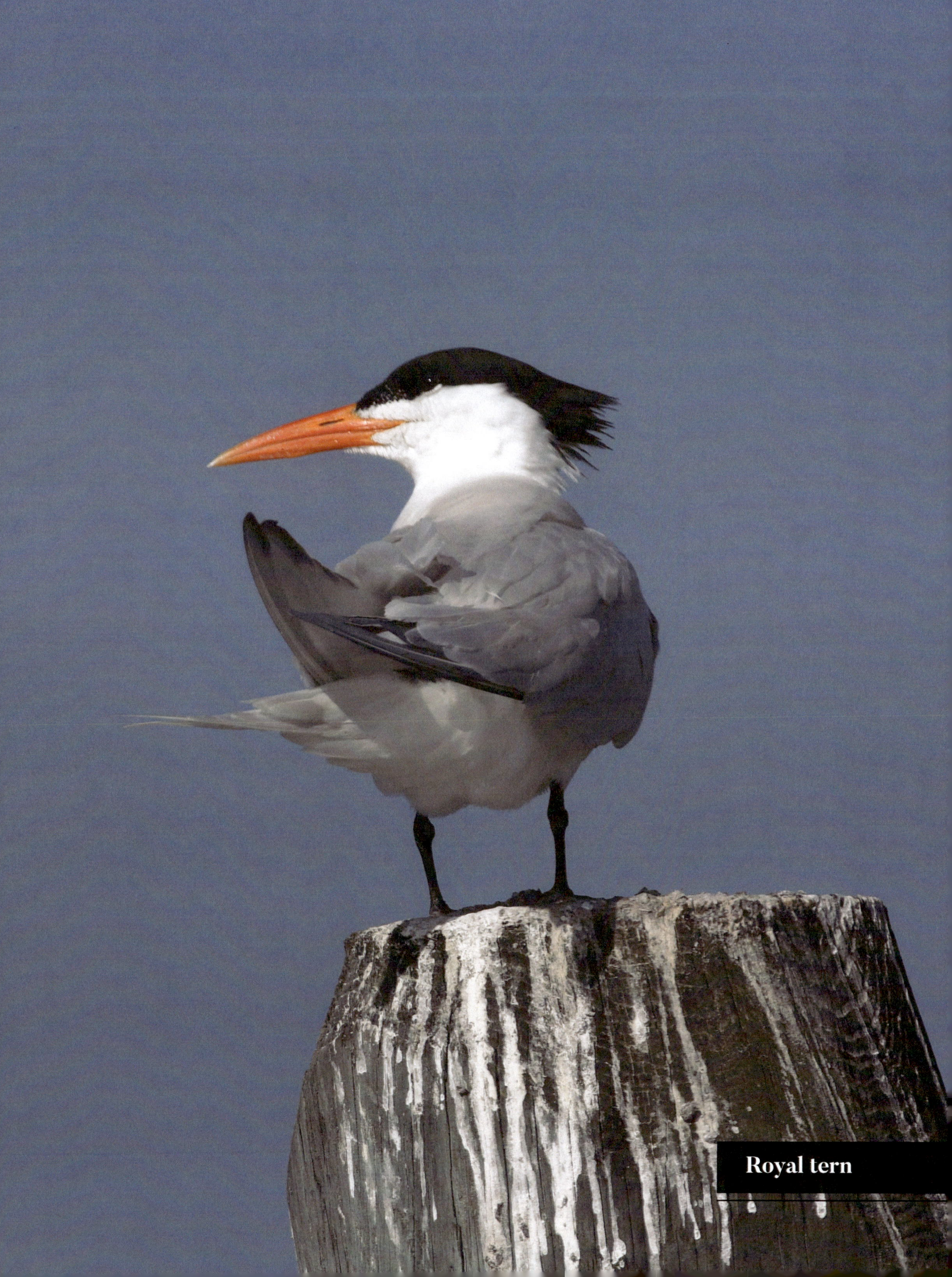

Royal tern

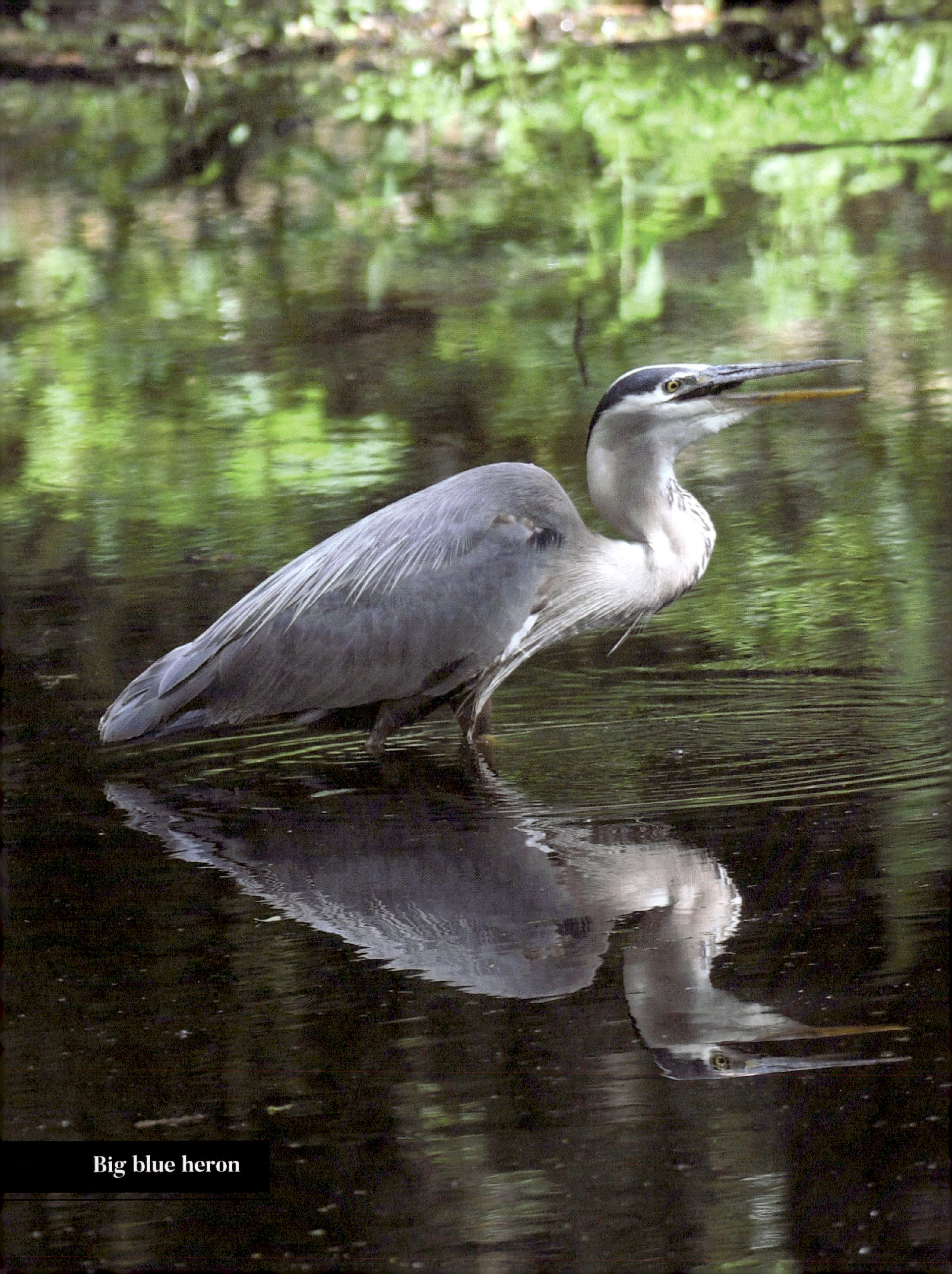

Big blue heron

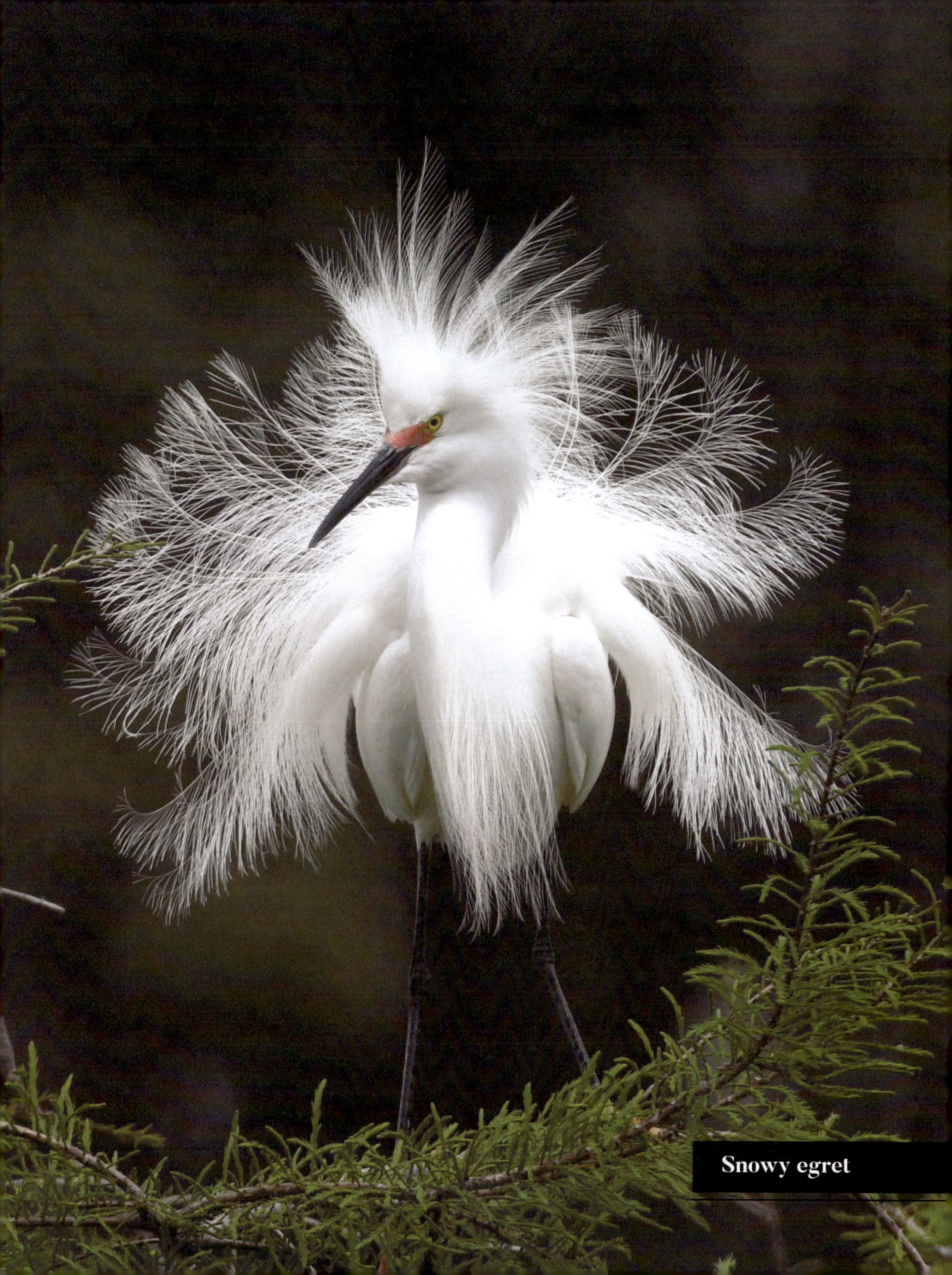

Snowy egret

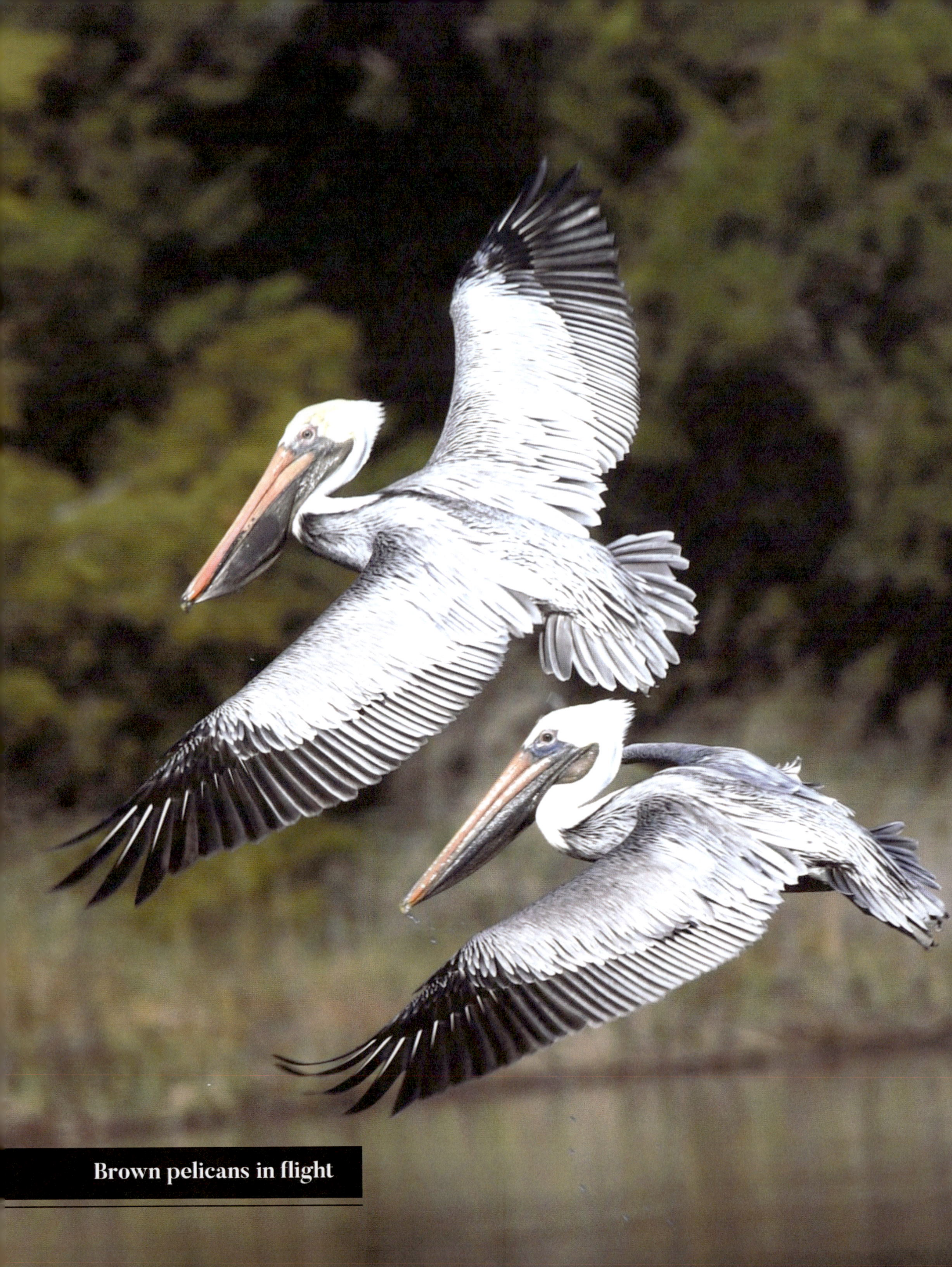

Brown pelicans in flight

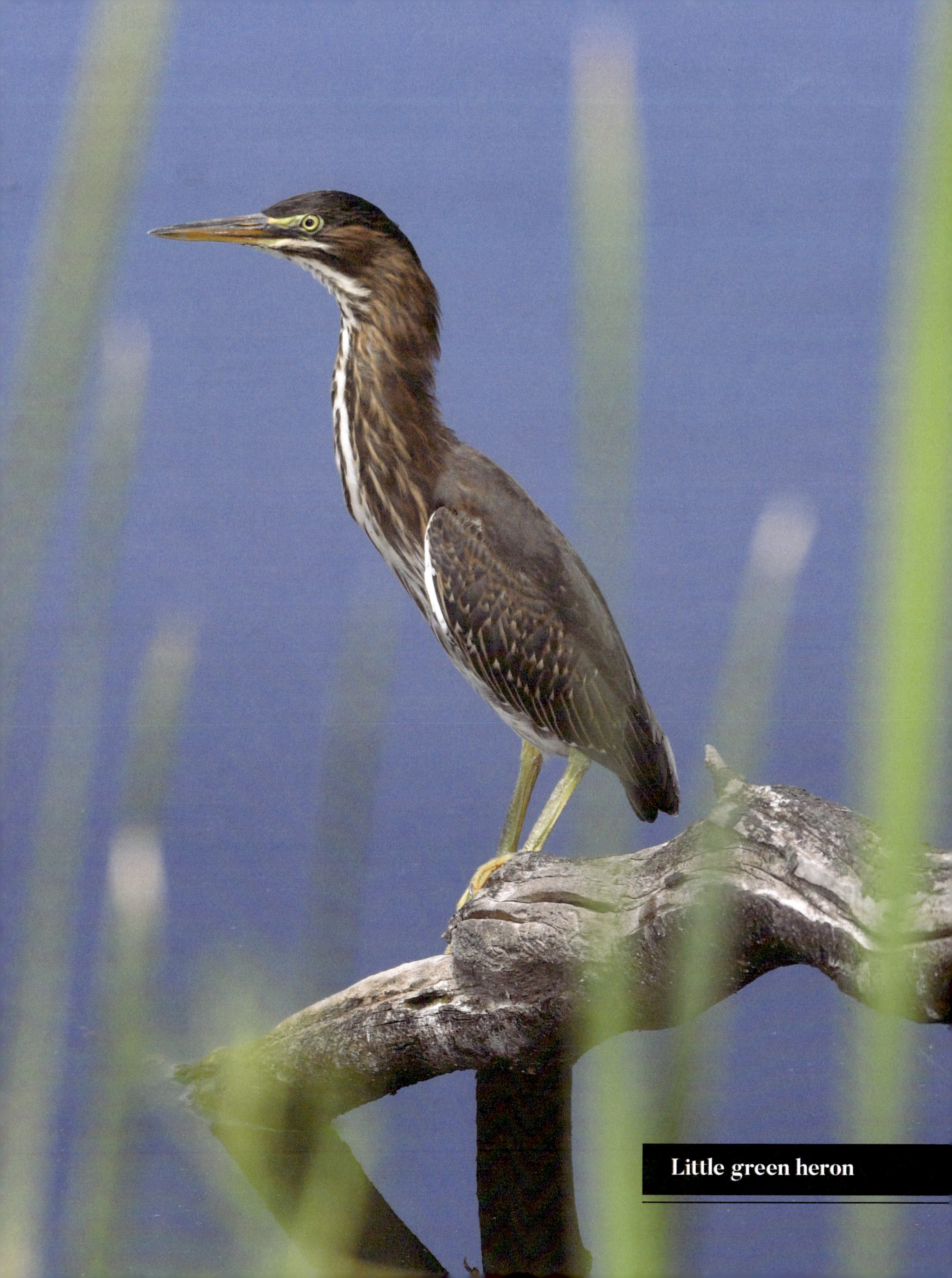

Little green heron

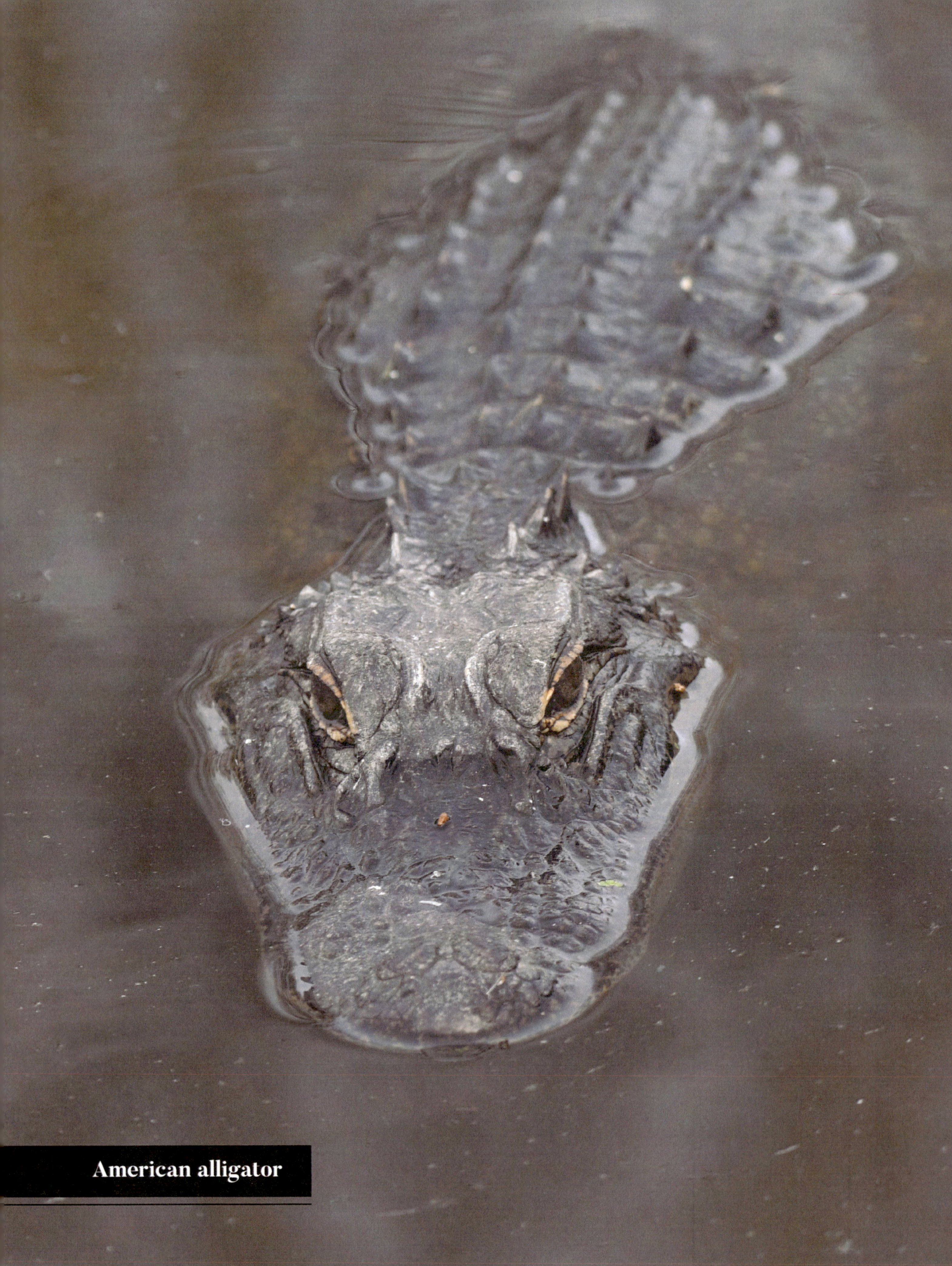

American alligator

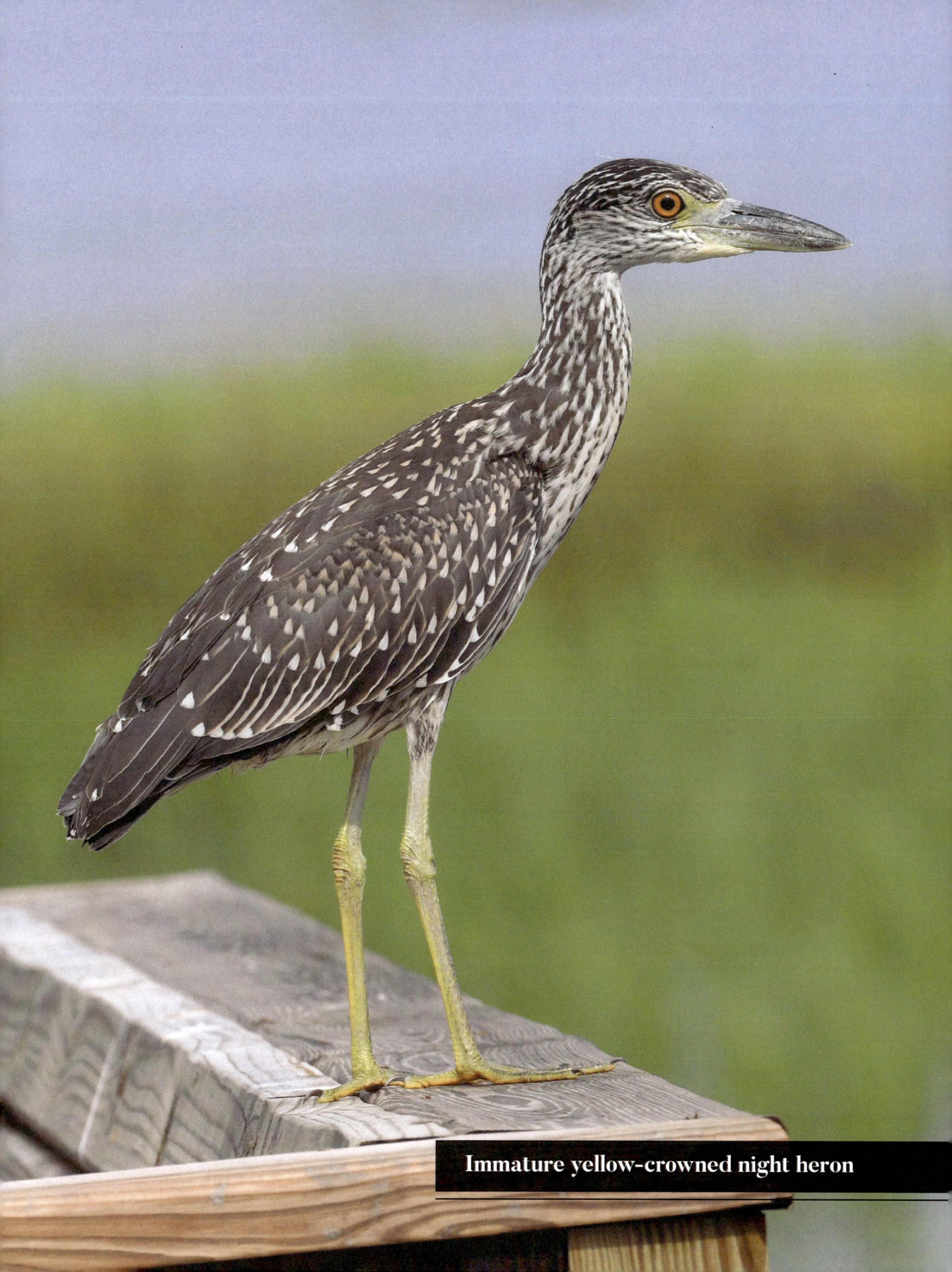

Immature yellow-crowned night heron

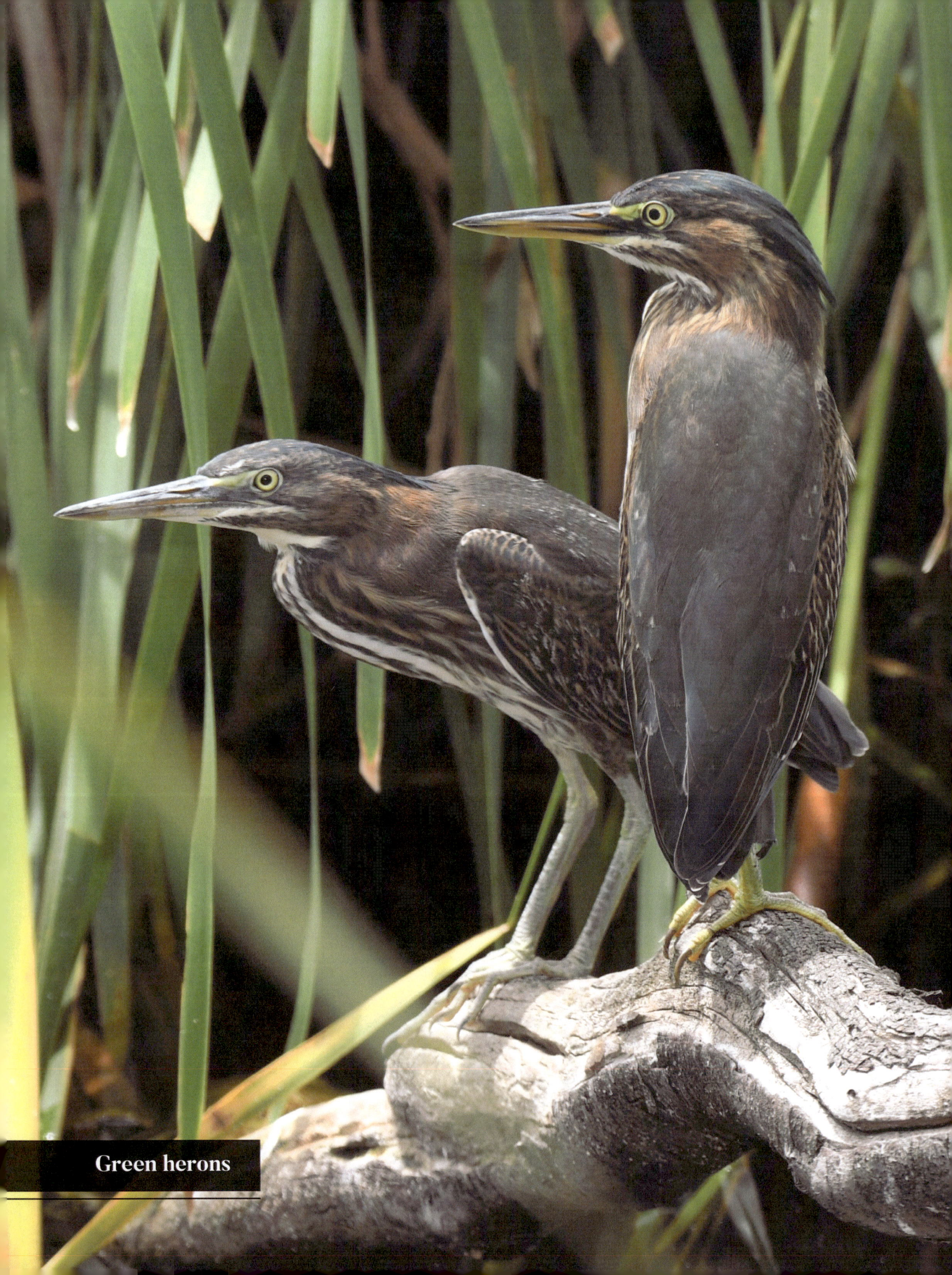

Green herons

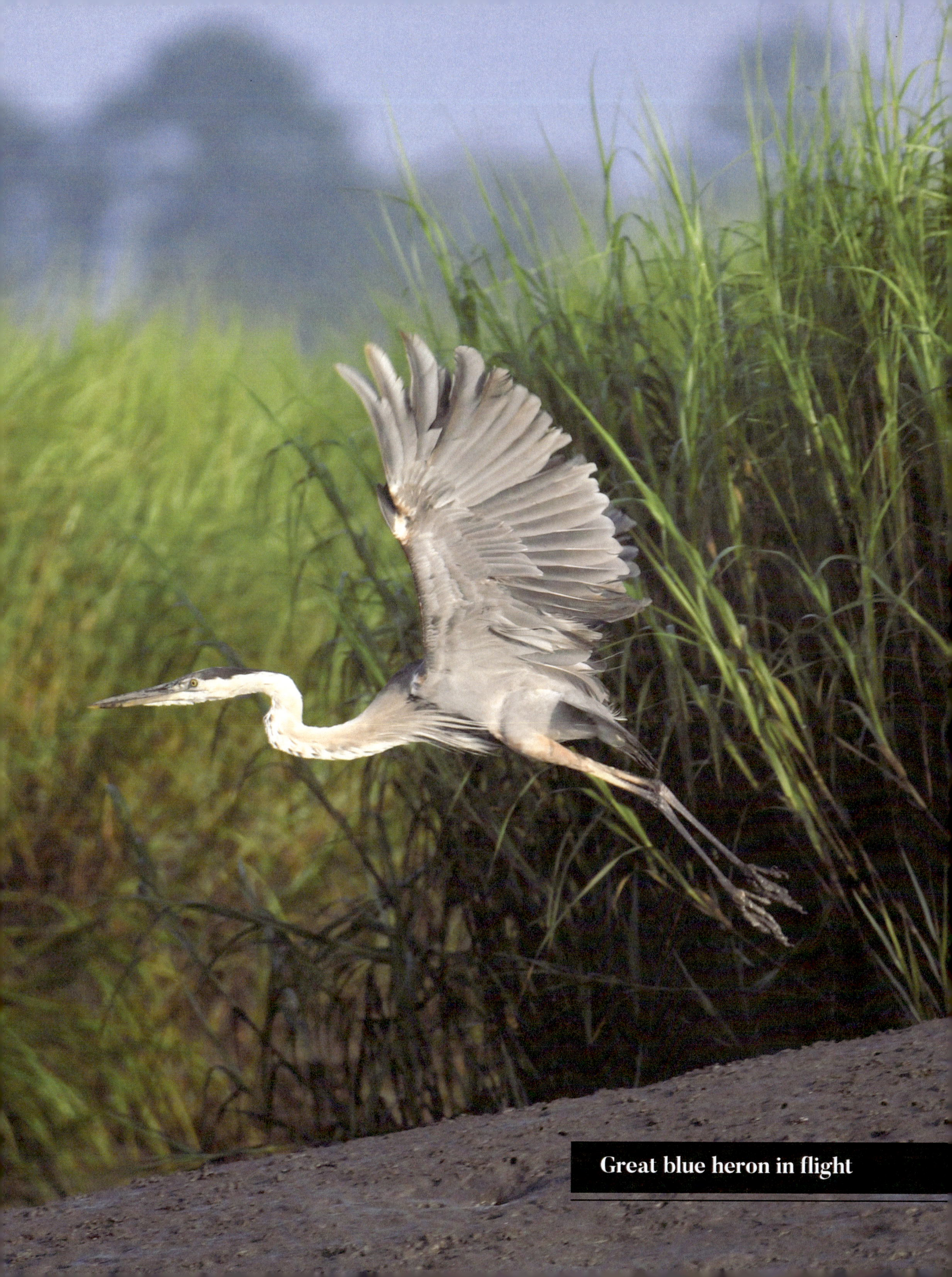

Great blue heron in flight

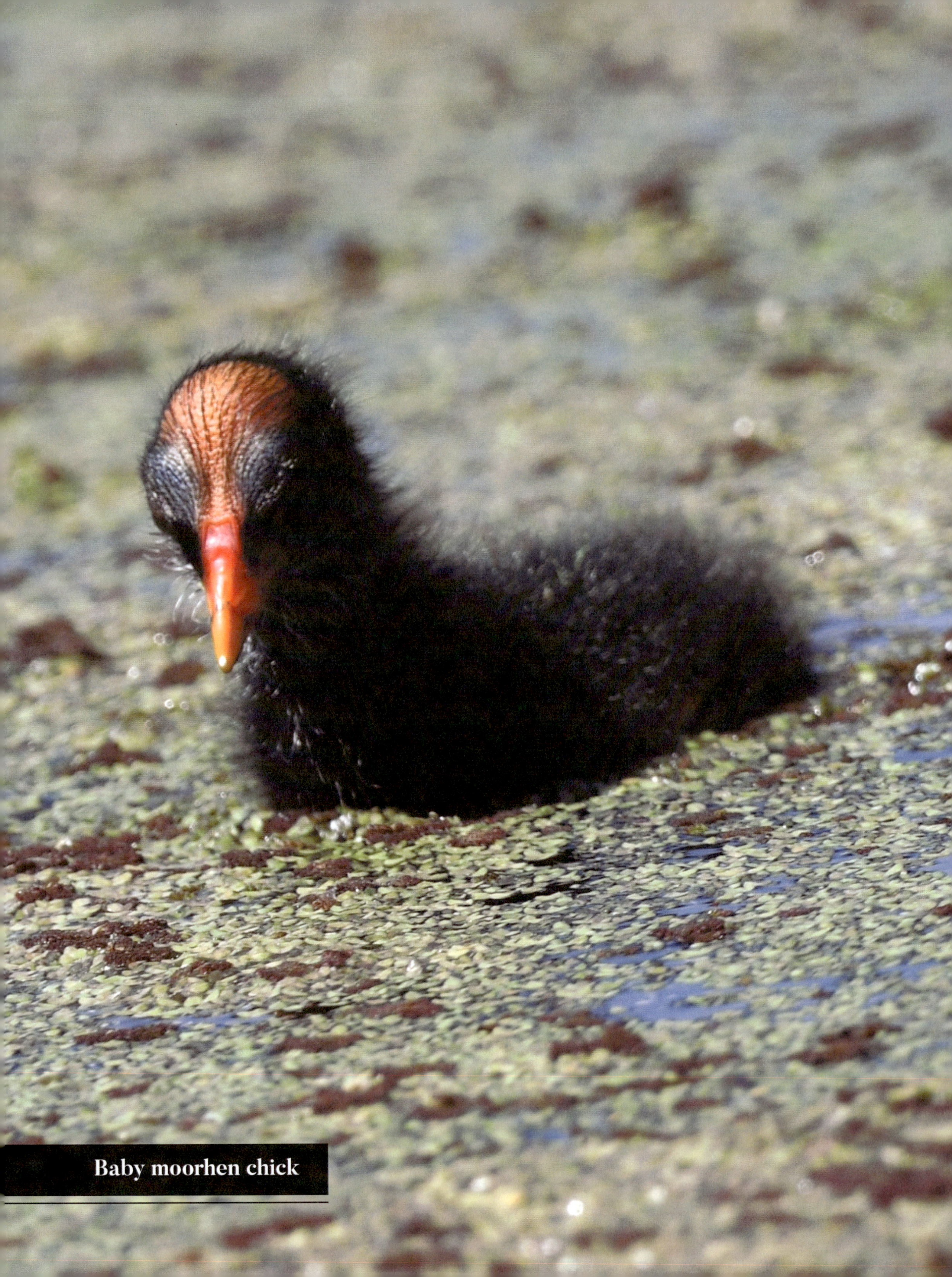

Baby moorhen chick

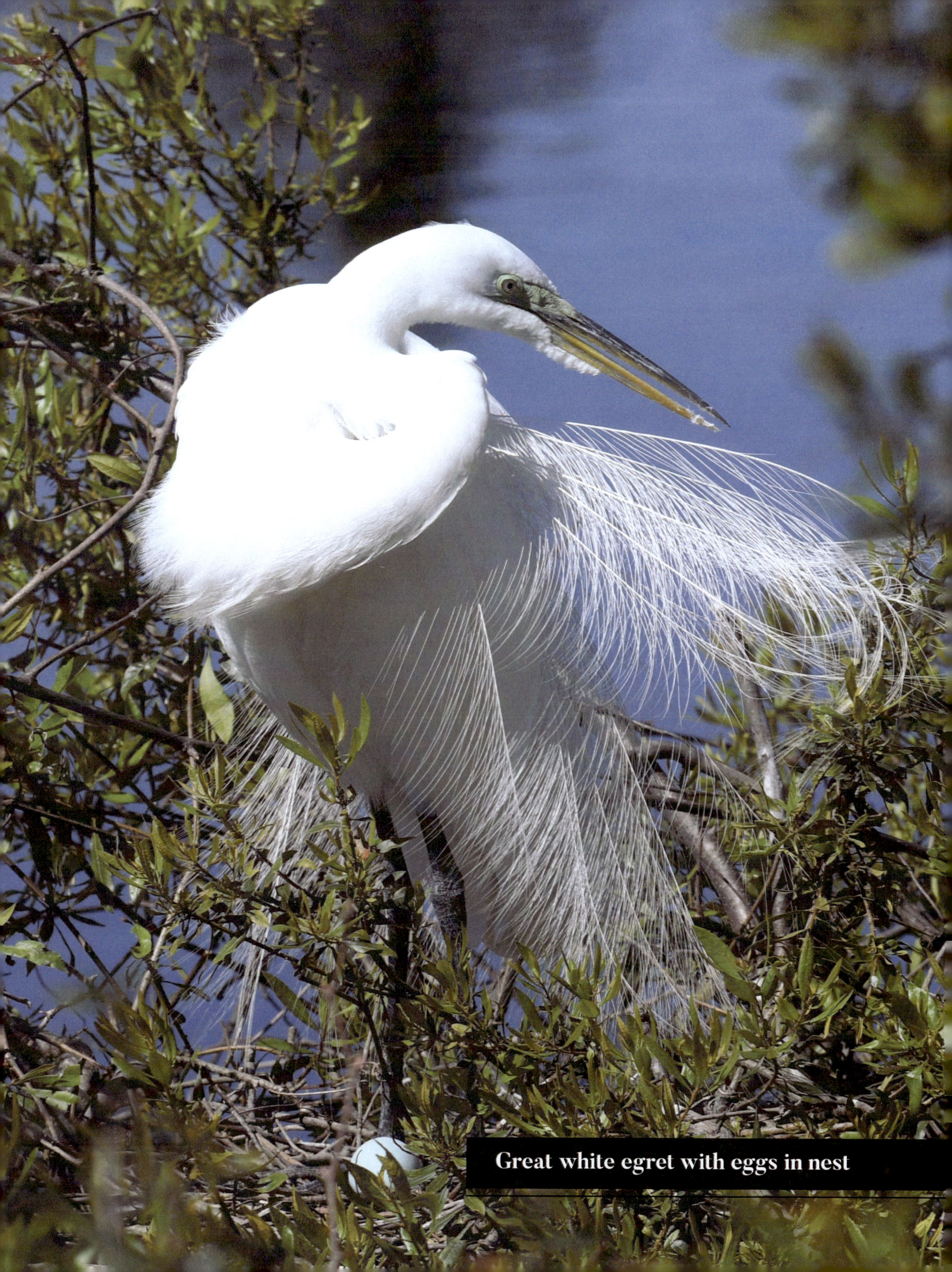

Great white egret with eggs in nest

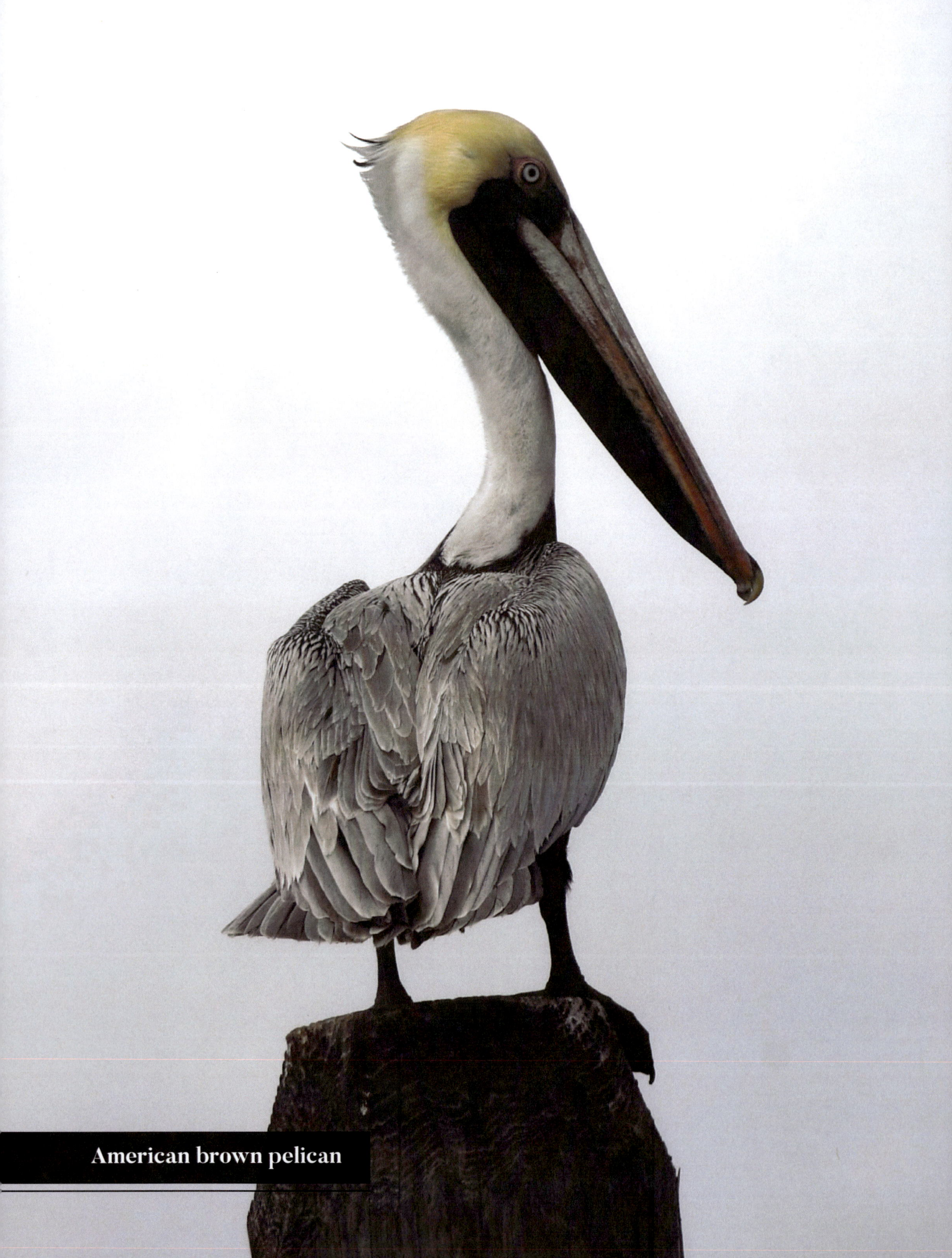

American brown pelican

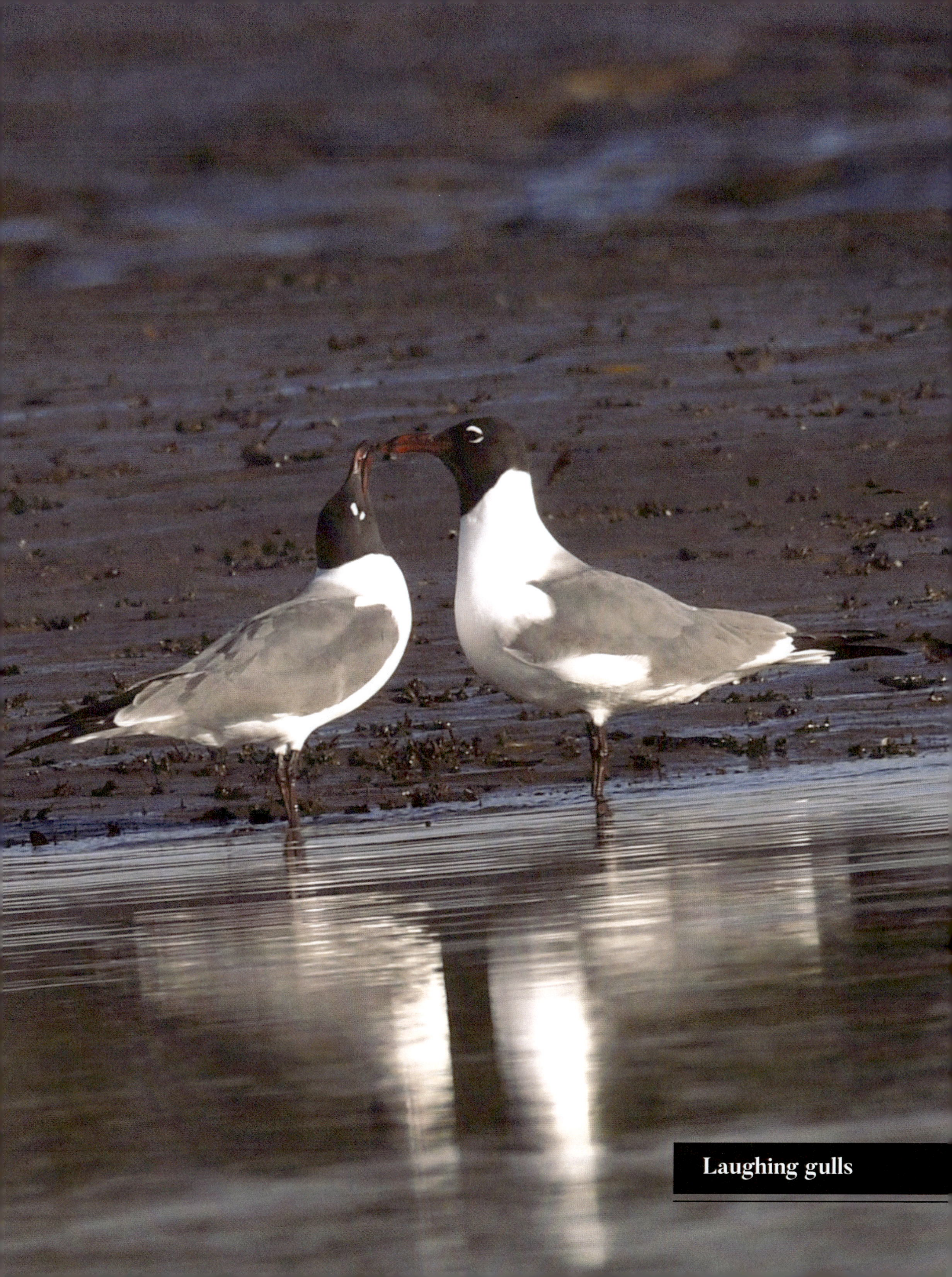

Laughing gulls

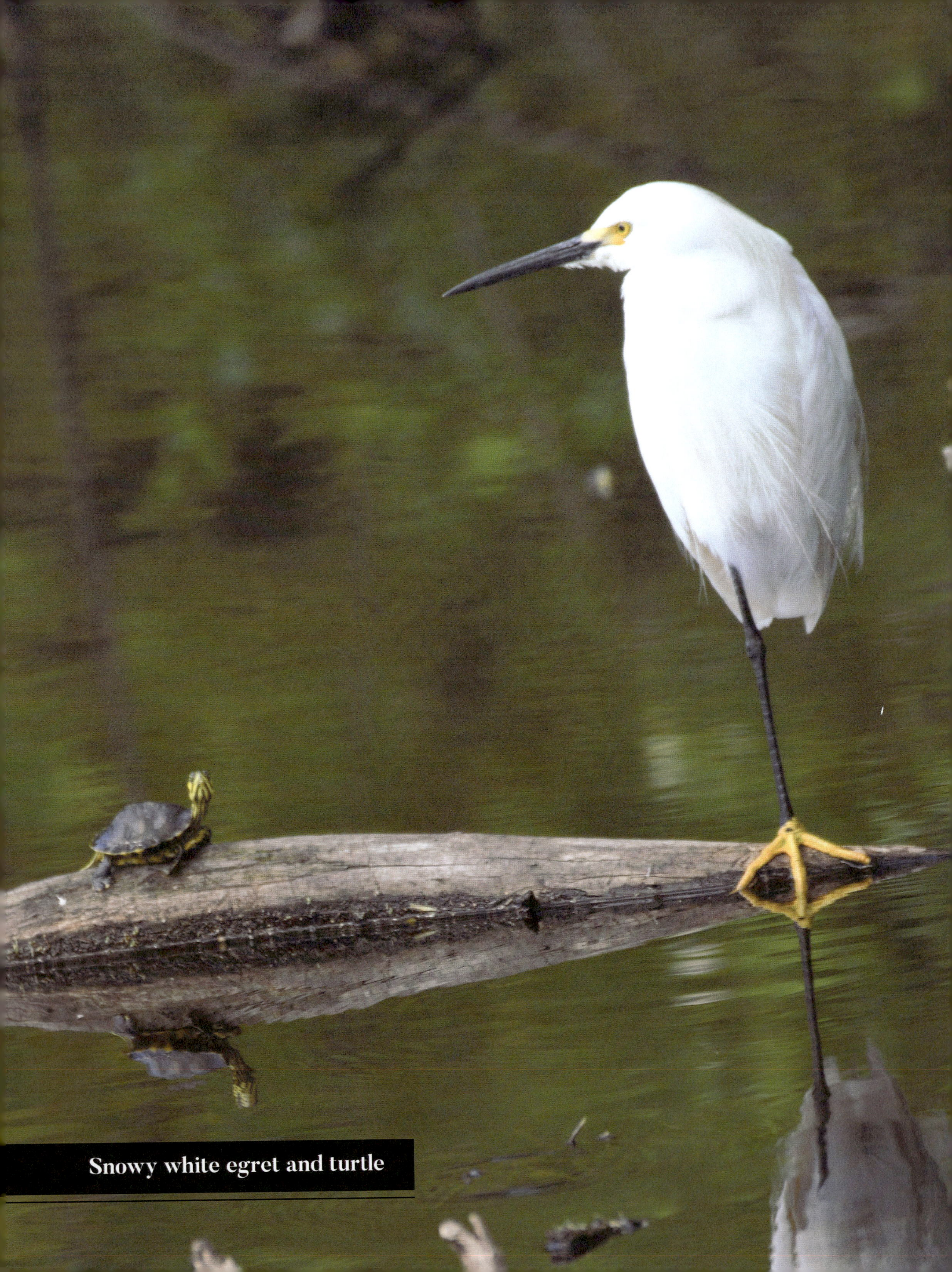

Snowy white egret and turtle

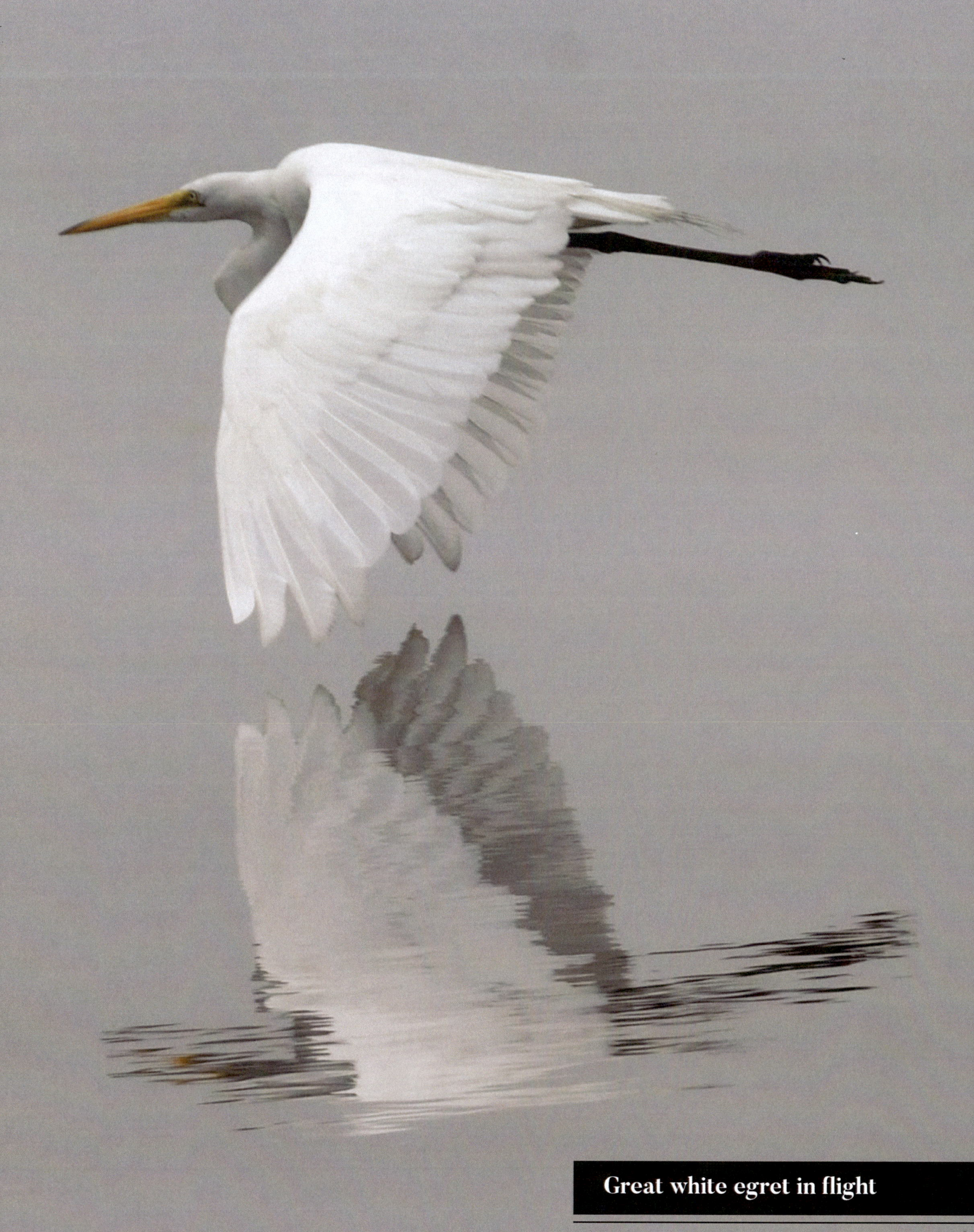

Great white egret in flight

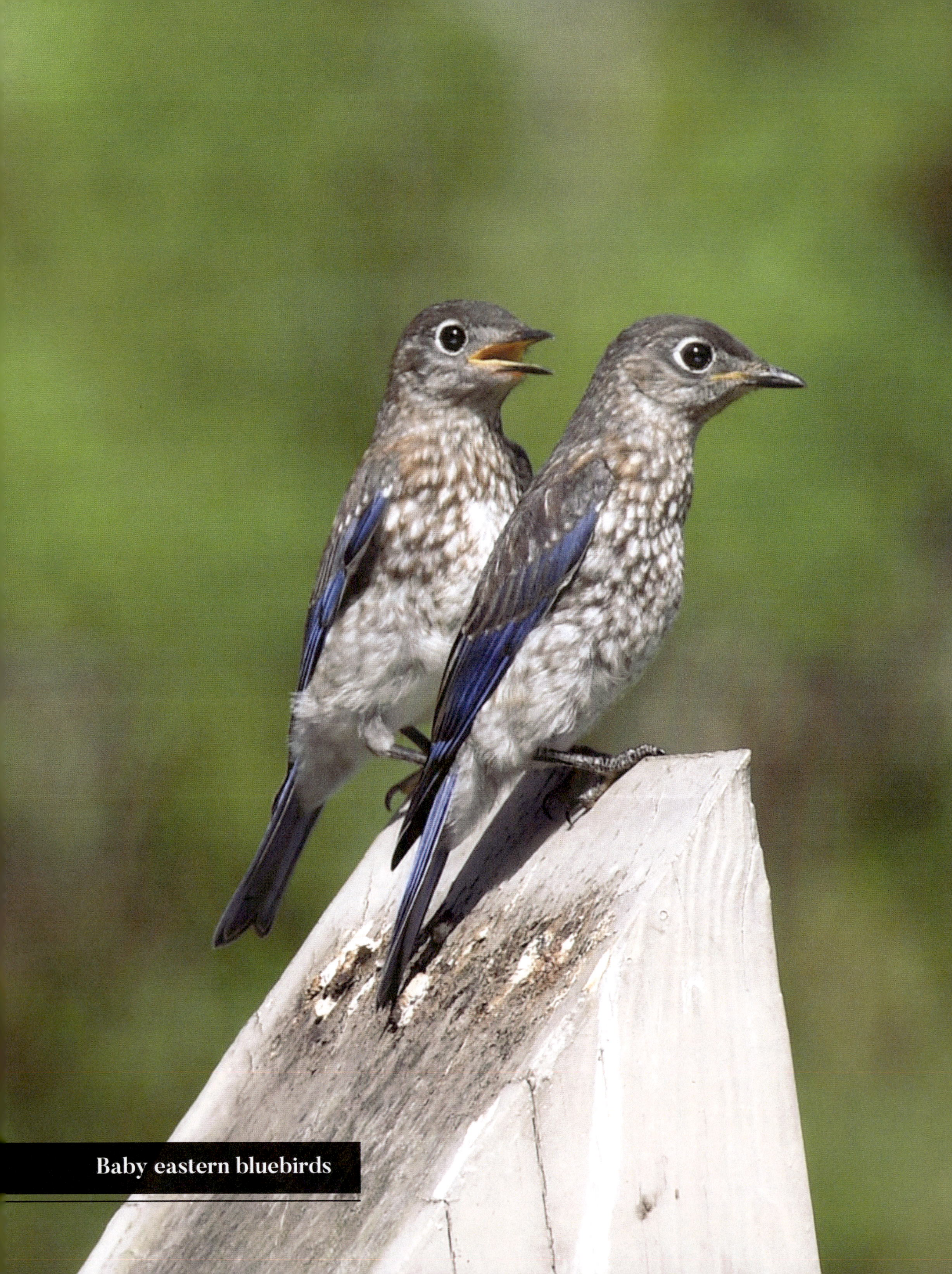

Baby eastern bluebirds

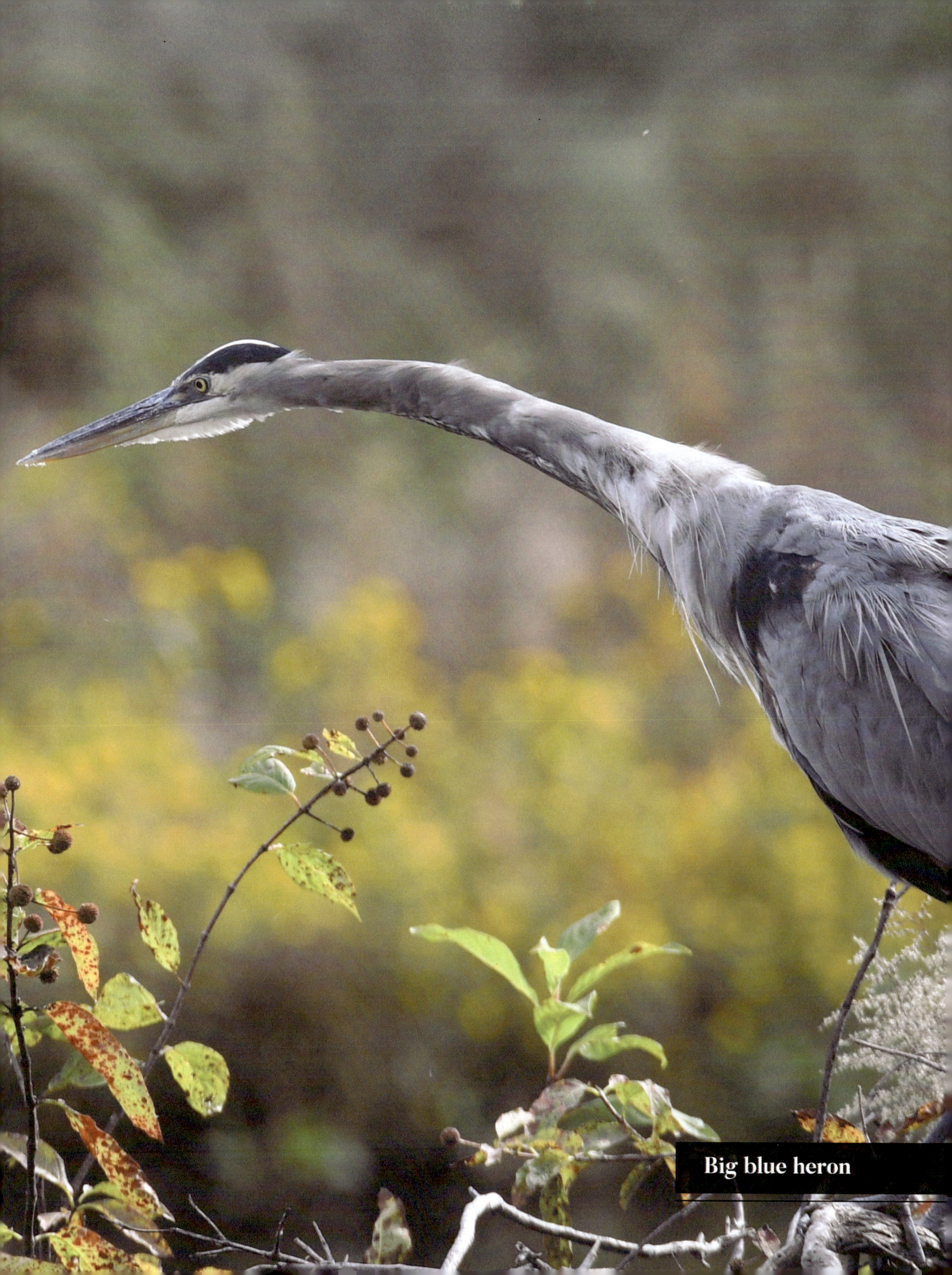
Big blue heron

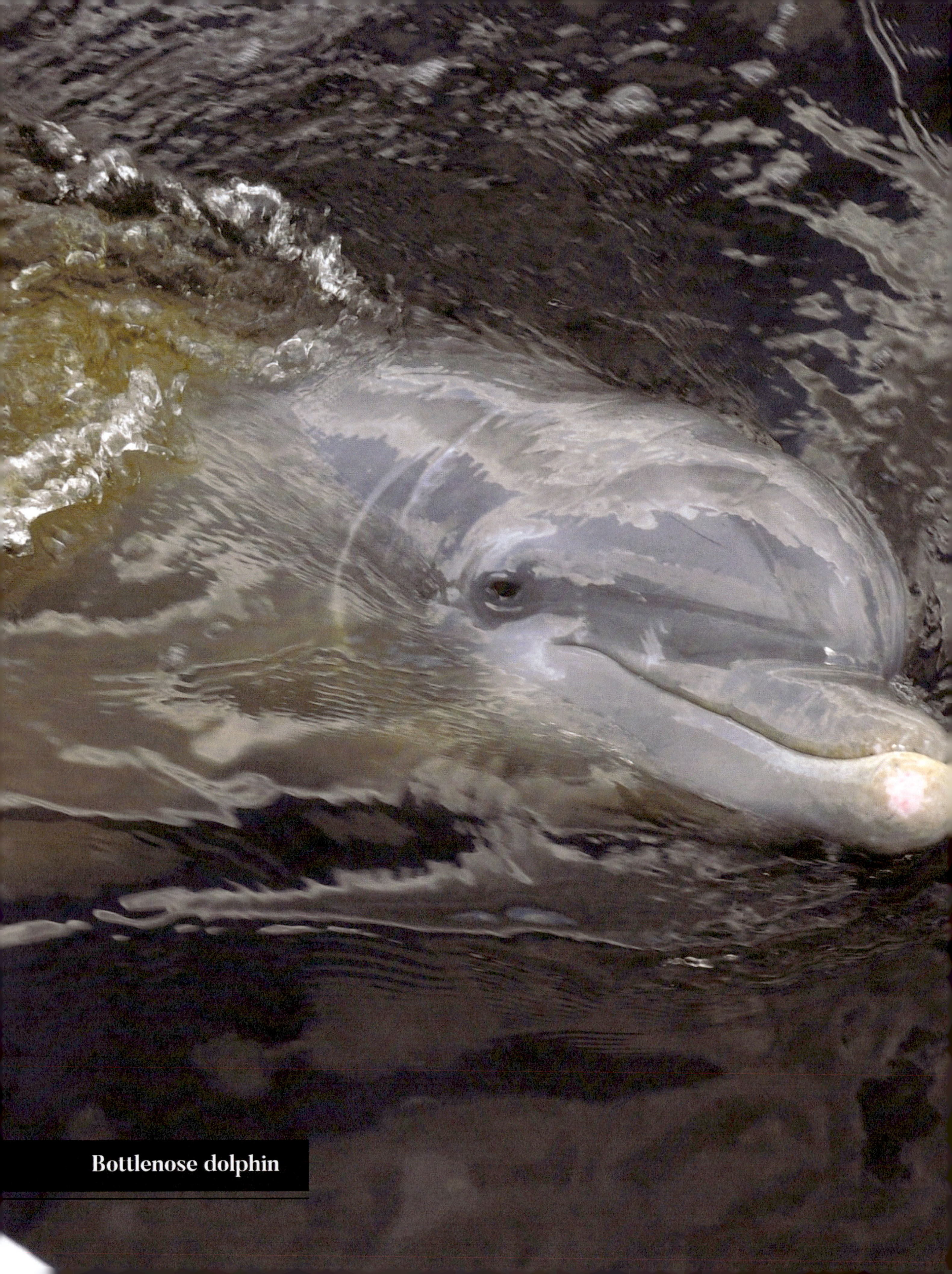

Bottlenose dolphin

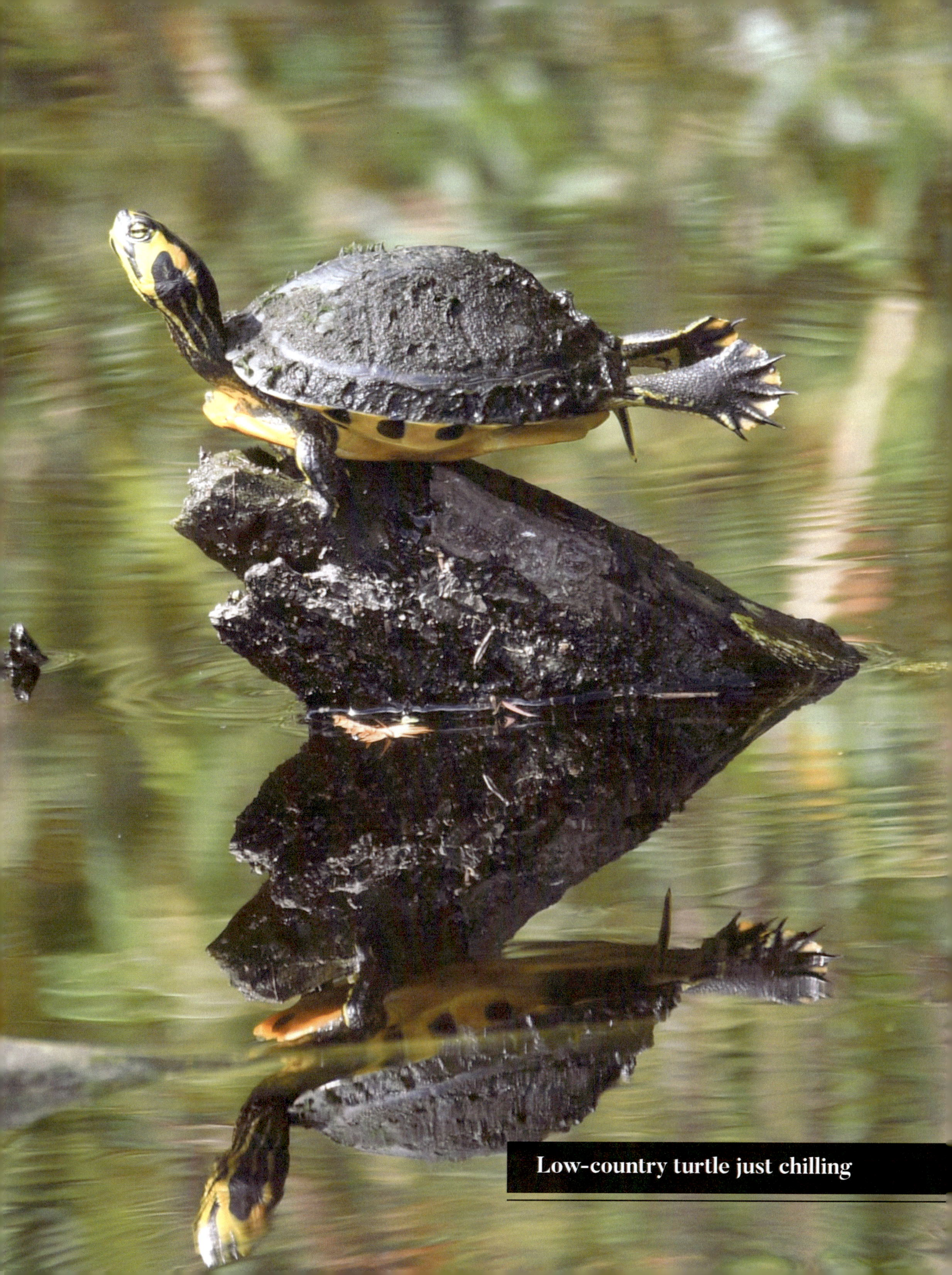

Low-country turtle just chilling

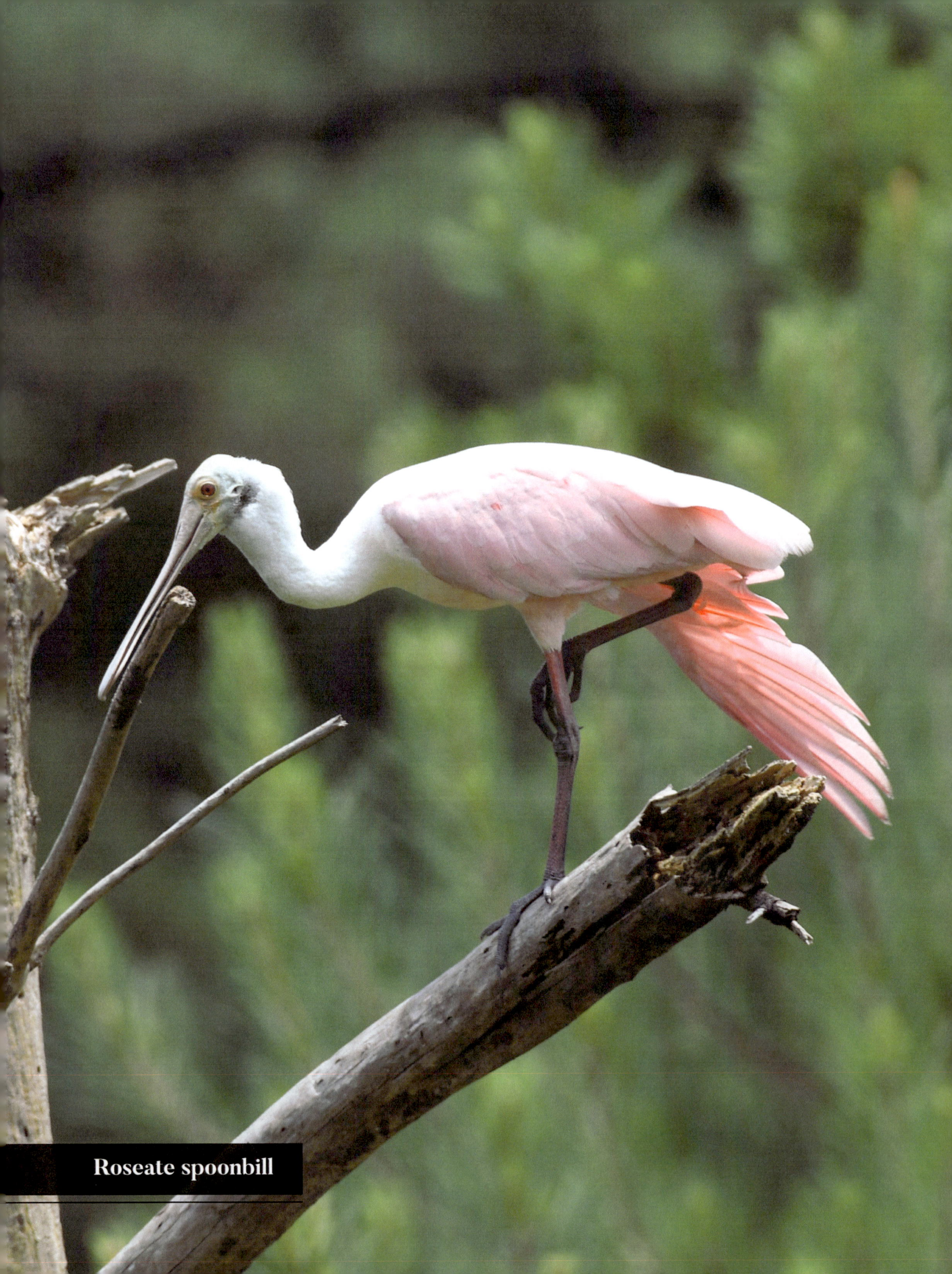

Roseate spoonbill

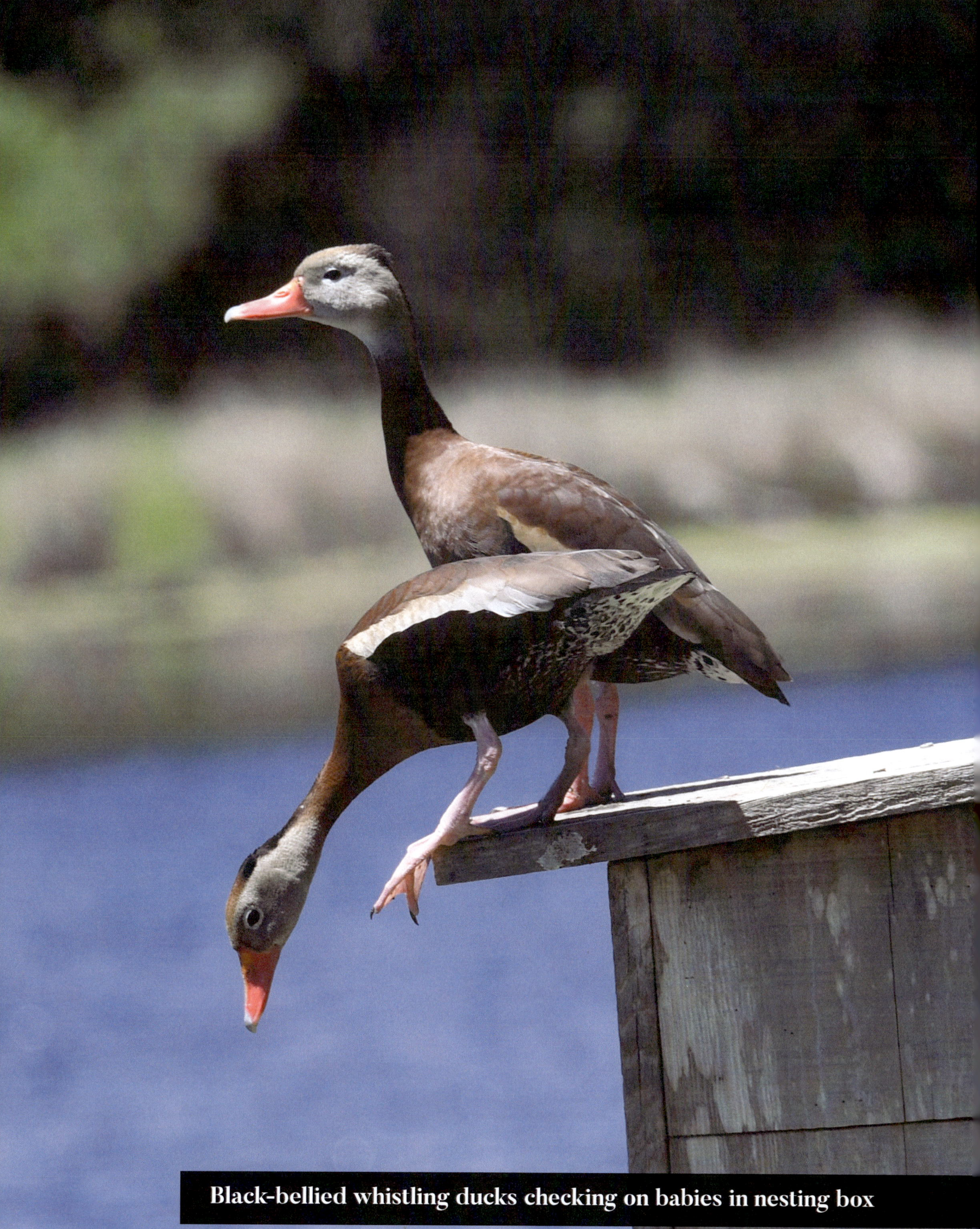

Black-bellied whistling ducks checking on babies in nesting box

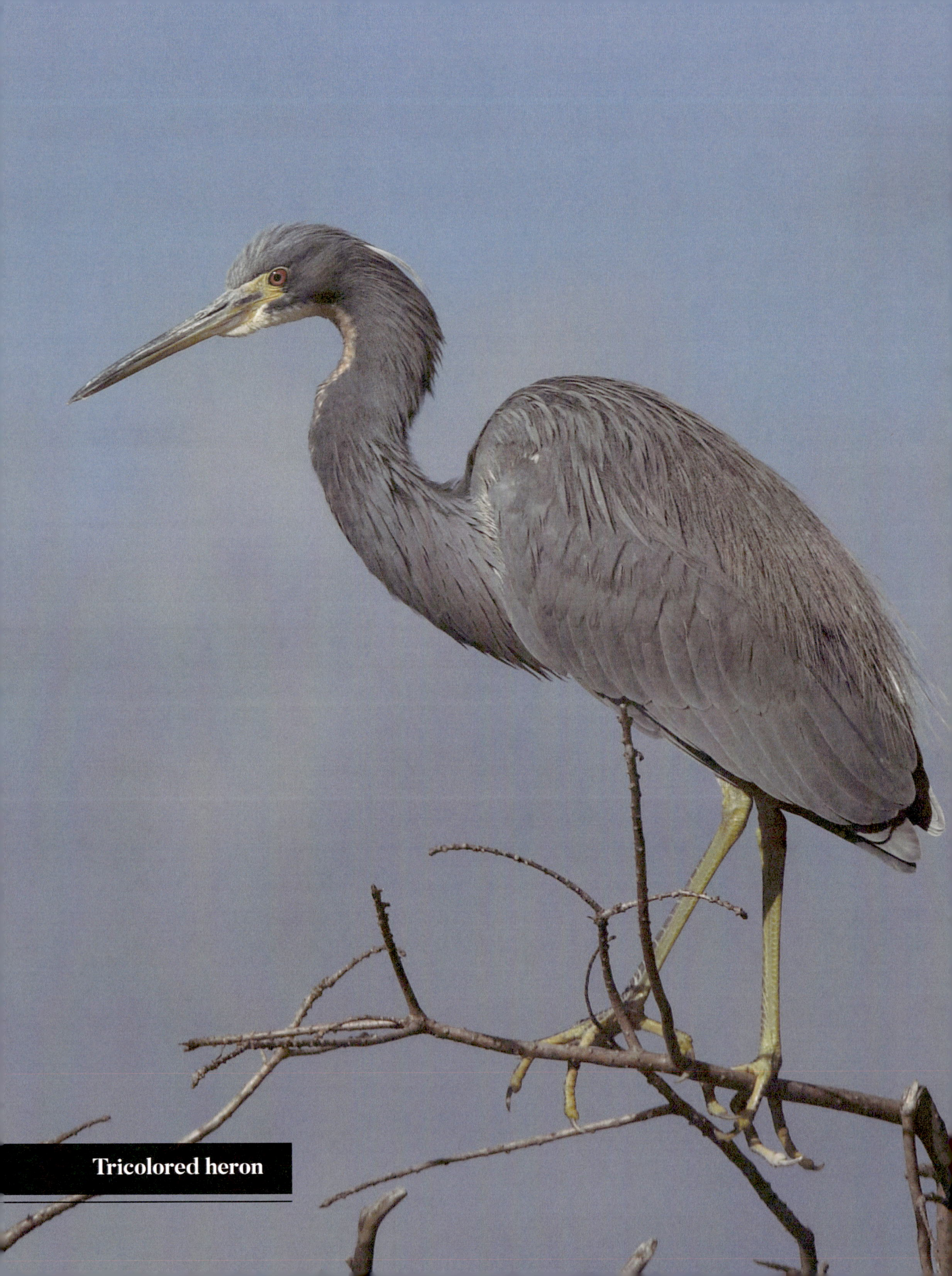

Tricolored heron

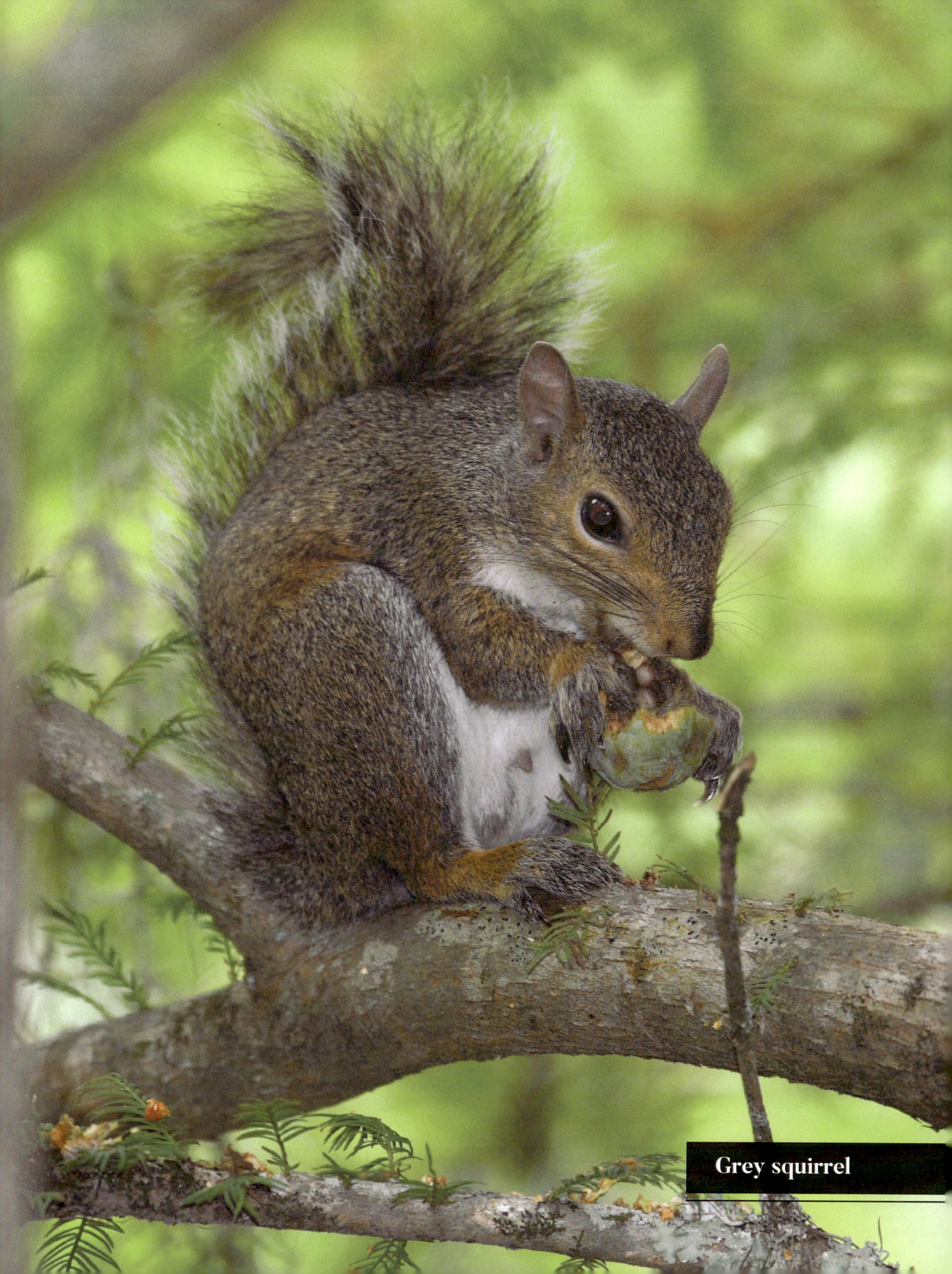
Grey squirrel

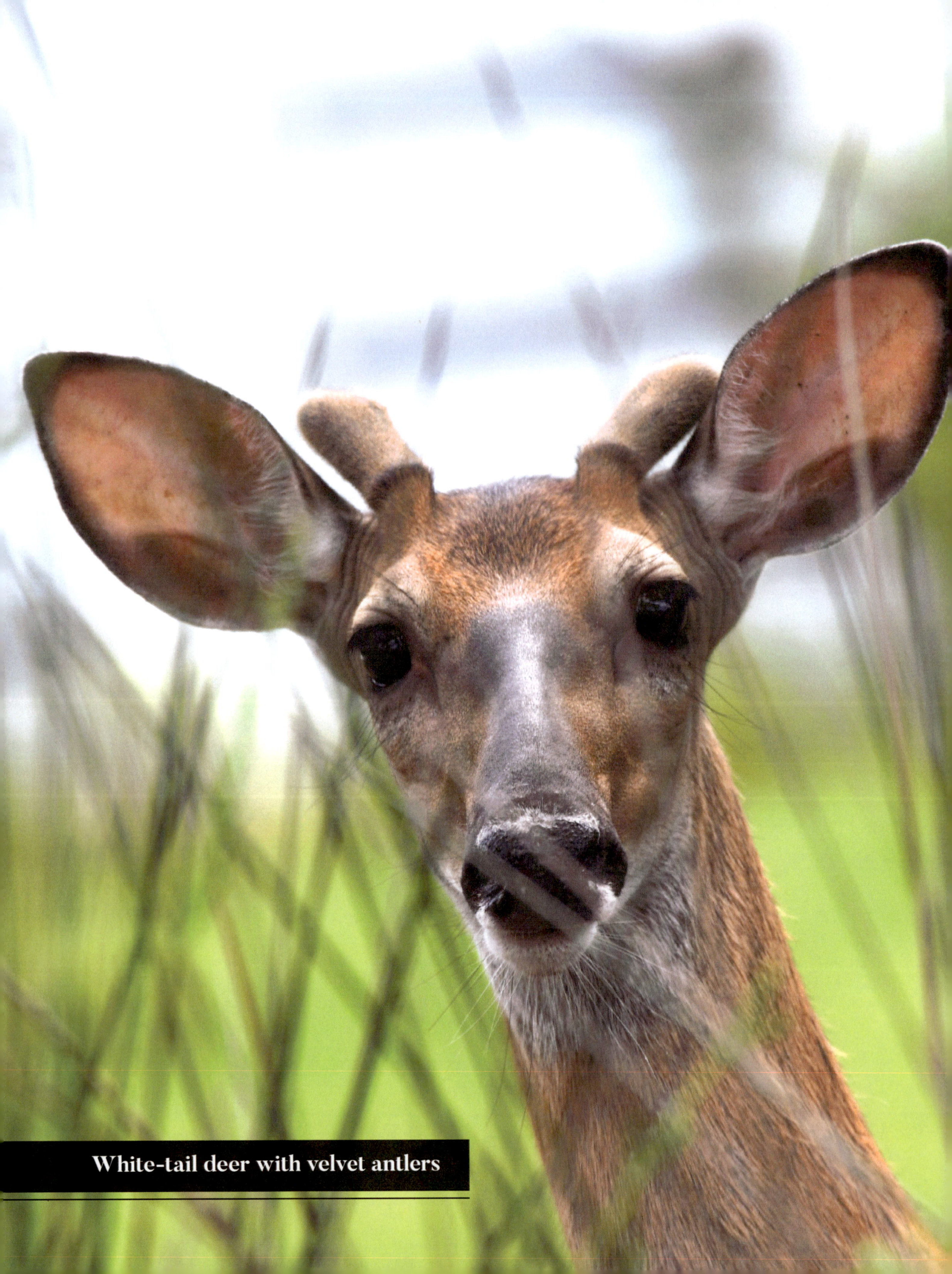
White-tail deer with velvet antlers

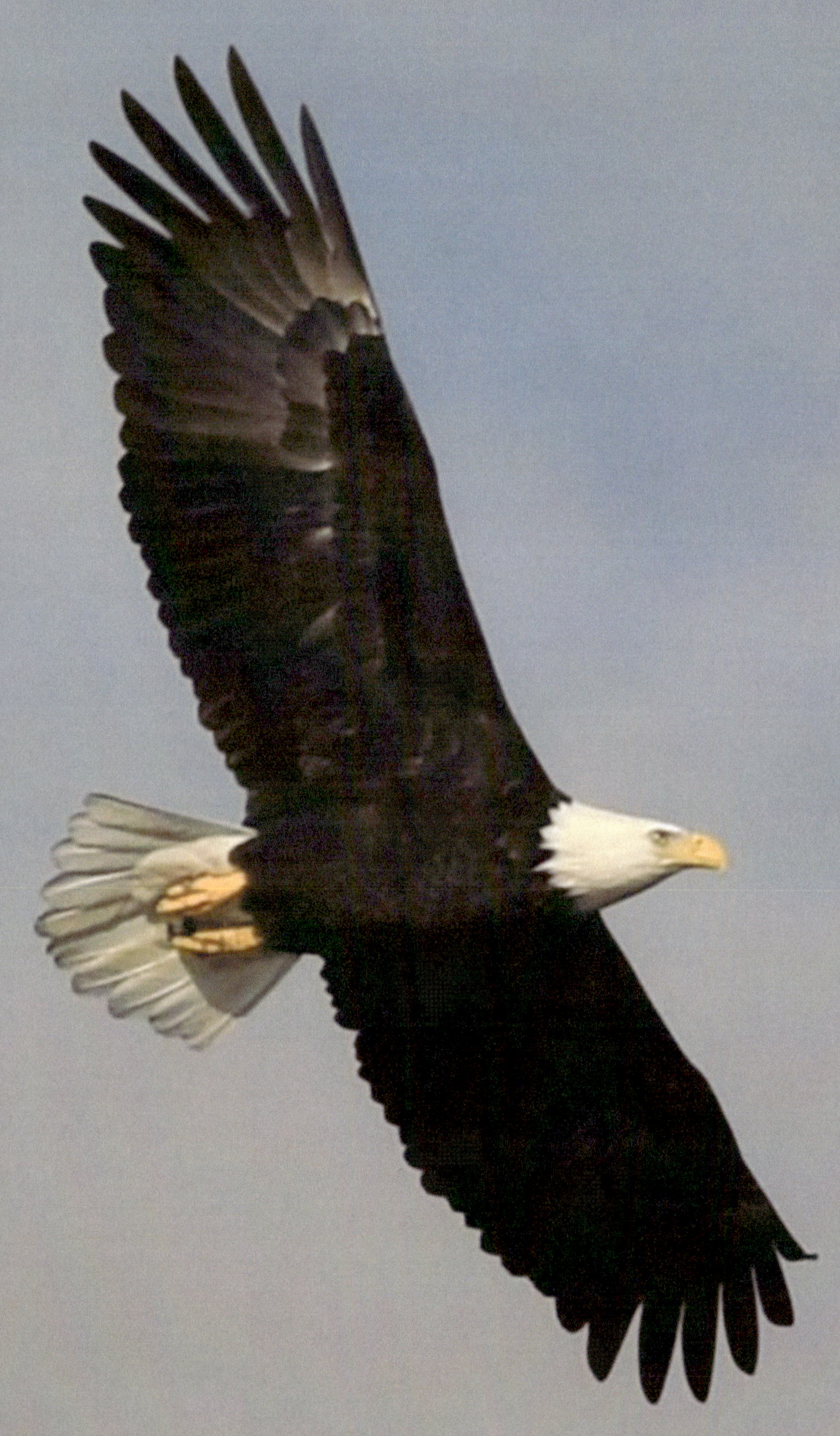

Great bald eagle

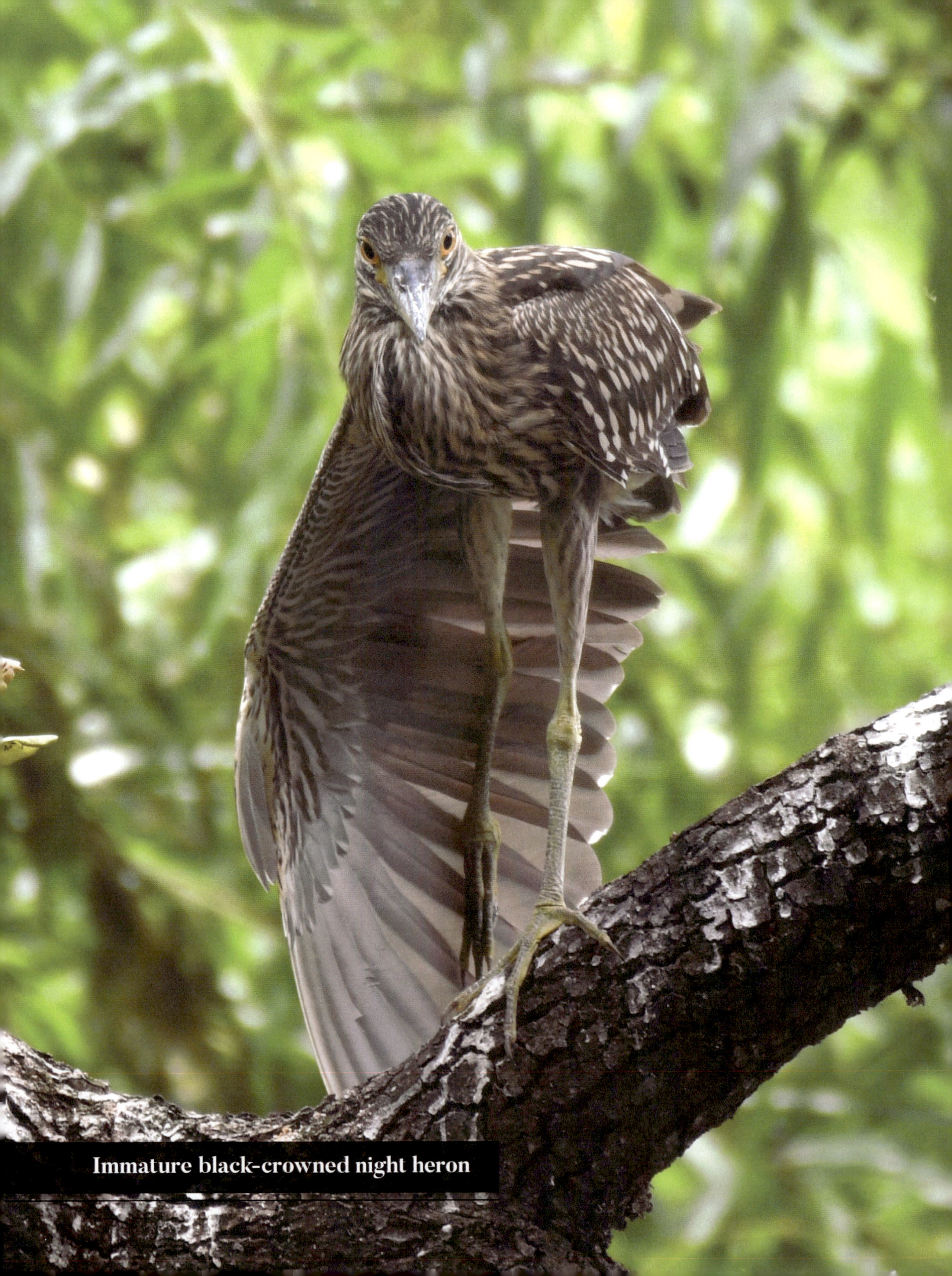

Immature black-crowned night heron

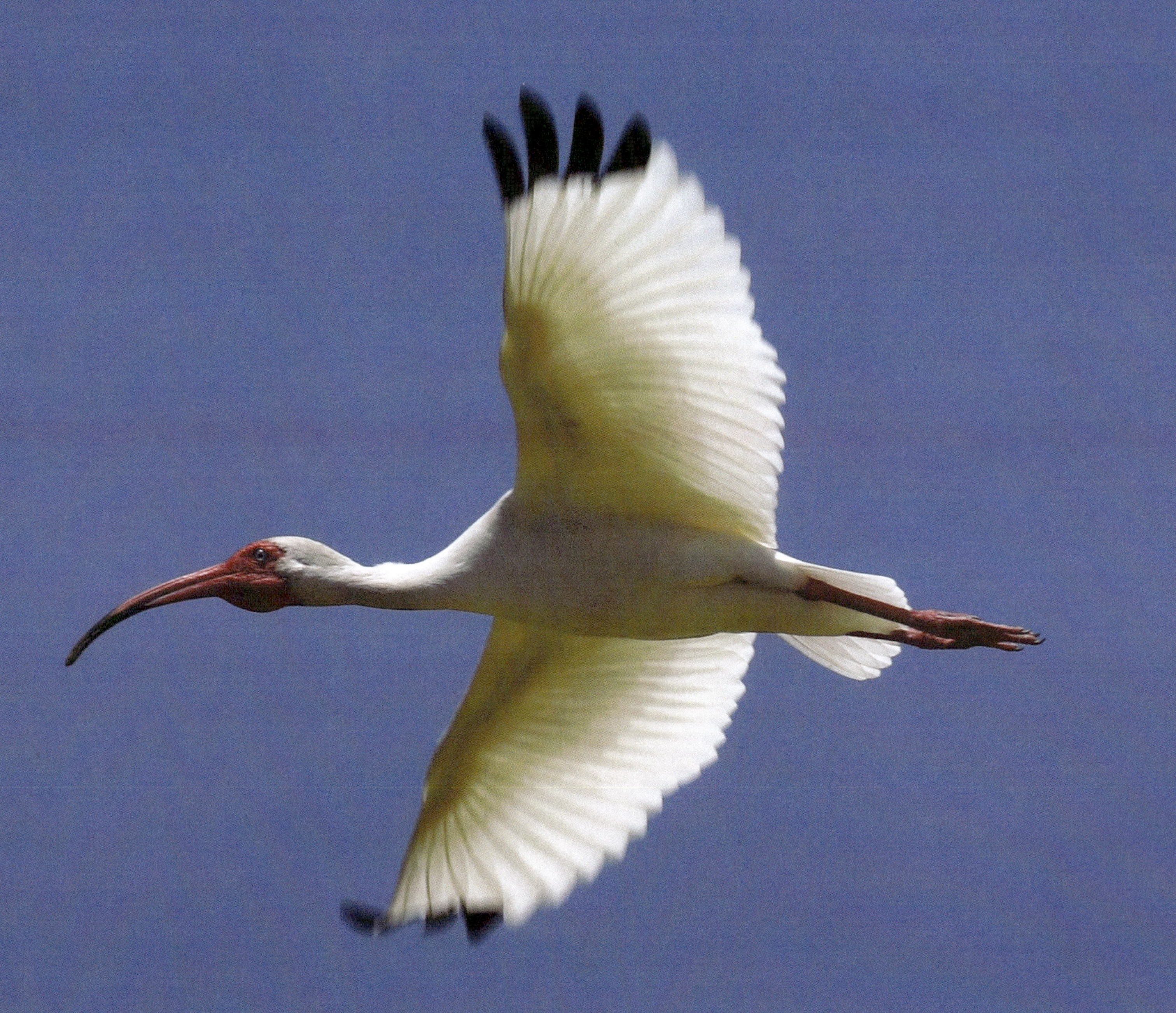

American white ibis

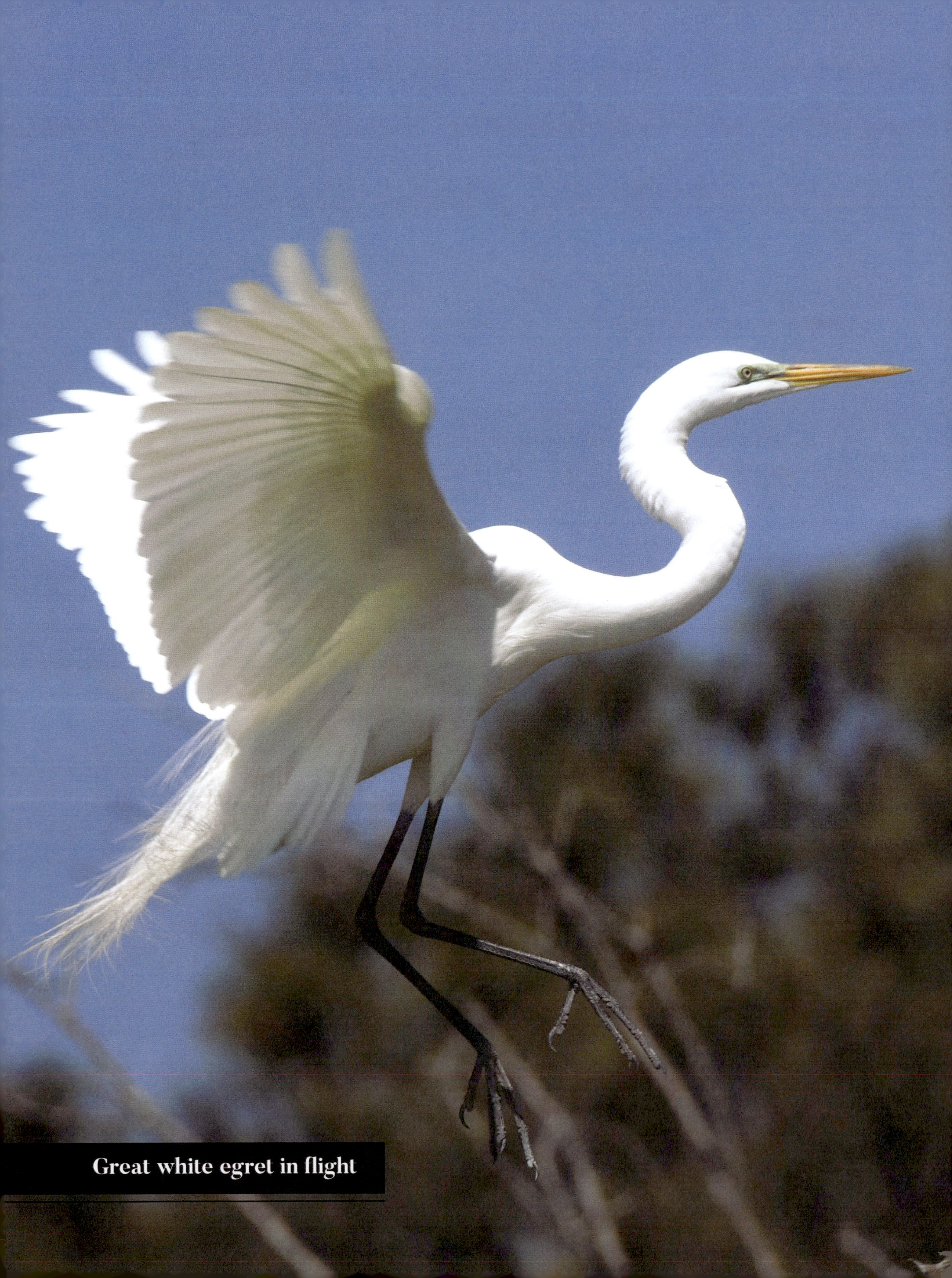

Great white egret in flight

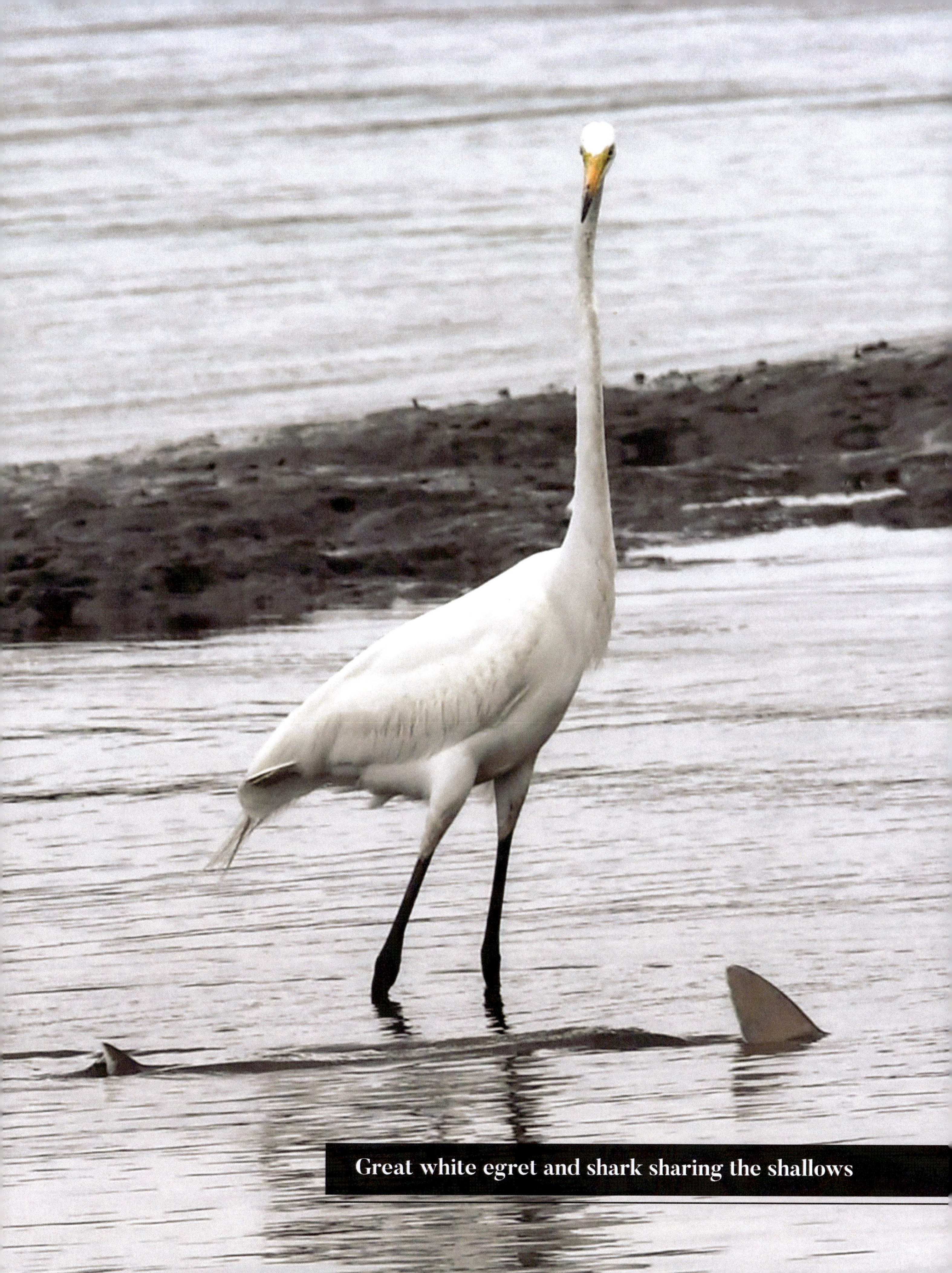

Great white egret and shark sharing the shallows

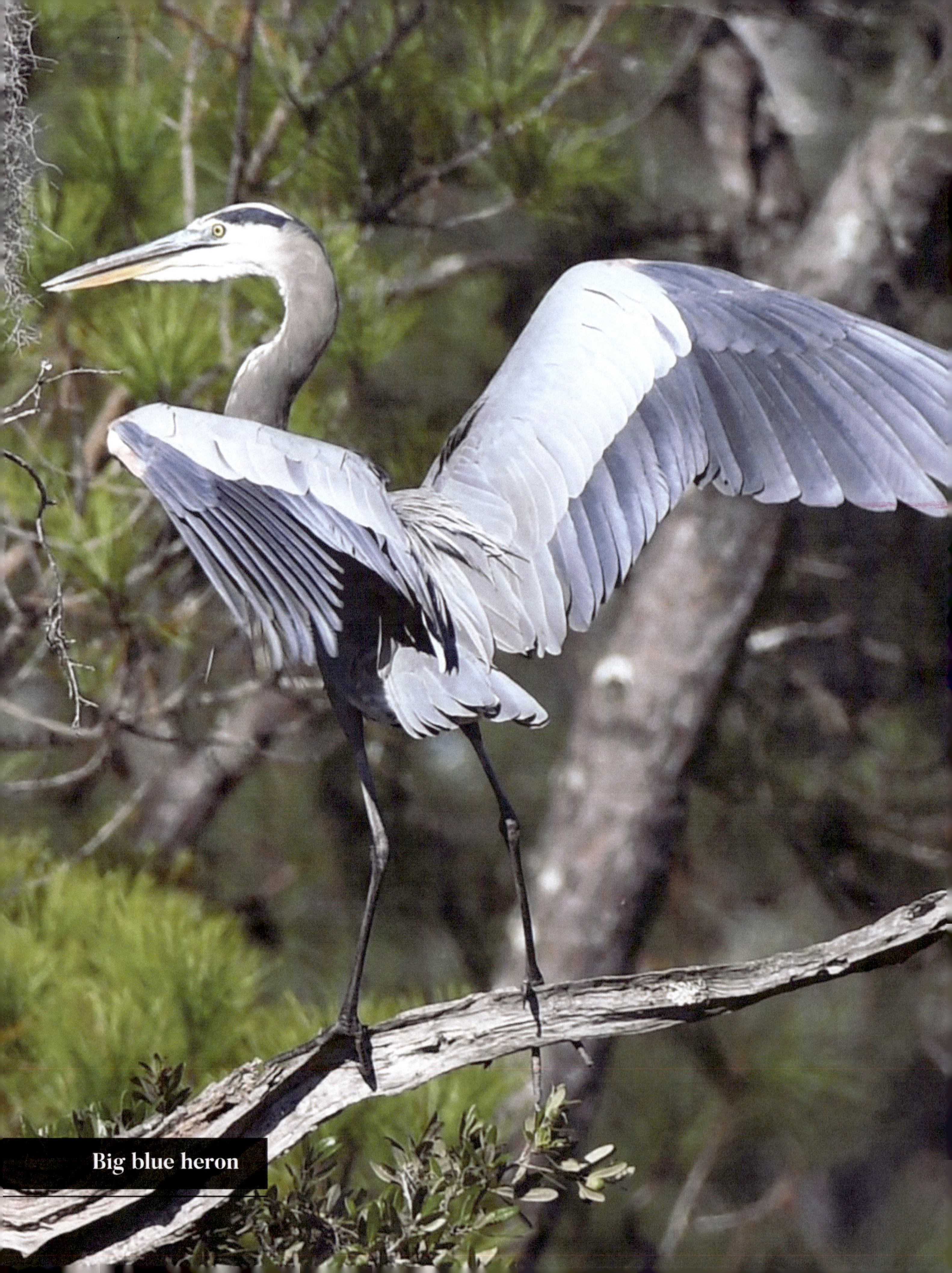

Big blue heron

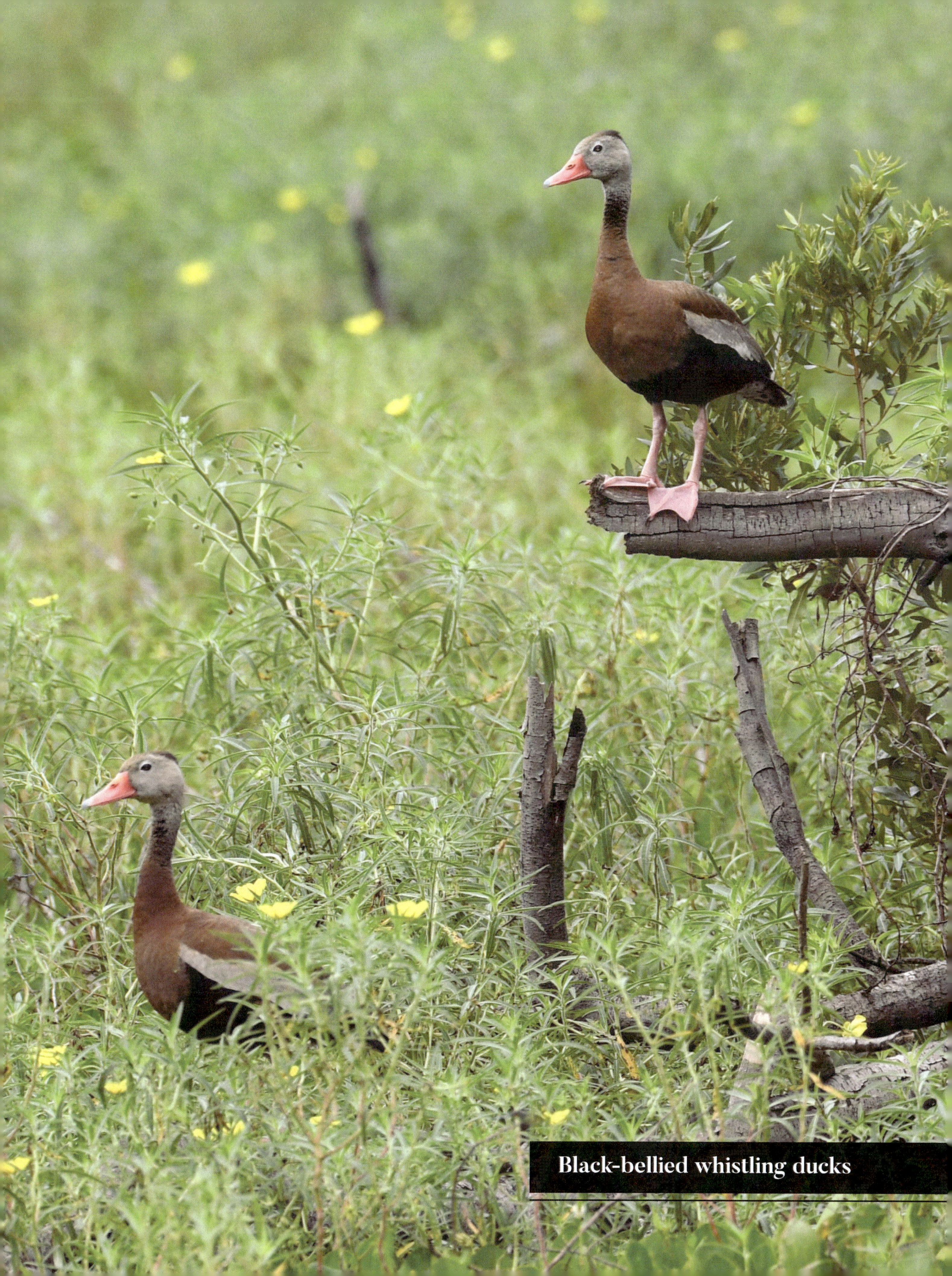

Black-bellied whistling ducks

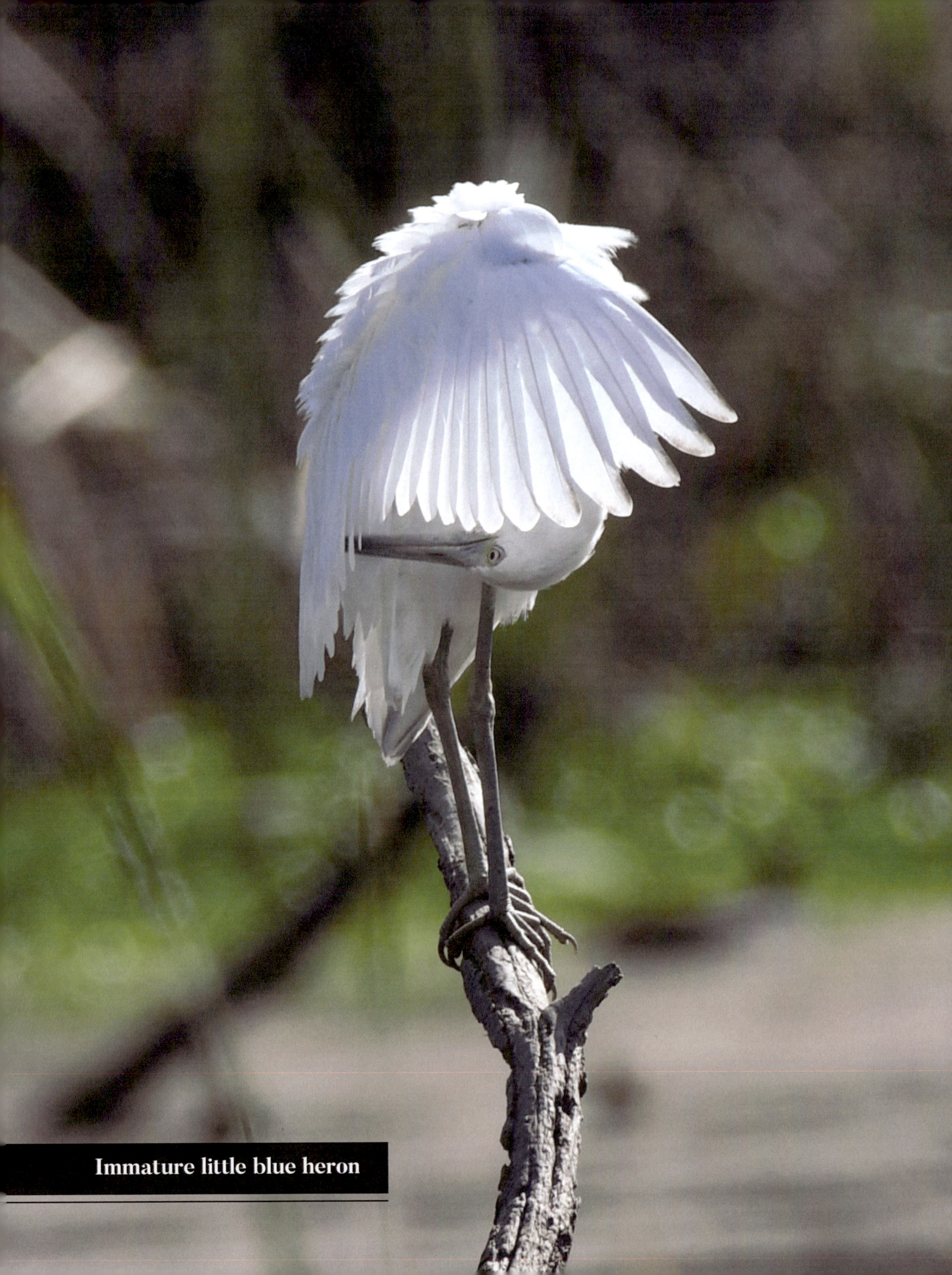

Immature little blue heron

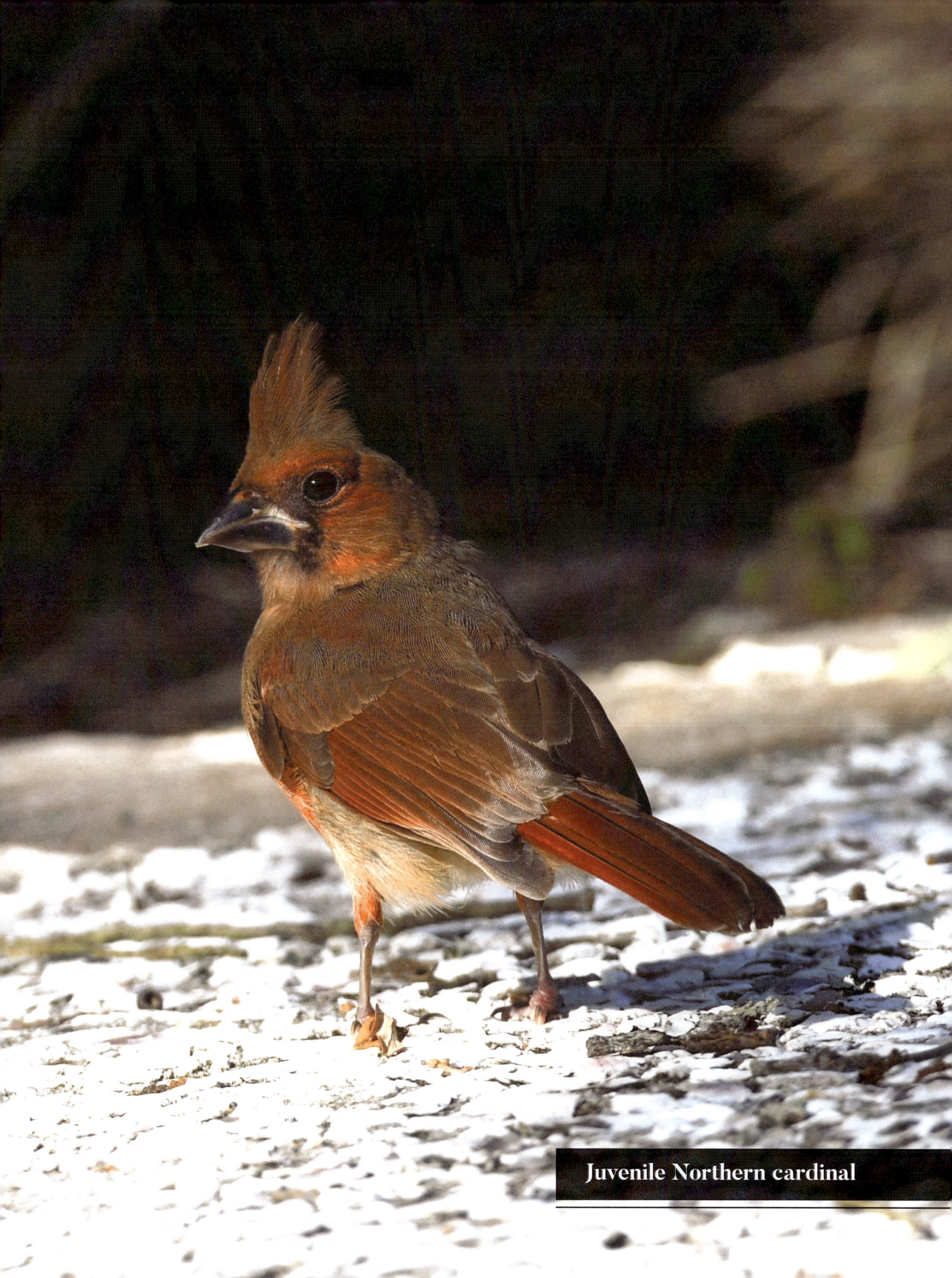

Juvenile Northern cardinal

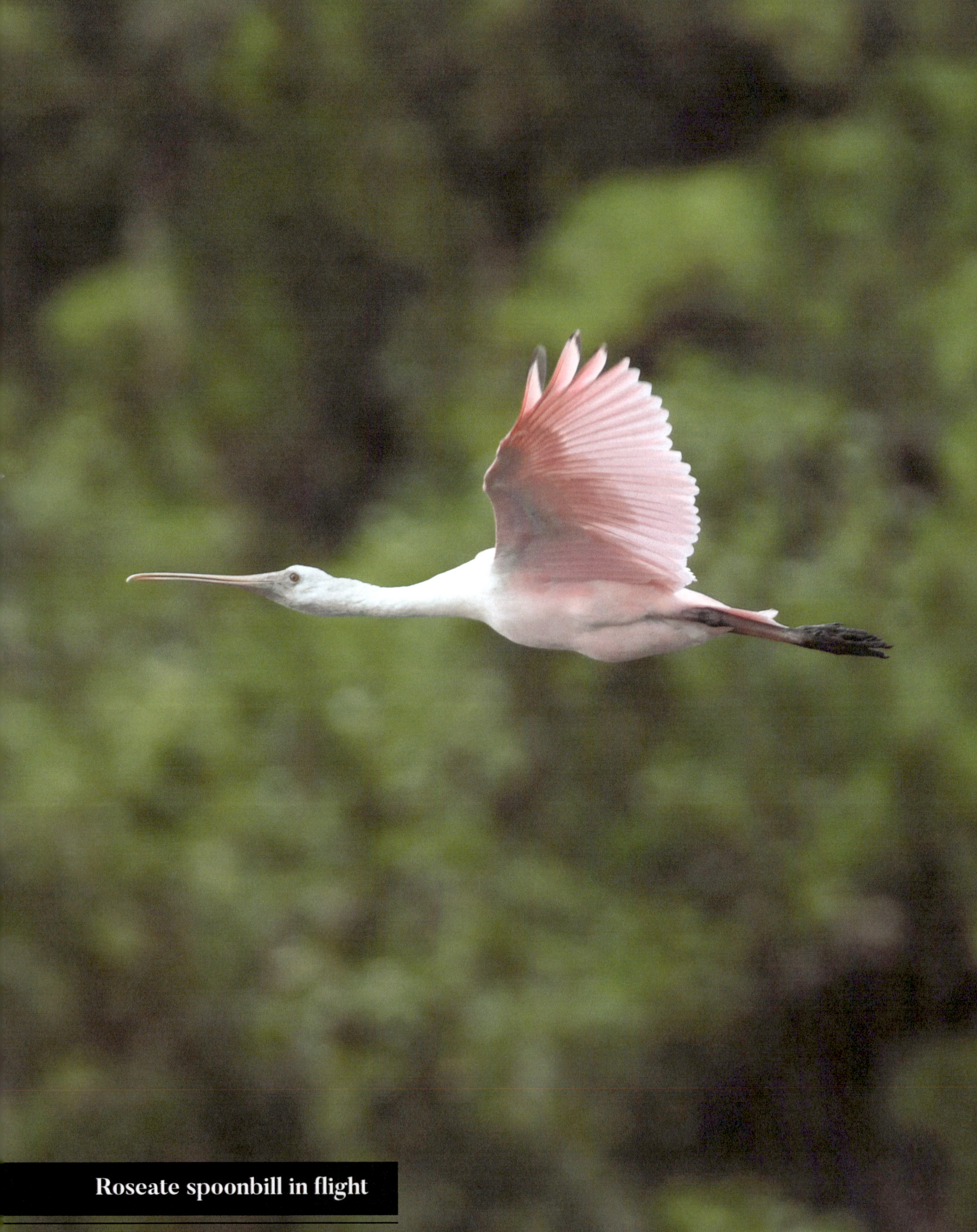

Roseate spoonbill in flight

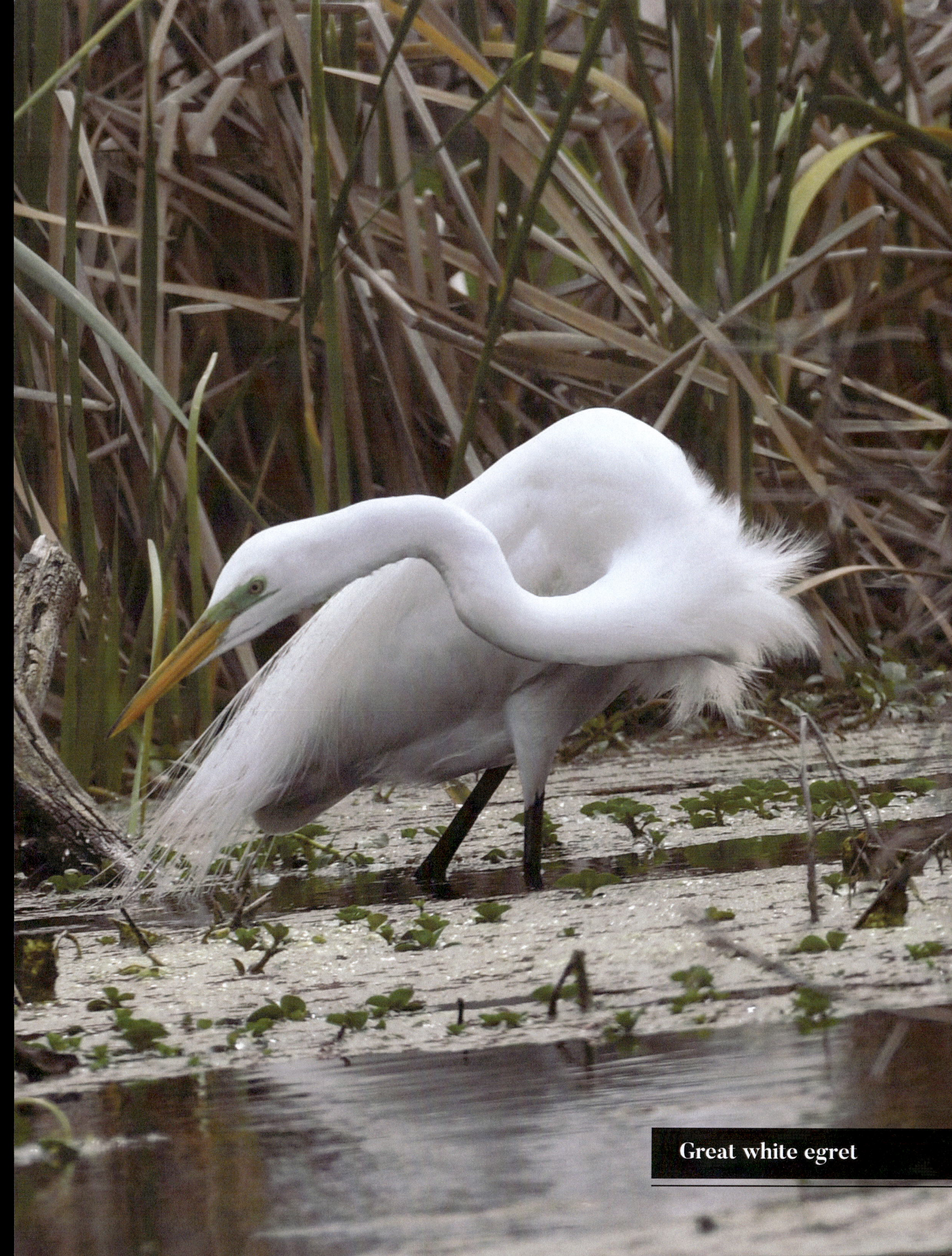

Great white egret

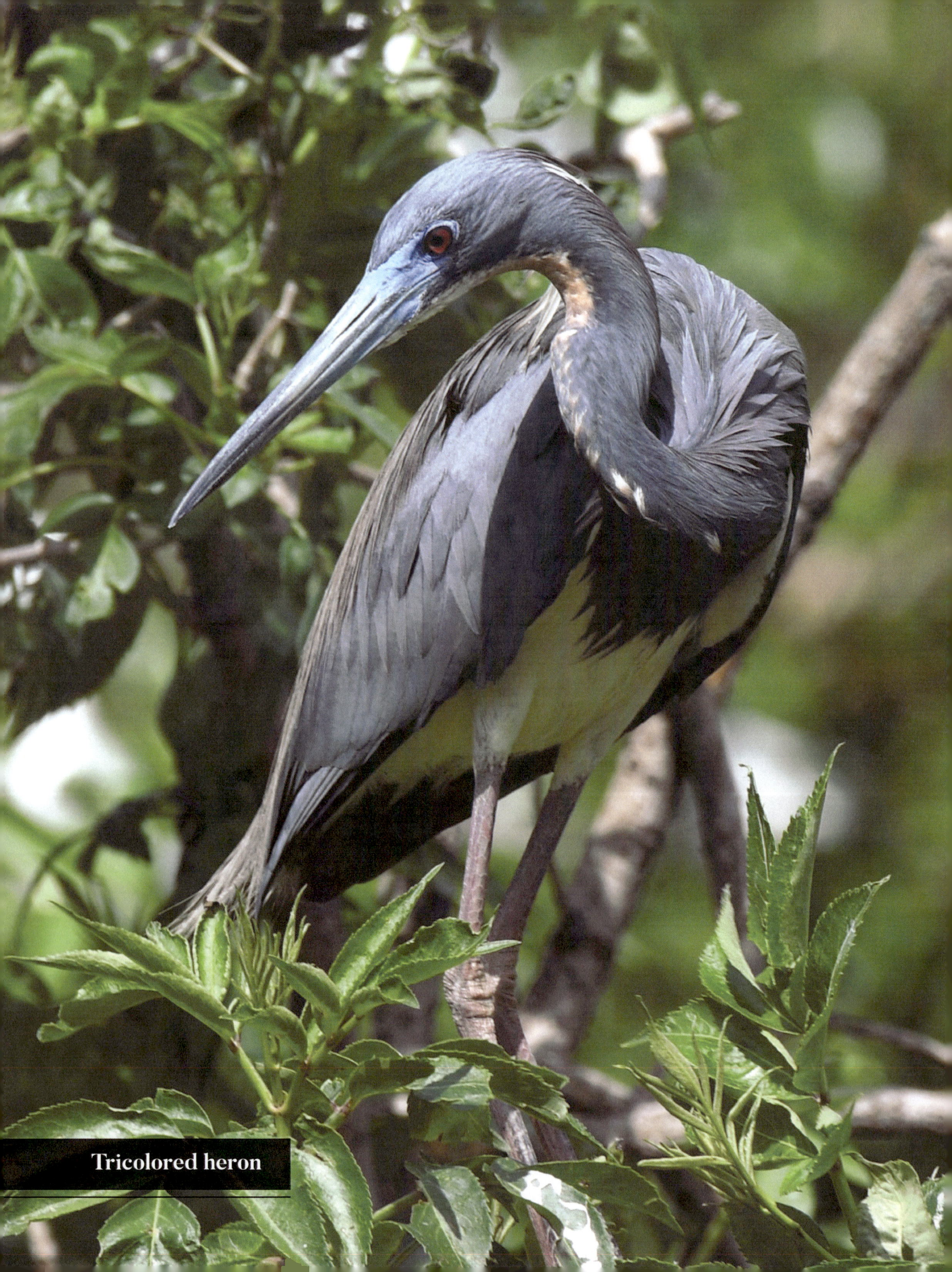

Tricolored heron

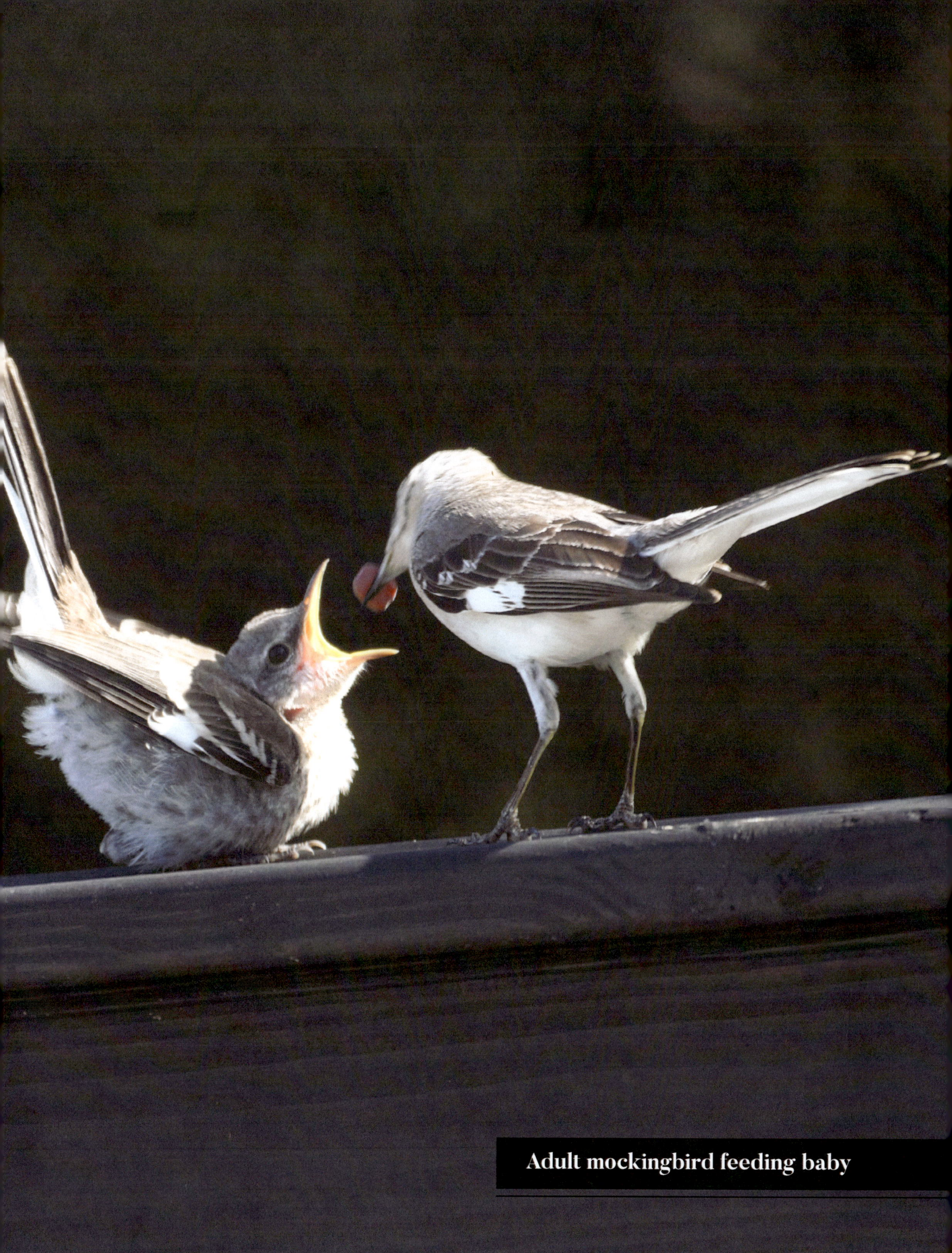
Adult mockingbird feeding baby

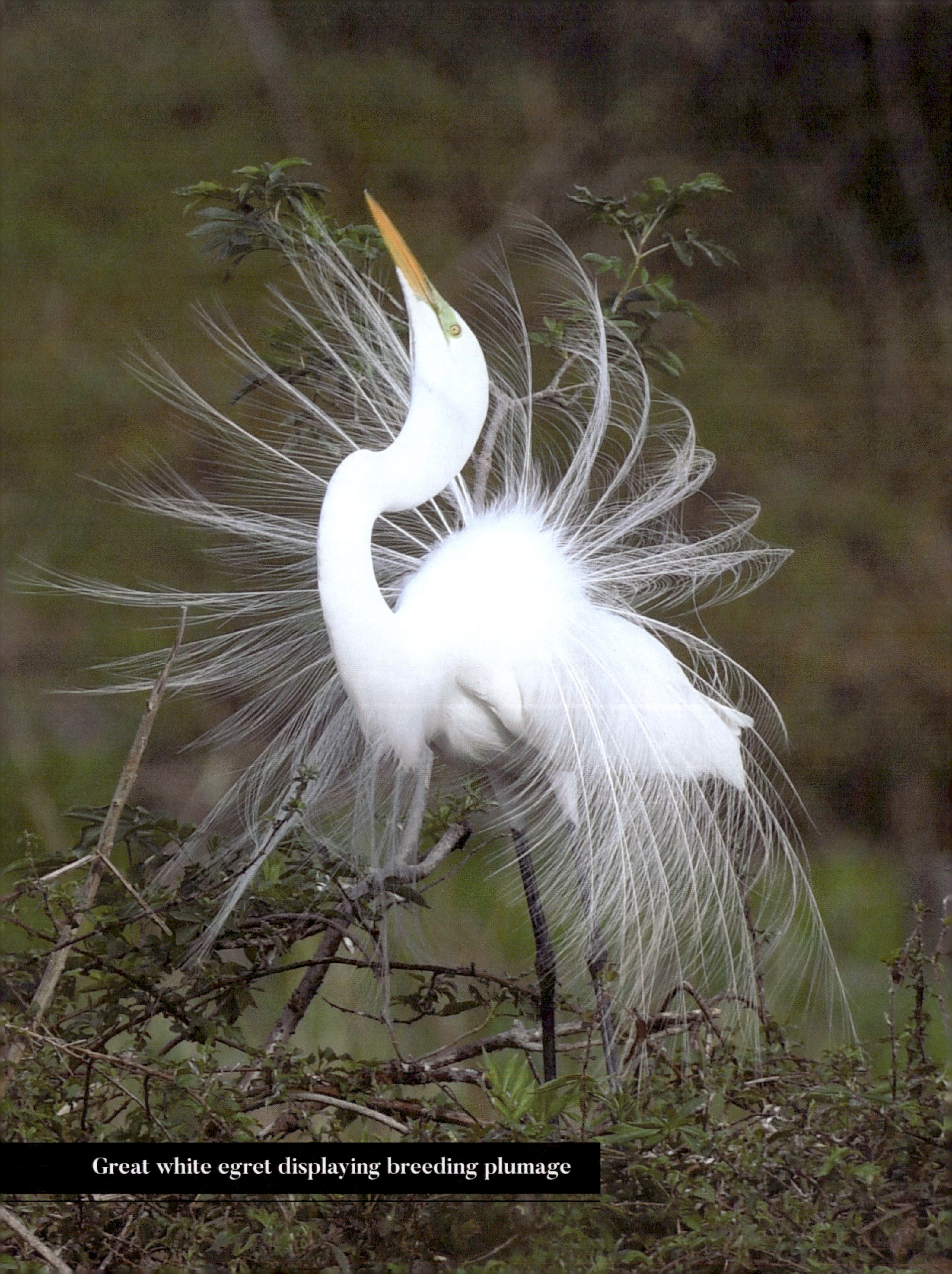

Great white egret displaying breeding plumage

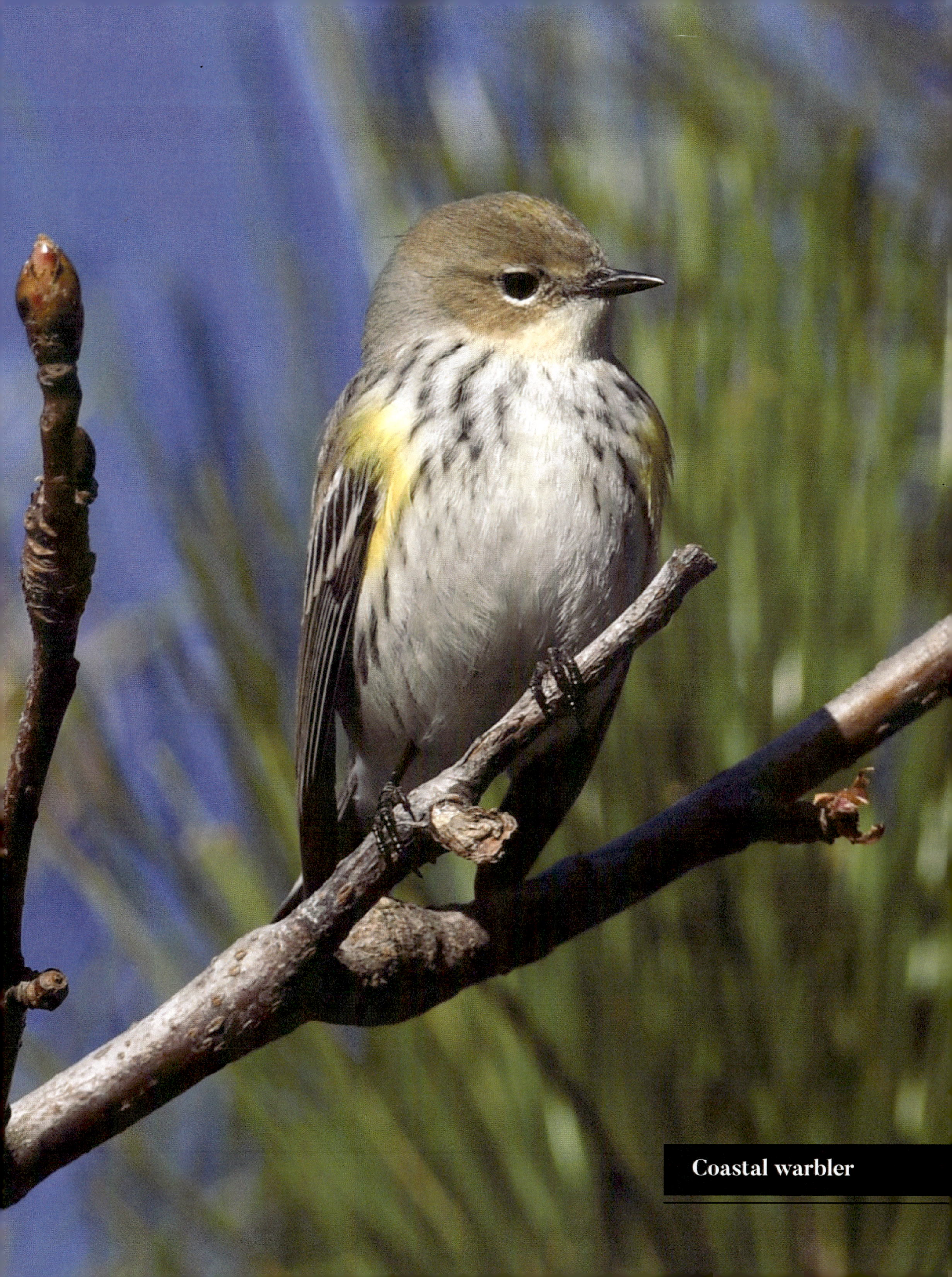

Coastal warbler

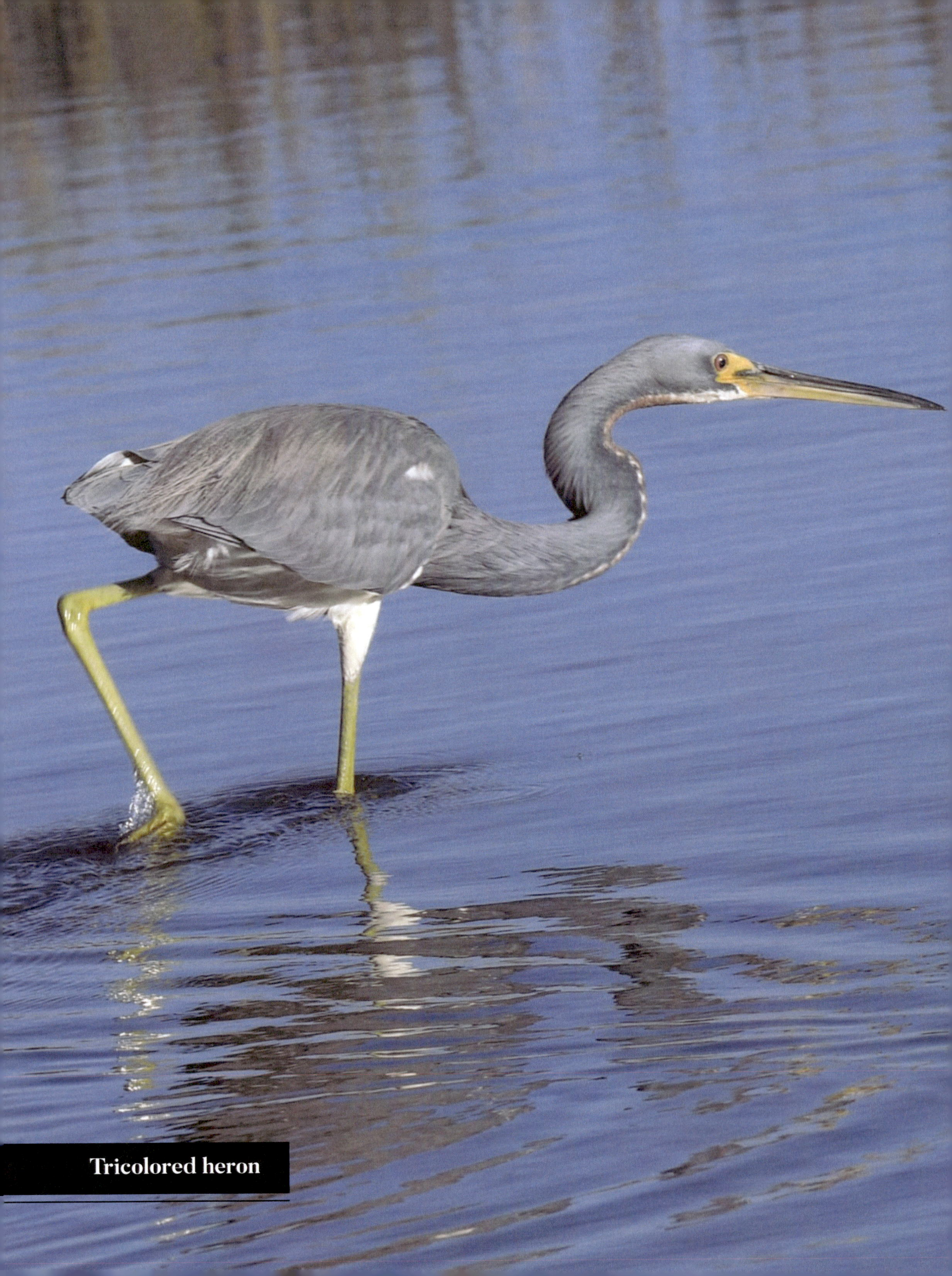

Tricolored heron

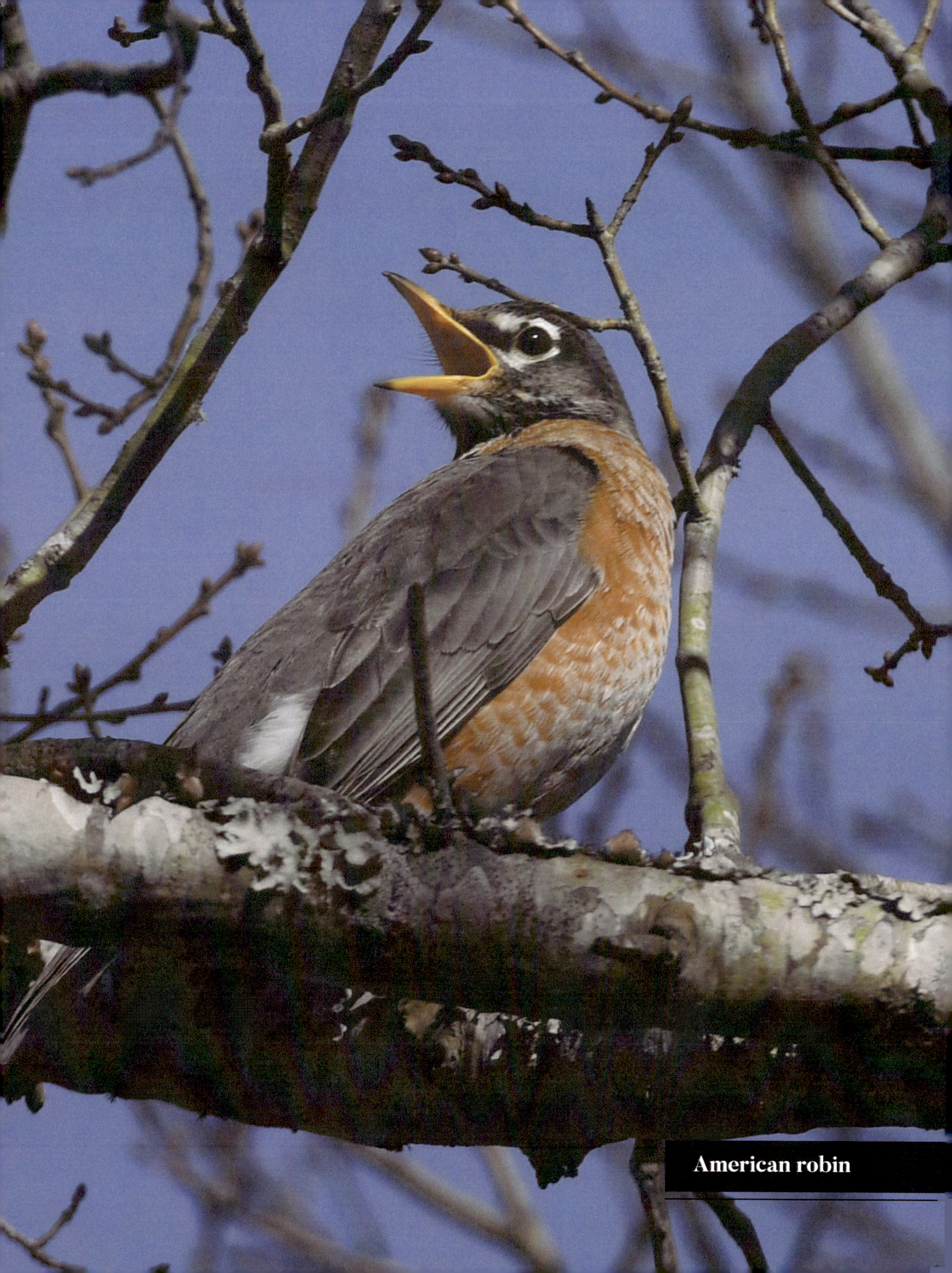
American robin

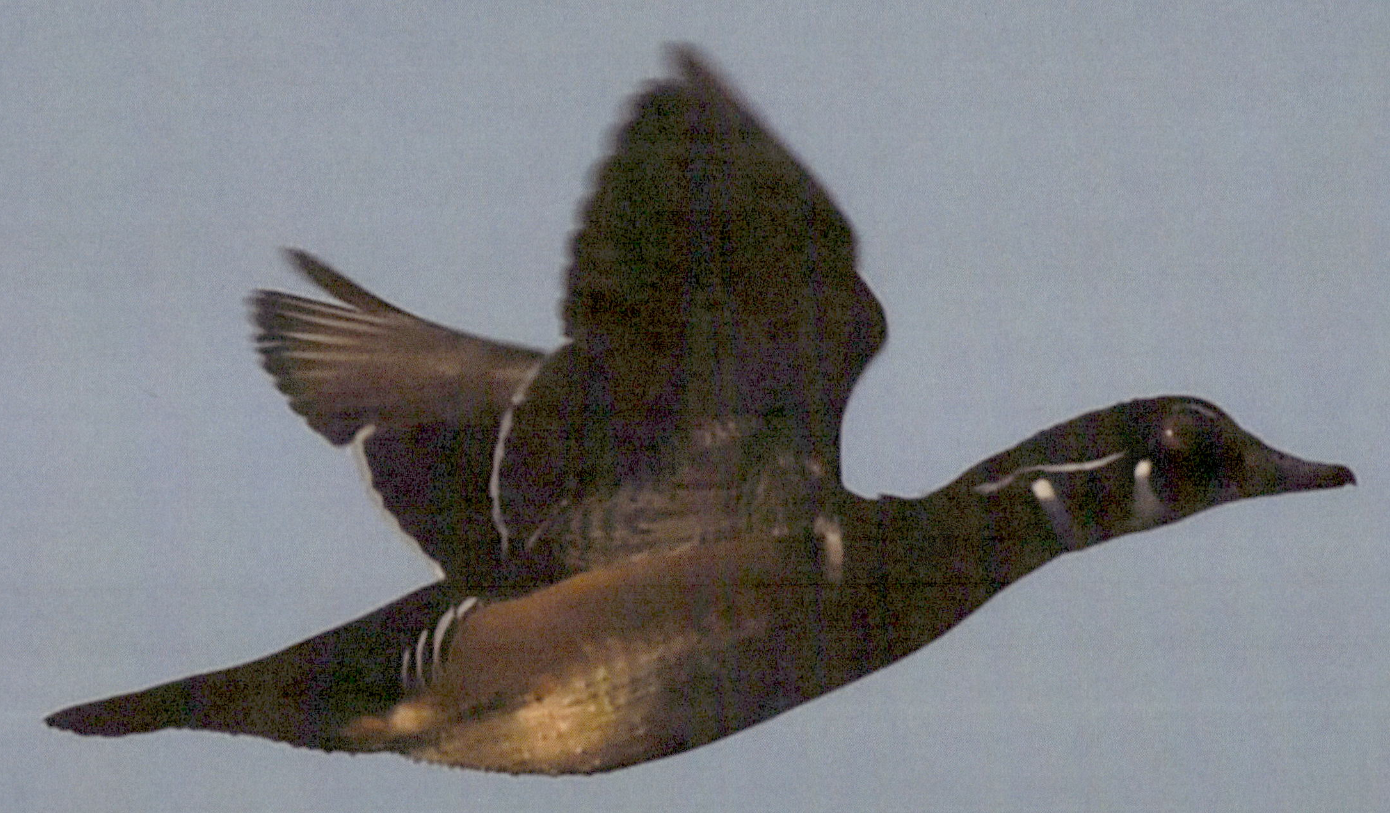

Wood duck in flight

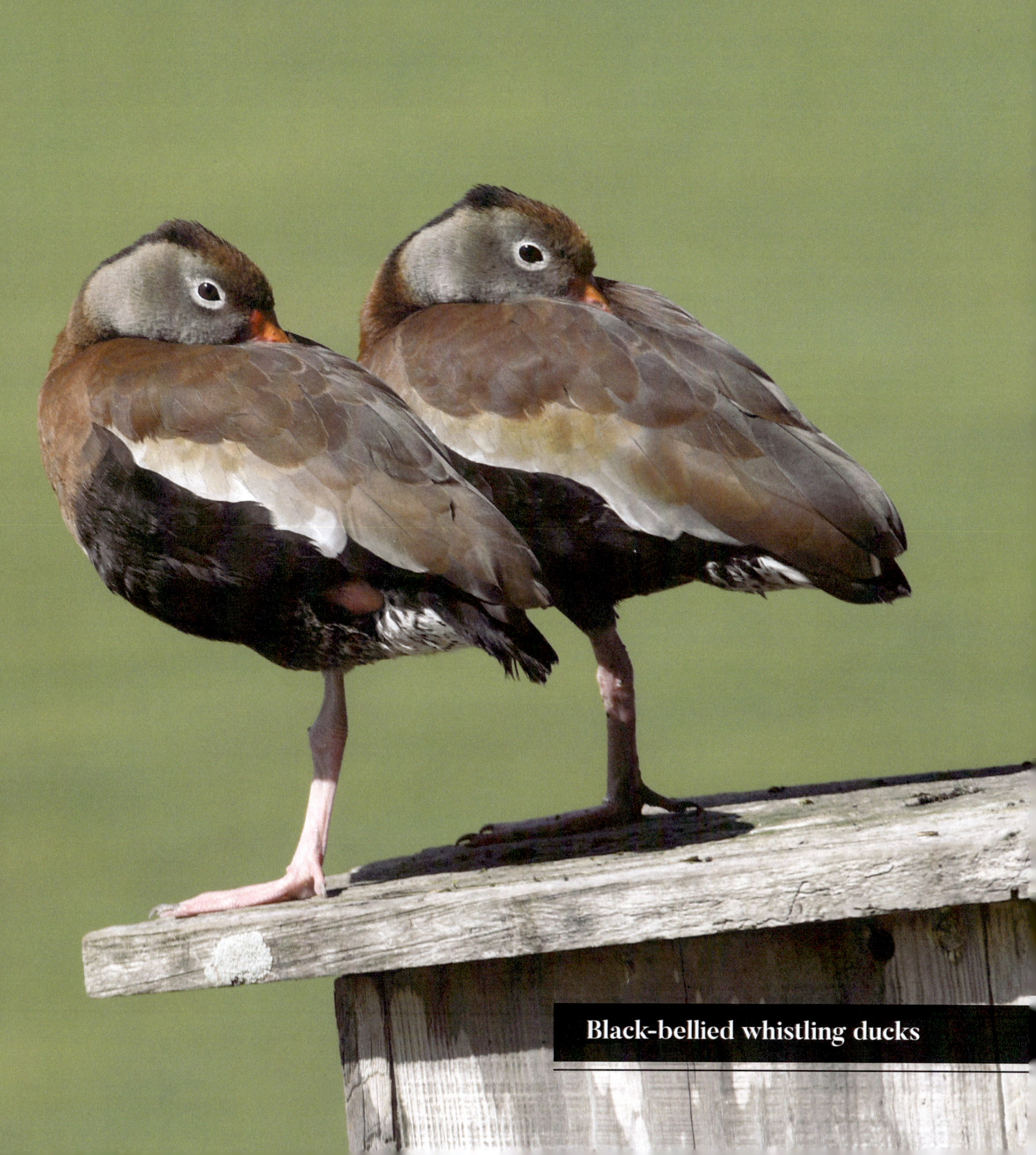

Black-bellied whistling ducks

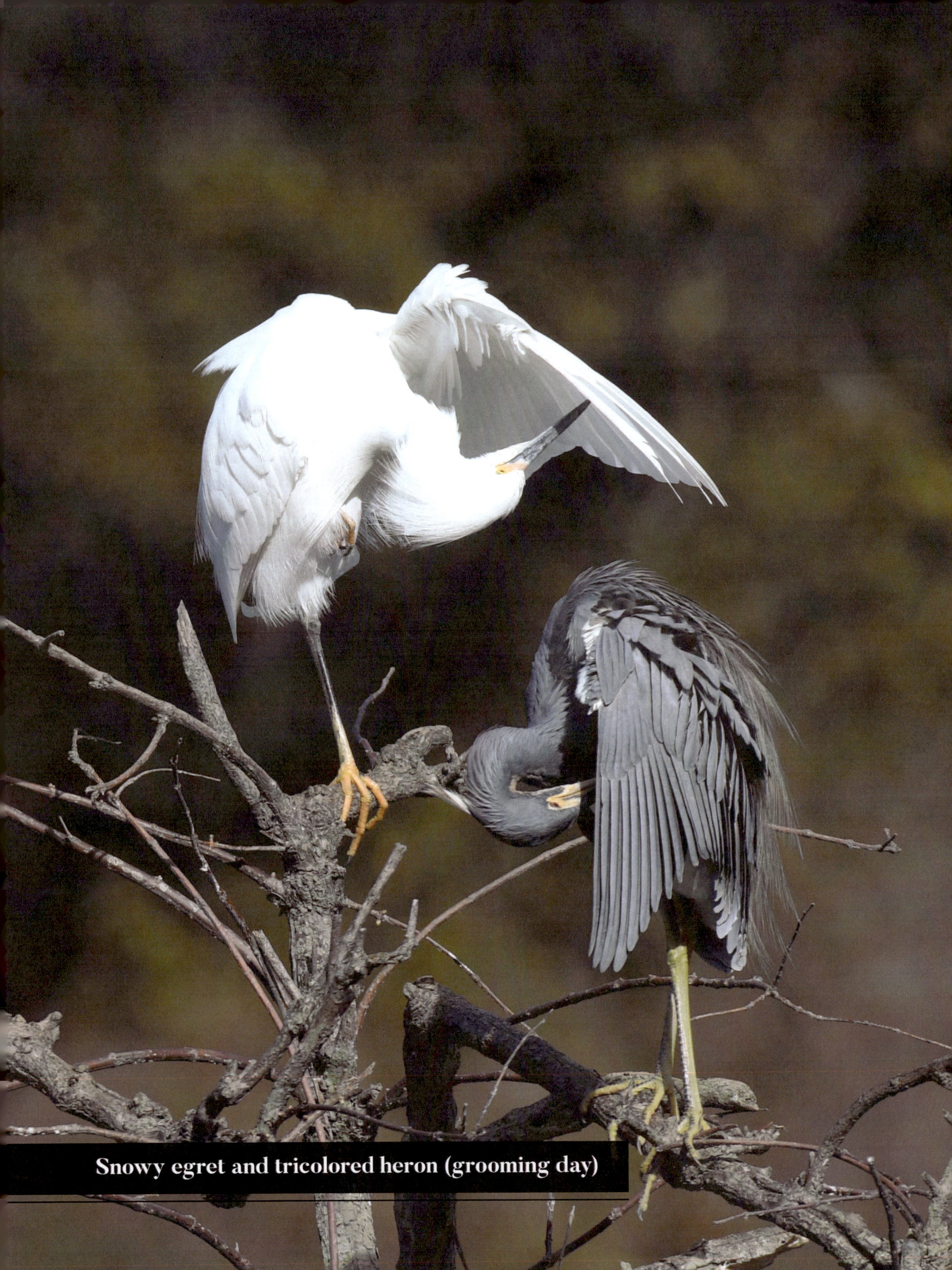

Snowy egret and tricolored heron (grooming day)

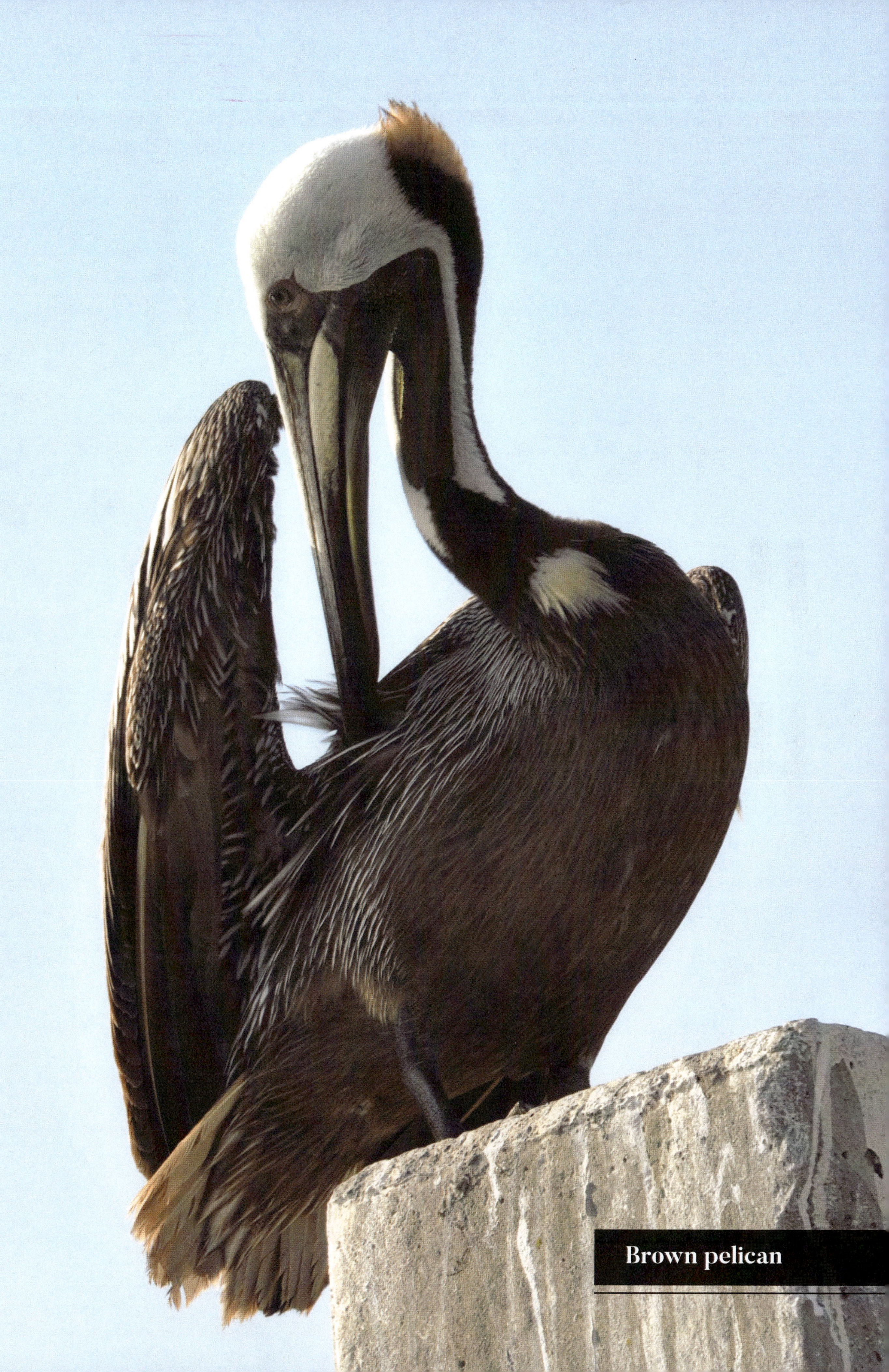

Brown pelican

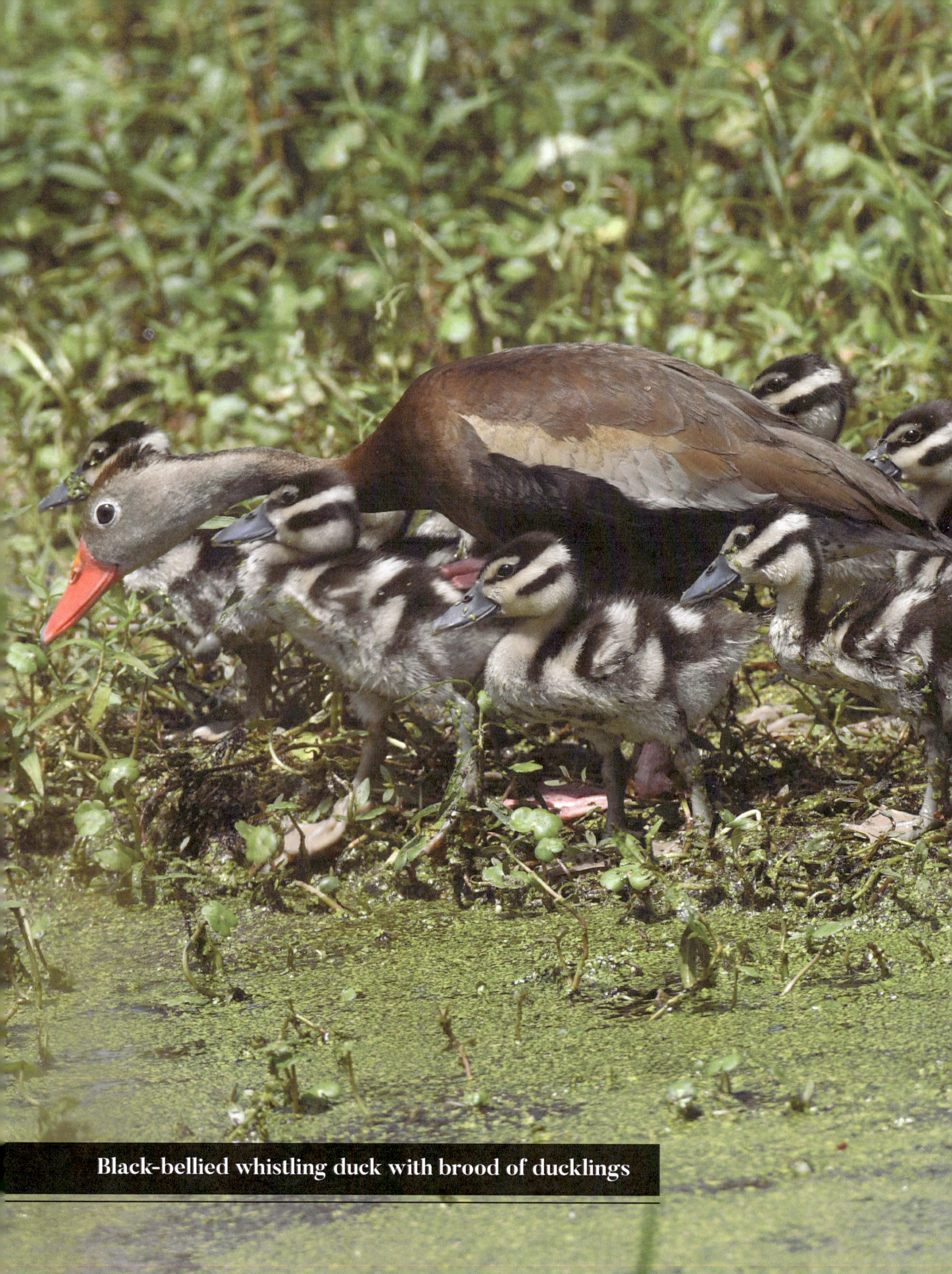

Black-bellied whistling duck with brood of ducklings

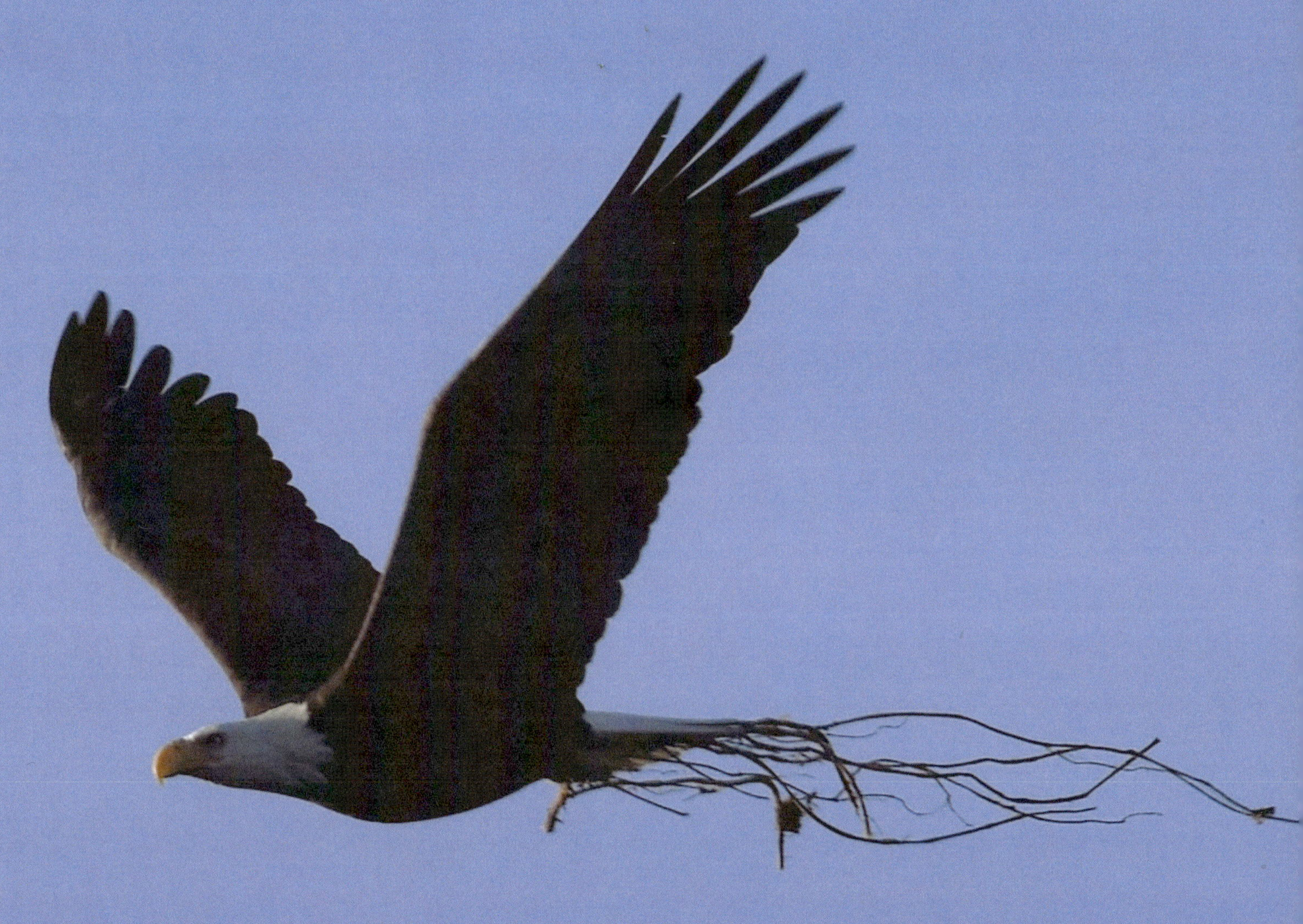

Bald eagle carrying nesting material

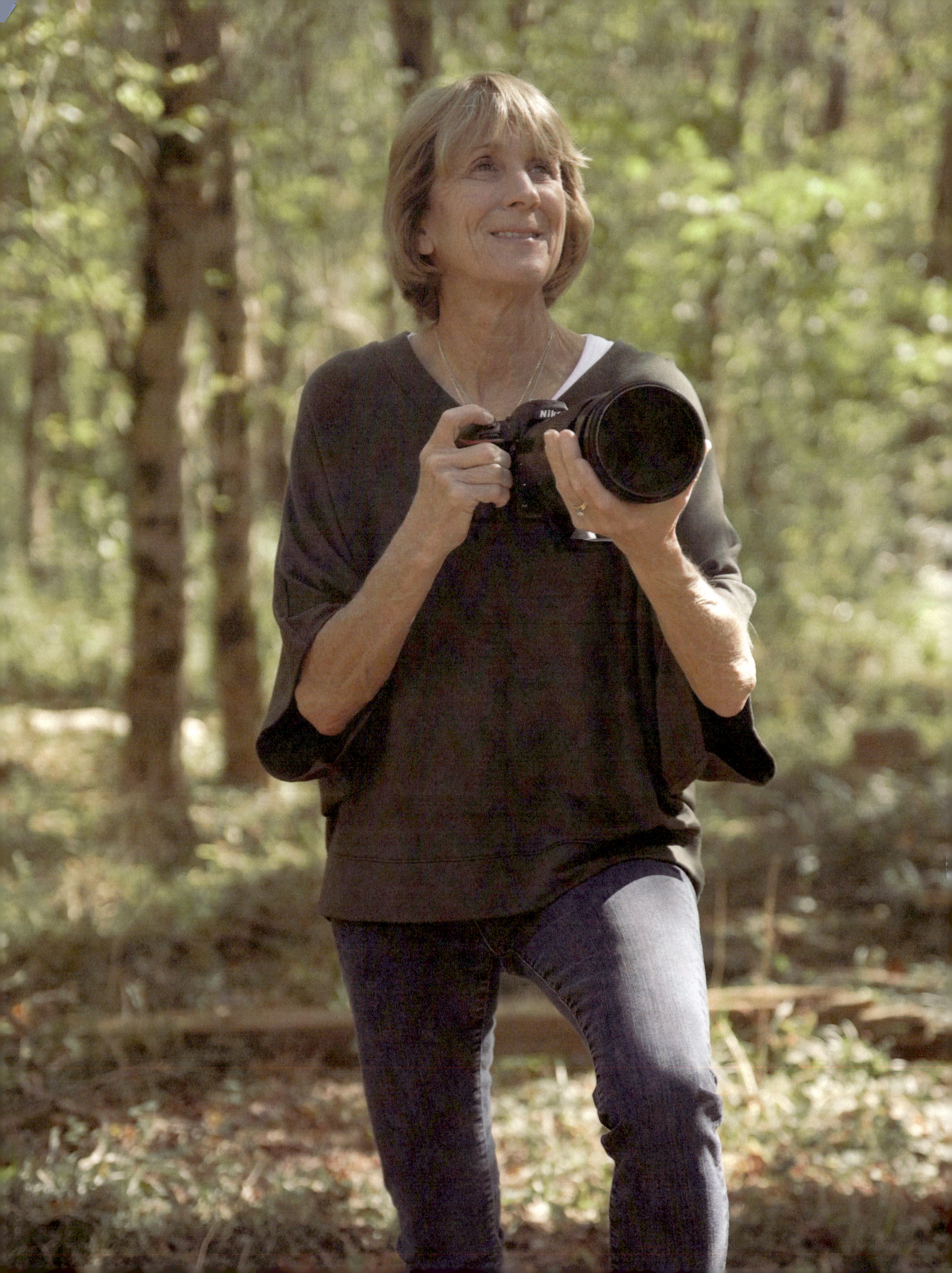

About the Photographer

Joanne Young was born and raised in the Lowcountry of South Carolina. After marrying her husband Steve, they relocated to Charleston, SC, where they raised their three children. After spending 35 years in Charleston, they returned to her hometown, building a house and embracing life on the river. Anyone who knows Joanne will tell you that her children and her grandchildren are the greatest joys of her life. Second to her family, Joanne has an unmatched enthusiasm for the breathtaking beauty of nature. You will typically find her, camera in hand strolling through one of the wildlife refuges or savoring life by the river, always striving to capture the incredible grace of these magnificent creatures that you will see throughout her debut book, *Wildlife of the Lowcountry.*

9 781647 048006